Earth: A Novel

Eric Van Meter

Published by Eric Van Meter, 2022.

EARTH: A NOVEL

First edition. November 8, 2022.

ISBN: 979-8201897840

Written by Eric Van Meter.

For Denise, Zachary, and Jonathan.

Because life is a group effort.

Cover design by Matthew Schwaerzler

CHAPTER 1:
LIKE A TUMBLEWEED
IN SPANDEX

In the least opportune moment, the Reverend John Wesley Denton had no words, neither for God nor persons, nor for the thirty-odd balding heads bowed before him. He took hold of either side of the podium, squared his shoulders and raised his eyes in hopes that a holy gaze or a holy posture might summon an appropriate text for his prayer. No luck, though. The things he needed most evaded him, Spirit and language alike. For all his striving, Dent could retrieve only one small nugget from his files of pastoral wisdom.

Keep in mind that the nearest exit may be behind you.

"Go ahead, Brother Denton," Jeff Burke said.

Dent nodded. Drew in breath.

Nothing.

Every drop of moisture fled from his mouth, popping up instead as beads of sweat on the three-inch swath of scalp that no longer grew any hair. It boiled there, fired by anger and embarrassment. Offering perfunctory meal blessings at civic events should be the easiest part of his job as pastor, a simple assemblage of platitudes using language every bit as prescribed as the Pledge of Allegiance. It didn't matter than Dent was only two weeks into his appointment to Earth, TX, or that it was his first time attending the Last Man Club's Tuesday breakfast, or that he was from the most liberal (and hence most suspect) denomination in town. Blessing meals for preachers was akin to boiling eggs for cooks. Failure here was a portent of a brief pastorate at Earth United Methodist Church, and what then? There was no less desirable appointment, even here in the Texas Panhandle. The next stop for Dent's ministry was not down. It was out.

"Let us pray," he said, this for the second time.

A rumble sounded in the street outside. Through the glass doors at the far end of the room, Dent could see Jack Schoendienst's blue GMC pickup pull to a stop in the middle of the street. Jack stepped out and glanced into the bed. Shook his head and commenced pacing back and forth along the sidewalk, occasionally slapping his green foam and mesh cap against his thigh.

"Brother Denton?" Burke said.

"Let us pray," Dent said, and summoning his last meager crumb of confidence, continued. "Oh, the Lord's been good to me, and so I thank the Lord..."

Dent winced as soon as the words left his mouth. It was a child's prayer—his daughter's favorite when she was little, and one many of those present had no doubt taught their grandchildren way back when. Awkwardness rushed through the room like the Spirit at Pentecost. Joe Dick Schieble and Jerry Sharp, who were both Catholic and thus used to following liturgy, joined in with the prayer. Dr. Omar, the lone non-Christian member of Last Man, cocked his head and looked for cameras, just in case he was being punked. The two-dozen or so who were left represented a wide swath of Protestant belief, but were all functionally Baptist and so dedicated to the every-head-bowed, every-eye-closed principle of corporate prayer. Dent wished the floor would open up and swallow him whole. But he was committed, and so soldiered on through the sun and the rain and the appleseed.

"Amen."

Dent released the podium, which shifted about an inch to one side with an unpleasant squawk. He shook Burke's hand and walked down the side aisle as though heading for the men's room. As the line for the breakfast buffet formed along the east wall, he slipped out of the glass doors and onto the sidewalk.

"Preacher!" Jack said. "I was afraid it'd be you."

"Morning, Jack."

"I didn't mean it like that." He held up his palms. "Sorry. I just—listen, I don't know what you've heard, or if you've heard anything yet. I just needed to tell you before anyone else did—or after if they already have—you know, Irene Ostendorf has lost her damn mind."

"Well," Dent said, and leaned against the pickup. He hadn't a clue what Jack was so worked up about—hadn't gotten any calls or texts or been pulled aside for a hushed conversation by someone in the Last Man Club. Hadn't even checked his email yet today, since this morning's meeting had cut into his usual quality time with his laptop over breakfast. But admitting ignorance too quickly might tip off Jack, might keep him from spilling what he really knew. And so Dent said "well" and then he waited.

"It was just right place, right time, so to speak. Or all wrong, as it were." Jack pulled his hat over his freckled scalp. Held up his hands as though explaining the length of a fish. "See, I happened to be going by on the tractor, that's all. I was moving it up to Hummelstein's to bale for him, since he just had a knee replaced. And all of a sudden, BANG!"

He brought his hand down flat onto the bedrail of the pickup. Dent jumped.

"I wasn't sure it was a rifle, at first. Irene's house is a ways off the road, you know, and I had to squint to see her. But sure enough, there she was on the porch, reloading."

"She was shooting at you?"

"Naw." He waved Dent away as though the preacher understood nothing. "The kid on the bicycle. Did I forget that part?"

"You did."

"Anyhow, the point is that he'd already fallen by the time I saw him—rolling down the gulley like a tumbleweed in spandex. And I was so busy watching him and Irene and the road that I never saw the bicycle. Swear to God I never meant to get Irene in trouble, crazy as she is."

"Slow down, Jack. It can't be that bad."

Jack grunted. "See for yourself."

He lowered the tailgate and motioned for Dent to look. Inside the bed lay the remains of an expensive-looking bicycle, its sprockets and seat smashed to oblivion in a slightly rippled pattern, crushed by the tractor's rear wheel. The front tire and handlebars were intact, but the fork that held the wheel was nearly shorn off, pierced by what might—but surely could not—be a bullet hole.

"Irene's the one pulled the trigger," Jack said. "Why so is between her and the Lord, far as I'm concerned. Now, I ran over the bicycle. That much I'll own, but—"

"Easy now, Jack. Let's take this one step at a time."

He got Jack to pull his pickup around back of the building and park in the alley—still an obstruction, but one that would garner less attention. Jack waited on the tailgate while Dent went back inside to pilfer two cups of coffee from the Last Man beverage table. Burke was still speaking up front, straight-backed and in command. Dent tuned in partway through a report on the Tall Tale Roundup, the club's signature event.

"—ready to go on November 5," Burke was saying. "That's less than a month, which means means all you subcommittees have to get busy. Rob, how we doing on that new stage?"

"Right on schedule," a man seated in the back said.

"Have you even started on it yet?" Burke asked.

"Nope. But according to schedule, that means we're right on track."

The other men laughed. The president clearly was not pleased. "All right," he said. "As long as it's ready in time for the Roundup."

"It will be."

A wave of relief washed over Dent at the sound of a familiar voice. Even in the fishbowl that was the Texas Panhandle, he was surprised to learn that Rob de los Santos, his old American Legion baseball coach, belonged to Earth's Last Man Club. He looked toward Dent, touched his nose and his chin and his nose again—the same sign he used to make twenty years ago to signal a baserunner to hold his ground. He had only coached Dent for one season down in Lubbock, and that years ago. But to know that he was not utterly unknown in this godforsaken town was enough to make Dent nearly weep for gratitude.

Dent looked around for coffee mugs, but found only the foam cups that were now anathema even in the little high country churches he was used to serving. The United Methodist Women were far too environmentally conscious to stock those things, or to allow the UM Men to do so. But the Last Man's Club was, as it forever had been, one hundred percent male and thus subject to all manner of thoughtlessness. Dent grabbed two cups anyway. Desperate times, these were, and so he filled one and half of another before the stream from the air pot slowed to a drip. He tilted the pot forward to finish it off, but it rolled to the side and onto his thumb. The skin sizzled against the stainless steel. He jerked away instinctively, knocking the air pot onto its side in the process. By the time he'd set it upright, every head was turned his way.

"Everything all right?" Burke growled.

"Fine," Dent said. "Just fine."

"Well then," Burke continued, a less-than-pleasant smile just visible across his face. "What do you think?"

Dent froze. "I think, well—I think—. What was the question?"

Burke let out a long sigh. "We need you to MC the Roundup this year. You're a natural choice, given the circumstances."

"Oh. Circumstances?"

"Give the preacher a break, Jeff," someone up front said. "He don't know what you're talking about. Hell, he hadn't been in town long enough to change his damn socks yet."

"That's five dollars for swearing," Burke said. The secretary made a note on his legal pad. Burke turned back to Dent. "This year's Tall Tale Roundup will feature one of your church members, Brother Denton. The guest of honor will be Old Mother Earth."

Dent felt a lump growing in his gut. He had heard the nickname before and was certain enough of its bearer that he swore under his breath, though not loud enough to get fined.

"You're talking about Irene?" he ventured. "Irene Ostendorf?"

"Of course. Miss Irene has more history in Earth than anyone still alive."

"She's lived here all her life," a voice chimed in.

"Ninety-six years," said another.

"Ninety-four, you mean!"

"Ninety-six. My granddad was the same age as her. They went to school together."

"Yeah, but I knowed them both. They wasn't the same age. She was just two years smarter than he was."

Dent looked at Rob, who tugged on his left ear. *Bunt.*

"How about I'm your understudy this year," he called to Burke. "I'm afraid I wouldn't do it justice."

"I'll vouch for him on that," Rob called. The other men laughed. Dent tipped his cup in Rob's direction. Jerked his head toward the back of the building. The former coach swiped left-to-right across his chest and then grabbed his right wrist. *Hit and run.* Rob got up from his seat. Moved around the room and disappeared through a door behind the American flag.

The argument over Irene Ostendorf's age picked back up, and Dent saw his chance. He wasn't quite sure where the door behind the flag led, and so he slipped through the front door with his coffee. Walked around back to where Jack now sat on his downturned tailgate, talking with Rob de los Santos.

"I yelled at her to hang on a minute," Jack was saying. "Said, 'Irene, he's just lost is all.' But she yells back, 'Then he needs to be lost somewhere besides here.' I don't know if she meant to pull the trigger just then or not, but—oh. Hey there, preacher."

Dent handed him a cup of coffee. Eyed him dubiously. "You sure that's how it happened, Jack? I mean, the law is going to want a statement from you, I bet."

"Well, now preacher," Jack said, shifting his bony old butt to a different position on the tailgate. "I was telling Rob here more the sentiment of the story than the facts of it."

Rob nodded as though this was a perfectly acceptable policy. He raised a hand ever so slightly to Jack. "If I hear you right—and please tell me if I don't—you were moving equipment and saw this bicyclist."

"Yeah." Jack nodded vigorously. "Japanese fellow. Least I think Japanese. He was bouncing along the highway—you know how uneven that pavement is out there, what with all the temperature changes and tractors and such. And he had a headwind on top of it all. I mean, it was a rotten day to be farming, much less bicycling. Why they call that fun I'll never know."

"But you said he was lost," Rob prompted.

"Right. He stopped at the edge of Old Mother Earth's—that's what we call Irene sometimes, preacher. Old Mother Earth. He stopped at Old Mother Earth's driveway and pulled out his phone and I'm thinking, good luck getting a signal out here, buddy. Nothing in the airwaves but dust and hawks. He punches some buttons and shakes it and beats it on his thigh, and then he mounts back up on his bike."

"Going down the road?" Rob asked. "Or toward Irene's?"

"That I couldn't figure," Jack said. "It's like he was waffling a little. Like his legs were trying to get him to follow the road and his chest was leaning toward the driveway. He ends up turning a complete circle and heading back in my direction for a good hundred yards. Then he turns around again and ducks his head and goes full speed back toward the driveway. Next thing I know, he's flying off one way and his bicycle's flying another, and Irene's standing on her porch with a smoking rifle."

"You could see it smoking?"

"Figure of speech. But I'm still trying to make sense of it all when I hear this weird crunch-ping type sound. That's when I realized I'd run over the bike. So I stopped the tractor and went back for my pickup and got what was left. Oh, and this."

He held out a coin about the size of a half dollar, dulled to a greenish-gray everywhere except across the back, where a shiny silver scrape cut across the bible verse printed there. Dent turned it over. A rugged sailor stared back at him from the "heads" side, his thick fingers gripping tight to the mast as though holding on against a storm.

"What is it?" Dent asked.

"No idea," Jack said. He motioned for Dent to keep the coin. "You think they'll send Irene to prison?"

Both he and Rob looked to Dent.

"I suppose they could," he said at last. "Seems a bit early to start that conversation, though. There's a lot we don't know yet."

A knob rattled on the building beside them, and a flimsy wooden door opened into the alley. Jeff Burke stepped out, Last Man Club gavel still in hand.

"Did y'all move the meeting out back and forget to tell me?" Burke said. His voice was big and pleasant, but tension showed around his eyes.

Rob clapped his hands together and hopped down from the tailgate. "No offense intended. Jack just had a story he needed to tell."

"I bet he did," Burke said. He waved his gavel back toward the Last Man Club's rear entrance. "Wayne Rogers just came barreling in. Said Old Mother Earth shot some bicycler this morning. Apparently they've got him down at Doc's, trying to stitch him back together."

Dent looked at Rob, who nodded once.

"Brother Denton was just on his way over there to offer pastoral support," Rob said. "Let's get back inside. I suppose this complicates our plan for the Roundup."

CHAPTER 2:
MORE TOWARD
THAN AT HIM

B y the time Dent neared the white two-story house where Doc
Schugart, MD, plied his trade, almost every citizen of Earth not
trapped in the public schools had gathered in the town square. Shop
owners, co-op managers, and even farmers dropped everything to
find out what manner of drama had pedaled into town. Catty-corner
from Doc's, the parking lot of Foodliner Grocery was filled to
overflowing with pickups and SUVs. Next door at the Super Chief
Diner, patrons squeezed onto the high deck out front so tightly as to
call to mind the erstwhile bustle of the old train platform it was
meant to resemble.

Dent made his way through the crowds, past curious huddles
of citizens who paused just long enough to register this stranger's
face and identify him as Brother Holloway's replacement at the
Methodist Church. "I thought he'd be taller," he heard someone say
as he passed. "Brother Holloway had his faults, Lord knows, but he
was so tall!"

He walked on, his cheeks flushed from heat and nerves. Sweat
dripped off his neck and down the front of the polo shirt. It pooled
atop his belly and soaked through the fabric in a shape much like
the diagrams of the female reproductive system he remembered from
eighth grade health class. Still, he made it through the gauntlet and
across the street. Before he could congratulate himself, an aging
couple stepped into his path.

"Brother Denton!" the woman said, her pearl earrings and blue-gray hair bouncing to proclaim her cheer. She stuck out her hand. "Mamie Martz. I don't believe we've met yet."

"Pleasure," Dent said.

"Vic and I"—she motioned toward the hunched old man beside her—"we're your neighbors. Right next door, as a matter of fact. I'm sorry we haven't been to call yet. Vic's been laid up for a few days with bowel trouble."

Her husband nodded gloomily.

"I bet you're on the way to Doc's, right?" Mamie said. "Checking on that poor man who had the accident. How sweet of you!"

"Well. I do what I can."

"Isn't that just the truth? That's all we can do. But—." She sidled up alongside Dent, glanced down the sidewalk to make sure no one else could hear. "Between me and you, I'm concerned. Word is that Old Mother Earth shot the poor boy. Is that true?"

"Not to my knowledge," Dent said. "I don't know a lot, really. I—."

"Word is that the bullet passed through both his hands and the bicycle frame." She turned to her husband. "What kind of gun do you suppose could do something like that?"

"Powerful one," Vic Martz said. "Hog killing gun might do it. Thirty-aught-six?"

"I doubt that's true," Dent said.

"And the wounds!" Mamie continued. "Why, he'd look like Jesus crucified. What is it they call that? When someone has the Savior's wounds on them?"

"Stigmata. That's different, though."

"I just can't imagine, Brother Denton. I really can't." She lowered her head. "And most of all, I can't imagine it here in Earth—*Earth!* This is the friendliest little town on the High Plains, Brother

Denton. Maybe the friendliest in all of Texas. I'm sure you've already found that to be true."

"Well."

"So for us to have a shooting—oh! I just can't even begin to tell you. We haven't had a shooting in, what, Vic? Fifty years?"

"That Nebholz boy shot himself, been seven or eight years," Vic said. "And then before that—."

"But those are self-inflicted. Don't you see that's different?" She squared up to Dent. Reached across and laid a hand over his arm. "Once you hear something about that poor woman, you let me know."

"You mean Irene Ostendorf?"

"Of course I mean Irene! I just know this is weighing on her. But also Mauri Beth, bless her heart. That's Irene's niece, who takes care of her. She lives out at the ranch. I'm sure you've met. No? Well, the woman is a saint for all she's endured. Irene never had kids. Lots of speculation as to why—."

"We need to let the preacher go," Vic said. "He's got work to do, I'm sure."

"Of course." Mamie stepped back, smiled broadly. "Welcome to Earth, Brother Denton. So glad you're here."

"Doc's not seeing any patients this morning," a young police officer said as Dent started up the steps. "You'll have to come back on Thursday, unless you have an emergency."

"I'm not a patient," Dent answered, a little snippier than he'd intended. "I'm a preacher. Came to check on the young man you got in there."

The officer eyed him doubtfully. He raised his walkie-talkie, but before he could speak Rachel Shugart poked her head out the door. Dent felt his shoulders relax. Rachel was not only Doc's nurse. She was his daughter, the child of his and his late wife's old age. She was only a few years younger than Dent, but cheerful and fit and easy to like. Had he not sworn off women after his divorce, he might have called her attractive. She put a hand on the officer's shoulder, and Dent could see a black stripe that fanned out along the seam of her bright pink scrubs.

"It's all right, Kyle. He can come on back."

She disappeared, but left the door cracked. The young officer tipped his hat and stepped aside. Another uniformed man, nearly triple the age of the deputy, rose to his feet when Dent entered.

"Can I help you?"

"I'm the new Methodist pastor. Came to check on my parishioner."

"The victim one of yours?"

"After a fashion, yes."

"Well."

Dent extended his hand. The Sheriff shook it and nodded once. "Paul Wayne Pearson. Pleased to meet you, I suppose."

"I can leave just as easy as I came."

"No. It's fine. I could probably use some pastoral comfort myself. Reverend...?"

"John Wesley Denton. Call me Dent."

"Okay."

They sat down across from one another in the little waiting area. The house had been Doc's family's home until his mother died a quarter century ago, when a heart attack ferried Momma Schugart to her eternal home while she watched Wheel of Fortune. Now, Rachel lived in the rooms upstairs. The downstairs provided the only medical services still available to the townspeople of Earth, now that the clinics had moved to Springlake or Portales.

The Sheriff laced his fingers together and dropped them onto his lap. Dent waited for him to speak, to tell his story, just like everyone else seemed to do in towns like this. How his family came in the wheat boon of the twenties and rode out the double hells of the Dust

Bowl and the Depression. How his grandfather helped to charter the local Last Man Club, whose members pledged to be the last man left in town when all others had deserted due to drought or bankruptcy. How his mother suffered as a child and almost died of pneumonia and went to Lubbock to find work during World War II, and then married a GI who had fought in the Pacific and came back with her to the Panhandle because God knew there were no jungles going to spring up here. How he'd fallen in love with a woman too good for this world, who'd had left it far too soon. How he hoped to retire, maybe move to Kentucky where his daughter taught chemistry at a private Christian college.

And as he listened to these stories, Dent knew just as well what people couldn't say out loud. I never intended to be old, but I am, sure as the world. I work and go to church and cheer at the high school football games and see the same people with the same desperate faces as mine. I would gladly trade this chiseled landscape for a lakeside cabin in Hot Springs, except that I myself have been chiseled by time in Earth, and I could not recognize myself were I to leave.

The Sheriff did not offer a story, though, and he did not ask Dent for one. After awhile, he sighed and turned his gaze toward the window to stare at this side of the blinds until Doc finally emerged from the back wearing a fresh white coat.

"Well, it's not a murder case," he said, peeling off his blue nitrile gloves. "He'll live."

"Glad to hear it," the Sheriff said.

"He took a pretty good blow to the head, and I'm certain he has at least a mid-grade concussion. His right foot is fractured, and that knee has some ligament damage. He broke a couple of fingers, too. Other than that, it's mostly scrapes and bruises and thorns. We'll be plucking goatheads out of him for a day or two to come, I bet."

"All right then," the Sheriff said. "No bullet holes?"

"Not a one," Doc said. "Doesn't look like attempted murder to me."

"A bad attempt is still an attempt," the Sheriff said. "Don't you think?"

"I reckon so."

"How's Rachel doing?"

"Fine, fine. She's stitching him up. He's already texting, if you can believe it."

"Wonder of wonders," the Sheriff said. "So can I talk to him now?"

"Not while we're still doing procedures," Doc said. "Give us an hour and we'll have him ready, assuming he's awake. He'll be in and out, what with all the pain meds."

"All right." The Sheriff rose to his feet. "I better go make the arrest."

"Hang on," Doc said. "Why don't you take the preacher here with you?"

The Sheriff narrowed his eyes at Doc. "Now why would I want to do a thing like that."

"Because she's an old woman who's had a traumatic day. If you rile her up more, you're just asking for trouble. And truth be told, Sheriff, you aren't exactly the seat of compassion."

"Compassion isn't my job."

"No, but it's his." Doc yanked a thumb toward Dent. "He might help keep things from escalating. Besides, Old Mother Earth is a Methodist."

"She is?"

"Much as she is anything."

The Sheriff folded his arms and glanced at the preacher. Dent sucked in his gut. Tried to look competent.

"All right," the Sheriff said. He turned to Dent. "We'll take your truck."

"Mine?"

"You've been out to see her before."

"Just once. Last week, right after I got to town."

"So she knows your truck. Or at least she knows it's not a Sheriff's vehicle."

"You think she'd shoot if she knew it was you?"

"I have no idea what she would or would not do," the Sheriff said. "And I've been shot at plenty. The objective here is to keep her from giving me a reason to shoot back."

"You boys be careful," Doc said. "Good luck."

"I'm an atheist in the luck department, but thank you anyway," the Sheriff said. He settled his hat onto his head and looked Dent up and down. "Lord help us," he said.

They drove down County Road 139 in silence, except for the occasional sigh from Dent. The Sheriff rode shotgun in utter serenity, unaffected by the potholes and washboards that lined the road or the awkwardness that filled the air. Dent marveled at the stillness of the Sheriff, despite the bumpy ride. When they crossed the cattle guard onto the ranch, he could feel the jiggle in every square inch of his body.

Dent eased the truck to a stop on the packed clay between the old woman's pickup and a familiar black SUV. Old Mother Earth sat on the porch swing, feet dangling over the boards below, a motley colored blue heeler at her feet. Her thin arms flayed out to either side, elbows dangling over the armrests, and her scrawny legs jutted out from beneath the hem of her cotton dress. She looked pieced together out of old pipe cleaners.

"Took you long enough, Sheriff," she called. "And what in the world are you running around with that fellow for? The last thing I need is another Methodist preacher around here."

Dent searched her wrinkled face for clues to her meaning, whether she was sardonic or serious. Before he could ask, the screen door from her house opened. A stocky man in khakis and tennis shoes backed out, a glass of iced tea in each hand. He wore a sky-blue polo with the Methodist cross and flame logo embroidered over one breast and a magnetic nametag clipped to the other. Dent's heart nose-dived into his chest.

"Hello there, Jay-Dub!" The man handed Irene a glass, leaned down and spoke loudly in her direction. "You remember Jay-Dub, don't you? John Wesley Denton? He's your new pastor."

Irene grunted.

Dent looked at his shoes. Gritted his teeth. No one on the planet called him Jay-Dub except Reverend Bud H. Cockburn, his district superintendent and so technically his boss.

"How are you, Sheriff?" Cockburn said. "Can I get you some tea?"

"Can't drink on duty," the Sheriff said. "Mrs. Ostendorf, what do you have to say for yourself?"

"I'm in a hell of a pickle," she said, smiling. "Boy ain't dead, is he?"

"No. Just beat up is all. You didn't kill him, thank God."

"Wasn't trying to," Old Mother Earth said. "I shot more toward than at him."

Dent raised a hand to his face.

"What if I told you that Schoendienst boy got it wrong?" the old woman continued. "Maybe I was shooting at a coyote or a hawk. I don't see how he could tell, fast as he was going on that tractor."

"Is that your statement or a hypothetical?"

Old Mother Earth grinned. "I figure you're going to tell me I got the right to remain silent. But old as I am, I aim to talk as much as I damn well please."

"Why don't you gentlemen excuse us for a moment?" the Sheriff said.

Dent ascended the stairs, squeezing in between Cockburn and
Old Mother Earth. He touched a finger to the barrel of the rifle that
leaned against the wall behind the old woman. The Sheriff nodded.
Dent picked it up and carried it with him into the house. He emptied
the shells from the chamber and set it just outside the back door.
Cockburn swooped into the kitchen behind him and leaned against
the stove.

"What the holy hell is going on around here?" he said.

"An arrest, I believe."

"That's clear enough," Cockburn snorted. "But I'm talking about
you—your judgment, or lack of it."

"Well."

"Don't 'well' me! Your wealthiest church member gets in trouble
with the law, and you side with the Sheriff?"

"She tried to shoot a guy."

"You're jumping to conclusions."

"And you're caught up in money."

Cockburn blew out a quick stream of air out his nose. In the
two weeks since Dent's move to Earth United Methodist Church,
the D.S. had noted on at least a dozen occasions that Old Mother
Earth might be worth quite a bit of money, which could be put to
use in the Lord's service if Dent played his cards right. Cockburn
sent at least three emails per day advising him on this and various
and sundry other aspects of how to do his job. Cockburn had served
as Earth's pastor for two years before giving way to Reverend K.D.
Holloway four years ago, and he implied to Dent that such a tenure
was more than enough to grant him perpetual wisdom in all matters
Earthen. Coaching, Bud Cockburn called it, although it certainly
felt like meddling to Dent.

"Jay-Dub, listen, I'm sorry if my showing up gets you off on the
wrong foot. I'm not trying to undercut you."

"Well."

"Stop, okay? You've got to understand. I've got a relationship with the people here—a history. You can't replace that overnight. Take Irene's husband, Harlan Brantley. He got cancer back in the late seventies, when you couldn't do much about it. Ended up digging his own grave out back of the ranch and shooting himself in it, so that all Irene had to do was cover him up. I've seen the grave myself, Jay-Dub. Those are not things that people just up and tell you. You have to earn their trust first, which you don't have. Am I making sense?"

"I suppose."

"Not that I blame you," Cockburn continued. "What I'm talking about takes time, which you haven't had—here, or any other place you've ever served. But that's beside the point. Once I heard that Irene was in trouble, I knew I needed to drive down. I should have checked with you first."

"You'd have come anyway."

"Probably," Cockburn said, and he managed a laugh. "Well I suppose there's nothing to do but forgive and forget. But there's another wrinkle in this I bet you don't know about. Have you been back to see the victim yet?"

"No. Jack said he was a Japanese guy. That's all I know."

"More to it than that." Cockburn grinned, obviously in the know and enjoying it. His eyes twinkled. "He wasn't a kid, and he wasn't Japanese. He's a twenty-four year-old Korean American named—ready for this?—Lucas Lim!"

He raised his palms as if to show Dent the value of such prized knowledge.

"Well," Dent said.

"Lim, Jay-Dub! As in Peter Lim's son."

Dent froze where he stood. Removed his glasses and rubbed his eyes and pinched the bridge of his nose. The Reverend Doctor Peter Lim was bishop down in the Houston area, and best friends with Dent's own bishop and former father-in-law, the Reverend Doctor

James Emberton, who understandably hated Dent's guts. If one of Dent's wealthiest church members—who had yet to made a legacy gift to her home congregation—had indeed tried to kill Bishop Lim's son, Dent knew he would somehow get the blame.

"And how did you come across this information?" Dent asked.

"Bishop Emberton, of course. And J.B."

"J.B.?"

"Jeff Burke. I told you, didn't I? We played football together at West Texas A&M. I can't believe I didn't tell you that. The Buffalo Bruisers, they called us. I can't believe I haven't told you."

"Me either."

"I was the halfback, and a pretty good one if I do say so myself. But I never would have gained a yard without. J.B. We ran an I-formation back then, the one that made Mike Rozier such a stud, and J.B. was the fullback. I saw him demolish linebackers that outweighed him by seventy pounds. I never told you this story?"

"Not to my recollection."

"Crazy, isn't it? Neither one of us could think of a thing in college besides beer and tits, and now here I am a preacher and he's the board chair in your church."

"Right," Dent said, trying not to make a face. What were the odds that the person with the most direct power over him as pastor would be a college friend of Bud Cockburn? Best not to calculate those. Dent had never subscribed much to providence, but he had plenty of evidence for its opposite.

"Look, we'd better get out there before the Sheriff works her over," Cockburn said.

"I doubt he'll touch her."

"Of course he won't touch her! But he might get information out of her that hurts her defense." He drained the rest of his tea and dumped the ice into the stainless steel sink. "It'll be tough, playing to both Old Mother Earth and Lucas Lim. I'm sure you'll get it figured out, though. Call me if you need anything—and I mean anything. I've got a history here, Jay-Dub."

"You've mentioned as much."

"All right, then. Be stubborn. But a nice donation from Old Mother Earth could go a long way in getting back on Bishop Emberton's good side."

"I divorced his daughter, Bud. I don't think getting on his good side is all that plausible."

"Then do it to stay on my good side," Cockburn said, weary as Methuselah. "God knows you could use at least one friend."

CHAPTER 3:
MONKEY IN THE MIDDLE

T he Sheriff remained silent as the grave as they pulled out of the driveway, Old Mother Earth tucked into the back seat of Dent's truck. Before they crossed the cattle guard, her head toppled over onto her upright suitcase. She snored softly, her upper dentures poised precariously at the edge of her lips.

"So tell me about her," Dent whispered as Irene snored. "What do I need to know?"

"Can't say," the Sheriff said. "Depends on why you're asking."

"I'm her pastor, and she's in a bad spot. So as her pastor, what do I need to know?"

"She hates preachers."

Dent waited for more information, but none came. At last, he said, "I'm doing my best to help out here, Sheriff. Least you could do is give me something to go off of."

The Sheriff picked up his hat, just an inch. Dropped it back onto his knee. "Tell me what you know first. I'm getting too old to waste my breath on speculation."

Dent gripped the steering wheel. "All right then," he said. "Her given name is Irene Ostendorf, and people call her Old Mother Earth. She's a hundred years old, or near to it. No children. She lives with her niece, who is the child of her youngest sister. The sister died some time back, and the rest of the family has too. So it's just Irene and Mauri Beth, and I think maybe Mauri Beth's daughter."

"Ashley Hyatt," the Sheriff said.

"Ashley," Dent said. "I believe she's in college somewhere. Colorado State?"

"Correct."

"All right then."

"Keep going, Preacher. You're on a roll."

Dent tried to find something else to say, anything to buoy his approval rating with the Sheriff. He came up empty. "That's all I got."

"There we are then."

"Don't tell me you don't know any more."

"I do. I know plenty, as a matter of fact. Not mine to tell."

"Surely there's a public record. Marriage and death and the like. What about Irene's parents?"

"Fair enough," the Sheriff said. "I don't know her Daddy's name, but he died young. Her mother remarried a man named Randall—local legend that one. Died in one of the biggest dusters ever to hit the Plains. Irene married in her teens. Helped out some with her nieces and nephews, but no kids of her own. That enough to do you?"

"Almost. What about her husband?"

"Harlan Brantley. Married in 1935, separated 1974. Deceased 1978. Self-inflicted gunshot wound."

"That's what Bud told me. He said Brantley had cancer, and so he dug his own grave and shot himself in it."

The Sheriff's lips twitched. "Was Reverend Cockburn speaking literally or metaphorically?"

"I don't know. Literally, I think."

"Well."

"Well what?"

"Well nothing," the Sheriff said. "Like I said, it ain't mine to tell. You'd have to ask Old Mother Earth, if you can get her awake. That, or find someone who wants to talk."

When they arrived back at the courthouse, Mauri Beth Hyatt's truck was parked in front, although parked might be too strong a word. The pickup had skidded to a stop at a forty-five degree angle to the sidewalk, straddling the white lines that delineated the parallel parking slots in a manner that was the very definition of wampyjawed. Short, dark skids of burnt rubber trailed the tires. Dent hoped against hope that the driver of the pickup was not similarly unhinged.

Old Mother Earth awoke as Dent glided into a parking space three slots in front of Mauri Beth. She adjusted her dentures and looked around as if to make sure she was still part of the terrestrial realm. Satisfied that death had not yet come to call, she smoothed her dress and checked again on her suitcase. Dent gave the Sheriff a quizzical look.

"Mrs. Ostendorf," the Sheriff said. "You won't be needing any luggage."

"I heard you say that back at the house."

The Sheriff did not answer. Dent opened his mouth to ask her why she bothered to pack a bag then, but the Sheriff held up a hand. A second later, Dent felt his pickup lurch. The rear door swung open, and Mauri Beth Hyatt dove into the cab.

"Irene!" she called. "Thank God you're all right. You are all right, aren't you?"

"Peachy," Irene said.

Mauri Beth turned her head toward the two men in front, eyes boggled with adrenaline. She adjusted her blue US Postal Service shirt, took three deep breaths and moved one hand in a straight line in front of her, left to right.

"My God, Paul Wayne!" she finally blurted. "You could have at least come and got me."

"We had plenty of help. I figured you'd be tied up with the mail. Neither rain nor sleet nor dark of night, that sort of thing."

"You should have come by. At the very least called." She pointed at Dent. "What's he doing here?"

"Moral support," the Sheriff said.

Dent extended a hand into the back seat. "John Wesley Den—."

"Save it," Mauri Beth snapped. "I know who you are and I'm trying hard not to hate you already." She turned back to the Sheriff. "What's the plan, Paul Wayne?"

"Get her inside without breaking a hip, I reckon."

"Don't get smart," Irene said, but a smile had stretched out beneath her wrinkles.

"All right then," the Sheriff said. "Let's come on in and go over your rights. We'll process you through the system and I'll talk to Judge Hicks about bail."

"How much will that be?"

"Depends on how much risk you are to flee." He shot Old Mother Earth a stern look. "You aren't planning on running off, are you?"

"Be serious," Mauri Beth snapped.

"I am."

"You think this is funny?"

"I assure you I do not."

The Sheriff trained his unmoving eyes on Mauri Beth, who returned his stare without blinking. The only movement Dent could detect came from her hand, which again made the left to right motion, as though she were sealing some unseen ziplock bag. When she lowered her hand, her face relaxed, if only just barely.

"Let's get on with it," Irene said, loudly enough to make Dent and Mauri Beth jump. "At my age, I could croak any minute."

"I'll get your suitcase," Mauri Beth said.

"Nope," Irene said. She closed her eyes and raised an indignant hand. "I am a grown woman responsible for my actions. You get home and feed Henry Fifty-one. I'll call you if they decide to electrocute me."

"Irene!"

"All right then," the Sheriff said. "You do whatever you like, Ms. Hyatt, but Ms. Ostendorf needs to get in and see Marlena. She's expecting you. I need a word with the Reverend here." Mauri Beth came around and opened the pickup door and helped her aunt down onto the sidewalk. When she closed the door again, the Sheriff fished out a five-dollar bill and handed it to Dent. "Why don't you run over to the Super Chief and grab yourself some coffee. My treat. Stuff we brew in the office isn't worth spitting in."

"I might just go home if it's all the same to you."

"It's not all the same." He waved toward the crowd across the street. The Foodliner had cleared out a few free parking spaces and erected the two large tents they used for Fourth of July cookouts. Arranged in a square beneath those were several eight-foot tables lined with individually wrapped snack cakes and single-serve bags of chips and all manner of coronary hazards. They had even pulled out a griddle and deep fryer, which the cooks were warming up under the assumption that everyone would stay for lunch. Not to be outdone, the Super Chief set up their own tent and tables, these covered with pastries and pies, with their famed Depot coffee at the end, a thick black sludge the consistency of forty-weight motor oil that the old men guzzled by the pint. Balloons from Peggy's Flower Shop were tied to every post. This was not an arrest. It was a spectacle.

"This may be the single biggest gathering in Earth since the Super Chief Express made its last run," the Sheriff said. "Everybody wants to know what's going on, Brother Denton. I figured you might satisfy their curiosity."

"But you don't like telling other people's stories," Dent grumbled.

"I don't, since you mentioned it. But you do. Telling stories—God's or whoever's—is a preacher's job."

"This wasn't in my ordination vows."

"And babysitting murderous old women isn't in mine. What's your point?"

Dent rolled his eyes, and for the thousandth time already today questioned his calling. Everyone seemed to have an idea of what the preacher's job was, always around one agenda or another. And the Sheriff's request was basic triangulation, a game of monkey-in-the-middle with Dent as the monkey, and doomed to be such. A pastor had to earn his place in every new church and every new town. This was his opportunity to be connected with something that mattered. You know John Denton, right? Preacher who got mixed up in that business with Old Mother Earth here awhile back?

"Anything in particular you want told?" Dent asked.

"Tell them Irene Ostendorf allegedly shot at a bicyclist. Tell them I'm a heartless son of a bitch that hauls old ladies to jail. I really don't care. Just don't make anything up."

He reached for the door handle.

"Hang on," Dent said. "Henry Fifty-one?"

"The dog, I assume."

"Oh."

Dent pondered the implications sadly. It was a dangerous life, that of a country hound. Between coyotes and feed trucks, there were a thousand ways for a dog to meet his maker. Still, fifty-one? He made a note to be patient with Old Mother Earth. With luck like that, he ought to be compassionate—from a safe distance, of course.

CHAPTER 4:
THE VELOCIRAPTOR

A shley Hyatt flexed her throbbing foot, smiling despite the pain. It had taken two excruciating hours for Mondesi, her tattoo artist at Screech Owl, to carve the three-inch figure into her skin. He had balked at the feathers, thinking they would detract from the ferocity of the beast. But Ashley insisted. He had incorporated them beautifully, although he had warned her that greater detail meant greater discomfort. Indeed, nearly sixteen hours after she'd left the shop, the skin on her foot still pulsed and stung, glowing red like it had been pressed with a hot iron. No matter. She now had—and it was worth every wince and swear—a perfect velociraptor permanently imprinted upon her. She giggled out loud.

Sid, the owner of Longs Peak Music and so her boss, slid his bifocals down on his nose and looked over the top of the frames. "You all right there?" he called.

"I'm good."

He grunted and turned back to his electric guitar, checked the maze of wires and cables connecting it and the pedal board to the amp on which he sat, legs crossed as though he were relaxing on a park bench. Had he been born a few years earlier, or somewhere in New York or California, Sid might have been a punk rocker. But his Oklahoma roots had stunted his musical horizons to the point that, after twenty-five years of repairing band instruments and strumming folk music on his acoustic, Sid was only now beginning to learn the ins and outs of playing lead. He adjusted the headphones over his ears and let loose with another riff, visually pleasing but audible only to him. He stopped. Tried again. Frowned, and pulled the headphones down around his neck.

"You sure you're all right?" he asked again. "You just don't seem quite yourself."

"Oh, no, I'm fine. Really." She leaned forward and whispered loudly. "It's a female thing."

"Ah. Right." He yanked the headphones back over his ears.

Ashley rubbed the tender skin beneath the tattoo with her other foot. She hated herself for lying to such a genuinely good guy, and for playing him so easily. But she did not need anyone else meddling today, even someone as meek and lovable as Sid.

She slipped her smartphone from her apron pocket and placed it on the counter below the cash register. Two missed calls from Jen and five from her mother and twenty-eight text messages besides, all of them woven together in an anxiety-riddled testament of just how messed up the situation back home was. Her mother would be continually pulling her imaginary curtain, trying to wall herself off from the danger. The town would be in an uproar. Irene would be giving everybody hell, one way or another.

This last thought almost made her giggle again.

She twisted her foot this way and that, playing with the different motions she could coax out of the raptor. Turning down her toes caused it to lean forward as though preparing to run. Raising them made its legs pull back, its claw ready to strike.

And five hundred miles to the south, her family melted down without her. Her mother wanted to lean on her for support, but she had none to give. She should be there to translate Irene's diatribes to lawyers and judges and Sheriff Pearson, not to mention to talk the old woman down so that she didn't stroke out.

And Lucas? And Jeff? Her truest love and her worst decision, now in spitting distance from one another. God, what a disaster.

Breathe, she told herself. Not my apples, not my pie. She closed the text app and brought up the LinearLife app and scrolled through the directory.

Jobs I wish I had.

Books I wish I'd written.

Foods I should learn to cook.

She looked around instinctively. If anyone ever saw her lists, she might vaporize from embarrassment. *Movies that make me cry? Boys I should never have kissed?* These were not for public consumption. She should delete every one of them on every device she'd ever owned, or at least eliminate the most embarrassing among them.

Reasons I haven't deleted my lists:

1) They are mine, and no one else gets a say in them.

2) They are my most honest record of who I've been.

3) They allow me the delusion of order.

4) They remind me of things that used to matter and maybe still do.

5) They tell a version of the truth I can live with. Maybe.

The phone buzzed, and a text alert scrolled down from the top. "From JB," the ID line read. *Can we talk?*

She chewed her lip. We could, she thought. We could talk about why Lucas is in Earth and how much he knows about us. I could remind you how much we have to lose if we get caught, and you could tell me not to worry, that our affair is a separate sphere from the rest of our lives. But we've covered that ground already. Anything new that comes up will lead to another conversation, which will draw us into another, which will open others still. The deeper we go, the greater the likelihood that I will truly see just how fucked this entire thing is.

She swiped away the notification and LinearLife once again owned the screen. She scrolled down until she found *Things I want (frivolous).* Tapped it. The orange label blinked twice before giving way to a blue background, over which were printed in white letters the whimsical desires of her heart.

1) A velociraptor tattoo.
2) A movie theater.
3) The green journal Sid sells on his magazine rack.
4) Finn hiking boots.
5) An EV convertible.

Each of her lists had exactly five slots. If she couldn't think of enough to fill it, she deleted the list. If she thought of too many things, she had to narrow them down to five or find a way to break them into two genuinely separate files. It was a kind of disciplined journaling—a way to understand herself through patterns and repetitions.

Unfortunately, the exactly five rule meant that the "Things I want (serious)" list went through a never-ending cycle of write, delete, and repeat. She wanted meaningful relationships, but the phrase seemed too trite. A good career would be nice, but how to quantify it? She tried starting sub-lists like "What makes a good career" and "How I know a relationship is meaningful." But those seemed only to skirt around the larger question of what she truly wanted, like gathering toppings without ever making the pizza.

But that was another problem for another day. With a ceremonial flourish, she swiped away "velociraptor tattoo" and added "authentic Japanese tea kettle."

The door to the shop swung open, propelled by far too much force to be one of Sid's regular customers. Ashley dropped her phone back into her apron and looked up.

"Holy shit!" the young woman exclaimed as she spun through the door, a whirl of black hair and pink sweatshirt. She tore past the wall of hanging guitars, past Sid, past the waist-high swinging door that led to the back of the sales counter. It wasn't until after she spoke Ashley's name that she slowed enough to be recognizable.

"Jen?"

"Wow!" Jen said. "I just saw the news and, I mean, just—fucking wow!"

Ashley could see Sid's fingers slide to a stop. He looked up, ready to intervene. Ashley motioned for him to take the headphones down again. "Can you watch the register?" she called. "It'll just be a sec." She grabbed Jen by the elbow and led her through the storeroom and into the break area. "What is wrong with you?"

"Me?" Jen said. "I'm fine. But you!" She stepped back, looked Ashley up and down. Her eyes settled on her bare feet, on the new tattoo. "What is that?"

"A velociraptor."

"I thought those were dinosaurs."

"They are."

She scrunched her nose. "It looks like some sort of mutant chicken."

"Actually chickens would be the mutants." Jen cocked her head and stared, looking for all the world like a particularly confused ostrich. Ashley leaned over into her line of vision. "Focus for me, Jen."

"Right." She eyed Ashley again, concern clouding her face. "Tell me you're not upset."

"Why should I be upset?"

"Jesus, are you serious? Lucas! Your grandma shot him. On your doorstep!"

"Okay, everything you just said is wrong," Ashley protested. "He was at the edge of the driveway. And he wasn't shot. And Irene is my great aunt."

"Still—wow!" She patted down her wild hair. Took a deep breath. "Why do you suppose he was there? I bet he was trying to find you."

"He knows where to find me."

"Bullshi-uht!" Jen exclaimed, drawing out the syllables. She had grown up in Georgia, and excitement caused her to fling phantom vowels at random. "Y'all broke up—what, a month ago?"

"It's been four, actually."

"Oh my. Has it really? Well, however long it's been, you've just dropped off the face of the earth. Moved in with another boy and stopped replying to his messages and—oh, I should probably stop."

Ashley folded her arms. Stared at her friend. "You've been talking to him, haven't you?"

"Who?" Jen asked, too quickly to claim innocence.

"Lucas."

"Nuh-ooh!" Jen looked down at her hand, scrubbed intently at the back of one finger. "Well, maybe a time or two. I just hate the way it ended for y'all, Ash. You and Lucas had a connection—a *connection!* That's just not true with Connor, now is it?"

Ashley dropped her head. Stared at her feet. She hadn't exactly forgotten about Connor, the experimental boyfriend with whom she'd been living since August. He simply wasn't relevant to the trouble at hand. They had decided from the start to make theirs a relationship of convenience, a way to split bills and tend to biological desires and keep loneliness at bay until they finished their degrees in the spring. But he proved less mature than she'd hoped, and she was a hot mess of grief and secrets besides. The arrangement had not even made it to midterms before Ashley left their bed and set up camp in the living room.

"Connor and I are fine," Ashley said. "All good."

"All good is not good enough!" Jen answered. "If I had a man so passionate for me that he'd bike five hundred miles to get to my family's ranch, I would snap him up and not let him go."

"You sound like a kidnapper. And he sounds like a stalker."

"And you, Ashley Jane, are hopeless." She pressed a hand to her lower abdomen. "I shouldn't have drunk that second margarita at La Huerta. I gotta pee like a bandit. Don't go anywhere." She ducked into the bathroom and closed the door.

Ashley pulled her phone back out and checked her notifications screen. Another text, arrived two minutes ago. "From JB." She tapped the screen.

I want to see you.

I can't, she replied.

You can. This weekend. Usual setup. I need you.

She put a knuckle between her front teeth and bit down. She had yet to parse why she had rekindled the affair with Jeff Burke, disastrous as it had been the first go-round, and she had not been able to find a way to extract herself from it this time. Jeff was too forceful and she was too stubborn to think it would end without damage. He needed her, and so he presumed she needed him—an assumption that, no matter how much she hated herself for it, might be correct.

Too risky, she answered.

No more risky than coming back to Earth.

She extended her finger. Checked the teeth marks around the knuckle. Did Jeff know Lucas was in Earth, albeit incapacitated? Surely he did. In a town that small, only the worst things stay hidden. The chances of them running into each other were too high for comfort, even with Lucas laid up at Doc's. And if that happened, Jeff would beat the everloving shit out of him.

The toilet flushed. Ashley dropped the phone back into her apron pocket.

"You have to admit it's romantic," Jen called over the water running in the sink. "I mean, Lucas took a bullet for you."

"Uh-huh," Ashley said reflexively. Already, she was conjuring two new lists, *why I should go to Lubbock* and *why I should not.*

Jen emerged from the bathroom and clamped one damp hand over each of Ashley's shoulders. "You two are in love. And everybody knows it but you."

Ashley tensed, and Jen released her. The phone vibrated at the base of her apron. "I have to get back to work."

"Fine," Jen said with a roll of her eyes. "But you call me when you get out of here, okay? Promise?"

"Thanks for stopping by."

Jen dropped her shoulders in a pitying shrug, then leaned forward and gave Ashley two air kisses, one below each ear. A second later, she flung open the break room door and flew out to whatever new drama awaited her.

Ashley pulled out her phone. One unread message. JB.

I'll see you this weekend.

She lowered her head, weighed down by the inevitability of it. She was going to Lubbock—of course she was going! But she didn't answer the text. Instead she pulled up LinearLife again and began a new list.

Things I know about love:

1) My mom loves me. So does Aunt Irene.

2) Jeff doesn't love me, and I don't love him, and that doesn't matter.

3) I don't love Connor but I might have loved Lucas but that also doesn't matter.

4) I don't know anything about love.

5) No one else does either.

CHAPTER 5:
THE GAUNTLET OF GOSSIP

A s he walked from his pickup to the diner, Dent was accosted by those gathered around tailgates who had either arrived too late to get inside the Super Chief or who had been lured outside by the free treats. He moved from group to group, explaining what he knew and admitting what he didn't, mostly. He told the story to the people at the base of the steps, then again to the old men on the patio. With each telling, he learned a little more about what enquiring minds wanted to know. Did the Sheriff ask him to go with him to make the arrest, or was it Mauri Beth? Were they scared going up the driveway that Old Mother Earth would shoot them? How long would she be in jail? By the time Dent squeezed through the glass doors of the Super Chief, he had a speech far more polished than his typical Sunday sermon. He could recite it word for word, the way the ancients could *Beowulf* or the *Iliad* or the prophets. He entered the dining room with a confidence he hadn't felt since seminary.

Twenty people followed him in from outside, pushing him toward the center of the room. The other patrons caught sight of him, and a wave of silence rippled through the restaurant from front to back. Farmers at the counter spun on their stools to face him, coffee cups in hand. Customers left the two dining cars to stand along the walls of the main room. The hostess flipped a switch, and the model train wound to a stop overhead. Emilia de los Santos, who owned the Super Chief, came out of the kitchen, drying her hands on her apron.

"Nobody pays this much attention to me in church," Dent said, and the room burst into laughter.

Bolstered by his early success, Dent recited the story with near revivalist fervor, once or twice teetering on the edge of acceptable enthusiasm for these stoic Texans. He held court for half an hour before he concluded his tale. Once he'd finished, people began to trickle away, back to cold plates of food or deferred errands or livestock. Behind them came another wave however, a mix of newcomers to the party and returners who only wanted to hear the story again. He spoke to that crowd, which soon gave way to another crowd. Dent went on like an old movie reel, playing and rewinding over and over, each time for a different audience.

As the crowd shifted, Dent could see Jeff Burke, the chair of the Methodist church board, enter through the hall door that led to the offices. He was dressed in the same blue polo he'd worn at Last Man Club, but he'd swapped the pressed slacks for khaki shorts that revealed thick, muscled calves, the left one sporting a tattoo of the IronMan Triathlon logo. A fullback's tight muscles still rippled across his shoulders and upper back, and his biceps popped out from beneath his sleeves. His face was square and handsome, although unevenly tanned thanks to the sport sunglasses that now rested atop his thick black hair. He sat down at the bar and folded his arms and cast a thoroughly unreadable stare at Dent.

After his sixth recitation, Dent's story began to lose steam. He could feel a tightening in his voice box, which soon turned to a lump that he couldn't quite swallow. Before he could embark on telling number seven, Burke stood up and raised his hand to what remained of the crowd.

"I think we all ought to show our appreciation for Brother Denton's willingness to give us the latest news," he said. He brought his hands together, and the room burst into applause. Burke put an arm around Dent's shoulder and quieted the crowd again. "But before we let him go, I think it would be fitting if Dent here offered a word of prayer for our town after what I think we'd agree has been a troubling day. Pastor?"

Dent shuffled on his feet, his newfound confidence immediately drained. Preachers were supposed to be able to conjure eloquent prayers on the spot, regardless of the circumstances. But he had always been a failure at pray-on-demand, and anyway, what exactly was the appropriate prayer for a situation such as this? To intercede for Old Mother Earth, whom the town claimed as something near to a mascot? Lucas Lim, her poor victim, certainly could use a prayer. So could Dent, for that matter. Perhaps Burke had already forgotten the debacle of a blessing Dent had offered just a few hours ago at Last Man Club. Or—and this thought made Dent squirm more than a little—perhaps he hadn't.

Regardless of motive, Burke had opened up a door through which Dent must surely enter, and he plowed ahead, awkward though he was. He stumbled over simple words, let his mouth go too quickly. The content was also thin, a jumble of platitudes that even included a couple of "thee"s and "thou"s from the King James Version of his childhood. After a failed attempt to salvage his effort through a Scripture quotation, he decided to scuttle the prayer in Jesus' name. Burke squeezed his shoulder and echoed his amen, then invited Dent to join him in a back table for a late lunch.

"Congratulations," Burke said. "Seems like you're quite the popular fellow today."

"Right place at the right time is all," Dent answered.

"If that's what you think."

"What am I supposed to think, if not that?"

Burke smiled. "I'm sorry. We got off to a bad start just now, you and me. I don't mean to be an ass. My wife tells me I just can't help it. I guess you know how that goes, right?"

"I'm divorced."

"Well so am I," Burke said with a wave. "Twice, for that matter. Hell, half the people you meet anymore are divorced. But you were married how long?"

"Fifteen years."

"So you know what it's like to have a woman needle you about the way you are, right? You don't have to answer that. Look, all I'm saying is that the world might run a little smoother if we were just honest with each other, don't you think?"

A young waitress bobbed through the door at the end of the dining room, adjusting the dozens of buttons she'd pinned to her red apron as she walked toward them. Her nametag read "Maya," and that's how Burke greeted her. While those two conversed about Burke's twin daughters—apparently Maya babysat them—Dent tried to read the buttons without seeming to stare at her shapely chest. A few had slogans, the typical teenage fare of chasing your dreams and living life to the fullest. She advertised for Wall Drug, the EHS Senior Class, and of course the Texas Tech Red Raiders. She was a member of Future Farmers of America and All-Region Choir, as well as in inductee into Beta Club, for which she wore a blue rubber bracelet.

Impressive girl, Dent thought, albeit grudgingly. She must have been three years younger than Dent's own daughter Leah, a few pounds lighter and certainly attractive. Leah was prettier, Dent decided, with better skin and less makeup. Still. Maya was someone else's daughter, and who was he to judge? Life wasn't supposed to be a comparative sport. Maya wrote down their orders on her notepad and came alongside Burke, who put an arm around her waist and gave her a fatherly squeeze. He watched her go, ponytail swishing between her shoulder blades. When she disappeared through the swinging doors into the kitchen, he leaned forward to speak. Dent twisted in his seat. The vinyl emitted an unflattering squawk.

"I know the Sheriff probably sent you over here," Burke said. "I know you're telling the truth about what happened as you see it. But these people around here, they love a good story—and sometimes it's the story that becomes fact, rather than the other way around. And when the wrong story becomes the accepted one, well, people suffer. You follow me?"

"I suppose." He lifted his coffee to his lips, held it there an extra second. "No, I suppose I don't. Am I getting this wrong somehow? Did I say something out of line?"

"No, no. Not at all!" Burke folded his hands on the table. Leaned forward. "This town practically raised me, Dent. After my mama died, they all pitched in to help. I don't know where I'd be today without them, I truly don't. But I guarantee you I'd more likely be inmate number something or other instead of superintendent of Earth schools."

"Well," Dent said.

The young waitress whizzed back into the room with their food. She lowered a platter of chicken-fried steak in front of Dent and slid Burke's chef salad in place.

"Thank you, darlin'," Burke said. He stabbed a forkful of greens and raised them toward Dent. "Here's a fact for you. Seventy-nine percent of people who live in Earth were born within a thirty mile radius of where we're sitting right now."

"All right," Dent said. He chewed on that a moment. "So not everybody born in Earth stays, but almost everyone who stays is born here?"

"That's right!" Burke said with a wide smile. "So a bicycler just riding into town for no apparent reason? You can appreciate my suspicions."

"Maybe. There's still a lot to learn."

"Always is, Preacher."

CHAPTER 6:
THE BOOK OF KNOWLEDGE

Dent awoke in a strange room without the slightest inclination to rise. The light above the recliner where he'd spent the night was off, but the blinds to his left were closed at a downward angle, and rays of sunlight bore through the slats like lasers. Every muscle in his back was stiff, and his head roared in a way he hadn't felt since the morning after his wedding.

Slowly, with a dreamlike sense of dread, he raised his left hand. He examined the fingers, then turned them over to be sure. No ring. He laid his palm over his forehead.

The wedding had taken place at a retreat center in Lake Junaluska, North Carolina. Bishop Charles W. Emberton, episcopal leader of the High Plains Annual Conference and the father of the bride, had reserved the retreat center for the weekend after a Council of Bishops training event and invited his colleagues to stay for the ceremony. The Appalachian venue meant that the older members of Dent's Texas family couldn't come, owing to long drives and expense. But Janet was insistent.

"Daddy is used to getting his way," she said. "He thought this would make us happy, and so we're going to go to North Carolina and get married and be happy."

What Janet had failed to specify was the duration of happiness required. Dent estimated true marital bliss to have lasted only until a few minutes past their first lovemaking session as a married couple, a fumbling encounter in the dressing room where they changed into their reception attire. Still flushed, they exited through a back door onto a blazing white sidewalk that had been chalked in blue with an arrow and the words "Newlyweds this way!" Janet frowned.

"Who did this?" she said. She turned an accusing stare onto Dent. "The wedding policy didn't say we were allowed to write on the sidewalks."

"It'll be fine, honey," Dent said. He leaned forward until his lips brushed her ear. "The policy didn't say we could have sex in the dressing room, either, but—"

"Don't be juvenile. Someone will have to clean this up. Find out which of your friends is responsible and put them to work before Daddy sees it."

She walked a half step in front of him most of the way to the pavilion that housed the reception. When the well-wishers—a full two-thirds of whom could be greeted by the title "Reverend"—began to applaud, Janet slowed up and took his arm. Dent smiled broadly, but not for the happy throng, and not even for Janet. He had spotted Leah, their five-year-old daughter, born their freshman year at Lambuth College. When Janet had broken the news of her pregnancy—matter-of-factly, at the dinner table, to her parents and her boyfriend at the same time—Dent feared he had just lost both his love and his career. Half a decade later, tears dripped from his eyes as he thought about all they had overcome—the scandalized reaction from their churches, the loss of friends, the embarrassment to Bishop Emberton's family. And now there they were, little Leah's parents tying the knot after so long a struggle. He sniffled. Wiped his eyes. Leah waved at them with one tiny hand, clung with the other to her Grandpa Emberton's leg. The bishop leaned down and whispered something to the child, and she broke into a run toward them, straight into her mother's arms. Janet gave her a kiss and told her she needed to put her shoes back on before she ruined her stockings.

An hour later, as the wait staff was setting up the buffet, Dent snuck out the back with a wet towel he'd pilfered from the kitchen and began erasing the nearest chalk drawings. Leah must have seen him go, because she soon was there on her knees beside him, helping scrub until the picture was no more than a blue smudge on the white concrete. He asked if she wanted to help clean some more. She nodded, and off they went into the cool mountain evening, stopping here and there to admire a flower or listen to a birdcall. He pushed aside mental images of the disapproving looks guests were sure to give once they realized Janet's daughter and groom were missing. It was his wedding day too, dammit, and a half hour wouldn't kill anyone. Besides, but these were the moments he liked best—when he was alone with his little girl, when they were not in a hurry.

So filled with joy was Dent that he didn't notice the blue chalk lines that were forming along the hem of Leah's dress as they cleaned, or the blue handprints in her skirt until they were dug in to the fabric. He was trying to brush off what he could when he heard Janet's footsteps coming toward him, her very heels clicking disapproval. What the hell, he thought. She'd have to learn to lighten up if this marriage was going to last.

"Reverend?"

Dent turned his head slowly toward the voice. Reluctant though he was to lose the image of his little girl, he was more than happy to let it go before the visage of Janet got within shouting distance of his memory. He blinked. Floated back toward the present and its furnishings. Office chairs and bookshelves. Fluorescent lights. The old man's voice—Doc's voice. He started piecing his situation together. He had come by last night after his conversation with Jeff Burke to check on Lucas Lim and keep Doc company. He and the good physician had stayed up late talking, and Dent had closed his eyes, just for a moment. That had to have been what? Six hours ago at least. He blinked again. Doc sat in a straight-backed chair with his legs crossed, a cup of coffee in one hand and an iPad in his lap. He had changed out of the jeans and sweatshirt he'd worn the night before in favor of a lavender dress shirt and khakis, which he wore beneath a crisp white lab coat. He raised the cup in salute. "How you feeling?"

"Old," Dent muttered.

"At your age?" Doc said. "Boy, you don't know the meaning."

Dent pulled the lever to the side of the chair and was flung upright. "How's the patient?"

"If you're talking about Mr. Lim, he seems to be all right. Still sleeping, last I checked. But if we're talking about you, I'd say you're a mess. Two weeks on the job, and you're already stretched thin and stressed out, and you're developing sleep apnea. I had to go back to the waiting room to get away from your snoring."

"Oh. Sorry."

"Those aren't your most immediate problems, though. I'd say that list starts here."

He leaned across and handed Dent the tablet, open to the online version of the *Avalanche-Journal*'s website. "Earth Woman Fires at Cyclist in Possible Hate Crime." Beneath it was the byline crediting Megan Ross, alongside a picture of a young woman who had asked him several questions as he held court yesterday in the Super Chief. He wiped his hand over his face. Never had it occurred to him that there might be a reporter in the crowd. He should have known better, but what could be done now except fall on the sword of his own idiocy? He tried to focus on the screen.

"Hate crime?" Dent mumbled.

"Reasonable question, I suppose," Doc said. "Random shooting at a Korean-American. It doesn't look good." He motioned for Dent to scroll down. "Go on. It gets worse."

Halfway through the article, his eyes froze over a familiar set of letters. That could not be his own name, here in print, quoted in an article about one of his parishioners. Yet there is was, clear as day—"said Rev. John Denton, pastor of Earth First United Methodist Church, where Ostendorf attends."

Dent handed Doc the tablet. Wiped his hand over his face.

"People around here aren't going to like that," Doc said.

"I don't like it either."

"Well enough. I wish I could say it's not a big deal. But I've already had three calls from your church members asking me what I thought of your story."

"What are they doing calling you?"

"Because they trust me," Doc said. "You're still the new guy. I'm not saying it's fair. I figure you'll have some folks after your hide today."

"Burke," Dent groaned. "Damn."

Doc raised his thick gray eyebrows. "Jeff Burke? I didn't realize he was a Methodist. Must be a new thing."

"I think he married into the church five or six years ago. He's the chair of the church board."

"That doesn't sound good."

"And he's apparently friends with my district superintendent, too."

"Oh, right," Doc said. "Buddy Cockburn. I'd forgotten. They played college football together in Amarillo—the Buffaloes. Buddy was a running back, as I recall. But Burke was the fullback, the one who did the dirty work. Burke the Bull, they used to call him."

"You're not helping," Dent moaned.

"I guess not." He pulled off his glasses and wiped the lenses with the hem of his lab coat and smiled. "Well, I wouldn't worry too much about the Bull. He's more into triathlons than head thumping these days. Besides, he's got plenty to keep him occupied, what with two little girls to chase around, and one on the way."

Dent nodded. Paige and Kaylee, the twin daughters of Jeff and Crystal Burke, had spent the entirety of Dent's Sunday sermon playing hide and seek in the empty front pews. The thought of a third made Dent's temples throb.

"Burke's a tough bird," Doc said. "He had to raise himself from the time he was old enough to fry an egg."

"He said the town sort of raised him together."

"I suppose that's partly true. Most of us had our own worries, though, and I'm sure he slipped through the cracks at times. If he's rough around the edges, he comes by that honestly."

"So he's all right then? Good at heart, I mean."

"Now don't be putting words in my mouth." Doc tapped his iPad and checked the time. "Quarter after seven. I figure you'd want to sneak out of here and get cleaned up before the church folks start getting after you."

Dent hoisted himself out of the chair and slowly stood up straight. He'd walked over from the Super Chief yesterday afternoon, he remembered now, but that was before spending the night in a recliner. He hoped he loosened up some before he got out to the street in view of Earth's citizens.

"Hang on," Doc said. "I'll get you some ibuprofen."

While Doc went to get the pills, Dent nosed around the office. Next to the door, quartered off by a cubicle wall, was Rachel's neatly ordered workspace. The rest of the office belonged to her father, Dr. Walker Philip Schugart. Medical books with leather spines lined the shelves to his right, dusty symbols of authority that Dent guessed hadn't been opened since the dawn of the internet. The requisite diplomas and certifications hung on the wall behind the desk, which was covered with stacks of files ordered according to a system he could not decipher. The smaller stack of shelves beside the window held more personal items—photos of Doc with family members or regional celebrities, novels by Tony Hillerman and Cormac

McCarthy. On the top shelf, a glass case held an imposing black book with "Die Heilige Schrift" stamped in gold across the cover. The Holy Scriptures, bound together on another continent no telling how long before Earth was settled.

Dent walked around the desk to examine the old family Bible up close, but a cache of papers on the floor by Doc's chair caught his eye. It was loosely held by a white binder, whose four-inch spine had been duct taped together at each seam. Brightly colored tabs and sticky notes, some covered with Doc's chicken scratch, jutted out from all sides. On top was a new sheet of white paper, divided into sections by black lines. He reached down and picked it up, inch by inch in deference to his sore back.

It looked to be some sort of homemade patient info form, although not entirely medical in nature. The top third was a kind of curriculum vitae, in this case for Doc's newest patient. Lucas Lim, born on February 27. Age 24. Parents (divorced): Bishop Henry Lim and Cheri Gatlin. In the middle of the page, underneath the heading "Misc Notes," Doc had written a brief description of the incident with Old Mother Earth, and a few general medical notes. The bottom section listed people linked to the patient. "John Denton—Methodist. Ashley Hyatt—girlfriend?"

Dent lowered himself into Doc's chair to get a better look at the other sheets in the binder. He cracked it open and peered inside to find yellowed versions of the same form, reproduced in the purple ink of an old mimeograph machine. Most of the people listed were unfamiliar to him, although he did recognize some prominent family names. The sheets were filed alphabetically by first name. Surely Doc wouldn't have a sheet for his own daughter, though, would he? He carefully lifted the pages to about where he would expect to see "Rachel".

"I see you found The Book of Knowledge." Doc said. He stood just on the other side of the desk, looming larger than he had moments before.

Dent froze. *It was a test,* he thought. *He wanted to see if I'd go snooping, and I did, and now I'm busted.* He'd been set up before, but that was always within the confines of church—committee ambushes and the like. But this sting involved a doctor and a shooting and the fishbowl of Texas Methodists. Here Dent was—innocently enough, not that he expected that to matter—tampering with medical records. What would it be like, he wondered, to be a prison chaplain from inside the cellblock? Heat rushed to his cheeks. He stammered out an apology and put his hands against the armrests to push himself out of the chair.

"Keep your seat," Doc said, but without any apparent malice. He set his offerings down on the desk—pills and water, the physician's sacrament. He lowered himself into his straight-backed chair and motioned toward the binder. "Careful with that."

Dent raised his eyebrows and tried not to look guilty. "All right."

"You might find out more than you really want to know, if you look too close. That's forty-five years of Texas history right there. It would curl what hair you got to read what's in those pages—secrets that would bring about a localized apocalypse, should they ever find the light of day. People do remarkable things, you know—lovely, generous things, but also cruel things. And everything we do affects someone else. I don't know how anyone can hope to take care of people—physically or spiritually either one—without knowing a little about who they are and how they got that way. Who's cheating who and who's being true, as the old song goes. The Sheriff has his criminal files, but we professional helpers have to go beyond just legal or illegal—personal histories and family dynamics and so forth."

Dent shifted in Doc's chair. His seminary professors had warned him about keeping such records, how they might over time skew even the most noble pastor's view of his flock. Still, Dent had kept mental diaries of wrongs perpetrated at his expense. And his predecessor at Earth UMC, the formerly Reverend K.D. Holloway, had gone so far as to catalogue and index the facts and foibles of his congregation on one hundred and eighty-seven neatly typed pages, wrapped with a rubber band and stuffed into a yellow envelope with THE DIRT written across the front in permanent marker. Dent had not yet perused Holloway's vengeful opus. Thus far he had treated it as scrap, using it only to kill scorpions. But neither had he thrown it away.

"Well since you found my book, why don't you help me with it?" Doc asked. He reached around and took up Lucas Lim's sheet, grabbed a pen and set it on the paper. "The Lim fellow says his daddy's a bishop?"

"I believe so."

"Any reason you can think of he might end up here? Earth isn't exactly a place you hit unless you're aiming for it."

"Well. Your book was open, see—."

Doc smiled. "You saw the note about the Hyatt girl then?"

Dent nodded.

"The lock screen on his phone," Doc said. "It was a selfie of him and Ashley Hyatt. Looked to be on top of a mountain someplace."

"You sure it was Ashley?" Dent asked.

"I delivered her as a baby and I've known her ever since. So yes. Positive."

"So he came to Earth looking for her."

"I was hoping you might know. Anything you can tell me about him?"

"No. Not about him specifically. He is a PK though."

"A PK?" Doc scribbled the letters onto his page.

"Preacher's kids. They're expected to be perfect angels who know all the answers in Sunday school, but usually that's not the case. PKs are the ones who nap during the sermon and smuggle whiskey in shampoo bottles on the youth trips."

"Were you a PK?"

Dent shook his head. "My momma taught school and my daddy drove truck. But I have a daughter that gave her mother and I holy hell when she was a teenager."

"Well now. I didn't realize you had children."

"Just the one."

"You don't say much about it."

"Doesn't mean I don't think about her." He waited, letting the silence grow to the very edge of comfortable before speaking. "We had her when we were in college, before we got married. She's grown now. I try to give her space."

"I won't pry then," Doc said. He waved away the topic with his pen and went back to his page. "So what you're telling me is that this Lucas Lim's daddy is something like a super-preacher, then—somebody he'd have to work pretty hard to differentiate from."

"Right," Dent said. "But every kid is different. I've known bishops' children that joined punk bands or became Buddhists. Then there's my ex-wife, who instead developed this obsessive need to be the perfect Christian child."

"Kids comply and kids rebel," Doc said. "I don't think that has much to do with the holiness of their parents. You still keep in touch with—what did you say your daughter's name was?"

"Leah. And I try. It's complicated.

"Don't I know it." Doc nodded slowly, then drew in breath and raised himself up. "Well, find out more for me, please. Our friend tells me bits and pieces between morphine naps, but I don't trust all he's saying. We need a better idea of who Lucas Lim really is."

CHAPTER 7:
ARE YOU AN HONEST MAN?

Dent slipped away from Doc's to the parsonage, showered off the stress-infused funk of the previous day, and emerged once more looking like someone who, under the right circumstances, might be taken for a professional clergyperson. In fact, he dared to think he would cut a semi-impressive figure when he met Rachel for the joint pastoral-slash-medical visit they planned to pay Old Mother Earth. But his choice in attire—an athletic-cut maroon polo Janet had bought him one year for Pentecost—hung loose above his elbows, illustrating his dire need to get back into the weight room. And if Rachel wore the same kind of neon pink scrubs that she'd had on yesterday, they would emerge from the car together looking like some deranged valentine. That sort of aesthetic misstep used to drive Janet crazy, and her voice was screaming at him from inside his head. Only spite for her memory kept him from going back home to change.

He climbed the steps to the Super Chief, hearing every pop and creak of the boards below his feet. A day after teeming with curious townsfolk and junior members of the regional press, the Super Chief had fallen into ghostly silence. People were back at work, playing catch-up from the impromptu holiday or simply laying low so as not to appear too curious. The farmers, never a crowd to deviate from routine, had already come and gone, since no self-respecting man could justify beginning his work later than 7:00 a.m., and certainly not for two days in a row. Only Maya Jordan was there to greet him, seated at one of the metal patio tables and rolling silverware into napkins.

"Hi, Pastor Denton," she said sweetly. "Your friend not with you today?"

"My friend?"

"Jeff." She waved that name away. "I mean Mr. Burke. You were in here with him yesterday."

"Right," Dent said. "No. Just me this time."

"Sorry. He makes me call him Jeff at his house. I watch his kids." She picked up a handful of the rolled silverware and dropped it into a bus tub. "Can I get you some coffee?"

"Please. To-go."

He followed her inside. The main dining room was also empty, except for a half dozen old and presumably Baptist ladies whose breakfast plates were wedged in around Bibles and study guides. Emilia de los Santos stood on the ladder in the corner, a Phillips screwdriver between her teeth, examining the underside of the toy train she and Rob had installed not long after the Super Chief opened. The track snaked around light fixtures and through tunnels in the walls that led to the old dining cars Emilia had affixed to the building to serve as overflow rooms. The train even had a remote-control whistle that sent a *whoo-whoo* and a puff of steam out of the little smokestacks atop the engine. It ran in the same loop all day, as fixed in its course and fascinating in its movements as the storied rail line that had inspired it.

The real Super Chief Express had never officially stopped in Earth, although it had sped through town every other day during a historic six-week stretch. A bridge collapse near Amarillo diverted the train to a more southerly route while repairs were underway, and the famed engine dipped through Earth on its way to Albuquerque for its one fuel stop between Chicago and San Francisco. Old timers could still remember lining the platform to watch the bright red engine streak through, destined for cities far away as the moon. Those were, in fact, some of the first stories Dent had heard upon his arrival.

But even in those halcyon days the elders so wistfully spoke of, the demise of the rail was already flying overhead, prosperity arcing right over the High Plains in shimmering passenger jets. Within the decade, the rail lines would pull out of Earth, leaving its once lively station to rot. A few enterprising citizens, descended from the original Dust Bowl speculators, tried to flip the building into something new. It housed an auto parts store for eight years and a bicycle shop for two, but neither could do sustainable business, what with Wal-Mart now just over in Portales. The station's ownership fell to the bank, which sold it to the city, which let it go so near to seed that the city council seriously considered lighting a match and letting the volunteer fire department use it for training. When Emilia de los Santos offered to buy it so she could open a restaurant, the council almost refused to let the sale go through on the grounds that it would lead to her certain financial ruin. She told them just to drop their price, if they were so all-fired worried about her financial state, and the city relented. Ten years later, the old men who drank coffee every morning on her patio still predicted that the Super Chief Diner would fail within a month.

Emilia hopped down from the ladder and folded it up. She walked over behind the counter, took the two dollars Dent was getting ready to hand Maya, and dropped the bills in the girl's tip jar instead.

"Coffee's on the house this morning," she said. "Come on back." She led him through the swinging doors that opened to the kitchen, past the prep area and to the office. She stowed the ladder and the screwdriver in a small closet and began moving stacks of books and papers off the desk and folding chairs. "I suppose I should thank you for telling your story over here yesterday," she said as she worked.

"Biggest day of business we've done since the Centennial Rodeo four years ago. Look out."

She held up her hand, stopping Dent's butt in mid-descent toward the newly cleared seat. He straightened. Stepped to the side. Emilia reached behind the chair and drew back with a large white canvas, onto which was sketched a sleek train engine, so detailed that it might have chugged right off the mat and onto the Plains.

"You have quite the talent," Dent said.

"Don't I wish!" Emilia answered. She tucked the canvas beneath her desk, safely away from any clumsy movements Dent might make. "Dad did that. It's supposed to be a Christmas gift for Rachel. He'd kill me if she sees it before then."

"Oh?"

Emilia laughed. "She didn't tell you, did she? Well I see she didn't. Doc is my father too. Rachel and I are sisters."

"Sisters?"

"After a fashion, yes. Our momma grew up in Chicago. She got pregnant with me when she was nineteen, thanks to a boy she'd met her first year of college. She hid it pretty well until late in the spring. But then the dean got wind of it and told her parents, who were old-school Catholics. So instead of going back home after term to face them, she ran away."

"Ran away here? To Earth?"

"Not on purpose. The plan was San Francisco, I think, although God knows what she would have done out there. But she only made it as far as Earth before she went into labor. Doc delivered me that night, and three months later married my mother. Can you believe that?"

"Those were different times," Dent said.

"Were they? The old days, I mean. Were they all that different?"

He thought for a moment. "I couldn't say."

"Well, there are plenty who will say it for you. Memory is a funny thing. Ninety percent of the people around here are liars. I'm sure you know that by now."

"Truly I do."

Emilia looked at him, eyes asquint, for long enough that he began to think he'd said something terribly wrong. He told himself not to shift in his seat. Shifted anyway. Tried to change the subject. "Rachel and I are heading up to see Irene this morning. That's why I'm here. Meeting your sister."

"She told me," Emilia answered. "Said it was to make things easier on Old Mother Earth, so that she didn't have two separate visits to take care of her physical and spiritual needs."

"That's the plan, I believe."

"All right. Good for you both." She leaned forward, elbows on knees. "Are you an honest man, Dent?"

He felt his face go flush. Pretended to consider the question, if only to buy time so as not to stammer. "I like to think so."

"So does everybody else," Emilia snorted. "The mystics say we are hidden from ourselves. Do you believe that's true?"

"I think probably so." He watched her face for a reaction, but could not tell if his answer pleased her. He looked out the window. Prayed for Rachel to arrive quickly.

"I won't ask for perfection," Emilia said at last. "But you'd best be honest as you can, especially if things go the way they might between you and my sister."

"And what way is that?"

Emilia grinned. Shook her head as though marveling at a particularly dim-witted pet. "You got to pay better attention than that," she said. "If you expect to see people for what they are, I mean. It takes some work to tell the appropriate liars from the abominable ones."

Dent looked out the narrow window, vainly hoping for some clue as to what his response should be. Instead, he caught sunlight glinting off the windshield of Rachel's Subaru, leaving streaks of purplish green temporarily stamped across his retinas. He nearly sprang out of his seat, and in fact rose so quickly that the backs of his knees slammed into the seat of the chair, sending it crashing into the wall behind.

"Sorry," he said. "Good thing you move that painting."

"He hasn't painted it yet," Emilia said.

Dent glanced out the window again, wondering if he could get out to the car before Rachel came in to see her sister and thus kept him on Emilia's hot seat awhile longer. But Rachel merely waited, one arm dangling out the window to reveal—and this, if nothing else in this godforsaken town, seemed a grace to Dent—khaki scrubs.

Irene's niece, Mauri Beth, was on the front porch to greet them when they drove up to the ranch. She waved at Rachel, but her face hardened when she saw Dent. She put her thumb and forefinger together and moved her hand left to right. Turned and went inside, leaving the door slightly ajar.

"Why does she do that?" Dent asked.

"Do what?"

"That thing with her hand. Like she's closing up a baggie."

"Oh, right. That's the Curtain of Calm. I'm not sure where she got it from. Probably Dr. Becky. That was our counselor in town for years and years."

"But what is it?"

"It's a coping device." She wiggled so that she could face Dent. "When you're confronted with something that causes you anxiety, you let it take whatever shape it wants in your imagination—like a big cat or a rattlesnake or whatever. Once it's materialized in your mind, you pull across the Curtain, which separates you from the anxiety. It gives a chance for you to collect yourself before you move on."

"I see," Dent said, doubtful. "So you've tried using this imaginary Curtain?"

"No. It's more Mauri Beth's thing. I'm sure she'd tell you more if you wanted to know."

"I guess I don't need to know more. Not if it works for her."

"Well. I have my doubts about that. Shall we?"

Inside, the house was tidier than it had been yesterday during the arrest. Sunlight beamed through the back door and onto the linoleum in the kitchen. In the living room, blankets that had been tossed about were now folded into neat squares, and the room smelled like carpet freshener and lemon furniture polish. Rachel slipped out of her shoes and joined Mauri Beth in the kitchen for a debriefing. Dent stayed behind with Irene, who was watching Wheel of Fortune reruns on the classic game show network.

"Hello, Miss Irene," Dent said.

"Shush!"

Dent shushed. The game was in the bonus round now, and Vanna was unveiling the lighted tiles for the category "Trophy." The contestant, a band instructor from Pierre, SD, looked instantly and irreversibly lost.

"Sailfish!" Irene barked.

Dent jumped. Fifteen seconds later, Vanna turned over the remaining tiles. Sailfish indeed.

Irene clapped her hands together and flashed a told-you-so grin at Dent. Then she held up the remote and pressed the power button and got to her feet.

"Come with me, Preacher," she said. "I have to take care of Fido."

"Fido?"

She scooped a handful of peanuts from the dish on the end table and shuffled out the door. No sooner had she settled herself into the swing than the hound, Henry Fifty-one, squeezed out from beneath the porch and sat down in front of her. She held out her palm and treated him to a few peanuts and ordered him to sit. He rolled over so she could stroke his belly with her foot.

"You sit too," the old woman snapped at Dent. "You're making us nervous."

Dent lowered himself into a rocking chair beside the swing. He went through his usual bag of pastoral conversation starters—family, weather, food—but could come up with nothing that gave him enough confidence to speak aloud. Irene seemed perfectly at home with this silent state of affairs, swinging peacefully and almost smiling. After a few minutes, a fat prairie dog scurried in from the field to the west. He came to a stop a few feet from the porch, stood up on his haunches and sniffed the air. Irene lobbed a peanut that landed inches in front of him. The prairie dog gobbled it up, seeming to Dent more like Henry Fifty-one than any of his skittery cousins in the prairie dog towns. Nine peanuts later, Irene was out of ammo and Fido the Prairie Dog was out of patience. He waddled across the yard and back into the sparse grass.

"That's the craziest thing I've ever seen," Dent said. "How in the world did you get him to do that?"

"Prairie dog's got to eat," Irene said. She folded her hands onto her lap and let loose an enormous sigh. "The Sheriff took my gun, didn't he."

"I suppose he had to."

"The hell he did!" the old woman fumed. "How am I supposed to defend my own now? What happens if I see a coyote?" The dog raised an eyebrow. She scratched his head with her foot. "Don't think for a minute that Henry Fifty-one will take him on. He's a lover, not a fighter. And who's going to protect Fido?"

"To be fair, you did shoot at someone."

"I don't recall," the old woman said, pouting. "Then again maybe I do. I suppose it's just me and Henry Fifty-one that know the truth, right Preacher?"

Dent shifted forward, unsure what to make of the old woman's request for confirmation. He was wading into sticky ethical territory here, walking a line between privileged conversation and mandated reporting. He was beginning to wish he'd paid attention in those continuing ed classes on pastoral counseling. He decided to stall.

"So have all your dogs been named Henry?"

"Just fifty-one of them."

"You must really like that name."

"I can't seem to shake it anyhow."

"And you call them all Henry because...?"

"Because I'm not very creative." She glanced over at him, the nearest thing to an apology he had yet to encounter from either Irene or Mauri Beth. "I like the name is all."

"Was that your husband's name?"

"Lord, no," Irene spat. "Henry was my boyfriend, back when I first got married."

"Your boyfriend," Dent repeated. "From when you—."

"You heard me." She crossed her legs, tapped one foot on poor Henry Fifty-one's head. She extended her hand out toward the road. "About this time yesterday was when I saw that biker fellow riding yonder. I thought I knowed who he was, but hard to tell in that get up they wear—skin tight clothes and ducky-looking helmets. And I truly can't say what happened after that—maybe I got confused and thought he *was* a duck, I don't know. Next thing I know, the rifle's gone off and all hell's broke loose."

"Well," Dent said.

She leaned forward. Spit between the slats of the porch rail. "How's the boy?"

"Lucky. He's pretty beat up, but he'll be all right. You said you knew him. Because he's connected with Ashley somehow, right?"

"Who told you that?" she demanded.

"I can't say. But I did hear they're connected." He leaned forward. Touched his fingertips together in what he hoped was a contemplative gesture. "Irene, if you meant to hurt Lucas—."

"Now why would I want to hurt Lucas? I wasn't even shooting at him."

"But you did, remember? He was on a bicycle."

"I thought he was somebody else."

Dent pressed his fingers together more tightly. "And who was that?"

She worked her gums back and forth behind her wrinkled lips. Finally, she spit out a name. Dent pinched the bridge of his nose.

"Vic Martz?" he repeated. "You thought you were shooting at Vic Martz?"

"I did. And you can't tell nobody that. We have pastoral privilege here, don't we?"

Dent ignored her question. The unflattering image of Vic in bicycling gear having taken over his brain. Old Man Martz, eighty years if he was a day, would have to stuff his doughy body into those spandex bib shorts one wrinkle at a time. Even if he wanted to, Mamie would ever allow her husband to be seen in public in such a state. He sat back in the chair. Rubbed his hand over his face.

The crunch of tires on gravel sounded from the east side of the house. Mauri Beth's pickup rolled around the corner and toward the exit. She waved—this time at Dent as well as Irene—but traveled on without speaking, down the driveway and across the cattle guard and to some errand she no doubt promised would only take a minute. Rachel would surely have agreed to stay until she got back, which meant Dent was stuck. A preacher's life, indeed. Henry Fifty-one swung his gray head from the disappearing pickup back to Dent and gazed pityingly with his deep brown eyes.

Irene's checkup took less time than it had taken to feed Fido the Prairie Dog. Dent had barely fallen asleep in the rocking chair before the front door swung open and Rachel stepped out, her medical supplies gathered in a yellow backpack slung over her shoulder.

"I think we wore poor Irene out," she said as she dropped onto the porch swing. "She said she was going to lie down and rest her eyes a bit."

"Sounds marvelous," Dent said.

"It does," Rachel said with a laugh. She stroked the long hair of her ponytail and flipped it over her shoulder. Dent chewed on the back of his lip, wondering how he should interpret such a thing. She was what, thirty-five? Not that much younger than him. But he had lived the monogamous life for fifteen years, never so much as buying another woman a drink. When it came to reading signals from the opposite sex, he was semi-literate at best.

"Dent? Did you hear me?"

He blinked himself out of his musings. There was no mistaking Rachel's facial expression now. Annoyance was one thing he could spot.

"I'm sorry. What was that again?"

"I said that Dad told me you found the Book of Knowledge."

Dent felt his face redden. "I didn't read anything, though."

"Nothing?"

"Nothing much. Lucas Lim's sheet was on top. I couldn't help but see it. Maybe I shouldn't have."

"It's okay," Rachel said. "He wasn't mad about it. He's made up his mind that you're a trustworthy person, so I think he'd even show you more if you asked."

"I don't know that I want to."

"I'm pretty sure that you don't." She leaned forward, and Dent thought for a second she was going to touch his knee. Instead she grabbed hold of the arm to the swing. "You've got to be careful with how much you know. It changes things, the way you see people. Some secrets don't have handles."

"Handles?"

"Nothing to grab onto. No way to carry them. It's like, once you know a thing about someone, and you can't get a grip on it, it bogs you down. You trip over it at the worst times, but you can't just pick it up and move it out of your head."

"Because it doesn't have handles."

"Right."

Dent rubbed his forehead, trying to massage away what he knew he should not know. *Henry was my boyfriend, back when I first got married. I was shooting at Vic Martz.* He needed those things interpreted if he was going to get a grip on them.

"So Ashley is connected to Lucas," he mused. "Like a dating thing? Boyfriend-girlfriend?"

"Maybe. Or maybe a stalker thing. I wish we could get in touch with Ashley and find out. But Mauri Beth said she isn't returning her calls or answering texts. Oh! That poor woman."

"Ashley?"

"Mauri Beth," Rachel said. "She is trying to figure out so many things, but her daughter is non-responsive, and her great-aunt has always been a bear to deal with."

"I suppose so, if she's shooting at people."

"Well now that part is a first. But Irene does have a history of odd behavior. Don't get me wrong, now. She comes by it honestly. She grew up during the Dust Bowl, if you can believe that—way, way back. Her daddy drank himself to death, and then her momma took up with another man that wasn't much better. He got trapped out in one of the dusters and suffocated."

"Sounds like a bad way to go."

"Oh, it would be awful. Suffocating is—well, never mind the gory medical details." She reached out her other hand, again latching it onto the arm of the swing. "You can guess what that kind of upbringing does to a person. Just awful, to have to live through all the things she has. She's earned whatever crazy she is."

CHAPTER 8:
A LITTLE PERSONAL,
DON'T YOU THINK?

"Well this doesn't look good," Rachel said. She frowned at Sheriff Pearson's patrol car, which was parked in her usual spot in back of Doc's office.

"He's probably just questioning Lucas."

"About what? He already knows what happened."

"Maybe there are other things," Dent said. "Irene might not have told the whole story."

"You think?"

"Well."

She parked alongside the cruiser, closer to it that strictly necessary, in Dent's estimation. But she was able to crack the door enough to slip out of the car. She had to reach in through the open rear window to retrieve her backpack.

Doc was seated at his desk, scribbling on a notepad. "How is she?" he said without looking up.

"Fit as a fiddle, for a woman her age," Rachel said.

He grunted in a way that Dent couldn't quite interpret.

"What's wrong with you?" Rachel asked.

"Nothing," Doc said, but he clipped the word short. "Sheriff's in with our boy. He wanted to question him as soon as he woke up. I told him he had fifteen minutes."

"Want me to try to hurry him up?" Rachel said.

"It won't do any good," Doc grumbled.

"Well then I'm going to go upstairs for a minute. You'll come get me if you need me?"

Doc assured her that he would. Rachel dropped her backpack and snagged a breath mint off her desk and turned up the stairs to her apartment.

"I should be going," Dent said.

"No, you stay," Doc ordered. He took off his reading glasses and wiped the lenses absently. "Lucas Lim has no memory of the accident, according to what he told me. He said the last thing he could recall was trying to pull up a map on his phone and not getting a signal. He turned down the driveway toward Old Mother Earth's, and he woke up here."

"That doesn't sound like much to go on," Dent said.

"I doubt the Sheriff expects much, or needs it. You find out anything in your visit to the ranch?"

Dent looked around the room. Lowered his voice. "She had it in her mind that she was shooting at someone else. She thought Lucas was Vic Martz."

"Sure," Doc huffed. "And I think I'm Dolly Parton."

"So you don't believe her."

"I do not." Doc's gaze wandered downward to the Book of Knowledge, balanced precariously atop a stack of file folders at one corner of the desk. All those stories, some that would curl your hair. He motioned toward the paper cup in Dent's hand. "I see you've been by the Super Chief this morning."

"I met Rachel there."

"Still haven't unpacked your coffee maker?"

"Why do you ask?"

"I don't ask. I observe." He waved his pencil toward the cup in Dent's hand. "You've been here two weeks and still haven't located your coffee pot."

"Haven't needed it."

"All right then. Tell me something. How old are you?" Doc asked.

"Thirty-nine."

"Huh. Just a spry young chicken then. Did you know that your level of physical fitness in your forties is your best indicator of mental acuity in your sixties?"

"I did not. Is that a medical fact?"

"Could be. I heard it on NPR."

Doc reached for the Book of Knowledge and pulled it toward him. It fell from its perch and onto the desktop with a thud. He flipped to a page not quite halfway through and scribbled some notes. Dent squirmed. That would be the right spot for the "J" section, which might mean Jeff Burke, or might equally mean John Wesley Denton. He fought the urge to confess. He had sinned in thought, word, and deed, by what he had done and what he had left undone. He had not loved the Lord with all his heart, nor his neighbor as himself. His marriage was a failure, and however attractive Rachel Schugart might be, the thought of dating again made his stomach clench. He'd not yet accepted the fact that he—a once up-and-coming young professional—had been relegated to chaplaincy in a dying Dust Bowl town. He hadn't put much effort into his sermons so far, hadn't made any kind of strategic plan or done anything beyond the bare minimum for pastoral survival. And no, he hadn't unpacked his damned boxes yet, and he didn't know when or if he'd get around to it.

That was the power of the book. It was Doc's very own truth serum, and as much as Dent hated to admit it, it was working.

"So Lucas and Ashley," he blurted. "You think he's some kind of stalker?"

Doc shook his head without looking up. "Can't say for sure, but I suspect not. She looked happy enough to be with him in that background photo on his phone."

"That doesn't always mean much."

"No it doesn't."

Doc scribbled a bit more, then flipped to a different page in the book, about halfway through. Lucas? Mauri Beth? He scratched a single note and flipped it closed with a thud. A cheap doorbell buzzed from the wall to their right.

"That's our summons," Doc said.

The buzzer continued as they entered the hallway. Doc had installed it twenty years ago as a way for patients who needed assistance to alert him or his nurse, and it had the groaning cow quality of a device both old and seldom used. Dent could still hear it as they entered the room. The patient had apparently fallen back asleep with his hand still on the buzzer, which was taped to the bedrail. Doc gently lifted the young man's hand and placed it on his chest.

"He asleep?" the Sheriff asked.

"It does appear that way," Doc said.

"But he shouldn't be, right? The medicine is wearing off. That's what I understood you to say."

"Yes. By now he should be conscious."

"Son," the Sheriff said, louder than Dent thought necessary. "Listen, son, we are going to finish that conversation one way or another. You can play possum all you want today, but you're going to have to talk to me before this is over."

The young man lay there unmoving, lips parted, encased in a dramatic snooze. The corner of the Sheriff's mouth twitched once, then twice. "He's faking."

"Maybe," Doc answered. "Hard to say for sure. Everyone responds differently to medication."

"What do you suggest we do with this mess?"

Doc picked up the man's arm and felt for a pulse. He looked at his watch for a few seconds and then gave a satisfied nod.

"Just wait," Doc said. "It may take him awhile to come around. Until then, I think it behooves us to make a plan. We can assume—and I think it's logical to do so—that our friend does not have any near kin close by. We need to be thinking about his options for after he wakes, at least for the near term."

"Options?" Dent asked. He did not care for the way Doc and the Sheriff stared at him, as though they'd already talked to the bartender and were just waiting to inform Dent that he was picking up the tab.

"He can't stay here," Doc said. "I've got a backlog of appointments to get to, some of them for really sick people. I'm going to need this room for exams."

"And I don't have any cause to put him in state custody," the Sheriff said. "As soon as I get my official statement, I'll turn him loose."

"You know," Doc said, as if the thought had just occurred to him. "We might talk to the ministerial alliance in town. See if one of the churches could put him up for awhile. What do you think, Brother Denton?"

Dent let out a heavy sigh. He was not only the new guy in the alliance, but also the one from the most politically suspect denomination in town. Add to that his recent divorce, and it was one, two, three strikes you're out. He may as well ask for a spacecraft, so remote were his chances of getting his colleagues to pony up at his request on behalf of a Korean-American stranger. This was an ambush, and he didn't have so much as a water gun.

"Suppose I kicked in a little bit," Doc continued. "The ministerial alliance puts a small amount aside every year for me to use to help out poor folks with medical bills. That fund doesn't have a lot in it, but I think I could justify its use for groceries, should someone be able to house him for a few days. Would you know of any such person, Dent?"

"All right. Fine," Dent moaned. "Just a week, though."

"Damn decent of you," the Sheriff said. He put on his hat and moved toward the door. "We have our plan. Doc, why don't you see if you can wake this boy up sometime today and persuade him to be a little more helpful?"

The parsonage was, to put it kindly, a wreck. The former Mrs. J. W. Denton had often complained that her husband had no knack for housecleaning, and after ten months as a bachelor, Dent had to agree. In his efforts to set his house in order, he found himself merely shuffling from one room to the next, occasionally displacing a bit of clutter from one flat surface to another. The result was a realignment of junk and zero net gain in organization. He shook his head, looked for something that might make him feel better about his efforts. What he saw instead was a dark blotch on the wall. It turned ninety degrees and froze in place. The hair on Dent's neck rose to attention.

Another scorpion, bigger than the dime-sized varmints he'd been disposing of ever since he moved in. This one was more of the dollar-bill variety, nearly three inches long and with a stinger the size of a railroad spike.

Easy now, he told himself.

He scanned his kitchen for some suitable instrument of death, settling at last on the most versatile weapon within reach. He bent down very, very slowly and removed his shoe without any grunts or jerks. He paused to let his breath even out. But as he raised it to strike, the doorbell rang out. Dent instinctively turned his eyes toward the sound. His target didn't take time for such consideration. The scorpion put it in gear and lit out across the light gray wall. Dent sprang from his seat and let loose a shot worthy of young David against Goliath. But whereas David had nine feet of Philistine to aim for, Dent had only three inches of striped bark scorpion. The shoe met the wall with an anti-climactic "umphf." It rebounded off the wood paneling and dove lengthwise toward a table containing the basket with his wallet, keys, and cell phone. The toe of the shoe clipped the edge of the basket, sending the contents flying across the room. Dent heard his cell phone crack against the tile floor. Even from this distance, he could see the chip in the upper right corner of the screen.

Dent swore. Glanced upward. The scorpion was long gone, of course—ascended to the heavenly realms above the drywall ceiling. Dent retrieved his phone, shoved it into his pocket and went to open the door. Rachel stood on his welcome mat, grocery sacks in hand.

"Everything all right?" she asked.

"Fine. Just fine."

"Because I thought I heard—."

"I'm fine."

She eyed him doubtfully for a long moment before finally shrugging her questions away. "I come bearing gifts," she said cheerfully. Dent reached to take the sacks, but she slipped around him and carried them to the kitchen table. She began unloading bandages and tape and bottles of pills.

"The Sheriff is back with Lucas again right now, but I don't think Doc is going to let that go on very long. I came on over to get things set up before they come—if that's okay with you, I mean."

Dent picked up one of the bottles. "Hydrocodone?"

"Yes." She looked at him sharply. "Tell me you're not an addict. Actually, tell me if you are. Because there's no way I can leave these with you if it's a danger to your sobriety."

"It's your lucky day then," Dent said. "Pills are not my problem."

"Oh," she said. "So is it booze then? Or women?"

"That's getting a little personal, don't you think?"

Rachel smiled. "I sometimes have to insert catheters for people who used to change my diapers. Personal doesn't bother me so much. The pills are safe with you?"

"They are."

"Good." She clapped her hands together. "Where shall we set up Mr. Lim?"

"The master bedroom," Dent said.

"Then where will you sleep?"

"I'm usually on the couch anyway."

"Okay then. Mind if I look around?"

"Go right ahead."

She scanned the kitchen again, frowning at the tower of boxes that lined one wall, all just as tightly sealed as they had been when the moving company ferried them from truck to parsonage. When she turned and walked through the living area and into the spare room without comment, Dent let out a relieved sigh. Seconds later, though, he heard a scream and a cracking sound, like someone hitting the wall with a whiffle bat. Dent grabbed THE DIRT—his predecessor's thick file of the townspeople's misdeeds and Dent's preferred scorpion destroyer—and ran into the room.

Rachel stood on her toes in a boxer stance, her hands lifted in front of her as though she was ready to knock someone's head off. In fact, she already had. A female mannequin, shapely and naked, leaned against the wall. Next to it stood its decapitated male counterpart, propped up by another stack of boxes. The head itself had landed in a plastic tub filled with old cell phones.

"Everything okay?" Dent ventured.

Rachel glared at him, her eyes dancing with adrenaline. It took a moment for her to gather herself. She looked at the mannequin's trim body, its thin arms and perky breasts and muted nipples—far more anatomically correct than any department store dummy should be. She smoothed out her scrubs.

"Listen, Dent, whatever you do in your own time is your business. I mean that. You don't have to explain—."

"They belong to the church," Dent said quickly. "Annette Brady donated them for the Halloween booth."

She stepped toward the mannequin and looked it up and down. "Tell me you're not dressing this thing in scary lingerie."

"God, no," Dent blurted. He reached for the other, now headless dummy, clearly male but mercifully less detailed where it counted. "Annette signed our church up to decorate a booth at the Baptists' Halloween carnival. This is going to be Moses. That's Miriam. Annette is making costumes for them but didn't have a place to store the mannequins so they ended up here."

"Slow down, Rev. I believe you." She picked up Moses' head and kicked the tub of old cell phones. "What's with this?"

"I'm still working that out," Dent said, relieved to have any new subject. "The box was here when I moved in. Best I can figure they were donated as part of some phones for troops campaign, but never sent to the troops. I need to go through them and see which ones still work before I find a place to donate them."

"Okay." Her shoulders slumped as the adrenaline drained from her system. "Okay. Wow. Sorry about poor Moses. I just saw a shape and the self-defense training kicked in."

"Remind me not to sneak up on you."

"I don't think I'll have to." She tossed the severed head to Dent and moved past him. "Let's get your bedroom ready for Lucas."

CHAPTER 9:
THE SORRY DAMNED
TRUTH

In only a few days the good citizens of Earth were once again entrenched in their work-week routines, drinking coffee at the Super Chief, milking cows, repairing cars, making lesson plans. But the matter of Old Mother Earth and the bicyclist still had a death grip on the gossip circles. Still not quite sure what to make of this whole kerfuffle, the townspeople chose the only course of action that made any sense to them.

They cooked.

Within a matter of hours, Dent's parsonage kitchen was full to overflowing. Hash brown casseroles baked by Old Mother Earth's supporters sat on the same refrigerator rack as vegetable trays assembled by those who wanted her thrown in jail before natural causes ferried her into the hands of a forgiving God. Nine loaves of bread, six containers of salsa, and at least a dozen of every flavor of ramen noodle, the closest thing to Korean food between Portales and Plainview. Plates of ham and green beans swimming in a sea of butter and bacon. Buckets of chicken from the Speedy-1-Stop. Salads with strawberries and poppy seed dressing, fruit salads spritzed with lemon juice, creamy salads with mandarin oranges in a sauce Dent couldn't quite identify. Pans of green Jello with flecks of mixed fruit suspended inside. Corningware dishes full of baked yams, some topped with marshmallows and others with brown sugar crumble. Cakes, pies, chocolate chip cookies, brownies, cheesecakes, scotcheroos. By the time the Sabbath sun dipped below the horizon, the fridge at the parsonage had overflowed, and both units in the church kitchen were well-nigh to it.

And yet, to his own vexation, Dent couldn't help but eye it all with suspicion. Almost everyone who stopped by stood on tip-toes and looked past Dent to try and catch a glimpse of Lucas. Some played a game of awkward chicken after they delivered the goods, hoping that, as a way of breaking the silence, Dent might invite them in. A few—Methodists, mostly—pushed past Dent without said invitation and scanned the parsonage for anything amiss, anything they might report back to their quilting clubs or Bible studies or regular crowd at the Super Chief.

The delectable barrage continued throughout the next week, often with a knock just as the clock hit 7:00 in the blessed morning. On Friday, the first visitor came even earlier, when Dent was just pulling on his jeans and flannel for the Last Man Club stage-building workday. He buttoned his shirt and checked his zipper and opened the door to find Crystal Burke there, holding a grocery sack.

"Good morning, Pastor!" she sang. "Mind if I come in?" He stepped aside, and she set about unloading English muffins and no-sugar-added jelly onto the table. "How's your guest doing?"

"All right, far as I know," Dent said. "Still sleeping a lot."

"Oh, poor kid!" Crystal said. She wrinkled her nose in sympathy, and Dent wondered if she was in fact older than Lucas. Certainly not thirty yet, not with hips that trim despite having birthed twins. Dent could see another small baby bump had begun to form in her middle.

"Doc thinks he'll make a full recovery," he said. "It may just take some time."

"How much time?"

"A few weeks. Hopefully he'll be on his way around Thanksgiving, or maybe a little after. We'll send him on, soon as he's able. I know some people don't like him staying at the parsonage, your husband included."

"Jeff? Oh no. Jeff is fine. He just gets a little grumpy on occasion."

"He was a little worse than that at the Super Chief the other day."

"I heard about that." She looked down at her hands. "I don't know why this has bothered him so much. I mean, it's not like he ever really cared much for Old Mother Earth."

"Well. I didn't know they were at odds."

"They aren't, really. Or maybe they are—I don't know. There's some sort of family history, I think, but I try not to pay too much attention to small-town drama." She forced a laugh. "But for some reason he's decided that this Lucas is the one who stirred up the trouble—like he provoked her somehow to shoot at him. Please don't tell him I told you."

"It was plain enough already."

She glanced over her shoulder to make sure the blinds were drawn. "Listen, I know he's hard on preachers sometimes. You can't take it too personally. He's been through so much already. A man with his history, you know—growing up like that after both his parents died so young. I suppose you know all about that."

"I really don't, no."

She nodded somberly. "His daddy was killed in one of the wars—Korea? Cambodia? I get them all confused. Anyway, it was someplace foreign and awful. He died in some sort of covert raid that the Army never would even acknowledge. They never even sent a Purple Heart to the family."

"That's awful."

"Oh, it was a necessary sacrifice. That's the way Jeff views it, and he said his daddy would have thought the same thing. His momma, now that was tragic."

"How so?"

"Well—and I almost hate to tell you, because it sounds so embarrassing—she was electrocuted. The power company had their limb crews out in front of their house, the one on Eastgate where the Tuckers live now. There was a nest of baby birds she'd been watching up in one of the trees, and she could see their branch was going to get cut. So she got out the ladder and went up to move the nest before the crew got to that tree. She managed to bend down and lower it to a safe spot, but the ladder slipped on her as she was raising back up. It hopped off the branch and onto the power line and, well."

She looked down at the floor respectfully. Placed one hand on her tummy. Dent thought she might weep.

"It's all right," he said.

"I know it," Crystal said. "It's affected Jeff more than he lets on, though. I mean, he's had to deal with all these questions about why his daddy had to be the one to give his life for his country, and whether or not his momma loved those baby birds more than she did her own son. He knows she didn't, of course. It was just her nature to save the powerless. I suppose a person can't help but wonder, nevertheless. Oh!"

Tears dropped from her eyes, splattered against the tile. Dent rummaged beneath the stacks of paper on his table and extracted a tissue.

"Thanks," Crystal said. "I'm fine. It's these hormones." She dabbed her eyes. Took deep breaths through her nose. "Jeff hates it when I cry."

"Take your time," Dent said.

"Can I tell you something, Pastor?"

"Sure."

She watched him for a second. At last she blew out a breath and lifted one hand. "Might as well," she said.

"Might as well what?"

"Tell you the story. You're going to hear it anyway." She turned her wedding band a full circle around her finger before she finally spoke again. "Jeff is connected to Irene Ostendorf through a scandal. It was indirect, of course, but still. A town like this, everything has ripples." She took in a deep breath. Let it out in short spurts. Repeated the process again before she spoke. "About four years ago—this was right before Jeff and I started seeing each other. That's important. I don't want you to get the wrong idea."

"About what?"

"The way things happened. Jeff has always been faithful to me, but when he was a single man—and I'm not saying this was right, mind you—he was involved with a younger woman for awhile. One of his former students. Ashley Hyatt. Do you know her?"

Dent shifted. Tried to keep his face neutral. "I know who she is. Irene's great niece, if I recall."

"Right. And this sort of thing happens in Texas, you know—nothing illegal about it. She was eighteen and graduated and perfectly willing to—well, you can imagine. But like I said, it was all legal. But it caused quite the uproar. The school board got all up in arms, and the girl's mother, oh my *god!* Anyhow, it was a wake-up call for Jeff, I can tell you that. He returned to the Lord, which is not a thing you can say to everyone, Brother Denton, but I know you understand. And the Lord blessed his repentant heart. Six months later, we were married, and the twins came along a year after that. So it all worked out, you see. But people around here, they have a hard time letting things go."

"I don't doubt that," he said sympathetically.

"You were bound to hear it somewhere," Crystal said with a shrug. She dabbed her eyes, smoothed her dress and checked her face in the reflection of the microwave door. "I'm all right. Thank you for listening, Brother Denton."

He walked her to the door amid thanks and y'all-take-cares. Closed it behind her and stared through the tiny square of glass at eye level. He could hear the clack of her heels on the concrete as she stepped quickly to her car. When she turned to glance back at the parsonage, her face showed no more emotion than if she'd been leaving the grocery store.

Dent grunted to himself. Wondered. He turned around to see Lucas Lim now standing in the kitchen, leaning on his crutches and looking like the sorriest sad-sack on the High Plains.

"I take it you overheard that conversation," Dent said.

"Enough of it," Lucas answered. He shuffled his way to the table and sat down. Dent retrieved a pan of breakfast casserole from the fridge and made plates for them both. Despite being a week and a half into their living arrangement, this was the first time the young man had indicated a desire to converse. Dent approached with caution, keeping his voice low and his movements slow.

"How you feeling?" he asked.

Lucas shrugged. "I've been worse."

"You have?"

"A couple of summers ago I was I was doing some hiking in the Tetons and got mauled by a mountain lion. I think she was trying to protect her cubs, but I never saw them. That was worse than this." He stopped, fork midway to his mouth, and considered what he'd said. At last he nodded once and continued eating.

"By 'this,' are we talking about your injuries? Or about what Crystal said just now."

The young man shifted, winced, swallowed. "That's complicated."

"I suppose it is."

Lucas thought a moment longer. "You saw the lock screen on my phone. Ashley, I mean."

"I think people have started to piece together your relationship, if that's what you're asking."

"Okay." He pushed a chunk of sausage across his plate. Pushed it back again. "I had my suspicions about her and Jeff Burke."

"Like what?"

Lucas shook his head. "I'd rather not say. My faith in preachers isn't exactly the highest."

"Mine neither." Dent put down his fork. Tried to sound earnest. "I know a little bit what it must be like for you. My wife was a bishop's daughter."

"Oh," Lucas said. "Is she—did she, ah, pass?"

"No. Sorry. I meant that she is no longer my wife."

"I see." He pressed his fork down onto the crumbs from the biscuit.

"I saw the kind of stuff Janet had to deal with because of her father. She was always under a lot of pressure and carried a lot of anxiety. It weighed on her."

"Did it weigh on you?"

"A little, yes. Sometimes a lot."

"But you understood her."

"Well, no," Dent confessed. "Not entirely. But there were reasons behind most of her problems. I think I understood those pretty well."

"And she divorced you anyway."

Dent wiped his mouth with his napkin and stared until Lucas looked away. "It's all right," he finally said. "She did divorce me, and that's just the sorry damned truth. I'm only trying to help you, that's all."

"I know."

Lucas reached across and dropped his half-eaten meal into the trashcan. Stared at it for a second with what might have been regret. "I've got a lot of questions about Ashley's past. I didn't really know it when I set out from Ft. Collins, but that's part of what brought me to Earth in the first place. I'm just trying to get things sorted."

"With Ashley's history?"

Lucas turned his palms up. Almost smiled. "With life."

CHAPTER 10:
JUDGED BY THE MESS

Dent walked the five blocks to Heinmann Downtown Theater, thinking some fresh air might help him with his own life sorting. Here he was, exiled in the Panhandle, playing nanny to a heartbroken son of a bishop, waiting for enough time post-divorce to pass that his daughter would start speaking to him again. None of it seemed quite real. Certainly nothing made sense, whether in his own life or his experience of the town so far. He needed time and perspective. He thought again of THE DIRT. Decided for the thousandth time he'd best leave it alone.

Clarity still eluded him as he arrived at the worksite. Renovation, on the other hand, stared him in the face. Last Man Club members had already carried in the piles of lumber and sheets of plywood from Rob's trailer and were now busy with their first coffee break. The Daughters of the Prairie, the Last Man's sister organization, were huddled over a table of fabric samples for the new drapes they would sew. Jack Schoendienst caught sight of Dent and pointed in his direction.

"Just the man I was looking for!" Jack called. He pulled Dent into a huddle of old men and draped an arm over his shoulder. "Lonnie here is saying that there is no such thing as the Devil, right Lonnie?"

"It is possible that the Devil is merely an abstraction," a chubby-faced man of around seventy said.

"The rest of us, now, we're skeptical of that notion," Jack said.

Lonnie held up his palm, spoke with the slow drawl of a farmer. "I'm not saying evil doesn't exist. I'm simply suggesting that it may not be made manifest in a personal being."

"You'll have to excuse Lonnie," Joe Dick Schieble said. "His TV went out a few years back and he took to reading books. It's ruined him for conversation."

"I'm just offering a hypothetical," Lonnie said.

"Well it ain't either," Joe Dick said. "Devil's as real as you or me. I seen him."

"What, you mean, you seen him?" Jack asked. He glanced at Dent, eyes twinkling. "Like when you was in the war?"

"Nope. In church."

"Church!" the men exclaimed together. Dent eyed them suspiciously.

"I was sitting next to an old farmer," Joe Dick said. "Right up on the front row, not far from where you stand every week, Brother Denton. And I mean to tell you the preacher was laying it on about sin and the lake of fire. I don't know exactly, but all his carrying on must have conjured the Devil to offer a defense, because next thing we know the pulpit topples over, and through a hatch beneath it crawls Satan himself. He starts snarling and spewing fire. People can't get out of there quick enough. The preacher dives right through a stained glass window, he's so spooked. But this old farmer, he just sits there like it was nothing. And the Devil comes up to him, says, 'Do you not know who I am?' Farmer says he does. Devil says, 'Then why do you not tremble?' The old farmer takes out a cigarette and lights it from the very fire of the Devil's beard, leans back and says, 'You ain't so bad. I've been married to your sister for forty-nine years.'"

Dent laughed, but he was alone in it. The other men nodded somberly, as though something had been settled. They all shuffled away, back to their work, leaving Dent to wonder just how good-natured this set up had been. Jack winked at him, the hint of a smile hidden beneath the wrinkles around his mouth.

"Reverend!" Rob called. "Welcome to work. Just find a place and be useful."

The Roundup had been held for fifteen years in the fellowship hall of First Baptist Church, the most spacious auditorium in the entire county. But the FBC elders board balked at the frequent mention of alcohol in last year's tall tales and determined that such a subject belonged in a more secular building. Johnny Heinmann, the owner of the only movie theater in town and a man of limited religious convictions, offered his cinema's Theater #4, which had been awaiting remodeling since before the ugly divorce that drained most of Johnny's capital. "You fix it up, and you can use it for free," Johnny said, with "free" being the operative negotiating point for the Last Man members.

Thirteen days before the Roundup, however, Theater #4 still looked like a scene from a zombie movie. The old screen hung in tatters up front, and the stage below it was barely wide enough for an upright piano. Last Man volunteers had removed the seats and floated a new floor over the pitched concrete, but it was only level in the general sense. A cherry tomato dropped by a guest was likely to roll for thirty feet, although in which direction was something of a crapshoot.

Dent looked for some task that was not currently being done, or some person who appeared as lost as he was. But everyone seemed occupied with sweeping or hammering or measuring—except Jack, who was still trying to engage Lonnie in theological conversation. Jack motioned for Dent to join them. He pretended not to see, opting instead to head out the back door.

Sunlight and a piercing whine greeted Dent as he stepped outside. He squinted. Plugged his ears. When the noise stopped and the sawdust cloud began to dissipate, he could see two women in safety goggles examining a section of plywood.

"Dent!" one of them said. She slid her goggles down around her neck and smiled. Even with raccoon eyes from the sawdust that stuck to the non-goggled part of her face, Rachel looked ready for anything.

"Glad you could join us," Emilia said flatly.

"I got tied up," Dent protested. "Pastoral matter."

"Well, we're just happy to have you here now," Rachel said. She turned to her sister. "Is that everybody?"

Emilia was bent over a clipboard on the table saw platform. She penciled in a checkmark, presumably beside Dent's name. "Almost. We're missing Dr. Omar."

"Oh, I forgot to tell you," Rachel said. "The Goldammers had a calf break its leg this morning. He went out to take a look."

"Then we've got everybody but the president." Emilia dropped the clipboard and shot a puff of air toward the unruly strands of black hair that had fallen onto her face. "Jeff Burke is not the most reliable leader we've ever had."

"Where is he?" Dent asked.

"At school," Emilia answered. "Presumably he couldn't take off work on the day of a home football game. And he won't be here tomorrow either. Says he has an educational coop in Lubbock. Ten to one he spends half an hour there and ends up at the Red Raider game."

"Emmie!" Rob called as he stepped into the daylight.

"Robbie!" Emilia yelled back, her voice dripping with sarcasm.

Rob grinned. He pointed to the slab of plywood the women had just cut. "That going to fit?"

"I cut it how you measured it," Emilia said.

"Well go see then."

"Go see?" Emilia said. "Jump when you say jump?"

"Honey," Rob sang, "would you please go make sure that I measured that impeccably cut piece of plywood correctly so we can get on with this project?"

Rachel saluted. Emilia rolled her eyes. They each picked up one end of the plywood and hauled it inside toward the stage. When Dent looked back up, Rob was grinning even wider.

"What?" Dent said.

"I was just wondering about what you told me about your divorce," Rob said. "I'm unclear. Did you swear off all women, or just your ex? Because the way you're looking at my sister-in-law makes me think you're reconsidering."

"You're seeing things," Dent said.

"I'm not, either. And for the record I think you should know that some marriages are great. You can see what kind of bliss Em and I live in. She's crazy about me."

"New topic, please."

"Fine, fine." He swept some wood scraps into a pile with his foot. "Joe Dick tell you about his run-in with the Devil?"

"Not that topic."

"All right, how's this? I hear your new roommate has ties to Earth after all."

Now it was Dent's turn to start kicking scraps, although he did so with more fervor than Rob.

"I don't mean to put you in a bad spot," Rob said. "You can keep whatever secrets you like. But Doc told me he thought Lucas was somehow mixed up with Ashley Hyatt, and I made the short leap into thinking that your situation is more complicated than people realize."

"I believe it is."

"You got some strong personalities at work. Irene, of course, but both the Hyatt women can be a handful."

"I've met Mauri Beth already. She doesn't seem all that stable."

"That may not be entirely fair," Rob said. "But it's not that far off, either. And then you've got a messy history between Ashley and Jeff Burke. I take it you've heard about that?"

Dent's heart dove through his chest and splashed into his gut. "A version of it, anyhow."

"Sad tale indeed," Rob said. "But don't think too poorly of Ashley. She's just the one he got caught with."

"You think he was sleeping with other students?"

"Students? No, he's too smart for that. But he does have a history with younger women. I wouldn't be surprised if—well, regardless. The incident with the Hyatt girl was pretty spectacular. She'd been making tea late one night at his apartment and forgot to turn the burner off. She fell asleep on the couch, and it caught a dishtowel on fire. Sent the whole kitchen up in flames. Jeff somehow woke up and grabbed her and carried her out. The problem was that all she had on was one of his Dallas Cowboy t-shirts, and there wasn't any way to cover herself while people gathered. Someone finally brought her a blanket, but she'd been exposed to what might as well have been the whole county. Burke had managed to pull on some clothes first, of course. He even became something of a hero to some folks in town, the guy who saved the damsel in distress."

"And the school board just looked the other way?"

"There were a lot of meetings, but not much more than that. Jeff can be very persuasive when he needs to be."

Dent felt beads of sweat forming on his brow, despite his lack of tangible contribution to the building so far. He wiped his hand across his face. "Well, I hear it worked out for the best. Crystal said that getting caught turned his life around."

"Maybe so."

"What's that supposed to mean?"

Rob stepped toward Dent. Lowered his voice. "Mr. Burke isn't one to let go of things too easily. You are harboring a man connected a woman for whom Jeff has—let's call them complicated feelings."

"So I'm in a minefield here."

Rob answered with a single, slow nod. Then he hitched up his carpenter's belt and took in a deep breath. "I suppose I better get back to work. I'd hate to die and be judged by the mess I leave."

CHAPTER 11:
THE TRUTH IS
WHAT YOU MAKE IT

Ashley stuffed trash into an empty Carl's Jr. sack and gave in to a yawn she'd been stifling since crossing the Colorado border. Almost no one was out this early on a Saturday morning, and so she'd made good time on the drive to Lubbock—just over eight hours, and at speeds that would send her mother scrambling for the curtain of calm. Her lower back ached, and the muscles in her shoulders burned. Teachers were always telling her that she acted older than her age. She hoped this wasn't what it felt like for her body to catch up to their prophecy.

She dug around beneath the driver's seat until she found her socks and tennis shoes and slipped them on her feet. It was warm enough for sandals, at least by Colorado standards. But the football game she and Jeff would attend that afternoon was a terrible place for exposed toes. Besides, she wasn't sure she wanted him to see the tattoo, which was still tender and swollen, and on top of that none of his damn business. She had kept her only other tattoo—a tiny praying mantis above her left hip—a secret for nearly two years. Even if she took her clothes off later, as she assumed she would, she could divert his attention. He was a man, and men were easy enough to fool, if you could keep their eyes and hands occupied elsewhere.

She took the stairs up to the fourth floor apartment, carrying only the crushed Carl's Jr. sack and her sunglasses. She let herself in with her key, wrapped her fingers around the draw cord for the curtains. Stared down at the sectional. She had slipped away from Fort Collins at three a.m. after only two fitful hours of sleep, folded up the tent she'd been sleeping in these past few weeks and stuffed it behind the couch in her and Connor's apartment. She left a note saying she was going camping alone and drove until the black sky to her left turned purple and then pink and then yellow. Even now, the full blue of a fall day on the Plains hadn't quite taken hold. It was still morning, for Christ's sake. A little nap couldn't hurt. Twenty minutes tops.

She slapped herself across the cheek. Tried to focus.

She tromped back down the stairs and to the old gray Taurus Irene had given her as a graduation present. In through the passenger door and up the stairs again, carrying only her backpack. She made three more trips, each time toting only a single item, until the muscles in her legs began to loosen and her lungs to open and her mind to clear. Today would be her watershed, her moment of no return. Her continental divide, over which the past and its sludgy mess would slide away in one direction while her life ran clean and clear in the other, filtered of past humiliations and present secrets.

She opened LinearLife and flicked through the lists with her thumb.

Secrets I hope my mother never finds out

1) That I knew about Dad's girlfriend at the lab before she did.
2) How I lost my virginity and to who.
3) That I'm sleeping with Jeff Burke again.

She stopped reading. Numbers four and five dealt with venial sins—petty things that had seemed life-or-death at the time of the list's creation and even now retained some modicum of importance. But number three on the list jumped out and kicked her in the gut. She had made this list years ago and transferred it over to three different cell phones. It was birthed at the far edge of her adolescence, when the circumstances of her parents' divorce still weighed on her and youthful explorations still left an imprint of guilt. Jeff had been an experiment at that point, and his attentions made her feel worldly and grown up. She had thought him temporary, and so convinced herself that she had no attachment to him.

She counted on her fingers. Five years now, since their first night together. Damn.

She tapped Number Three on her list and solemnly dragged it into the top spot. The highlighted rectangle moved halfway up, froze, and disappeared as the screen bled into a notification. Video call from Mauri Beth Hyatt. She rolled her eyes. This would be the sixth time this morning her mother had tried to call, and would certainly not be the last. Might as well get this over with. One tap later, Irene's kitchen appeared. Ashley's mother walked by, left to right, with a wine glass in her hand. A second later, she paced back across in the opposite direction.

"Hello?" Ashley said. "Mom?"

Her mother pulled up short, sloshing red wine over her fingers and onto the linoleum.

"Shit," her mother said. She turned and faced her phone and squinted down at Ashley. "Is that you, sweetie?"

"It's me."

"I'm sorry for swearing, hon," her mother said. She sat down in the chair, wiped off the bottom of the glass. Looked down at her lap and brushed at a stain. "Shit."

"Did you mean to call me?"

"Of course! I've been trying all morning. Where have you been?"

"Asleep. I had my phone off."

"Oh." She leaned closer to the screen and squinted. "That doesn't look like your apartment."

"I'm over at Jen's."

"Doing what? Don't tell me studying. I know better than that."

"Mom, is there a point to this?"

Her mother lifted her shoulders and drew in a sharp breath, then let loose a dramatic sigh. She dropped her head into her hands, teetering on the verge of some inconsolable meltdown. Then she reached for the curtain and tugged until it had closed off the threat and sat back in her seat.

"It's been awful," she said slowly. "I've been getting call upon call all week. At first it was only friends, and then reporters looking for quotes. One was even a television station in Lubbock, which of course got a big 'no thank you' to their interview request. Lately, it's been well-wishers and do-gooders, like that new Methodist preacher. Have you met him?"

"I haven't been home since he's been there. Remember?"

"Right, right. When *were* you home last?"

"I don't know. Easter?"

Mauri Beth swigged a third of her wine. Reached with an unsteady hand to draw another layer to the curtain.

"Do you have to do that?" Ashley said, exasperated.

Her mother stiffened. "I do, sweetie. You have no—and I mean this with all the love in my heart—you have no idea what it's been like here. Without my Curtain, I'd be curled up in bed with a bottle of Jose Cuervo by now."

"How much wine have you had to drink?"

"Not nearly enough, which is a fact."

"It's not even lunchtime yet."

Her mother emitted an unsteady hiccup. Shook it off. "Did you know Dr. Becky moved to Houston?"

"You've mentioned that a few times."

"Just up and left," her mother continued. "Said she didn't want to stay around after her divorce. Well who *does* want to stay around a town like this? We're here because of family, because of community. You don't just convince a new therapist to come to a place as bass-ackwards as Earth overnight. What about all of her patients?"

"Mom."

"I'm serious!" She rested her elbows on the table and looked earnestly into the screen. "You have to learn to talk, sweetie. I mean it. To be able to get it all out, the really—excuse me, but—the really shitty parts of your life. When you don't release those feelings, they come out in other ways."

"Such as?" Ashley said wearily.

"Well, you flip off the Wal-Mart trucks that tailgate you on Highway 70 from Portales, or you yell at the manager because the teenage server spilled iced tea on your table. Or you drink too much, which I am not doing, by the way."

"Mom."

"Or you fire a rifle at a stranger on a bicycle. Had Aunt Irene gone to see Dr. Becky, like I told her to do, none of this would have happened."

"I have to go."

"Wait," her mother said. "I'm sorry. I just needed to hear your voice. It's lonely here, hon."

"I know, Mom. I'm—I just don't know what I can do."

"You can come home."

"I can't."

"Yes you can." She leaned in closer. "Is there something you're not telling me?"

Ashley felt a cold sensation rush down her head and through her arms. "No."

"Are you sure, hon? It's not that I'm mad at you, or ever would be mad at you. I just want to know that you're okay."

"I'm fine."

"Irene hasn't quite been herself since shooting at that cyclist. She keeps bringing him up. By name even. She's been asking about you a lot, too. I think it would do her good to see you."

"I just can't, Mom."

"Why not?"

A key rattled in the door. The cold feeling shot through the rest of Ashley's body. Her heart jumped up into her throat.

"I have to go," she said again.

Before her mother could protest, she ended the call and shoved the phone in her pocket. The front door made an unpleasant *thud* as it caught against the safety latch. A man cursed from outside.

"Ashley?" Jeff called. "What the hell?"

She flew into the bedroom on tiptoes, yanked the suitcases off the bed and dropped to her knees to shove them beneath. They caught on something else, however. Ashley pressed her head against the floor to look. Another suitcase was wedged between the box springs and the flat carpet—a pink one she had bought in high school for a science-club trip to Dallas. She'd assumed her mother had donated it to some charity garage sale along with the rest of her unwanted childhood artifacts. But now she remembered. She had brought this one with her—what, a year ago? Planned to fill it with her clothes before Jeff got there and walk away from this place forever.

Knuckles rapped on the door. "Ashley?"

She shoved the new suitcases under the bed along with the pink one. Checked the other side of the bed to make sure nothing was sticking out. Everything was hidden, thank God, if only barely. All she could see was a blue rubber wristband with the Earth high school mascot printed on it in gray. She picked it up and read the writing on the other side. "Beta Club," it said. She squeezed her eyes tight. Tossed it onto the nightstand.

"Be right out!" she called as she moved into the bathroom. She flushed the toilet, grabbed a can of air freshener and squirted a tiny mist of potpourri to make her excuse more convincing. She replaced the can onto the rust-colored ring in the corner between the cabinet and the toilet. When she ran her fingers over her hair, she could tell it was a mess, but no time to worry about that now.

She walked out without checking the mirror and unlatched the door.

Twenty minutes later, while Jeff was in the bathroom, she slid out from beneath the sheets and dressed in her socks and underwear, which covered both the mantis and the raptor. Jeff emerged naked from the bathroom and frowned.

"What's with this?" he asked.

"I'm cold." She pulled a t-shirt on and slipped back under the blanket.

"Turn the heat up then."

"It's fine." She picked the rubber bracelet up from the nightstand. Traced its words absently.

Jeff dropped down on top of the covers, grabbed the remote and turned to the Big 12 channel. A loud-mouthed announcer was holding up an enormous burnt-orange cowboy hat and ranting about the Longhorns' game against Kansas State. Jeff muted the channel in disgust. He looked down at Ashley's fingers, nervously twirling the Beta Club wristband. He gently lifted it from her and sent it flying across the room. It arced soundlessly into the small trashcan next to the TV stand.

"Something wrong?" he said.

"You should know that answer."

"Maybe."

"There's no maybe to it." She turned her head, locked her eyes on the tip of his nose. He kept his gaze fixed on the television, looking, she thought with some irritation, a little bored. "So you want me to say it out loud? Fine. I will."

"Don't."

"I will!" she said, her voice far more pouty than she'd intended. "Be serious for a minute. There's a whole shitstorm of trouble back home."

"The rule is that we don't talk about our lives outside of us."

"Maybe that *was* the rule. Listen to me. Jeff? Lucas knows about us."

"Not if you didn't tell him."

"I didn't have to," she said. "He's smarter than you give him credit. He *knows*, I'm sure of it."

"Then he's a disgruntled ex trying to stir things up." He opened his mouth in a giant post-coital yawn. "He can't prove anything, and he's got no credibility. Relax."

"What if your wife finds out?"

"I'll deny it, and she'll believe me."

"But what if someone I know finds out? What if Lucas tells Irene, or my mother?"

"Then you'll have to deal with it." He let out a heavy, patronizing sigh. "Ashley," he said, as if she were a child. "It'll be fine. The truth is what you make it. Hush."

He unmuted the pregame show, which had moved from the UT-K-State affair to Texas Tech's homecoming this afternoon. The graphic at the bottom showed the Red Raiders as 2.5-point favorites. Jeff elbowed her, as though drawing her attention to some joke.

"So are you wearing red or green today?" he asked, and seeing her puzzled expression, added, "We're playing Colorado State."

Ashley froze. Every time she went to a game with Jeff, she feared someone from Earth would find them out, or that Jackie and Todd—the two old WT A&M teammates who always met him at the games with their wives or girlfriends—would leak her name to someone with connections to her hometown. Today, she would have the added danger of someone from CSU recognizing her. A slim chance, given the disdain her small circle of friends had for football, but still. It would only take one casual acquaintance with an Instagram account to ruin her life.

"I don't think I should go," she said. Jeff rolled his eyes. "I'm serious! Too many people know me."

"You're paranoid," Jeff said. "And thinking too highly of yourself. Out of the sixty-thousand people in that stadium, how many do you think know your name, outside of our usual crew? Maybe two? Three would be pushing it. No one's looking for you, and especially not there."

"What about Connor? He likes football."

"Who's Connor?"

"My boyfriend."

"Boyfriend?" His voice turned mocking and mean. He moved to face her. "Look, I don't care who you fuck or how often you do it. But I don't want to hear about it." He stood up and reached for his clothes. "We better get going."

"No."

He whirled. Nearly dove in her direction. Landed with his fists buried in the mattress, one on either side of her hips, his face even with hers.

"Go on back home if you need to," he said, talking low. "We don't have to be together today. Of course we don't! Get this little girl fit out of your system and we'll just start new next time."

"It's not like that."

"Sure it's not."

He leaned forward to kiss her. Ashley pulled her head back, but he had her pinned and was approaching fast. She tilted her head to the side, resigned to meeting his lips, and closed her eyes. Nothing. When she opened them again, he had stopped, his mouth only millimeters from hers. He pulled back and smiled. Lifted one hand and placed it high up into the bend of her hip, his thumb just beneath the elastic of her underwear. He smiled, strong and mean.

"Get dressed," he said.

CHAPTER 12:
SUNDAYS WILL SUNDAY

Dent cast a pastorly gaze over his flock at Earth United Methodist Church and saw the thing he feared most.

Disappointment.

A hundred and fifty people had shown up for his first Sunday at the church, planting seeds of hope that the congregation's fortunes might turn, now that cranky Rev. Holloway was out of the pulpit. Only a few weeks into Dent's pastorate, however, the congregation had once again dwindled to a mere forty souls. He could see defeat in the eyes of his truly invested members as they entered the sanctuary—Mamie Martz's disapproval, Jack Schoendienst's desperation. Today was but another flop in the death throes of their mainline church, and it showed on their aging faces. The sparse choir dutifully donned their robes and lined up in the narthex for the processional. Mrs. Paisley hit the downbeat on the prelude, jolting them all. But eight measures in her right and left hands were at odds with one another, warring for both key and tempo. She stopped altogether. Started over. Dent pinched the bridge of his nose.

Before he could feel too sorry for himself, however, a new problem arose, called to his attention by a chorus of little-girl squeals and jolly men's voices. A second later, the outer door closed behind two broad-shouldered men in gray suits. Bud Cockburn swaggered into the narthex along with Jeff Burke and family. Crystal grasped her daughter's wrists, one in each hand, and dragged the screaming girls along. She glanced toward the front just in time to catch Dent's eye, and in half a second a saccharine smile replaced the harried-mother look on her face. But her teeth remained clenched, the skin at the corners of her eyes tense. She marched down the aisle and plopped down, twins still screaming, in the third pew from the back. Burke and Cockburn, unfazed, settled in beside them.

"What do you suppose that's all about?" Jack Schoendienst whispered.

Dent held a finger to his lips. Tried to look prayerful.

But no amount of prayer could save the ecclesial disaster as it unfolded before his eyes. Mrs. Paisley's prelude ended not in triumph, but confusion. Once the octogenarian sopranos finished warbling their way through the opening hymn, Jack launched into seven minutes worth of church news and fundraiser announcements. He concluded with, "Remember, folks, we're open every Sunday!" Dent wanted to pull his black robe over his head and hide behind the altar.

By the time the anthem had ended, everyone could sense that this service was a lost cause. The energy drained from the room, and even Jack did not have enough bounce left to plug the leak. He read the Scripture with barely a hint of optimism, and finished it as though disappointed that David had killed Goliath. The poor congregation stared down at the backs of the pews in front of them, looking as forlorn as if they themselves were the Philistines now enslaved to the Lord's chosen.

Dent ascended the pulpit in defeat, resigned to the coming failure. He stared down at his manuscript. It lay on the pulpit, limp and agonizingly thin. He scanned the congregation for help, but the faces that weren't glossed over with boredom were smeared with pity. Jeff Burke leaned over to Cockburn and whispered something that elicited an unpleasant smile. Nothing to be done about it, Dent thought. He filled his lungs and opened his mouth and preached on until the bitter end. When Mrs. Paisley rang the chimes after the benediction, it sounded for all the world like the bell tolling for John Wesley Denton's pastoral career.

Dent trudged down the center aisle after the benediction, hauling failure with him. It clung to bottom of his stole, threatening to topple him over onto his face in front of God and everybody at Earth UMC. Disappointment clutched at the hem of his black robe, pulling the neck so tight that he thought he would choke. He wanted to rip the damned thing off. But when he turned the corner into his office, he saw his entire sacerdotal wardrobe in a pile on the floor, his spare robe and stoles crumpled in a heap beside his desk, their hangers sticking out of the pile like the frame from a wrecked airplane. He swore loudly.

Jack Schoendienst appeared in the doorway, his weekly offering report in hand. Dent winced. "Sorry for my language."

"It's okay, Preacher," Jack said. "I feel sort of the same way."

Jack placed the folded sheet of paper on the desk with an expression so deflated that it reminded Dent of his mailman in Tucumcari, a morose stick of a man who looked positively ghost-like on the day he delivered word that he'd just run over Janet's cocker spaniel. Jack patted the paper and backed away slowly, as if it were a dangerous and particularly ill-tempered snake.

"That bad?" Dent asked.

"I've seen worse."

"But still bad?"

"Dollar for dollar, given the crowd we had? Yes. Real bad. We usually get a nice check on the Sundays that the Burkes come, but...well, nothing, this time."

They stared at the paper for a few seconds, Jack apparently waiting to see Dent's reaction when he read the figures. But Dent had no intention of letting his disappointment slide any further today. He turned his attention again to the crumpled vestments.

"Your hook thingy broke," Jack said.

"Thank you, I am aware of that."

"You need—I'd be glad to help if—"

"I'll get it, Jack. Thanks for the offer."

"You bet."

Dent waited in silence for Jack to leave. He did not. The longer he stayed, the more Dent suspected that more was coming, and he tried to brace himself. Had Jack overheard something from Burke or Cockburn? Was he upset about the scant crowd or pitiful offering? Twice Jack moved as though about to speak, but he held back each time—aware, Dent hoped, that one man can only take so much, regardless of his ordination credentials.

Footsteps swished across the carpet in the hallway. A second later, Burke himself appeared.

"Well," Jack said, his voice thick with cheer. "Be seeing you."

Jack slipped past Burke, taking the last of Dent's hope with him. Burke closed the door behind them. Sweat beaded on the crown of Dent's head.

"I understand you visited with my wife the other day," Burke said. "You had her in the parsonage."

"She stopped by to drop off a meal for me and Lucas," Dent said. "It was a nice gesture."

"I'm sure she meant it to be. But I worry, Brother Denton. I worry about her lack of discretion. And I worry about the start you're getting off to here at the church."

Dent felt his face go hot. "I'm afraid I don't follow."

"This is the Panhandle, remember. Think of how it looks to people around here, a single man like you inviting a pretty young woman into your house at a time when you think no one is looking."

"It wasn't anything like that."

"Oh, I know. But truth is never quite as important as interpretation. Did you know Mrs. Martz is usually awake at that hour, and that her treadmill faces out toward your house? I'm sure she's overreacting. Well, I'm reasonably sure."

"I don't like where you're going with this," Dent said. He tried to bow up his shoulders, but knew it was no use. Clerical robes made every wearer look puffy and insecure. He might as well dive into the pile of vestments on the floor and hope to disappear.

"I'm not going anywhere," Burke said evenly. "Just drawing natural conclusions. The new pastor had an attractive early morning visitor, whom he invited to be alone with him in his house."

"Lucas was there."

"An outsider who was incapacitated and probably asleep. Understand, Reverend. I'm not accusing you of anything. Except perhaps poor judgment." He stepped closer. Lowered his voice. "Crystal is not the most reliable person you'll meet. I love her dearly, Brother Denton. I truly do. But she does not always process the world in a clear way. I would hate for things to get confusing for her. Wouldn't you?"

The day of rest for parishioners had never been anything of the sort for Dent, nor, he suspected, for any member of the Christian clergy. Rather, it was a day of demand and chaos and, as the morning service clearly showed, failure. As a mentor once told him, "Sundays will Sunday."

No sooner had Burke disappeared from his office than Vic and Mamie entered, wanting to talk over a concern that Dent could never quite get a handle on. He finally ushered them out so that he could get lunch, but a call from Pete Eberhardt about the impending death of his Uncle Clif sucked him back to his desk. He ate stale crackers he found stashed in the food pantry for lunch, prepped the youth lesson, and delivered it to two exasperated teenagers whose attendance clearly was not voluntary. When it was over, Dent wanted nothing more than a fast-food hamburger and a long shower. Instead, he got a phone call from Doc.

"You busy this evening?" the old physician asked as soon as Dent picked up.

"I'm fine," Dent said. "How are you?"

"Too old for pleasantries. And in need of a pastoral visit."

Dent wiped his hand over his face. "It's been a long day."

"Ain't they all," Doc said. "You coming? I need a fishing buddy."

"It's too cold to fish."

"No it isn't. May be too cold to catch anything, but not too cold to drink beer and throw out a line. I'll have Rachel text you directions to the cabin. Come on around back when you get there."

Before Dent could deliver his next excuse, the line went silent. He shook his head. Loaded his gear into the bed of the pickup and left a note for Lucas.

The lower edge of the sun was just touching the horizon when he turned off the gravel onto the single-track road heading east to the cabin. A teenage boy raced his ATV out in front of Dent's pickup, sunlight glinting off the giant stainless steel scrotum that swung from a wire tied to the rear rack. When he got out of the truck at Doc's, Dent could still see green and yellow streaks across his vision.

Doc was seated on a swivel chair in a small flat-bottomed boat twenty yards from where the shoreline once was. Three summers of drought had taken their toll on the reservoir, and the boat was wedged a foot deep into dried mud and six feet back from the water's edge. A yellow nylon rope connected an eyelet in the boat's stern to a support post of the cabin's deck, just in case the floods of Noah once again floated Doc's boat. Dent walked out across the dried earth and climbed in.

"Think you could make a little more noise?" Doc grunted. "The fishing wasn't bad enough already." He motioned toward his orange bobber, thirty feet beyond. "The lakebed takes a pretty sharp turn down about there. Plenty of water, but the best fishing is usually further back toward the house, when the lake is high enough. Damn climate change." He reached into a foam minnow bucket filled with ice and pulled out a beer for Dent and another for himself. "How's the detective work going?"

"Detective work?"

"The Sheriff tells me you've been asking around about some town history. What is it you're looking for?"

"Anything that will help me figure out the people in this town," Dent said.

"Yeah?" Doc said with a grunt. "You got a better chance fishing in a dry lake. Find anything good?"

"Not much, really. A lot of conflicting stories about Irene. Like this Brantley fellow she was married to."

Doc's hands tensed. He spit onto the cracked dirt. "What about him?"

"According to Bud Cockburn, Brantley was a pillar of the community—taught Sunday school, was past-president of the Last Man Club. Bud tells me he dug his own grave before he shot himself, all to save his family the trouble of watching him die of cancer. But Old Mother Earth gave me the impression that he wasn't all that near and dear to her heart. When I went to see her she mentioned a boyfriend she had when she first got married. But she never even uttered Harlan Brantley's name."

Doc's bobber jerked violently to the left. Doc tugged at the pole to set the hook, but the swirl of the water around it told Dent it was no use. A second later, the turtle surfaced a few feet away, apparently scanning the water for another courtesy meal. Doc reeled in his line. Turned deep, cold eyes on Dent.

"Harlan Brantley was a no-account son of a bitch that the world is better off without."

"That's harsh."

"I mean it though."

"Why?"

"Nothing I care to repeat," Doc snapped. "Now are you here to fish, or are you here to piss me off? Because that's what you're doing, and it's my damn boat."

Dent lowered his head and lifted his palms. He dropped his pole over the side of the boat so that its handle rested in the dust of the once and perhaps future lakebed. He skewered a worm onto the hook and cast it into the water several yards from where Doc had dropped his newly baited line. They fished in silent futility until Doc reached in for two more beers and handed another to Dent—an act which, in Texas, amounted to reconciliation. Dent took it and tilted the top of the can toward Doc.

"You helping with the Tall Tale Roundup?" he asked after a long drink. "It's all anybody in Last Man Club seems to care about these days."

"I'm not a member of that fraternity," Doc said.

Dent pinched the bridge of his nose. "Okay."

"It's all right," Doc said. "Hell, you don't know any better. So let me tell you a little bit about how things work. The Panhandle myth is that people in these parts bond together, enduring the harsh conditions and all. But that's only true for certain people. I can still remember a day when last Man Club didn't let in Catholics or Jews. Well, my daddy was a Catholic, and my momma was a Jew. I'll admit it's an odd pairing, but that was the way of it."

"The club won't let you in for that?"

"They would now," Doc said. "Maybe I just haven't overcome my own prejudices yet."

They watched the bobbers loll in the fading daylight. A light wind stirred what leaves remained on the trees, sent tiny ripples over the water. Dent felt as though he could sleep, sitting straight up right here in the boat. It was Doc's voice that yanked him back into the waking world.

"What?" Dent said.

"I said Irene Ostendorf is dying."

Dent let that settle in. "Well."

"Pancreatic cancer," Doc continued. "Her heart won't survive aggressive treatments, and she could drop dead of a stroke any time. But I suspect that the cancer will get her first."

"How long does she have?"

"Everybody always asks that question. Truth is nobody knows. I suspect a matter of weeks."

"She know this?"

"She does."

"How's her mind?"

Doc shook his head. "That's what I can't figure out. She seems just as alert and together as ever. No Alzheimer's, certainly. She's on a lot of meds, but none of them are known to produce dementia or paranoia. I've checked it three times."

"So she's perfectly sane."

"Let's not jump to conclusions." He tapped his head. "I'm just saying that the hardware looks good. There's no physiological reason that I can find for her to have shot at anyone. And psychologically speaking, I've known that woman all my life. If she were going to kill somebody, she should have done it long ago. I can't figure it. Can you?"

"Not a bit," Dent said. He thumbed through his mental files. "This boyfriend she used to have—some guy named Henry. What's the story there?"

"Well now," Doc said, a smile lighting up his face for the first time tonight. He turned his whole body to face Dent. "Henry Turzanski. That's someone I haven't thought of in a long time."

"Who was he?"

"Irene's true love, if you believe in such things. His parents moved here during the wheat boon of the 20's and got off to a pretty good start, or so the story goes. He and Irene were playmates when they were kids, and it was just assumed around town that they'd marry someday. But then Irene's daddy died, and her mother took up with this no-account man from back East. Henry's parents didn't think him old enough to marry yet, and Irene decided she couldn't wait to get out of her house, and so she took up with someone else."

Dent opened his mouth to say Harlan Brantley's name. Thought better of it.

"I don't know the whole story," Doc continued. "Folks always speculated that he got mixed up in some kind of bad business, the way he lit out for Albuquerque in his old Model A. He hopped the train to San Francisco from there and that was the last anybody ever heard from him."

Dent traced the thread of the narrative through his limited knowledge, but could not make the stories weave together in a way that made any sense. "I haven't heard anybody else talk about this Henry fellow. He can't still be alive."

"Likely not. He'd be nearly 100 by now."

"Then how do you know so much?"

Doc sat up straighter. His smile widened. "He was my uncle. The brother to my momma. She was still little when he left town. I never met him, of course. She used to talk about him from time to time. I never heard Irene mention him, though."

"She may not know your relationship," Dent said.

"You can bet that she does, which may explain even more." He turned his hands around and clasped his knees. Stared into the bucket with the two scrawny bass that constituted their evening catch. "I believe the fish have spoken. Let's go make some sandwiches."

CHAPTER 13:
YOU CAN IMAGINE
THE SCARS

The cabin was roomier than it looked from the outside, clean and ordered to a degree that suggested some sort of compulsion on the part of its owner. Dent set to work spreading peanut butter over bread, glancing up and over the bar occasionally to examine the trophies of stuffed fish and deer heads on the far wall. He rummaged through the cabinets, searching for jelly or honey and marveling at the organization. A place for everything and everything in its place, just like Janet would have done. He shuddered at the thought.

Back at the parsonage, his own kitchen was a disaster area, a junk pile of recycled pots and pans Bro. Holloway had not seen fit to pack. And all the while infinitely better cookware was entombed in cardboard boxes a few feet away. How long would it take for Dent to unpack them? A day? Half a day? When the bishop had sent him to Odessa, he and Janet had managed to have their house set up less than seventy-two hours after they first pulled up in the parking lot, and that with an eleven-year-old girl in tow. Some of their success, no doubt, was due to Janet's compulsive organization. But her attention to detail had also slowed them down. The spice rack had emptied when Dent accidentally picked its box up upside down, sending Janet into a fifteen-minute tirade. She lost another half hour reorganizing the jars based on some system of herbal classification Dent had never been able to decipher. They had more or less made up by evening, and they finished the day by making love in their new bedroom. But Janet let him know in subtle ways that she had condescended to forgive, and he was in her debt not just for the spice rack, but for her patience with his failure to move up the ranks of church hierarchy more quickly. He had dragged her from one nothing town to another, slightly bigger nothing town, but she'd made a promise—taken vows, for God's sake. He lay awake, miserable, until 4:00am.

Unpacking alone should have been a privilege by contrast. He could put things where he wanted them without any nagging voices. What he didn't need could be thrown out or donated to Goodwill. He took a mental inventory of the boxes' contents. Electric skillets and swimming trunks. Books, of course. Every pastor had books enough to sink ships. Curtains, diplomas, office supplies, throw rugs—things people needed in another kind of life or place. Some of the items in the boxes had been wedding presents. He and Janet had started their new life together under a blanket of gifts and prayers and blessings. And what to show for it? Worn out mixers and 9"x 13" pans. Chipped stoneware with out of date patterns. Fifteen years he would never get back.

A disappointing buzz sounded in his pocket. He had not expected to get cell signal here at Doc's cabin, located as it were on the very edge of civilization. But when he reached into his pocket, sure enough he felt the phone vibrating against the tips of his fingers. He silenced it without looking at the screen, knowing it would be Bud Cockburn, his district superintendent, wanting intelligence about Old Mother Earth or Lucas—how they were doing, what people were saying about them, what plans they had for handling their screwed up lives. He had called three times in the past two days, none of which Dent accepted. He would see Cockburn soon enough—in only a week, as a matter of fact, when he traveled to Amarillo for his yearly checkout meeting with the DS. Until then, those under his care had a right to keep their secrets. And if that irritated Cockburn, all the better.

The phone buzzed again. This time he pulled it out and checked the screen. A large red "X" showed as the photo ID. The contact name read *Janet*. He declined it even quicker than if it had been Cockburn, but a half second later it buzzed a third time. He looked out on the deck, where Doc was finishing off the last of the beer, watching the sky like a man at peace with the world. Dent suddenly wanted to knock him on his wise old butt.

He swiped the screen. "Hello?"

"John, hi," Janet said. "Sorry to bother you so late."

She waited for him to respond with the standard Texas deferrals about it being okay and he wasn't doing anything anyway. He said nothing.

"John? Hello?"

"What can I do for you?"

She cleared her throat. "Well, I'm looking for something. A box, to be exact. I think I must have left it behind when I—after we separated. It's got a lot of Emberton family history in it. You understand."

"Well."

"John," she said, exasperated. "It's my family stuff. You have no need for it. Don't be a—just don't."

A sound in the background caught Dent's ear—their daughter's voice, maybe. "Is that Leah?"

"No, no," Janet answered. "My question first. Do you have the box?"

"Probably. I thought Leah was away at school."

"You thought? John, if I were you—and we both know full well I'm not—I would try contacting Leah directly if you want to know something. She's an adult now."

"She told me she was going back to Kansas State this fall."

Janet sighed patiently. "When did you last talk to her?"

"When I found out I was moving to Earth." Dent counted on his fingers. Squeezed his eyes shut. "Maybe three months ago. In my defense, she wasn't exactly happy to hear my voice then."

"You two have to work out your own issues. It's not good for me to try to be a go-between."

"Tell me what's going on with her."

"If you—no. I'm not going to get into another fight." She drew in a deep breath. "Bud told me you have a meeting with him in Amarillo next week."

"Cockburn? Why are you talking to that—?"

"It's my business, John. How about I meet you halfway. Tucumcari? I know it's a little out of the way for you, but—well, there's no good way to connect, really. Let's meet at that espresso shop on Route 66."

"Seems like a shady rendezvous," Dent said. "I thought you were a married woman again."

"I'll take that as a yes," Janet said. "Find the box, John. Please. I'll see you next Tuesday."

Doc sent him home with a square foam cooler, inside which he had packed the bass fillets from their night's meager catch. Dent took a mental inventory of his available pots and pans and utensils, deciding after only a few seconds that he could not do the fish justice unless he unpacked his cast-iron skillet. Perhaps Doc had picked up on that. Perhaps this was his way of forcing the new preacher to actually start living in his new town. Dent turned over the possibility with no small measure of resentment, deciding as he did to toss the fish over the fence to the Martz's dog as soon as he got home.

As he drove down Main Street, however, another thought occurred to him. He slowed as he passed the old Schugart house, where Doc had his office, and looked up. Sure enough, a warm yellow light glowed from Rachel's upstairs apartment. He drove around back and parked next to her car and pulled out his phone to text her. Before he could even open her contact, she raised a window.

"Give me two seconds," she called. "I have to find pants."

Dent could hear her footsteps thud through the old wooden bones of the house. True to her word, she emerged at the backdoor a few seconds later, wearing an orange Broncos sweatshirt and pink scrubs.

"Don't laugh," she said. "It's laundry day. Come on up."

He tried to protest, held the cooler out and mumbled something about her father sending fish. She turned without seeming to hear, into the hallway and through a door and up the stairs. Dent followed, an awkward feeling growing in his chest. Another private meeting with a woman, and this one in her apartment. If Mamie and Vic were out for an evening walk, and if they told Jeff Burke, and if Burke told Cockburn—or worse, Doc—well. He should set the cooler down on the table and be on his way.

"I can't stay," he said as he entered her apartment.

"Oh now." She set a teakettle on the stove. Pulled two mugs from the cabinet. "You wouldn't have come by if you didn't want to stay. I'm a grown woman and I don't go to your church. Relax."

"I don't know. My truck—."

She held up a hand, signaling the end of his protests. Opened the cooler and wordlessly placed the baggie of fish in the freezer, on top of what appeared to be other baggies of fish.

"Black tea, or chamomile?" she asked. Before he could answer, she clapped her hands together. "Black."

"I should probably go."

"You're committed now. Tea first. Then you can leave."

"Well, all right."

"So how was fishing with my father?" Rachel asked. "Be honest."

"Fine, I guess," Dent said. "Water's way down, of course. But it's a lovely cabin. Y'all have really kept it up well."

"It's not a 'y'all' thing. I mean, look." She swept her hand around the apartment, which was littered with piles of clothes and stacks of paper and various crafting projects. "It's always like this, I'm afraid. I give good advice, but I don't live it out so well. Not in the domestic arts, anyway. Dad and Emilia take care of the cabin. It's all I can handle to work for him day in and day out."

"Oh," Dent said. "I thought you and your dad got along pretty well."

"We do!" Rachel said quickly. "But we are together all the time, and after awhile enough is—." She froze, turned slowly toward Dent. "He sent you out here, didn't he."

"Doc? No. He had no idea I was coming by. I didn't even know I was coming by until I saw your light on."

"You sure talk fast to be an innocent man."

"I'm not. I mean, I am innocent, but I'm not talking—listen, I should go."

"Sit!" Rachel ordered. She turned to the stove and lifted the squealing kettle. Poured steaming water over Irish breakfast tea bags and let them steep. After a couple of minutes, she lifted a teabag and dropped it into the bowl of a spoon. Wrapped the string around it and pressed lightly. She did the same over the other mug, then spooned in honey and took them by the handle. When she finally turned again her expression had lost its edge.

"Sorry," she said. "It's just that, with Emilia happily married despite the odds, Dad can't figure out why I don't have someone—a husband or a wife, he wouldn't care. It doesn't make sense to him that I could be happy alone. You'd think that someone who has lived by himself for fifteen years would understand."

"Unless he's not really been happy."

"And that's the problem." She lifted the cup to her mouth. Winced as the tea scalded her lips. "I'm sorry. You didn't come hear to listen to me whine. The truth is that the amount of emotional baggage my family carries could sink a freighter."

"I would not have guessed that," Dent said.

"Probably because you see what you expect to see, and not what's really there."

Her voice stayed as even and conversational as if she were diagnosing a common cold. Dent rubbed his fingers together, unnerved by her lack of passion. He tried to remember if there was anything embarrassing he'd heard about the Schugart family since he'd moved to town, some factoid of scandal.

"Emilia told me about your mother," he ventured. "About how she ended up here from Chicago and met Doc. It's got to be tough, growing up without ever knowing your father."

"She had a father. Doc."

"Maybe I heard her wrong."

Rachel thought this over while she swirled her tea. At last she sighed. "No, you probably didn't. She just usually doesn't talk that way. I can tell you for certain that Dad never treated her as anything other than his own. You knew she ran away, though, right?"

"Nobody's mentioned that."

"Back when she was a teenager. I don't think this is much of a secret, really. She had some trouble in school, and I think at home, although I was really too young to pick up on all that was going on. Anyhow, she stayed pretty tight-lipped about what happened while she was away, but I think she was able to track down her biological father at some point."

"That seems like something she might have told you."

Rachel shrugged. "She keeps a lot to herself. Besides, our mother died while she was AWOL. So you can imagine the scars that left."

"Well. Runaways never have it easy. That must have been a tough time for her."

"Of course," Rachel said. She lifted her hands, let them drop against her thigh. "Everybody has sympathy for the prodigal. It wasn't the easiest of times back here, either, trying to nurse Dad through his grief and figure out womanhood without a mother. God! I'd forgotten how awkward that was."

She laughed, but not in a way Dent trusted. These were old wounds she was opening before him, and he was not sure whether to be honored or terrified. He was so busy wondering what to say next that he almost didn't notice that Rachel had begun to cry very softly.

"Oh wow," she said, fanning herself with her left hand. "I don't normally do this sort of thing. I'm sorry."

"It's all right," Dent said.

"No it's not. I hate crying. It makes people anxious."

Dent shook his head. "I'm used to tears."

"I don't see how."

"Well."

He waited, eyes cast down at the space between them. Her left hand was on the mug, but her right lay on the table. This was not a time to reach for it, he reminded himself. You had to be careful with touch in situations like this. People forgot themselves when emotions ran too high. Pastors forgot themselves too.

"She had a Sunday school teacher who was an abuser," Rachel said. Her words were soft, but filled the apartment.

"Emilia did?"

"Yes. It was Irene Ostendorf's husband."

Dent blinked. "Harlan Brantley?"

"Yes." She wiped her eyes. Placed her hands back on the table. "I don't know what exactly he did or how long it went on. I know he got into some kind of trouble when she ran away, but not enough to go to jail. They wouldn't let him teach Sunday school anymore, though. Which is good for me, since—."

She drew in a quick breath. Her shoulders jerked.

"You would probably have been next," Dent said.

"There's no way of knowing," Rachel said. "I think I would have been. Dad didn't find out until after Emilia ran off."

"It's not your fault."

"I know."

"You don't always get to choose what kind of past you're going to have."

"Maybe not. I don't know what I'm telling you all this. Fuck!"

The swear wasn't loud, but its intensity sent another missile through Dent's insides, tearing at his comfort with the world. It must have helped Rachel, however. Her face relaxed, if only a bit, and she almost smiled. He waited—the one skill he'd picked up in years of failed pastoral work. He let her cry and did not reach for her. He waited to see and waited to hear, and he did not run away.

CHAPTER 14:
THE PATRON SAINT OF
DESPERATE SITUATIONS

Sunday morning was half gone when Ashley awoke in Lubbock, alone and panicked. With Plan A for extraction thrown out the window when Jeff arrived before she could pack, Ashley had hastily constructed a Plan B while the Red Raiders were getting walloped by CSU. She would play nice during dinner with Jeff's buddies, go with him to the apartment and let him take her to bed—no dramatic scenes, no shouting or threats. Then she would feign sleep until he gave up trying to rouse her and dressed and left to be with his family. She would pack her suitcases and slip away and never—this time—never come back to him.

Her own plan had been her undoing. Rather than pretend sleep, she succumbed to it, falling into a long and fitful slumber from which she couldn't quite wake through dream after exhausting dream. She finally dropped into a sound sleep sometime after dawn, but two hours later the light through a crack in the curtains bore into her face. She peeled herself up off the sheets and willed her legs to stand, and when her thoughts finally began to order themselves she remembered she was supposed to work this evening at 5:00. No way she could make the drive in time, not now that she'd slept in. She texted Sid that she was not feeling well, and half hoped that he would fire her, or at least express how annoyed he was by her recent flakiness. Instead he responded with understanding, and even concern. Damn the innocent, she thought, for making the guilty feel even worse.

She showered and dressed and waited until the fog lifted from the mirror to brush out her hair. The left side of her scalp hurt, and she remembered how she and Jeff had gone at each other last night after the game, all rage and desperation. Could he sense her fury? If he did, he gave it back, and more. But he had not kissed her goodbye. Had not even tried to wake her before he left. If she believed in God, she would have thanked Him for that, at least.

She slipped a few items she wanted to take home in her backpack—a stocking cap she'd left here last winter, a novel she'd forgotten to finish, a bottle of contact solution. She clicked off the bathroom light and glanced into the bedroom as she exited. The blue Beta Club bracelet caught her eye from the wastebasket next to the dresser. Who was the girl, she wondered. Was she as old as Ashley had been? Was she any less incapable of not screwing up her life?

Ashley flipped over the bracelet, looking for any small identifier. Nothing but the club logo and the colors of Earth High School, a token of solidarity. She slipped it onto her wrist. Closed the door behind her.

Three hours into the return trip, Ashley was engaged in a full-on assault against her past life. Without making a conscious decision to do so, she had missed the onramp to I-27 and instead taken Highway 84 North out of Lubbock. It wasn't until she saw the faded Chamber of Commerce sign urging visitors to "Make us your No. 1 spot on EARTH!" that she realized what she had done. She slumped in her seat and pushed her sunglasses up against her face and drove exactly four MPH over the speed limit until she was safely out of Lamb County. She expected to feel a weight lifted from her as she crossed into Castro, but the burden persisted through Deaf Smith and Oldham and into Hartley. She tucked her sandals beneath her seat, rolled down the windows and tried to sing over the rush of wind—tried to feel free, or at least what she imagined "free" might feel like. Instead her fingers and ears got colder the further north she drove, and her voice grew pained and raspy, and loss opened up behind her like a parachute. By the time Dalhart came into view, she was afraid she might actually cry behind the wheel. Instead she pulled into a gas station, hoping a full tank and a large coffee would do for her what time and distance had not.

She went into the bathroom first, washed her face with cold water. When she came out to pump her gas, a man about the age of her father was leaning against her back fender, grunting out the lyrics to the Dire Straits song that played over the grainy speakers overhead.

"Afternoon, miss," he said once he caught sight of her approaching.

"I'm sorry," Ashley said. "I didn't know there was a—what do you call it?"

"A full service lane?" the man said. He laughed. "It's not."

"Oh." She took a step back.

"I see," the man said, narrowing his eyes. "I'm coming off as creepy."

"A little."

"My apologies then," he said cheerfully. "I'm just trying to help out. Name's Carl." He pushed up his sleeves and extended a hand. Scents of grease and cigarette smoke clung to his Dalhart Wolves hoodie. "It's a slow day around here. Didn't mean to worry you."

"You don't," Ashley said.

Carl looked down at her sandaled feet and grinned. "With ink like that, I'd guess you're a hard one to spook. Pigeon from hell, that thing is."

"It's a velociraptor."

"Ah!" Carl exclaimed, clapping his hands together. "I knew that. I should have guessed it. Well, it's a beauty, no matter what you call it. You got a good hand working on you."

"Thanks." She glanced at his forearm, where a stunning phoenix stretched over his brown skin. "You too."

Carl flexed his hand open and closed. "I'm proud of her. Not gonna lie." He returned the nozzle to its hanger. Dropped his hand onto the hood of the car. "I heard your engine squealing as you pulled in. Pop the hood and I'll give her a look."

"I'm kind of in a hurry."

"All the more reason," Carl said. "You can't afford to be stranded, right? Neither time nor money to spare, I'd wager."

Ashley smiled, reached beneath the steering wheel and pulled the handle. A loud *pop* sounded as the latch gave way. Carl raised the hood, reached his fingers under a graying rubber belt and tugged. He let out a dissatisfied grunt.

"I hate to be the bearer of bad news," he said. "But what you have here is the potential for multiple catastrophic problems."

"Okay."

"How old is this car? Fifteen years?"

"About that."

"Well, I think your belts and hoses are originals." He motioned for Ashley to look closer. "See those cracks in the rubber? A few are just natural, but you've got them all over the place. I would not let my daughter drive with it like this—no offense to your father or nothing."

Ashley shrugged. "Well then," she said. "I guess I'll have to get that fixed when I get home."

"How far away is home?" Carl said, but threw up his hands before she could answer. "I'm doing it again with the questions. The whole creepy thing. Listen, I'm just trying to help, honest to God. Give me an hour and I can have you up and going."

Ashley shook her head. "It's all right. I've made it this far with whatever is on the engine. I can make it a little further, can't I?"

"Well, I suppose you could," Carl said. "But you're tempting fate the longer you go."

"I guess I'll just have to tempt it then."

"All right, all right," Carl said. He took her credit card between his fingers like a cigarette, flapped it once against the air. "Just give me one second." He trotted through the glass door and around the counter and disappeared below the register. When he returned, he held her card and receipt and something that looked like a half dollar coin. It depicted a square-jawed man with a ragged beard and determined expression, clutching the mast of a sail with one hand and a cross with the other. A Christian Poseidon, unapologetic and wild.

She examined the coin, tried without success to decipher the Latin. "Thanks. I guess it's good luck?"

"He's more of a guardian than a charm," Carl grunted. "That's Jude, patron saint of desperate situations."

"Oh," Ashley said, and smiled despite herself. "Am I a desperate situation?"

"Not yet," Carl said. "But you'd be surprised how quickly that can turn. I gave one of these to a guy passing through on his bicycle a couple weeks ago. Found out later that some old lady in Lamb County shot it right out from under him."

Ashley laid the coin on top of the pump. "I have to go," she said.

"Now don't be like that," Carl said. He scraped St. Jude off the top of the pump and handed it back to her. "You can throw him out the window when you get out of town, but I'll feel better knowing you at least carried him that far."

Ashley opened her mouth to argue, but stopped before the words could form. The primary mission was not debate, but extraction. She set the coin onto the dash. "Thank you."

"It's Catholic," Carl said. "I hope that's okay."

"Sure. Fine," Ash said.

"I admit I don't know as much about it as I should," Carl said. "I go Christmas and Easter, same as everybody else. But my sister never misses a week at St. Anthony's. She's always giving me these icons to aid my spiritual journey—handfuls of them every month. I usually just toss them in the trash."

Ashley slipped through the car door and turned the key. The engine squealed to life. Sure enough, the belts whined in an unsettling fashion. How had she not noticed that before? She held St. Jude up, examined his face in the light through her open window.

"Why didn't you?" she asked.

"Why didn't I what?"

"Just drop these in the trash along with the other icons?"

"Oh," he said sheepishly. "I never could throw away a good piece of metal." He backed away and lifted his hand, rising upward above the phoenix tattoo. "Keep Jude with you, all right? At least until you get them belts fixed."

CHAPTER 15:
EVERYBODY'S HIDING
SOMETHING

Tasked with the short-term preservation of John Wesley Denton's pastoral career, Bud Cockburn reviewed Dent's personnel file with the morbid cheer of an embalmer. He sucked on his lips and frowned and grunted in a mildly pitying way. In the reflection of the glass doors over the bookshelf behind the desk, Dent could see the leaves in Sanborn Park dance over the fading grass on this crisp fall day, passing by without the slightest concern for those trapped in evaluative meetings.

"Mercy, J-Dub," Cockburn said. "You have managed to amass quite the portfolio here." He took off his reading glasses. Narrowed his eyes at Dent. "How are things going in Earth?"

"It's only been three weeks."

"A hell of a three weeks, though. And it looked like you were struggling a bit yesterday, if I may say so."

Dent blinked. With all the running around on Sunday, he'd forgotten that his district superintendent had been there for worship that morning, seated on the pew next to his fellow Buffalo Bruiser as if they were back on the sidelines at WT A&M. Dent had to lay one hand on top of the other to keep from covering his face. Cockburn went on.

"Everybody has a bad Sunday on occasion, of course—weak sermon or small crowd or bad music. God knows you've got to overcome that awful choir somehow, which was always my frustration when I was pastor in at that church. But let's talk about you, J-Dub—*you!* You've developed a pattern of ineffectiveness over these past few appointments. The bishop is concerned."

Dent watched the swirling leaves. In his first year in ministry, he had sat in this office before a former district superintendent, Reverend John Bill Hollis. While Hollis told him war stories of when he was fresh out of seminary, Dent had watched his wife and little girl through the window behind the desk. Leah heaped leaves at the bottom of the slide, ascended the ladder and hurled herself down into the pile. Even Janet got into the act, helping kick the leaves back together once their daughter had scattered them. God, they had been beautiful.

"J-Dub? You listening? I said the bishop is concerned."

"I don't doubt that."

Cockburn leaned forward on his elbows. "Give it to me straight, J-Dub. Are you in trouble?"

"Trouble? I don't believe so."

"Janet seems to think you might be."

A cold sensation spread through Dent's chest, as though he'd downed a glass of ice water too quickly. He repeated her name. Cockburn raised up his palms.

"Now don't get the wrong idea. Your personal life—the divorce and all—is your business. I'm not trying to stir up trouble with the your ex just because she's the bishop's daughter. I'm just trying to get a clear picture of what I'm dealing with here."

"Well."

Cockburn picked up his glasses and flipped open the file on his desk. "We've appointed you to six churches in fifteen years, none of which has seen significant growth. You had a pretty good run as an associate pastor, but stumbled every time the bishop put you out on your own. And this last congregation—well, frankly J-Dub, we thought it was a slam-dunk. Hell, we could appoint the devil himself there, and that church would still grow. You actually lost members. And then you divorced your wife. Right in the middle of it."

"She divorced me."

"You divorced each other. Listen, I'm not here to assign blame. A failed marriage is a terrible thing for everybody, Lord knows. How's Leslie?"

"I don't know a Leslie."

"Your daughter," Cockburn said. He furrowed his brow. Looked back down at the open manila folder. His lips moved as he scanned his notes. "Leah. How's Leah?"

"All right, far as I know," Dent said. "We don't talk as much as we used to."

"That's what Janet said. That's got to be hard on a fellow. You can tell me about it if you want."

"Thank you."

"I need more than a 'thank you.' You've got to be able to trust me, J-Dub. That's the only way I can help. Can I speak openly to you? Your career is in the toilet, and your marriage has already been flushed. The bishop and I both want to know. What are you hiding?"

Dent set his gaze beyond the DS again. Watched the play of the leaves. Thought of the words of confession he spoke at Eucharist the first Sunday of every month. *We have sinned in thought, word, and deed.*

"I'm not hiding anything," he said.

"Everybody's hiding something," Cockburn insisted. "And nine times out of ten, it's honey or money. You have a girl stashed somewhere I need to know about? Been skimming a little of the loose plate offering?"

"Lord, Bud."

"Answer the question."

"No."

"No, you won't answer? Or no *is* your answer?" Cockburn waited for Dent to respond. When he did not, Cockburn spread his hands wide. "I'm not looking to condemn you, J-Dub. I've had my own temptations, back when I was a local church pastor, and God knows I wasn't perfect. I just need to know. Confession is the first step to redemption."

"All right."

"All right what?"

"Go ahead," Dent said. He felt his anger pushing downward from his brain, forcing sarcasm out of his mouth. Already he could see that this wouldn't end well. Already didn't care. "If you have something to confess, I'll be glad to listen."

"Quit it, J-Dub. We're talking about you, now. I'm here to help *you*."

"I'm overwhelmed with gratitude."

Cockburn pushed back from his desk. Threw up his hands. Stood up and began to pace. "See, this is what I'm talking about," he fumed. "It's not that you don't have any talent at all, John. Clearly you had some sort of potential, once upon a time. But you won't get out of your own way. Something good comes along, and you just have to blow it up. I don't understand that."

"That sounds like your problem."

"Fine." Cockburn sat down again. Folded his hands together, his index fingers sticking out, their tips pressed against one another. Here is the church, and here is its steeple. "You're on borrowed time here, John. I'm not kidding around. It's not your fault that you walked into a shitstorm of trouble, practically on day one. If we'd known that Old Mother Earth was going to shoot at Bishop Lin's son, we would certainly have put someone else there to handle it."

"That's kind of you to say," Dent said.

"Enough!" The irritation drained from Cockburn's face, replaced by as pure an anger as Dent had ever seen on anyone not named Janet

Emberton Denton. An unpleasant smile crept across his lips. "I can't help, not with you like this. You're bringing it on yourself."

"Bringing what?"

"Whatever is coming. Just remember I warned you."

Dent drove toward Tucumcari as though trying to outrun the devil, although at this point who could stay on which end of his journey the devil resided. Cockburn hadn't even bothered capping off the checkout meeting with the standard exit prayer, preferring instead to let the wreckage of Dent's career smolder on the two-thousand-dollar rug in his office. Dent walked away with his chest puffed out, a hero unsinged by the flames. But it was all bravado. Misery had descended upon him the minute he got back into his pickup. Woe to those who set fire to what they have, for they will be left in ashes.

The more he tried to outrun this latest failure, however, the larger his errand loomed on the western horizon. He had located Janet's box of Emberton family mementos when he'd gotten home from Rachel's on Sunday night, buried in a haphazard stack of miscellany guarded by the Moses and Miriam mannequins. It was labeled with a single identifier at one end of the box, *Emberton/ J's Office*, printed in Janet's impeccable script. He opened it, just to be sure. Inside, was a time capsule of his ex-wife's maiden identity, foundations of a life into which John Wesley Denton had made a fifteen-year cameo. Neatly bound stacks of photographs. An infant-sized baptismal gown. A file containing life insurance documents for her father, which made no mention of Dent as a beneficiary of any kind. Nothing she couldn't live without for a few months. He had considered no-showing, letting her sit at the window of the espresso bar and sip her latte and feel superior. Maybe she'd bring her new husband, an artsy fellow who owned a costume company in Albuquerque. The thought made Dent want to drive the truck straight into a bridge embankment.

But what if Janet didn't bring Mr. Costume Guy? What if she brought Leah instead? He'd always told himself he'd wade through hell in a kerosene jacket for his little girl. She wasn't so little anymore—nineteen years old. How did that happen?—and she blamed him for the divorce more than he thought was fair. But a good father had to be able to withstand his child's raging and even her rejection. So bring on the devil and her play-dress-up boyfriend. Douse him in fuel and light the match. At least Dent had the courage for this one thing, however small.

These thoughts buoyed his spirit, but also weighed on his right foot as he sped into town. He noticed the speed limit sign and the state trooper at the same time, and in an instant his dread was realized. The cruiser whipped into the westbound lane and turned on the blue lights. Dent panicked. He was in sight of the coffee shop now, and anywhere he pulled over his truck would be visible to customers seated by the window, which would surely include Janet and quite possibly Costume Guy and Leah. He slowed to five below the limit and cruised right past the espresso bar, telling himself not to look to see if his ex-wife was watching. He did anyway, and immediately laid his eyes on Janet's army-green Subaru. She was only just now getting out of the car, but her eyes were tracking Dent's pickup as he passed. He wished a cement mixer would plough him under, then and there.

What happened instead was much worse. In the same instant that he noticed Janet, he spotted someone else sliding out of the passenger seat. A young woman in maternity clothes, a strip of elastic dividing her heavy breasts from her round belly, pulled herself up with the doorframe. And Dent saw what he could not have seen—what could not possibly be so. Behind the mirrored sunglasses on the expectant mother's face were the features Dent loved more than any on the planet.

Leah.

He blinked. Looked away and looked back again, just to be sure. Stared for a long moment. Her back was to him now as she shuffled into the espresso shop, but there was no mistaking her identity. His daughter was about as pregnant as any woman could be, and he could neither make sense of nor turn from it.

The pickup lurched, and Dent snapped back to reality after what seemed like hours away. How long had he been staring? Not more than a couple of seconds, surely, but long enough for the pickup to veer off course. The jolt had come from his front tire, which had hopped a nine-inch curb. The rear tire followed, and for several feet Dent drove half on the street and half on the sidewalk. The trooper punched his siren once, and then flatly ordered him to sir-please-pull-over, his voice sounding through the megaphone like the very wrath of God. Dent managed to guide the pickup behind a gas station and skid to a stop, kicking gravel forward onto the cashier smoking on a bench. She dropped her cigarette and flipped him off and disappeared behind the gray door.

The cruiser pulled to a stop behind him. Dent leaned over to open the glove box and retrieve the requisite documentation. A shadow passed over him, and he realized in an instant how he must look, rummaging through the glove box with his hands shaking so. The cop would think he was searching for his gun, and might even have his service pistol pointed at Dent right now. Dent threw his hands up. Pushed himself back into a seated position.

"For heaven's sake, John," the woman's voice said.

Dent lowered his hands and turned his head and saw certain humiliation standing beside his vehicle, arms crossed.

"Hi Janet," he said.

"Have you been drinking?"

"No. Just driving. I'm a bit preoccupied at the moment."

"Well, you may get off lucky," she said. She jerked her head toward the cruiser. "Your state trooper turns out to be Johnny

Schmidt. Remember him? He was in your youth group when we served the church here. I think you may have confirmed him."

"Wait." Dent held up his hands. Blinked. "What are you doing? Isn't this interfering with an arrest or something."

"I doubt you get arrested just for driving like a maniac, but I suppose it's possible. Anyhow, Johnny said I could talk to you while he ran your plates. Such a sweet young man." She stepped to the side and peered in the back seat. "Is this my box? I'll go ahead and take it now, if you don't mind. I need to get going."

She opened the back door and reached in. Dent unbuckled the seatbelt and turned around in one swift motion. He planted a hand on top of the box and pressed it to the seat.

"No!" he shouted. "Tell me what's going on with Leah."

Janet let out a long sigh. "There's nothing to tell."

"The hell there isn't. I saw her walking into the coffee shop. She's—when did that happen?"

"About eight months ago," Janet said. "She tried to tell you several times this summer, but never could find a way. You aren't always the best of listeners, you know. Not when your family is concerned."

"Then you should have told me. Who's the father? Is she still with the guy? When is she due?"

"I'm afraid you'd have to ask Leah. Some other time, though. She thought she was ready for this, but the closer we got the more she knew she couldn't face—well, you know how it is."

"I don't have the foggiest idea how anything is," Dent said. He glanced up to see Officer Schmidt moving toward the pickup. He pulled his hand off the box. Janet peeled back one flap, noticed the baptismal gown on top. Tears shimmered in her eyes. "Wait on me, Janet. Please. Just til I can talk to her."

She hoisted the box onto her hip. Smiled politely as she walked across the empty lot and back to her vehicle. Seconds later, as his broad-shouldered former confirmand approached with what was sure to be a massive ticket, Janet's SUV rolled by, Leah in the passenger seat. His daughter turned her head toward him. Raised her fingers in an uncertain wave.

CHAPTER 16:
YOU KNOW THIS CAN'T
END WELL

Ashley scrubbed a gooey pasta-like substance from the inside Jen's saucepan, mentally spelling out every possible microorganism that three days of neglect might produce on such a surface. *Salmonella. Campylobacter jejuni. E. Coli.* If entered into her phone, the list would easily extend beyond five slots, no matter what parameters she set. No use bothering with that, not when she was so busy playing maid and nursing Jen through her microbiology midterm. Neither was her job, of course. But she did not have friends to spare, which made the thought of Jen flunking out both irritating and unnerving. And if she wanted to eat something besides pizza on a surface not made of paper, the dishes had to be done.

"The first person to observe microorganisms with a microscope," Jen mused. "Pasteur?"

"Van Leeuwenhoek."

"Damn it."

Ashley turned the pot over in the strainer. She glanced at her forearm as she pulled her hand back. She didn't remember exactly how she got the faint purple and yellow bruises on her wrist, but neither did they surprise her. A little rough sex, that's all. She pressed her forearm against her stomach and pulled down her sleeve.

"Are you listening? Hello?" Jen said, tapping on the table. "Phospholipids?"

Ashley sighed. "You know I'm just enabling you," she said.

"Uh-huh." Jen gnawed on her pen, drummed her fingers on her laptop. "Never mind. I found it."

Snow fell outside the kitchen window—the big, wet goosefeathers of mid-fall in Colorado. The temperature was barely at freezing, which meant the snow would thaw and refreeze into the clear, deadly-slick sheen that could lead to bodily harm or, worse, social media infamy. She considered texting Connor to let him know she'd be staying at Jen's tonight but decided it wasn't worth the price to be paid. He would find some reason to be pissed, and anyway she would never get any sleep with Jen's Micro 101 test coming up in the morning. For once, she longed for the warmer temps and pillow-soft solitude of Irene's ranch in Earth.

Well, almost.

She did long for Irene and her wisdom of years, to hear the stories she told when Ashley's mother wasn't around—life without the filters. The old woman had seen and endured as much as any person her age might expect, but more than anyone deserved, from her desperate mother to evil stepfather to no-account husband. Her great aunt understood things in a way that made Ashley feel like she wasn't so screwed up. One more conversation, one more late night session over ice cream might be all she needed to come clean about Jeff. To find out what to do.

Footsteps pounded outside, heavy and determined, obviously a man. The door flew open. Ashley felt the muscles in her shoulders knot up. Jen peered over the top of her laptop as Connor trudged inside.

"He-ey there," Jen called, as though his unexpected presence was just the greatest thing. "I didn't expect you."

Ashley turned to face him. He stopped in his tracks. Glared. She fought the urge to roll her eyes. "So how was your day?" she asked instead.

"Shit," Connor said. He kicked the door closed with his foot. "It was absolute, unqualified shit."

"That's dramatic."

"No." He shuffled out of his coat and pulled a beer from the fridge. "It's just accurate. I failed my organic quiz, got a parking ticket, locked my keys in my car, and had to walk all the way over here in the snow because my roommate wouldn't answer the phone."

"Oh," Ashley said, heat rising in her cheeks. "I left it in my backpack, out by the couch. I must not have heard it. Sorry."

"It's freezing out. Do you know how far it is from campus to here?"

One and a half miles, Ashley thought. *Not too far to walk. Suck it up.*

"I'm sorry," she said instead. "You want me to take you back to get the car?"

"Not yet. I need to warm up." He lifted his beer toward Jen. "Thanks."

"Anytime," she sang.

Ashley pulled a towel from the drawer and offered it to Conner. "I'll wash and you dry?"

"Maybe later," Connor grunted.

He dropped into a chair across from Jen. Hunched his shoulders and stared down toward Ashley's feet. She felt his anger engulf her for a moment before it retreated and settled into the space between them. True, Connor was not exactly being fair. His rage was excessive and petty and totally devoid of perspective. But there was something pure in the emotion, a kind of clarity that she found refreshing. No obligatory apologies for his behavior, no tense words of forgiveness. Just you screwed up and now I'm pissed.

Still.

"Look," she said. "I didn't hear my phone, okay? It's not the end of the world."

"Just do your dishes," he muttered. "You're so damn busy."

"I didn't say I was busy. I was helping Jen, for God's sake. You know things are crazy for both of us right now."

"Yeah?" he said. "How so?"

She folded her arms. "You don't care, do you."

"I asked."

"You didn't mean it."

"It's been a shitty day. I just want to rest for a minute and go get my spare key. Can we worry about this other stuff later?"

"My problems, you mean? They can wait?"

"Whoa there, people!" Jen said, lifting her hands like an umpire. "Jen's kitchen is a no-fighting zone, all right? Let's kiss and make up."

Ashley stared at Conner, who stared right back. She held his gaze until he finally blinked. He grabbed his bottle by the neck and stomped into the living room and turned on the television. Ashley raised her middle finger toward the back of his head.

"Psst!" Jen waved Ashley closer. "Are you okay?"

Ashley nodded.

"You sure? We can find someplace to go talk."

"I'm fine."

She turned back to the dishes. Took a deep breath. Applied as much logic as human relationships allowed. Crappy boyfriend though he had been, Connor was at least reasonable in his assessment of her, and of their relationship as well. He didn't idealize her, and they had never discussed a long-term future together. He treated her as a stubborn and clueless child who didn't understand a thing about the world. God, could she ever feel the truth in that.

"Oh sweet Jesus!" Jen exclaimed.

Ashley looked over her shoulder. Jen was staring at her laptop screen, hands clasped over her mouth. Connor did not stir from the couch.

"What?" Ashley said.

"Shh!" Jen wrinkled her brow and waved her palms. She looked at the screen, then at Ashley. Back to the screen.

"What?" Ashley mouthed again.

Jen swiveled her laptop around. The screen lit up with photos on some social media website that Ashley couldn't place. Jen tapped her touchpad, and one of the photos expanded into the forefront—a selfie taken by a young African-American woman in a green-and-gold CSU sweatshirt, surrounded by fans attired in Red Raider gear. The caption, posted by someone named Maddison, read, "Cheering on the Rams in Lubbock! Wish you were here, Jen MacGehee!"

Ashley's stomach flipped. Over Maddison's right shoulder, two rows back, Jeff Burke was raising his hands in disgust, apparently complaining about some Red Raider failure to the fan next to him. On his other side, hands in her pockets, was Ashley, staring blankly in the direction of the photographer.

"Hey, Connor?" Jen sang. "If you want to pay me back for that beer, would you mind running down to my car and bringing up my micro lab workbook? I think I left it in the backseat."

Connor mumbled something to himself and lumbered into the kitchen. He dropped his bottle into the recycling box under the sink. Jen closed the notebook and tossed him her keys. "You're a doll," she said.

When the door closed, she stared open-mouthed at Ashley.

"You're supposed to be studying," Ashley said.

"I'm taking a break. Oh god." She tapped again. The next pic was another selfie, this time snapped from a different angle to get the press box out of the frame. Judging by the number of fans clapping or raising their hands in the air, Tech must have just scored. Burke held one fist aloft, his other arm draped around Ashley's waist. She was leaning into him, her hand playfully smacking his chest. She was smiling, her expression suggesting a happiness she did not remember feeling.

"Ash?" Jen said. "What. The. Fuck!"

"It's nothing," Ashley said. "I went to a game with my uncle."

"Then your uncle's a perv. His hand is practically on your ass. And—pardon my saying so—but you don't look exactly innocent. Who is he?"

"Nobody. Just a guy I know from back home."

"Who looks about forty. He's way too old for you."

"Let it go."

"All right, all right," Jen said. She turned to face Ashley, pulled her knees together and dropped her palms on top of them. "He's married, isn't he."

Goosebumps crawled up Ashley's neck and scalp. "That's not your worry."

"Ash, honey," Jen said. "You know I love you. But you are a piss-poor liar. Does he at least treat you well?"

"Yes," Ashley said, turning her palms back so that the inside of her wrists didn't show. The noise in her ears made her own voice sound far away. She flexed her right foot. Felt the tender skin where the velociraptor vainly waved its claw.

"Bull-shi-uht," Jen said. "Whoever he is, this guy is trouble—*trouble!* And he has a wife, too. You're in commandment territory here, Ash. Adultery. That's one of the big ones—one of the 'Thou shalt nots.'"

"I don't believe in God."

"You say that," Jen began, but pulled up as Connor's footsteps approached. "Fine. I won't preach. Just think about it, okay? You know it can't end well. Stories like this have a way of following you down."

CHAPTER 17:
A PRETTY SORRY MESS,
AND NOTHING FOR IT

D ent hustled along the sidewalk toward the Last Man Club breakfast, sweat beading on his scalp and a prayer tucked into his pocket. He was not so naïve as to think anyone had forgotten the Johnny Appleseed fiasco, even if no one would have such bad manners as to speak of it. And, Dent realized sadly, he had forgotten least of all. That was the curse of failure. It lingered not as an image or even a memory, but as a full-body program that took over both the psychology and physiology of the victim. You didn't just remember failure. You relived it.

So it was with the sight of his daughter, the young mother-to-be, whose puzzled visage had passed through his thoughts a thousand times during the sleepless night. The other memories of the previous day—the joyless meeting with Cockburn, tense exchange with Janet, even the $314 traffic citation—felt like nothing more than life as he'd come to expect it, demoralizing and expensive. But to be rejected by his only child? She had not even spoken to him, and her befuddled wave as she and her mother drove away conjured every dance recital he'd missed for the sake of a Council meeting, every family outing he'd cancelled to tend to a dying parishioner. Had he been too hard on her, grounding her for something so small as getting a B- in geometry? Or had he been too lenient, turning the other way when he smelled beer on her after a high school party?

Every unfair word he'd spoken, every tear he'd dismissed as teenage drama lined up in his memory to accuse him.

Dent veered off the sidewalk without intending to, his ears ringing as he stepped down a darkened walkway that led to a round garden on the courthouse lawn. He walked until he ran out of pavement. Leaned a hand on the white stone monolith in the center of the garden. Sweated despite the cool morning, and tried not to weep.

As a diversion, he tried reading the message carved in the monument against which he rested. Another one, a mirror to the first, stood three steps beyond. Dent expected them to contain the familiar "Thou shalt nots" of the King James Bible, the Ten Commandments chiseled in stone as a sign of the town's collective civil disobedience. Instead, the angular letters were names and ranks, all stacked together to form lists divided according to American military conflicts. WORLD WAR I. WORLD WAR II. KOREA. CAMBODIA. VIETNAM. DESERT STORM. AFGHANISTAN. IRAQI FREEDOM. Beneath each header were the names of local boys who had gone to war and not come home. Dent studied them. Frowned. Crystal told him Jeff's father had died in active duty, but no one named Burke appeared on any of the lists. Hard to believe that a town that so venerated its military might leave one of their native sons off the memorial. Perhaps Crystal was mistaken, or perhaps she was lying. Or had been lied to.

The thought of someone else's familial dysfunction made Dent feel not quite better, but at least no longer alone. He offered a silent prayer for the fallen soldiers and the trauma their absence induced. He retraced his steps back to the street. Continued on his way.

His heart rate rose as he approached the front door of LMC, but he soldiered on. Pasted on his best preacher smile and reached out his right hand to greet Jack and Lonnie and even Joe Dick Schieble, whom he had come to believe deserved the awful name his parents had saddled him with. Moisture continued to collect on Dent's palms and torso as he struggled to remember names. He reached his left hand into his pocket and felt for the slip of paper folded there, the prayer of St. Francis, which he'd copied from the Book of Worship. *Lord, make me an instrument of your peace.* It wasn't exactly a table blessing, but it was versatile enough to justify using in a variety of settings. The plan was to keep it upon his person at all times, at least until he could somehow re-develop a capacity for public prayer. When Burke called on Reverend Dunham from the Church of Christ to bless the meal, Dent was almost disappointed.

He exchanged greetings and handshakes as he moved to the back of the line. By the time he made it through the buffet, all that was left were the crusty edges around the pan of eggs and a few sausage links swimming in a greasy puddle. He shook them out the best he could, dropped them on his plate and chose the only seat left, at a back table between Jack and Dr. Omar. Jack clapped him on the shoulder.

"Settle an argument for us," he said.

Dent shook his head. "No more Devil stories."

"What?" Jack said, wrinkling his nose. Joe Dick chuckled. "Oh that," Jack said. "No, I'm serious about this one, Preacher. We could have an issue. Lonnie?"

Lonnie wiped his fingers on his napkin and reached for a folder beneath his chair. He passed it over to Dent. Jack motioned for them all to keep quiet. Dent eyed the others at the table, half convinced he was being set up again, but opened the folder anyway and began to read. Inside was the sign-up sheet for the Tall Tale Roundup, which had been posted in the Super Chief for a week in an effort to solicit storytellers from among the patrons. Dent scanned the list. Looked up. Raised his eyebrows. Lonnie made a circling motion with his finger. Dent turned the paper over. Three more names were scribbled on the back in hand-drawn blanks. The last one was written large in an unsteady hand that sloped off near the end. *Irene Ostendorf.*

"I thought being the guest of honor meant people told stories about *her*," Dent said.

"That was the plan," Jack said. "People can tell any story they like, so long as they keep it PG-13. But we usually pick a theme or a person to help guide our storytellers. We've never had a guest of honor ask to tell their own story before."

"Why not?"

"Well, why would they?" Jack asked. "It just doesn't seem fitting, leastways not to us. What do you think?"

Dent looked around the table for clues as to what he should think, but saw only the same stoic faces that always greeted him in this circle. Only Dr. Omar registered any kind of emotion, and that no more than amusement.

"I think I'm missing something," Dent said. "What's the harm in letting her tell her story, whatever it is?"

"Well then let me tell you," Joe Dick said, not unkindly. "Old Mother Earth ain't your average old widow, as I'm sure you've figured by now. She's been around these parts since the Apostle Paul was in diapers, and she's paid attention over the years. Every tangle of sin and gossip that's ever blown through town has passed her ears."

Dent felt the sweat beading up again on top of his head and in his armpits as his own secrets—unknown to Irene Ostendorf, of course, always near the surface for him—blanketed his conscious thoughts in shame.

"I see," he said. "She can't keep her mouth shut."

"Actually the opposite," Joe Dick said. "She's not known for telling tales, good or bad. Once she knows a thing, she holds onto it. What we can't figure is her sudden change of heart."

Lonnie nodded solemnly.

"You're afraid she's going to spill the beans on someone."

The men exchanged nervous glances.

"That is a plausible outcome," Lonnie said.

"Here's the thing," Jack interrupted. "She knows enough stories about enough people to put half the town to shame for one thing or another. Joe Dick here says we oughtn't even give her a microphone."

"No good to come of it," Joe Dick said.

"You think she'd really dredge up dirty laundry?" Dent asked. "I mean, a woman of her age, and in the predicament she's in with the law."

The other men's eyes fixed on Dent and, almost as one, shifted to Jack, who cleared his throat and leaned forward.

"That's what we need you to find out," Jack said. "Now don't give me that look, Preacher. We don't want you spilling pastoral secrets or anything like that. We just need to know if Old Mother Earth plans on doing anything that might embarrass anybody."

"Embarrass?"

"Unduly embarrass," Jack said. "Just talk to her, is all we're asking."

Dent stared down at the Roundup sign-up sheet still before him, marveling as he did at this town's uncanny ability to give preachers jobs they couldn't refuse. He wiped his hand over his face. Jack slapped the table.

"We'll take that as a yes," Jack said.

The air was still chilly early in the afternoon, when he arrived at Old Mother Earth's ranch. Henry Fifty-one roamed the yard in front of the house, zigging this way and that and taking in the new smells offered by the first cold day of the fall. When Dent stepped out of the pickup, the dog trotted up to him and wagged his entire butt, as though Dent was his oldest of old friends. He scratched the dog's ears and told him he was a good boy. Henry Fifty-one lolled his tongue happily, then systematically peed on each of Dent's tires.

Old Mother Earth sat in her usual spot on the porch swing, although she had exchanged her cotton dress for gray sweat pants and an old denim jacket. Her head was bowed in what looked like prayer, and she did not seem to hear Dent as he climbed the steps. He approached slowly, dread filling his chest. He spoke her name and reached for her shoulder. All at once she sprang into motion, so instantly animated that he half thought she had been resurrected before his eyes. She brought up her right hand to block his and whipped her head around to face him.

"Touch me and by God you'll draw back a nub," she snapped.

Dent pulled away. As he did, he noticed the tablet in the old woman's lap. The screen was alive with an animated desert landscape, populated by cats that zipped across from behind rocks and cactuses. Irene dropped her hand back into her lap and tapped with a crooked finger. A rope shot across from outside the frame, lassoed the kitty and whisked it into a corral in the top right corner. She tapped again, this time landing not on a cat, but on an animated horned lizard. The landscaped faded and "Game Over" spun into the foreground.

"It's called 'Cat Ranch,'" Irene explained. "Ashley showed it to me last time she was in, and now I'm hooked." She closed the folio lid over the tablet and laid it on the swing next to her. "You come to pray for me in my addiction?"

"If you think it'll help."

"Save your breath then. I know why you're here."

"That so?"

"It's that storytelling thing for Last Man Club. I got them all worked up."

"Right," Dent said. "You have people really worried."

"They should be." She nodded once, smartly. "But if they wanted me to speak kindly of them, they all should have behaved better."

"I'll not argue that," Dent said. "Surely you can understand them being nervous, though."

"I've outlived nervous," Irene said. Her eyes twinkled. "What if I told you? What the story is, I mean. Could you keep a secret?"

"I suppose."

She shifted beneath the oversized jacket, which barely seemed to move. "I had a brother Todd who'd moved out to San Francisco in '36. When things got bad here after Elzie Randall died, Henry high-tailed it out West to work with him."

"We're talking about your boyfriend Henry," Dent said. "Right?"

"He wasn't my boyfriend."

"Oh. I thought you said—."

"Are you going to let me tell my story or not?" She waited a beat to make sure he wouldn't interrupt. "Todd got Henry a job dredging up the Bay to build Treasure Island, where they had the World's Fair in '39. He even found him an apartment in the building where a lot of the workers lived. Every time I saved enough for a train ticket, I'd go stay with Todd and look in on Henry."

"Look in?"

"That's what I said, Preacher, and that's what I mean. We weren't having wild sex on the beach, if that's what you're thinking. He never even knowed I was there."

"You just...looked in on him."

"I figured I'd made my choice and he'd made his, and it was all a pretty sorry mess but there weren't nothing to do for it."

"So you never talked to him?"

"I did. After a while, I surely did." She sat still a long time, petting the dog with her foot until even that lazy motion stopped. Dent called her name softly, and she straightened back up. "Asthma. That's what kept Henry out of the war. The Army was swearing in anybody with two legs and a pulse, but Henry's lungs disqualified him. He got a civilian job at the naval base and married a girl—I never did know her name. They rented a house not far from Treasure Island, which by then the Navy had taken over. Henry used to ride his bicycle on the way to work, on account of it helping his lungs to exercise. There was an old Catholic Church on the route—St. Jude's—and we'd meet there on a bench outside it and talk until the priest chased us off. Uncle Sam may have passed on Henry, but they snatched my brother Todd up quick enough. Shipped him to the Pacific to fight the Japanese. Once he was gone, I lost my place to stay in the City. So I saved up what I could and decided I'd make one more trip, and see if Henry would come back with me."

"Back to Texas?" Dent asked.

She raised her palms. "I didn't know quite where else to go. I know it would've been adultery, Preacher."

"I'm not casting stones."

"Good, because I'm just telling the story like it happened," Irene said. "I told him to meet me at St. Jude with whatever he wanted to bring and we'd run off. But he wouldn't do it."

"Wouldn't meet you?"

"He met me all right," Irene said, and for the first time, Dent could see a sadness fall across her wrinkled face. This she had not yet outlived. "He was too honest to lie to his wife, and I don't think he wanted to leave her anyhow. He wished things could be different, he said, but they weren't and that was that. I watched him get back on his bicycle and ride away. He went back to his life and I went back to mine."

Dent placed his hands on his knees. Sat quietly for several seconds. "That's quite the story," he finally said. "Is that what you plan to say at the Round Up?"

She waved him off. "Truth is I don't know what story I'll tell. But I figure this year is my last chance. I better make it good."

"So what do you want me to tell last Man Club?" Dent asked. "I don't believe they'll be satisfied with that answer."

"Tell 'em I got a story about a dog. Everybody worth anything likes dogs." She rubbed her foot across Henry Fifty-one's belly. "Nobody gets satisfactory answers. I figured a man in your profession would have learned that by now."

CHAPTER 18:
KNOWLEDGE IS NEVER
THE PROBLEM

The Lamb County Library occupied three-thousand square feet of space in a maroon brick edifice that housed the preschool associated with G.H.W. Bush Elementary. Dent had to do almost a full circle around the building to find the public entrance, afraid with each step that Crystal Burke might see him in the school yard and report back to her husband that their pastor was creeping on children. He finally located the glass door and walked through the electronic scanners set up at the entry, hoping they could not detect the contraband in his backpack—cheese-on-cheese crackers and a 20-ounce cold drink and the tools necessary for his afternoon's errand. He pulled up at the librarian's desk, realizing too late that he still carried the cup of gas-station coffee he'd picked up on the way back from Irene's ranch. He could already hear the "no food or drink" speech in his head before the librarian even spoke.

"Hello, Reverend Denton," she said. Sure enough, she motioned at the mug. "Need a little jolt to help with your sermon prep?"

"Hi. No. Sorry. Have we met?"

"We have now." She extended her hand. "Judy Watkins. I know it's not fair, how five hundred people seem to know you as soon as you get off the truck, and you've got to try to learn all of them at once. I still remember that feeling from when I moved here, and that's been forty years."

Dent let out a respectful whistle. "Forty years. You're practically a native by now."

"Gracious no," Judy said with a laugh. "You never really stop being an outsider in a place like this. But it's all right. So how can I help you? We just got a new shipment in—my favorite is one of the historical novels, but there's also a new biography of Santa Ana that is fascinating. Please tell me you came for more than magazines."

"I came to do a little research," Dent said. He lifted the coffee cup. "Should I pour this out?"

"Absolutely," Judy said. "If that coffee tastes like it smells, you'd be better off without it. I'll brew a fresh pot if you'll promise to check out at least one book before you leave. I could use the circulation boost."

"You don't mind if I drink in the library?"

"As long as it's not stronger than coffee. The fewer barriers I can put between people and books, the better."

Dent thanked her and slipped through the stacks to a small round table against the wall. He opened his backpack. Took out its lonely contents. Brushed the dried scorpion guts off the yellow envelope that housed THE DIRT.

He had resisted opening the file before now, preferring to take the high road and judge the townsfolk for himself. But THE DIRT's very existence had suggested to him the inevitability of its reading, and he'd given up hope of finding out anything useful from those who should know—Doc and the Sheriff and Irene Ostendorf. He put on his reading glasses and slid out the stack of papers and bent over the first page. The author, the formerly Reverend K.D. Holloway, had included a handwritten preface to his opus—a three-page diatribe against hypocrites and malcontents and his meddling District Superintendent. Church people had wrecked his ministry to the point that he gave up his credentials entirely, he said.

If there was a road to heaven, he would pursue it not as a pastor, but as an appliance salesman in a chain store in Wichita Falls.

Dent flipped past the introduction. He drew in a deep breath. Let it out. Contained in these pages were the secrets everyone had but no one wanted shared, things that most people would rather not know about their neighbors—that the banker had fathered a child with a teenager, or the grocery clerk was hooked on meth, or the chair of the altar guild suffered from hemorrhoids. It was Doc's Book of Knowledge in expanded form, and he didn't doubt that it would tell him plenty.

He backed away. An unpleasant warmth began at the top of his head and washed down over him. He recognized the feeling instantly, the same one that had plagued him in dozens of meetings surrounding his divorce—with Cockburn, with the bishop, with lawyers and church committees. It was the same one that sometimes took hold of him when he opened his laptop at home, knowing that he would not be able to stop himself from clicking on the illicit internet sectors that had been his comfort since his marriage began to crumble. The same emotional heat lamp that would sear him with shame when he was finished. The DIRT was gossip porn. He had no business engaging in it, and couldn't go back once he did. And yet—he knew it and hated it and hated himself for it—he would go over every damned page before all was said and done.

Dent wiped his hand across his face. What was he doing, here in this backwater library, divorced and exiled to the furthest outpost of Methodism in all the High Plains? A washed up preacher who would be a grandfather before he turned forty, yet whose daughter would not even speak to him—and whose ex-wife seemed to be actively keeping him away from his family. He had always known Janet was high maintenance, but when had she become cruel? And why could she not see the efforts he had made on her and Leah's behalf, all these years?

The answer was damage. Some people carried deep scars that sliced through everything good in their lives, wounds that taught them to keep others at a safe distance. Beneath every human skin was an arsenal forged in a furnace of grief and guilt and unresolved conflict. The very best people Dent knew understood this about themselves, and so were able to reign in their need to attack. And because they had plumbed the depths of their own souls, they were able to see through the motivations of others, to absorb shots fired their way as a mother might absorb the rage of her toddler. They may not attend worship every Sunday or populate committees—in fact, they often didn't. But those who could see how utterly fucked up people are and translate that into compassion were the real saints among the sinners.

In Dent's experience, however, few had the desire to be truly good, much less the discipline. He included himself in the number whose want-to never quite translated into just-did.

He flipped the page and read.

THE DIRT turned out to be one giant closet with ten thousand sordid skeletons, all recorded in the haphazard prose of a crumbling preacher. Holloway's manuscript had neither chapters nor flow nor index. He had simply copied things down as they happened, or at least as they came to him. Affairs, grudges, swindles. Wars and rumors of wars, but insight along with it. Why did the Haurwas family hate the McClendons? Because of a dispute over mineral rights in the 1960s. Why did Mrs. Rausch change the subject when asked about her children? Because one had died of AIDS and another of alcohol poisoning, and the third blamed their mother for both deaths. Why are people the way they are? Because humans were cultivators of sin, ancient and uncreative as the Devil himself, and had always been that way, from Babel to Amarillo, across time immemorial.

Ten pages in, however, something new appeared—notes in the margins, scribbled in sloppy handwriting with red ink. Dent frowned. Flipped ahead. The rest of THE DIRT's pages had greater or lesser degrees of the same scrawl, sometimes with reference notes in the margins—"see p. 103" or "contradicts p. 51." Occasionally a page would have keywords circled, linked together by solid or dotted lines. It was the diary of a madman annotated by a paranoid code breaker. Dent could not make heads nor tails of it.

"I can give you a blue pen if you want to make your own notes," Judy said from behind him. "Or green, but that might be too Christmasy against all the red ink."

She sat down in the chair opposite him. Set a "Reading Is an Adventure!" mug in front of him and cupped her hands around her Dr. Seuss mug. Dent stacked the papers. Set the empty yellow envelope on top of them.

"Don't worry," Judy said with a laugh. "I don't want to read it, even though I probably know a lot of what's in it. There's some knowledge you're better off without, which is what I tried to tell Lucas."

"Lucas Lim?" Dent said. "He made these notes?"

"He did. Hobbled in with that folder yesterday and spent most of the afternoon with it." She reached across and flipped the envelope over so that "THE DIRT" was face up. Tapped her finger on the words. "That's it all right. I thought surely you knew. He is living in your house, isn't he?"

"We keep to ourselves, mostly."

"Well, I'm sorry then. It sounds like a tense situation."

"Not tense. Just—I don't know." Dent wiped his hand over his face. "There are a lot of secrets in here."

"I don't doubt that. Can you tell what he was looking for?"

"Not yet. I can't read his handwriting. But I imagine it has to do with Ashley Hyatt."

"Ashley?" Judy repeated, raising her eyebrows. "Why on earth would she be—oh."

"The apartment fire," Dent said. "I assume that's in there."

"That, and her relationship—or whatever you call it—with Mr. Burke. I'd just about blocked that out of my mind."

"Was it that bad?" Dent asked. "I only know the basics—that she left the stove on and caught the kitchen on fire and Burke carried her out."

"That's the way it's told, usually." She turned the wooden stir stick through her coffee. Watched it swirl. "I have a hard time blaming Ashley for any of it. She was just a girl, you know."

"So I've heard."

"No one wants to blame Mr. Burke for any of it, given his upbringing. But I just don't know. It seems like—well, I shouldn't judge, I suppose."

Dent leaned forward. "Crystal Burke told me last week about how both Jeff's parents died tragically."

"Tragic doesn't begin to cover it."

"Right. But I'm having a hard time believing her story." He looked up, a new thought unfolding in his mind. "She said her father was killed in the war, but he's not on the town's memorial."

"Well now he wouldn't be," Judy said. She shook her head. "I'm not one to spread rumors."

"I'm not talking about gossip," Dent said. "I'm looking for hard research. Surely there has to be something in the archives about Burke's parents, right? Obituaries, at least. And if they died the way Crystal said, I'm sure there'd be some news story."

Judy furrowed her brow and let out a long sigh. "Okay. Give me just a minute."

While he waited, Dent turned again to THE DIRT. Apparently, Lucas had also been interested in Ashley's family. He had dog-eared several pages that detailed the story of the tumultuous union between Harlan Brantley and Irene Ostendorf. The two married in 1936, only a few months after Irene's mother wed Elzie Randall. As a bride, Irene was young even for the times, barely fifteen and raging at the world. She and Harlan snapped and clawed until he went off to fight the Nazis, and she seemed none too pleased when he came back. After the War, Brantley took a job at the railroad and worked his way up so that, when he finally retired in the mid-1960s, he commanded quite the pension. On top of that, Irene had been a saver, and she quietly amassed what qualified as a fortune in Earth's standards.

Dent scanned through the pages, looking for any mention of Henry and finding none. He flipped back. Read on.

Harlan Brantley's sins were better known to Holloway. He recorded the names of a half dozen women—including Mrs. Paisley, the organist—rumored to be among his infidelities. His wicked ways finally caught up with him not long after Nixon resigned the Presidency. In September of that year, he bragged to Irene in a drunken fit that he had gotten a local woman pregnant. Irene, who had never been able to conceive, threw him out of the house, brandishing a rifle and threatening to shoot him dead if he ever set foot on the place again.

Judy took her seat across from him so quietly that he almost didn't notice, so wrapped up was he in the narrative. But he set the sheets down and folded his hands on the table. Judy slipped another piece of paper in front of him, thin and yellowed at the margins. It was an ancient mimeographed copy of a police report filed by Deputy Paul Wayne Pearson, also signed by Sheriff William J. Pearson.

"What's this?" Dent asked.

"The real story about Jeff Burke's parents."

Dent stared at the names in the first paragraph. Irene Brantley. Harlan Brantley. "I don't understand," he said.

"Just read it."

The report detailed a complaint Irene Brantley, nee Ostendorf, had called in against her estranged husband on September 3, 1978. He had driven his car up to the ranch, obviously drunk, and called Irene to the window. He was cussing and crying and making threats, babbling on about the way of things, the way of things. While this was going on, his young mistress pulled up in her old pickup. She hopped out screaming and carrying a rifle, but she was too out of control to do much with it. He wrestled it away from her and knocked her down and fired a shell at the house. Irene came running out, thinking she could reason with him. But before she got there, he turned the gun around and shot himself dead.

"God Almighty," Dent whispered.

Judy eyed the page. Chewed on her lip.

"This happened right after Donnie and I moved to town," she said. "One of the saddest stories I ever heard," she said. "That poor, poor girl."

"You mean Irene?"

She shook her head. "I mean Sarah Burke. She was only nineteen at the time. She never did recover."

The fragments of the story floated through Dent's imagination. He let them hang for a long moment before he could finally pull a few pieces together.

"So Harlan Brantley got Sarah Burke pregnant? She couldn't have been more than a kid."

"Fifteen," Judy said quietly. "She was sixteen when Jeff was born." She reached across for the police report. Turned it around and tapped her finger onto the second paragraph, which listed only two named witnesses to the scene: Irene Brantley and Sarah Burke. But after Sarah's name were two words that chilled Dent. *And child.* She shook her head sadly. "It's awful to think about. She'd been in

Harlan's Sunday school class. So had a lot of other girls, we found out later."

Dent's head pounded. "Jeff saw his father shoot himself?"

"As a young child, yes."

"But Crystal doesn't know what happened?"

"Probably she does. Knowledge is never the problem. Telling it is." She rubbed her forehead. "You can know a thing well enough, but if you can't find a way to share it, the thing might as well not exist at all. This town never found a way to tell the stories of what Harlan was doing to those girls, and so they never confronted it."

"That's why Jeff makes up his own story."

"Right," Judy said. "By the time Sarah started going off the rails, folks were committed to ignoring it. It was alcohol, mostly, although I'm sure she was doing some kind of drugs too. People really did try to rally around her then, but she was just so angry all the time. It's a wonder Jeff was able to pull any kind of life together after that. I just don't know."

"Don't know what?"

Judy frowned, stared down at the paper again as though searching for an answer in the purple ink. "I don't know anything," she said. "Just like everybody else."

CHAPTER 19:
STINGS

J udy kept the library open half an hour after closing time so Dent could complete his excavations in THE DIRT. At last he drained his coffee and thanked Judy and walked homeward through the gathering dusk, feeling much worse about the human condition than he had few hours earlier. Along the way he stopped at the Quik Pik and bought a six pack of beer, which he tucked under his arm and tried to conceal from Mamie Martz' vigilant gaze as he walked up his driveway. He didn't need her spreading rumors about the new pastor's drinking habits. He did, however, need a shower in the worst possible way.

The door had not finished closing behind him before he descended on his wall of boxes. He tore into the one he deemed most likely to hold his bottle opener. Stirring spoons and spatulas and ladles. Coffee filters, if not the pot. He was just about to expand his search to a second box when he heard his name being called.

"Dent!"

It came in a whisper, urgent and pleading. A cold feeling washed over him. The voice sounded hollow, human-like but not exactly human. He did not believe in ghosts. He did believe—most of the time, anyway, he believed—in God, and that was worse. He knew the Bible stories of Samuel and Isaiah and Paul and a dozen others. God never called anyone by name unless it was important. God also never did anything important without leading his most faithful people through inordinate amounts of suffering. He closed his eyes and willed it away, but the voice came again, a little louder than before.

"Dent!"

This time, the call was followed by an anguished groan. That led to a string of curses, which certainly didn't seem like language the Lord might use. He hustled off in the direction of the voice, which led him to the spare bedroom he'd been using for storage. He pulled up short at the threshold and came to a stop, precariously balanced on one foot. The shadowy body of the Moses mannequin—beheaded last week by Rachel's ninja chop—stood to his left. Beside him, Miriam's sensuous silhouette beckoned him, arms outstretched. He could have sworn he saw her head swivel.

While these things flashed through Dent's mind, his weight continued forward. He pressed down with his toes, tried to stop himself. But his fall was inevitable, maybe even predestined.

"Shit!"

The voice didn't belong to Dent, but it expressed his sentiments. He toppled forward into the lascivious arms of the naked mannequin. The two crashed against the blinds over the far window, pulling them down as the tangle of bodies—human and human-like—crashed to the floor. He scurried to his feet, still clutching the newly severed arm of poor Miriam. The orange light of the safety lamp in the Martz' yard flooded into the room, revealing the frightened and still cursing visage of Lucas Lim.

"What's wrong with you?" Dent spurted.

"Get the light," Lucas hissed.

Dent waded through the carnage to the wall and felt for the switch and flipped it. Lucas sat in the center of the room, Dent's old laptop on the floor beside him, his foot propped up on a box labeled "Misc. Office." Sweat poured off his face, which was devoid of color. His eyes were wide, frozen open in panic. Dent wiped his hand across his scalp. Wondered how his day had gotten so out of hand. He reached down to clear away the boxes.

"Don't!" Lucas yelled. He gave a barely perceptible nod toward his broken leg.

"Scorpions," he whispered. "Two of them at least."

"In your cast?"

"Yes."

"They sting you?"

"Seven times." He shifted, only a bit. Clenched his teeth and trembled.

"Eight?"

Lucas nodded. "Every little move sets one of them off. I got two when you barreled in here over the mannequin."

"Right. Sorry about that." He rubbed his forehead. Reached down gently and picked up the laptop to move it out of harm's way. The screen flickered to life at the movement, and Dent could see what Lucas had been staring it—a selfie of a young woman, obviously wearing her happiest face. Over her right shoulder, however, was a more familiar figure. Jeff Burke, in full Red Raider gear, lifted one arm over his head. His other was wrapped around the waist of a young woman next to him. "That's Burke," Dent said.

"Yeah."

"And Ashley?"

"Yeah." He made a winding motion with his index finger. "Scroll through."

Dent tapped the mouse pad. There were three more pictures, all from the same football game, all with Ashley and Burke in the background.

"How did you find these?"

"It doesn't matter. Can we please take care of these scorpions now?"

"Right, sorry," Dent said. He pinched the bridge of his nose. "Okay."

"Okay what?" Lucas said, his voice sliding from impatient to nervous. "You know how to get rid of them?"

Dent gave a confident nod. "Be right back."

He jogged to the garage and took a pair of leather gloves from the utility shelves. Shook and squeezed them until he was satisfied that they were scorpion free, then pulled them on and started jerking open the boxes stacked along the east wall, hoping something might suggest to him what he should do. How would one get at these hidden demons? Smoke them out? That seemed too dangerous. Cut the cast off? A handsaw would only give the scorpions all the time they needed to really work Lucas over, and however pissed Dent might be at life, he was not cruel. A power saw would certainly mean greater injury, if not all-out amputation.

At last he found a rusty can of bug killer and stole the straw from a can of spray lubricant. He prayed as he zipped back into his spare room that it had enough to do the trick. He didn't remember the last time he used this particular can, and his vermin killing method in Earth had so far been limited to direct shots with the crusty folder that housed THE DIRT.

He planted his feet one step inside the door. Froze.

"What?" Lucas said.

"Tell me why you were going through my files."

Lucas stared up, dismayed and confused.

"THE DIRT," Dent said. "Judy Watkins said you spent all day yesterday reading it in the library."

"Okay, yes," Lucas said, his words rushed and pleading as though he were at the edge of the Inquisition. "I was trying to find out more about Ashley's family, okay?"

"And how is that your business? Especially considering you did your looking in a private document."

"I know, all right! It was probably wrong. It was wrong, okay? I just want to understand why she does things—Jesus!"

He clenched his teeth. Pounded the floor with his fists. Guilt washed over Dent. He fixed the aerosol straw to the trigger and shook the can of bug killer.

"Does it work on scorpions?" Jeff said through his teeth.

Dent held the can at arm's length, but without his reading glasses the only word he could make out was CAUTION.

"Says so right here."

He placed a hand firmly on Lucas's leg just above the knee and slipped the aerosol straw between skin and cast. Lucas blew out two sharp breaths, like a weightlifter grabbing the bar. He nodded. Dent depressed the trigger.

Lucas went rigid as the cold stream slid across his skin. A second later, he growled in pain. He grabbed at the boxes, at the windowsill above him, at his hair, at his thigh, at the prone body of the mannequin, all in desperate search of someplace to hold on to until the pain ended. He thrashed and swore and screamed for Dent to stop. When he didn't, Lucas beat him on the arm until Dent could feel a knot rising up. Still, Dent held firm until two small brown scorpions wobbled out of the cast and onto the poor man's toes. One of them instantly dropped to the floor and died. The other lingered a moment and, before Dent could swipe it away, arched its tail and struck at the very tip of Lucas's second toe.

Lucas screamed again. He cursed the scorpion. He cursed Dent. Sweat dripped down his nose.

"I thought you said that stuff killed scorpions?" he said, his voice weakening.

"It does. Well, I think it does. It may be a little old." Dent released his grip and stepped back. "We had to try something."

"Yeah, something that might work."

"It did work."

"Jesus."

Dent locked his fingers on top of his head and stared down at his miserable guest. What exactly should a pastor do in a time such as this, filled with violence and adultery and pestilence? The Bible might have something to say on the matter, but he was too tired to go searching tonight.

"You need me to call Doc?" he asked.

Lucas did not answer. He wobbled for a moment, eyes rolling up into his skull, and passed out on top of Miriam.

CHAPTER 20:
NATURAL RHYTHM

Almost before Lucas had finished slumping over on the carpet, Dent phoned Rachel in a near panic. The thought of watching Lucas go into anaphylactic shock in his spare room caused every pre-guilt synapse in Dent's brain to fire. And of course—he didn't like admitting it, but it was true enough still—he worried that this might be the last nail in his professional coffin. After such a spectacular string of failures as he'd endured, letting a bishop's son die on his carpet probably spelled the end.

"Six minutes, tops," Rachel said, and ended the call.

A few seconds later, however, Lucas groaned and rolled back upright, groggy but alive. Dent wanted to hug him. Instead he pulled him up and helped him hobble to the kitchen. He spread a towel over the table so that Lucas could prop his foot up, wondering if the bread knife he'd found while searching for his bottle opener would slice through the cast well enough. He had pulled it out of the knife block to examine it when Rachel burst through the front door.

"Stop!" she called without breaking stride. She pulled up a chair across from Lucas and began digging in her bag. "Dent, I had better not see that knife out again unless you're making French toast. Are we clear on that?"

"Yes ma'am."

"Good! Now, let's see if we can't get this cast off and take a look."

Her hand emerged from her bag with a rotary tool. Attached to its tip was a gritty, disk-shaped blade. She turned it on, pressed it against the palm of her hand. Opened her fingers to show both men that she was yet unscathed, that the tool was perfectly safe. She donned a set of safety classes and made two long slices down the sides of the cast, then cut through the cotton batting with scissors. When she was finished, the top section lifted off like a lid.

"All right," she said cheerfully. "Let's see what we've got here."

Angry red welts covered Lucas' swollen shin and calf. Rachel made a face, as though the sight caused her physical pain.

"Two of them, you say?"

"Yeah," Dent answered. "That's how many we found, anyway."

"I see," Rachel said. "Hey Dent, why don't you go have a seat on the couch while I tend to Mr. Lim? It looks as though you've had a long day."

"I'm fine."

"Bless your heart," Rachel said, and looked up to face him. "Go sit somewhere that you won't be in my way, please?"

He wandered into the living room, doing his best not to look as chastised as he felt. Before he could fall too far into his pouty pit, however, Rachel began asking questions to Lucas. Her hands kept at the work, peeling off the cast to reveal two more dead scorpions—enough to make Dent feel at least somewhat vindicated. She pulled out ointments and checked ingredients and applied salve, all the while masterfully drawing Lucas out of his self-protective shell. Dent learned more about his roommate in fifteen minutes of eavesdropping than he had in a week of sharing the same house.

Lucas was wandering the halls of LBJ High a decade earlier when he got word that his father had ascended to the episcopacy. He had expected as much, given Reverend Doctor Lim's ambitions and not-so-subtle campaigning. Success was as natural to his father as hunting to a shark. All of the father's achievement left the son with one clear and irresistible path of rebellion. If the Reverend Doctor justified his existence through success, Lucas did so through failure.

He excelled at flunking out, made failure both his message and his medium. After making straight A's for virtually his entire career as a student, Lucas flunked three classes in tenth grade. His GPA dove. His parents grounded him in anger at first. But he remained polite and thoughtful, a courteous young man who perhaps was going through a phase. This vexed his mother to no end and caused his father to grumble at his good behavior, suddenly suspicious that it masked deeper issues. They took him to a therapist to check for depression and to a physician to look for a brain tumor. Neither found anything worth the money they charged. When, just for kicks, Lucas scored on the ninety-fifth percentile on his SAT, his mother scheduled a therapist appointment for herself.

He bounced around the private Methodist colleges to which his father's politics gained him entry, dropping in and out of classes and majors and extracurricular activities. At twenty-three, he settled on engineering as a career path and enrolled at Colorado State, where he met Ashley Hyatt on a backpacking trip to Bryce Canyon with a group of mutual friends. They were the most outdoorsy in the group by far and often found themselves a half mile or more ahead of the pack. As they talked, they discovered mountains of similarity between them. Both were children of divorce with successful fathers and mothers who, despite their loyalty, had nonetheless been replaced, his by career and hers by another woman. Both slept with one foot outside the covers, even in winter, and both preferred white cake to chocolate. They shared affinities for books and television shows, and although they disagreed on movies, this imperfection only served to cast their commonality in greater relief.

They arrived at Angel's Landing early in the afternoon and slipped out of their backpacks. They ate their lunch while overlooking the Virgin River, which snaked across rocks and occasionally disappeared beneath a green canopy below. Ashley gathered their trash and stuffed it into one of the innumerable compartments of her backpack, then sat down next to Lucas, so close that their hips and shoulders touched. He reached across and laced his fingers through hers. They stayed like that for what seemed like forever, until they heard their friends approaching and she, with a tender squeeze, let go of his hand.

"Well that all just sounds wonderful," Rachel said. She motioned for him to lower his foot. Patted him on the knee. "Doc will probably want to look at it again tomorrow. You might get lucky and end up in a boot rather than a cast, but no way to tell for sure. Stay off it tonight and come by the office tomorrow about nine."

"Anything special I need to take? Medicine of some kind?"

Rachel shook her head. "I can't give you anything stronger than you're already taking kiddo. You just rest up. I think Dent is going to walk me home."

A north wind had brought the temperature down ten degrees from when Dent had come home from the library, the harbinger of winter storms to come. He offered Rachel one of his jackets to wear over her scrubs. She zipped it up and pulled her hands back into the sleeves, leaving her bag for Dent. It felt like high school again, carrying a girl's books—exhilarating and terrifying all at once. He felt the urgent need to speak before his mouth dried out completely.

"Thanks for taking care of Lucas," he said. "Sorry to have called you out so late."

"No trouble at all. He's going to be fine by morning. Maybe a little itchy, is all. I think I was treating anxiety more than I was stings."

"I suppose. But why did you let him off so easily?"

Rachel looked up, surprised. "Let him off?"

"Well, I mean—you had him talking all about his past. I think he had a lot more to say about Ashley Hyatt."

"I'm sure he did. But he wasn't ready to tell it."

"How do you know?"

"Maybe because I'm a nurse, or maybe because I'm a woman. Or maybe I just pay attention."

"Well. I suppose."

"I'm just teasing," Rachel said. "Lucas was in a vulnerable spot just now. I didn't think it was fair to ask him to tell us about him and Ashley, not with so much going on in his body and his mind. If he wants to share more when he's good and strong again, then I'm sure he will. And I'm sure you'll be the one he comes to."

"I doubt that."

She punched him in the arm playfully. "What's this crisis in confidence? I think you're doing great."

He lurched onto the grass, as though she had walloped him with ten times the force. She laughed, and he listened to the sound and liked it very much.

"I'm just trying not to screw things up here," he said. "People's souls are at stake."

Rachel laughed again. "Calling bullshit on that one," she said.

"Excuse me?"

"Bullshit. That's a word normal people use when someone is trying to pass off something ridiculous as true."

"Right. But I don't see—."

"People's souls are not in your hands," she said. She swung her arms at her side. Brought her fingers out of the sleeves and flexed them. Her smile was still there, but not quite as easy. "Okay, here's the truth. I mostly believe in God, all right? But church seems pretty silly to me. Folks get so worked up about what other people believe, and preachers have these grand notions that they are ferrying souls across—is it the River Styx?"

"Christians might say the Jordan," Dent said.

"That's it. Well, I've seen inside a lot of bodies over the years, and I've never come across a soul, much less a person carrying one for somebody else."

Dent shook his head. Tried not to let his tone get defensive. "Just because you don't see it doesn't mean it's not real."

"Oh, I know that," Rachel said. "But, while we're on the subject, your believing something doesn't make it real either." She slipped her arms around his elbow. "I'm not trying to criticize your faith, or even to renounce what faith I have. I just don't see how what I believe has to do with ultimate reality. Either God is real and heaven is waiting, or he's not and it isn't. Nothing I think or believe has much impact on what is finally true."

They walked in silence a long time, Dent turning the problem over in his mind. He searched for words suitable to the moment. His training in pastoral care taught him to ask questions, to help her dig through the sediments of faith and doubt so they could examine them together. But was he on the clock right now? He didn't feel like a professional caring for souls, not with Rachel. And yet he had not felt this way about a woman in years, Janet included. He walked beside her in silence, wishing more with each step that he had something wise—or at least impressive—to say.

He was still formulating his thoughts when he realized that his left hand was now occupied with Rachel's right. She had not laced her fingers with his—that he would have noticed sooner. But she clasped it surely nonetheless, letting her arm swing with his in the natural rhythm of their strides.

CHAPTER 21:
SHE'S FOND OF YOU,
GOD HELP US

The light above the stove in Rachel's kitchenette was still on when Dent finally slipped out from beneath the blanket and off the couch. He knelt on the floor beside it long enough for her to settle back into sleep and then watched her a while longer, wondering what to do with the covers. She looked warm enough. But she had fallen asleep between the back cushions and Dent, with the quilt pulled over them besides. Probably best to let her be, he decided. But he folded the blanket back over her bare shoulders anyhow and got dressed and made his way slowly across the creaky floor of the old house, trying with little success to predict where the joists were to minimize the noise. It took him the better part of two minutes to weave through the maze of housekeeping and reach the door, and a minute more to ease it open without its hinges emitting a piercing squeal. He stepped onto the landing and pulled it toward him and turned the knob to soften its closing. Just before the last sliver of light disappeared, Rachel called to him in a sleepy voice.

"I had a wonderful time," she said.

He waited for more, but she laid her head back on the pillow and nestled into sleep. He let the door click shut and walked halfway down the stairs to put on his socks and shoes, trying to sort the events of the last few hours into more coherent categories—things that happened and things I wish had happened and things I could get in trouble for. He hadn't spent the night with a woman in more than a year, and had never before awakened with any other than Janet. What was protocol for this situation? And would Rachel understand how important it would be to keep their night a secret? He took comfort in remembering how she treated Lucas in his vulnerable state. She would understand, surely. Maybe she would understand everything, if he had the courage to say it.

He pulled his shoelace tight and walked down the stairs and felt his way through the office toward the back door. Halfway across the room, he heard the slide of a shotgun's forestock. A voice growled at him from the darkness. Doc.

"You better get real still and talk real quick," he said. "You wouldn't be the first to die in this house."

Dent raised his hands. Turned in the direction of the voice. "I'm sorry," he said, and then, sensing his doom, added, "Really sorry."

More clicking sounds, and the whish of the old man's khaki's. A second later, the fluorescent overheads flickered to life. Both men blinked and squinted. Doc shielded his eyes as he looked Dent over.

"Can't say I expected this," Doc said.

"I can explain."

"I wish you wouldn't." He sat down on top of his desk and rubbed his eyes. "I figured you for a thief. Looking for drugs or something. That's happened once before. Turned out to be a couple of high school kids. Rachel heard them and called it in to the Sheriff. I was afraid this might be worse."

"So did you call the Sheriff?" Dent asked.

"No. I wasn't going to do that until after I shot you." He raised his hand to his mouth, but could not stifle the laugh. "Sorry, Preacher. I doubt you find the same humor in that as I do."

"It'll be funnier once daylight gets here," Dent said, but he could feel himself starting to sweat. "Rachel and I got to talking last night—."

Doc raised his hand. "Will you shut up please? About that, anyway." His face sobered. "There's something else you should probably know."

"All right."

"The reason I'm here," Doc said. "I got a call about a half hour ago saying that there were lights on in Rachel's apartment and the back door wasn't closed all the way. Said he saw somebody moving around and that I might want to check it out."

"I suppose that's reasonable."

"I might think so too, had it been somebody else that called."

"Well. Who was it?"

"Jeff Burke," Doc said. "Told me he was out for an early morning run and found it. I hate to jump to conclusions, but do you think he could have known that you were over here already?"

Dent wiped his hand over his face. Thought of the incident with Lucas. The blinds crashing down in a window facing Mamie Martz' house. He silently cursed cellular phones. Wished Mamie had a landline he could cut.

"It's possible," he said.

"Well then," Doc said. "You think he's out to get you?"

"I couldn't say. Maybe."

"Come on now."

"All right. I think I've been here less than a month and he already wants me gone."

Doc tapped his fingers on his knees thoughtfully. Narrowed his eyes at Dent. "You find out about his daddy yet?"

Dent nodded. Doc blew a quick breath out his nose. "It's taken considerable effort not to hate Burke for the sins of Harlan Brantley," Doc said. "We have some history there."

He did not look up, and Dent did not reveal what he knew about Emilia. But the story surrounded them nonetheless. Doc unloaded a shotgun shell and fidgeted with it. "Don't you let my daughter get caught up in your squabble with Burke," he said. "If he tries to use her to get rid of you, than I'm liable to do something I'll regret."

"It'll be fine," Dent said.

"I don't know. I hope." Doc stood up and raised both arms over his head and yawned. "Big day coming up."

"Big as any, I guess."

"It's not either," Doc said. He checked the clock. "Just about the whole town will turn out for the Hallelujah Halloween. I hear you're putting up a booth."

Dent's heart sank. With all the drama piled on to the basic stress of moving, he had forgotten about the festival. He lowered his head. Pinched the bridge of his nose.

"Annette Brady is taking care of that," he said. "But I suppose I'll have to help."

"Annette?" Doc shook his head. "She's not doing anything with anybody for awhile. She turned a knee playing tennis. Tore her ACL."

"I hadn't heard."

"I'm not supposed to tell you, of course. HIPPA and all. But it's the middle of the night and I'm too old to care as much about regulations as I should. Let's just say she's not doing anything more active than Netflix until I can get her into surgery. I thought Rachel might have told you."

"No."

"Makes sense that she didn't. She's a lot more concerned about following protocol. Probably a good thing." He dropped the shell into his pocket. "Ask Rachel to help you with the booth. I believe she's fond of you, God help us."

A soft gray was beginning to dawn on the Panhandle as Dent made his way to the sidewalk. The coming dawn would have to plow through a fog before it shed much light, which seemed a gift from God. Perhaps the Almighty was shielding Dent from the watchful eyes of his neighbors, save Doc. Perhaps God was covering his own eyes from Dent and Rachel, knowing that however unsanctioned their union, it was nonetheless a grace to them both.

Could a preacher get fired for being in love? Stranger things had happened, he knew. Rev. J.A. Molitor, one of his early mentors, had been forced into retirement after an unfortunate preaching slip. Instead of referring to the choir director as a "fiery packet of pepper," as had been his intent, he had gotten tongue-tied and called him a "fiery little pecker." It didn't take much to sink a pastor. Get crossways with one or two influential people, and you might as well turn out the lights. And regardless of his being a genuine asshole, Burke was influential.

Then again, so what? Was this pastoral gig so fantastic that he couldn't risk losing it? Of course not. The question was where he would go next, and he needed time to figure that out. This morning, with Rachel's sweet scent filling his thoughts, Earth seemed as good a town as any to try to get his bearings.

He nearly floated as he made the turn onto his street, but he forced himself to slow nonetheless. He kept to the shadows. Focused his eyes on the windows in the Martz house. The blinds were closed, which made it possible that Mamie wasn't still watching. He quickened his stride, thankful for safe passage. Less than twelve hours now until the Hallelujah Halloween, and if Annette was out of commission, he'd have to repair the mannequins and set the whole thing up himself, lest that public failure put even more bullets in his detractors' guns.

The to-do list was still spooling through his head when he saw that he was not alone. A dark figure stood next to his pickup, watching. Dent pulled up, startled, and bore through the fog with his gaze just enough to see the blurred features of Jeff Burke.

"Good morning, Pastor," Burke said.

"Morning."

"It's awfully early for a preacher to be up exercising, isn't it? But I'm proud of you. Really, I am. Such dedication to your own health. Am I right?"

"I don't believe it matters," Dent said. "You seem to have your mind made up on things."

"You misunderstand me," Burke said. "I'm rooting for your success, Brother Denton. Of course I am. And if your body is healthy, your mind will be sharper, and you will make better decisions. Better than you've made recently, at least."

Dent bit the inside of his lip. He badly wanted to accuse Burke to his face of trying to get Doc to shoot him for trespassing. But that would be admitting that he'd spent the night with Rachel, and that was a can of worms he could not afford to open.

"My morning run takes me by here sometimes," Burke continued. "It's a peaceful street, low traffic. And your house is almost exactly three miles from mine, which helps me gauge my progress. Of course, it also gives me a chance to pray for my pastor."

"All right," Dent said. "Did you want to pray for me now?"

"Not at the moment, no. I meant that I can pray on my own time, as I go by your house. Prayer for me is a private thing, very special. You might even say intimate. And there is both a peace and a danger in what is intimate. You have to be careful who you let see you naked, Brother Denton. I'm sure you are aware."

Dent's heart hammered against his sternum. He counted backward from ten, waited until he could speak without his voice wavering. "Say what you mean, Jeff."

Burke grinned. "I always do," he said. He bounced on the balls of his feet once, then twice. Then he resumed his run, disappearing into the morning fog.

CHAPTER 22:
PEOPLE DO CRAZY THINGS

Dent poured his rage into housekeeping, which was the nearest, if not the most logical, point of attack. His hands shook as he swept up the plaster fragments of Lucas' cast and straightened up the kitchen. How should he have responded, after all? Punch Burke in the face? Certainly not what Jesus would have done, and a bad idea besides. That Dent would lose a fistfight with Burke was clear enough. But to stand there mute while Burke used one of the best nights of his life to threaten him? It was a kind of losing worse than a bloody nose.

He stomped into the living room. Gathered up papers and files and library books, stacked them so that their edges aligned and placed them in the built-in shelves. He cleared out a dozen paper coffee cups from the Super Chief in the living room alone, plus five more in the spare room. Judging by the crusty remains of the mocha flavoring Lucas preferred, about half of them must belong to his guest. Dent shoved them into a trash bag along with paper plates and takeout boxes. How could two men create such a mess in such a short time?

He was reaching for the ruined blinds when pain seared into the webbing between his ring and middle fingers. He yanked his hand back. Searched the floor for any sign of the little scorpion that had gotten him, any window of opportunity to exact his revenge. He kicked and swore and searched, all for naught. At last he gave one final sweep of his foot. His toe caught in the pull string of the downed blinds, stopping his momentum short and ruining his balance. He landed on his butt between the mannequins. Decapitated Moses and dismembered Miriam, freed from Pharaoh's bonds only to meet their doom in the house of an inept Methodist preacher.

"I think it's the boxes," Lucas said. He stood in the doorway, the knee of his busted leg resting on the padding of the wheeled scooter Rachel had gotten for him.

Dent grunted.

"Scorpions love cardboard," Lucas continued. "I did some research last night while you were out."

"I was—."

"With Rachel, I know. Good for you, man." He twisted on the scooter so that he could lean against the doorframe. "Listen, I'm sorry about going through your files, okay?"

Dent blinked.

"And about logging on to your laptop without permission. To look up those pictures of Ashley and Burke."

"Oh. Right." Dent paused to reconstruct the previous evening. Winced at the memory. "And I'm sorry I made you answer for it before I helped you with the scorpions."

"It's all good."

They waited for a long moment, each lost in whatever remorse or regret he could conjure this early in the morning. Lucas finally broke the silence.

"Ashley's thing with Burke. It's not good."

"I can imagine not," Dent said. "You said there was a history?"

"Yeah. But even I'm not sure exactly what it is. I mean, they were together right after she graduated high school. You know, the apartment fire story."

"She told you about that?"

"No. She doesn't talk about her past. I've found out more of her history in a week in Earth than I did in all the months we were together. But it explains a lot." He stood on his good leg. Twisted his body and sat down on the pad of the scooter. "She's been hurt."

"You're one to talk."

"What, this?" Lucas said, motioning at his injured leg. "This is nothing. Doc thinks everything should heal pretty well in a few weeks. It's predictable enough. Her wounds go deeper."

"From Burke, you mean."

"Yeah," Lucas said. He picked up an old flip phone from the donation box the former Rev. Holloway had left behind. Ran his thumb over the casing. Worked its hinges. "Will any of these even power on anymore?"

"I haven't tried them."

"Mind if I play around later today?"

"Suit yourself."

"Thanks." Lucas tossed the phone back into the box. "Why do you think she got back together with Burke?"

"No telling," Dent answered. "Maybe he's a safety net for her. Or maybe he's manipulative enough to string her along."

"Ash isn't one to be manipulated," Lucas said. "Not by another person, anyway."

"How do you mean?"

Lucas took in a deep breath. Let it out. "I mean that the past is always right there with you. Some bad shit can happen when you let it steer, you know?"

They had eggs for breakfast, fried in a cast-iron skillet Dent had located in the box he'd started unpacking the previous night. Lucas did the dishes on one foot while Dent sorted through the other boxes, their work now purposeful as a step toward eradicating the scorpions. He separated them into two stacks—one that contained necessary things that should be unpacked soon, and another, much larger stack filled with stuff he had little use for. Lucas donned his spare set of gloves and pitched in until he came across the coffee maker. He extracted it from the box. Held it over his head in triumph and set to brewing the first pot in the parsonage since Dent had moved to Earth. They drained it in fifteen minutes, then climbed into the pickup so Dent could drop Lucas off at his appointment with Doc.

Alone once more, Dent's mind buzzed from the caffeine, sending him into a near panic when he considered the tasks of the day. He called Annette Brady, who told him through a hydrocodone fog that she was in fact incapacitated for the foreseeable future, and he would need to make other arrangements for the Hallelujah Halloween. He dropped his phone into the cup holder between the seats and backed the pickup into the driveway. Two minutes later, he had the mannequins and all their pieces loaded into the bed of the truck. He covered them with a tarp and wrapped the bundle with bungee cords, a la every mob movie he'd ever watched. As he pulled away, he could see Mamie Martz standing at the window, snapping pictures with her phone.

He stopped by the hardware store and picked up the strongest epoxy Trefz had in stock and drove around to the Heinmann Theater to try to con Rob into helping him with the repair. Instead he found a note that Rob was dealing with some escaped livestock this morning, and volunteers should report back after lunch. Dent swore and hopped back in the truck and—citing the desperate times for his desperate measures—drove out to the de los Santos ranch.

He pulled into the driveway and passed the house and stopped in back on the concrete platform outside the shop. The big doors were rolled up on either end of the building. Inside, Emilia bent over an open repair manual, elbows resting on the workbench. She wore green coveralls smeared with grease along one arm and a red International Harvester cap, also dotted with black smudges. To her right, a large red tractor was split in two, each half held upright by thick chains wound through a come-a-long that hung from the I-beams above. She noticed Dent's shadow as it passed through the open garage door. Lifted her head and blew strands of hair out of her face.

"This doesn't look good," Dent said.

Emilia huffed. "We blew a gasket—literally—at the end of the summer, and it started leaking a lot of oil. Bad as it looks, it's closer to being fixed now than it was before we pulled it apart. I just have to get it done before that winter storm hits. What brings you out this way?"

Dent scanned the shop. It seemed more likely that he would sprout wings than that Emilia would be able to reassemble this machine. The floor was littered with its internal organs—bolts and sprockets and oddly shaped canisters that performed functions he could only guess at, all of which fit together in some greased 3D puzzle.

"I was hoping Rob would help me with a project," Dent said, but added quickly, "I can come back another time."

"Don't be an idiot," Emilia said. She waved her arm toward the mechanical mess behind her. "Who around here do you think is the more capable one? Let's see what you got."

He lowered the tailgate and peeled back the tarp to reveal the mannequins and their pieces. Emilia picked up the severed head and turned it over in her hands.

"Lover's quarrel?" she asked. She looked down at the female mannequin and its well-defined anatomy. Raised her eyebrows. "Doesn't leave much to the imagination."

"They're siblings," Dent said. "Or they will be tonight. Moses and Miriam."

"Oh right. The Hallelujah Halloween. It's a ridiculous event. Drag them on out."

Dent arranged the mannequins on some newspaper while Emilia washed the grease off her hands. Miriam's repair was easy enough—a simple matter of slipping the ball joint back in place and sealing a crack in the socket. Moses, however, had snapped at the neck. Emilia drilled a few strategic holes and fastened the head back on with brackets and plastic weld. Then she had Dent hold the head in place while she smeared the remaining epoxy in the new seam. She stepped back and admired her work.

"Now don't move," she ordered. "That'll take about eight minutes to set. You get jittery and we'll have to start over." She pulled up a yellow plastic chair and sat down across from him. "How's your roomie doing? I hear you had another eventful night."

Dent swallowed hard. "I guess your sister told you."

"Rachel?" Emilia snorted. "No way. She doesn't confide anything in me. Dad, on the other hand, can't keep a secret to save his soul."

"Ah. How much did he tell you?"

"Enough for me to bring it up."

"Is he, ah, concerned?"

"I'm not at liberty to discuss that," she said. "As for me, though, I can tell you that if you break my sister's heart, you'll be lucky to end up no worse than that mannequin you're holding. Clear?"

He scanned her face for a sign of playful banter. Results were inconclusive.

"So Lucas," he said. "I think he's doing all right. Apparently he and Ashley Hyatt were pretty serious, at least from his side. But he says he's learned more about her in just a couple of weeks in Earth than she told him in all the time he's known her."

"I don't doubt that," Emilia said. "Rachel keeps things pretty close, but Ashley is even worse."

"You know her?"

"Of course. She worked for me at the Super Chief for awhile. Brilliant girl—funny too. But private to a fault. She'll be mortified at those pictures of her and Burke at the Texas Tech game. You've seen them, right?"

"Lucas showed me."

"Did Lucas give any context to it? Any kind of excuse from Ashley?"

"Not that I know of."

"That figures," she said. She held a hand out in front of her. Rubbed the drying epoxy off the side of one finger. "You think she's in trouble?"

"I was going to ask you the same thing."

"That's tough to say," Emilia said, sadness flooding her face. "Tell me what you want to know and I'll fill in the gaps where I can."

"The story is one big gap," Dent said. "I think she must have been seeing Burke while she was dating Lucas. Do I have that much right?"

"Maybe. Like I said, it's been awhile since we talked."

"But you think that she was."

"Maybe. Feels like I just said that."

"Okay." He lifted his shoulder to wipe his forehead, careful not to let his hands slip from Moses' head. "Then let me ask it this way. How long have Ashley and Jeff Burke been together?"

Emilia chewed on a fingernail. Spit a fragment out onto the floor. "'Together' is a bullshit word."

"Then what word would you use?"

"Hard to say. People do crazy things to try to convince themselves they're okay." She leaned forward, elbows on knees. "I worry, Brother Denton."

"About Ashley?"

"She's one."

Dent felt a sickening gurgle swirl through his stomach. "You think there are other girls."

"I think there's a lot of danger.

"I see."

"Bullshit," Emilia said, her voice suddenly sharp. "Men always think they can see—even good men like Rob, and presumably you. Do you ever go to strip clubs?"

"No."

"Good for you. Ever watch porn?"

Dent's internal organs seemed to liquefy, flooding his system with shame. His face burned so that he did not bother with a denial.

"I'll take that as a yes," Emilia said. She knelt beside him. Looked down at his hands. "You've got a good heart," she said, but not so gently as he would have wished.

Dent stared down at the repair seam, breathed in and tried to slow his pulse. He was not a bad person, he told himself, nor did he stop being a man just because he was ordained or divorced. But the standard applied to him was different—maybe because of his religious claims, and maybe because of his status as clergy. He wondered if K.D. Holloway, his pastoral predecessor turned appliance salesman, could get him a job in Wichita Falls—if he could find work in some field in which it was okay to have needs and socially acceptable to fail. He blinked away tears. If Emilia noticed, she didn't let on.

"To answer your question, yes," she said. "I do worry about Ashley. Once this town gets hold of those pictures, she'll have a hard time walking the streets. But she's a grown enough woman to live with her choices. That's not so for everybody."

She stood and brushed off her hands and moved back to the workbench. Dent repeated her words in his head. There was a second message, something he was missing—a part of the story she'd been telling between her words. Another figure took shape in his mind. He waited until it emerged into the light of his consciousness. He closed his eyes. Tried to swallow the dread he felt when the face became clear. "Your waitress at the Super Chief. Maya."

Emilia narrowed her eyes, boring through him. All at once she laughed—as startling a sound as Dent had ever heard.

"You're better at this than I thought," she said. "Why Maya?"

"She fits his type for one—young enough to be dangerous. Then there's the way she and Burke talked when I saw them at the restaurant on the day of the shooting. She calls him by his first name. She—." He stopped. Shook his head. "I need to tell the Sheriff."

Emilia glowered at him. "No, you don't."

"Why not?"

"Because Paul Wayne won't do anything. Maya is seventeen. She can have sex with anyone she wants, at least in the eyes of the law."

"He's a school administrator and she's a student. That's got to be illegal."

"I'm sure it is, not to mention immoral. But the rules are different for men like Burke. Try taking it up with the school board, and good luck getting them to believe a teenage waitress over the town's golden boy."

"Then what do we do?" Dent said. "We need to do something, don't we?"

"You need to be more careful with your mannequins."

"We need to find proof," he continued. "Something to incriminate Burke."

"Is that what we're after here?" she snapped. She marched back over to the mannequin and knelt down inches from Dent. "You want to punish the bad guy, sure. But what's the cost? Don't get me wrong—I'm all for throwing his smug ass in jail. But you better be sure you can make that happen, because I will not have these girls put through hell just to keep the status quo."

Dent pulled his head back so he could study her face. "You've tried before, haven't you?" he asked.

She did not answer, except for the faintest of twitching in her lower lip. After a moment, she reached out and covered his hands with her own. Gently pulled them away from the mannequin. Ran her finger along the line of repair and gave a satisfied nod.

"It'll hold," she said.

CHAPTER 23:
SECRETS

Anortherly wind blew into Earth late in the afternoon as Dent was setting up in Booth 51, the chalk square in front of the FBC Youth Center to which the Methodists had been relegated for the Hallelujah Halloween. Dent framed up the base with 2 x 6 lumber using the screw holes from last year's booth. He squared the plywood sheathing on top and fastened it down with the last few sparks that remained in battery of his drill. Then he spread out the decorations according to the directions Annette Brady had given him. Palm trees here, fake rocks there. The scene looked more like Galveston than Sinai. But his was not to question why.

"Hey there!" Rachel called over the wind.

"Hey," Dent mumbled.

"Don't sound so excited to see me."

"No, sorry. Long day is all."

"Then consider me the cavalry. How can I help?"

They finished setting the scene and placed the man and woman in the center and waited to see what the wind would do. Sure enough, Moses began to inch his way across the Red Sea, his robe billowing up like a sail. After only a few seconds, he rocked past Miriam, who with arms lowered and song book in hand proved to be more aerodynamic than her brother. Moses wobbled back and forth, back and forth, tilting ever closer to the far side of Egypt. Dent stepped up as the mannequin neared the end of the platform and reached his hand forward just in time to keep Moses from toppling into the adjacent booth—Sodom and Gomorrah, brought to you by Earth Bank and Trust.

Rachel furrowed her brow, crooked a finger and raised it to her lips. "Sand around his feet? Or bags of concrete? I can run pick something up."

"Trefz will be closed by now," Dent answered. "I think we're stuck with what we got."

"Well, screw it then."

"My thoughts exactly."

He left her to hold things down while he retrieved a fresh drill battery from his pickup, which could not remain in First Baptist Church's parking lot because of the high number of participants in this year's carnival. He wove his way through the maze of Biblical panoramas, managing with some effort not to facepalm with every step. While not ghoulish or gory, the scenes nonetheless reflected a level of artistic literalism that might have embarrassed the likes of Jerry Falwell. Jeremiah weeping over the ruins of Jerusalem. Abraham preparing to sacrifice Isaac on Mt. Moriah. Jesus descending into hell to preach to the damned. The Beast of Revelation waging war against the archangel Michael who, perhaps understandably, wore an NRA t-shirt under his white toga.

At last, Dent returned with a fresh battery, a handful of washers, and a box of three-inch wood screws he found hiding in his toolbox. Rachel had stripped Miriam of her robe and was removing safety pins. The mannequin lay next to her male counterpart, naked and lovely despite the glue marks around her shoulder socket.

"What are you doing?" Dent asked. He stepped alongside Miriam. Looked both ways to make sure no one was watching, lest their host church be offended by her detailed womanliness.

"Oh, the robe wasn't hanging right," Rachel said casually. "It was easier just to strip it off to get the safety pins out. I'll start over in a second."

"Should we make her...decent?"

Rachel smiled, but did not look his way. "A body is a body, Dent. They're all decent. Does she embarrass you?"

"Of course not."

"I kinda think she does."

"Well."

Dent rubbed his head, felt its heat beneath his touch. He hoped she wouldn't see his face glowing its bright red. Hoped more fervently still that she would never find out all the convoluted emotions that caused him to blush. And that she never, ever talk about him with Emilia de los Santos.

"You'd never make it as a nurse," Rachel said with a laugh. "Pick her up so I can get this back on her."

Dent lifted Miriam, careful to obey the age-old youth group dating advice to not touch anything that a normal swimsuit would cover. Rachel threw the robe over the mannequin's head and tugged on the fabric, ordering Dent to tilt this way or that, to hold right there while she slipped the safety pins through the robe. She leaned in close to him, her warm body resting against his as she made her adjustments.

"My sister said y'all had a good talk when you were over to repair the mannequins."

Dent's heart wrenched. "Well," he said weakly.

"Well what?" she answered.

He started to say more. Thought better of it. "Why do you ask?" he finally said.

"Just curious." Rachel tilted her head toward him, half-smiled. "My sister doesn't give away content. I'm usually left to speculate, which is what I have to do in your case."

"Oh," Dent said, relieved. "Well."

"There you go again. 'Well.' Well listen here, cowboy, because I have an important request. Don't talk about me with Emilia, okay?

She is my sister and I love her. But I don't like being the topic of conversation. Maybe I'm a narcissist to think you even mentioned my name. You probably never did, and maybe she didn't either. What I'm saying—."

She stopped. Clamped her teeth down on a safety pin while she shifted Miriam's robe with no real purpose. She adjusted the fabric, placed it back in its original configuration. Stepped back to examine her work. Frowned. "I guess it'll have to do. This wind!"

They repositioned the duo in their proper stations, Moses gazing out over piles of blue fabric, parted as though they were the Red Sea. His hands were upraised in a manner that could equally mean prayer or dismay, but the posture could not be altered without risking a second decapitation. Miriam stood two feet away, hymns in hand, her manufactured womanliness now hidden beneath her blustering robes. Dent carefully drilled holes in the plastic feet and strategically screwed them into the platform. He had just driven the last one home when Rachel reached down and caught his shoulder.

"Look," she ordered.

Dent extricated himself from Miriam's skirt. Got to one knee and stared down the row of booths. Just beyond the parking lot, he could see Crystal Burke's burgundy SUV parked along the street, windows down to reveal her daughters trying to swat each other from their car seats. Crystal slammed the driver's side door and marched toward the sidewalk. A few feet out, she intercepted another pedestrian, a young and lovely girl wearing a black cap and carrying a dark blue server's apron.

"Maya?" Dent asked.

Rachel nodded.

Crystal reached out and took the girl by the elbow and spun her. Maya rounded, hands up, the ties of her apron slapping against the other woman's neck. Crystal flew into a rage, arms flailing and head bobbing and no doubt screaming, although from this distance Dent could not make out her words. Maya bowed up, folding her arms in defiance, until Crystal began to lose steam. At last the older woman dropped her face into her hands and wept. Maya seemed to shrink by several inches. She reached out a hand, pulled it back. Reached out again. Crystal saw her this time and swatted it away, hard. Maya backpedaled. Turned. Ran down the sidewalk in the other direction.

Crystal did not chase her. Instead she pulled the windblown hair out of her face and wiped her eyes and smoothed her clothes in a way that let everyone watching know she had regained her composure. She marched back to her vehicle in short, smart strides, and drove away as though just leaving a picnic.

Dent glanced at Rachel, whose face darkened with worry.

"You know what that was about?" she asked.

"I have my guesses," Dent said.

"How do you suppose she found out? Crystal, I mean."

"A town this small can't keep a secret."

Rachel shook her head sadly. "God, I wish that were true."

CHAPTER 24:
WHAT THE HELL
IS WRONG WITH ME?

Ashley cleared a space on the living room floor and set up her tent. She crawled inside, zipped the flap closed and lay down on top of her sleeping bag. She opened the lists app on her phone.

Why I am in this tent:
1) To make space so I can sort things out
2) I can't afford a hotel or a new apartment
3) I can't go back to Earth
4) I want to be alone without being alone
5) Connor

In hindsight, it was clear enough that her relationship with Connor was doomed from the word go. Had she really been able to fool herself those first few weeks, pretending that a warm body and second income were enough to justify an intimate relationship? No, she just hadn't paid attention. If she had, she would have seen the blowup coming, although she doubted she could have anticipated how quick the descent or how fiery the crash. Two days after she moved into the tent, Connor had brought home a girl from a party at the Zeta House and not even bothered to shut the bedroom door. Ashley tried to pretend it didn't matter, that this girl had no impact on her life, just as she had no impact on Crystal Burke's. She lay awake through it all, listening to the sounds of passion fade into gentle snores. And when she took stock of her emotional landscape, she found it just as barren as ever.

She re-read her list. Frowned. It sounded the same way she felt, dangling and frayed. She had rejected Connor's bed—when? Two weeks ago? Three? Since that time she had lived in a collapsible tent she set up in the living room. Connor had derided her for refusing the couch, but she didn't blame him for not understanding. She couldn't find a way to tell him how exposed she felt, how utterly scrutinized by everyone. She wasn't sure what to make of it herself.

She tried to turn that into a list, but gave up after only a few seconds. She stared at the apex of the tent above her and worried. If her lists stopped working as a means of understanding the world, what was next? Her mother's curtain of calm? The thought made her want to cry.

A key rattled in the front door. Connor. She checked the time on her phone. Only 10:16, and here she was, bedded down for the night. She dropped the device onto her chest. Tried to be silent.

"You sure it's safe?" a woman's voice said.

"She closes at Sid's on Wednesdays," Connor answered.

"I don't know. She's been flaking out on work a lot lately. Should we check the tent?"

"Just stop, okay?" Connor said. "She won't be back until midnight. I promise."

"Well, I guess o-kay-uh," the woman said, drawling out the words in a familiar Georgia accent that made Ashley's blood run cold. She sucked her lips back against her teeth until she could taste iron in her mouth. A fluorescent light flicked on in the kitchen. She could hear the shucking of winter coats.

"I just feel so bad for her," Jen said. "It's so much to take in all at once, you know? Lucas and her aunt, and this married guy."

"Do we have to talk about this?" Connor asked.

"I guess not," Jen said. "Do you think she suspects we're together?"

Connor swore. Opened a beer. "I keep telling you that it doesn't matter. She and I have been over for weeks. Besides, we never had any emotional connection."

"I know. Still, it seems like this would just add on to things, you know?"

"Then don't tell her."

"And you won't either?"

"You can see how much she talks to me anymore," Connor huffed. "She's sleeping in a tent in the living room, for god's sake. Listen." He lowered his voice. "I don't want to hurt her either, okay? But that's a separate thing from me and you. Right?"

"I guess."

"You do more than guess."

"I know," Jen said with a giggle. "You're right."

Ashley could hear the rustling of fabric and the gentle smacks of kissing. Seconds later the light in the kitchen clicked off and the couple moved to the bedroom. Ashley shielded her phone with her hand, tapped the screen to find the time again. Only ten minutes since she last checked—not nearly long enough for her to feel the actual weight of her shame. She needed to move before it pinned her to the sleeping bag. She pulled on the zipper slowly, quietly. Slipped out of the tent into the relative cool of the room. Saw only a flash of pale skin through the door to the bedroom. Turned away.

She slid into her boots and reached for her coat. Stepped out into the night. Let the door close behind her with what seemed a deafening click.

She walked quickly to campus, crunching salt crystals into the concrete sidewalk with her boots. Most of yesterday's snow had melted, and what remained wasted away in slushy gray piles at the edges of curbs and parking lots. She had forgotten gloves, and by the time she finished her first lap around campus her toes were numb and her fingers ached and the skin around her lips was raw and hot. She was breathing hard when she stepped into the student union, and fighting a thought that verified as much as any that she was coming unhinged.

I should call Lucas.

Call Lucas and what? He had been reaching out—that was his phrase, *reaching out*—to check on her, delicately asking her how she was making it without directly referencing any scandal. That wasn't exactly out of character for Lucas, whose selflessness sometimes bordered on tragic. But the timing was more than a bit suspicious. He had seen the pics of her at the game, she was sure. Jen had probably tipped him off sometime between lying to her face and screwing Connor. It didn't matter. Should she make excuses? Tell him to go to hell? Apologize? Grovel, even? History was not so easily dismissed. And even if it were, she wasn't sure she could withstand the absolution. In fact, she was sure she could not.

A drum fill sounded from the theater inside the union. On the downbeat, electric guitars boomed to life. She checked the time on her phone. The 11:Eleven Band, beginning their set at the precise minute advertised on the soggy fliers she'd seen tacked to poles and bulletin boards all week. The chords were heavy and distorted, the singer's voice anguished. She stepped closer to the side door to try to make out the lyrics.

"*My God, my God!*" the vocalist wailed. "*You cast me aside.*"

Ashley's heart jumped. Jesus music? Not her thing, and not her night even if it had been. But if this was a religious band, they hadn't gotten the positivity memo. They crushed onward, lamenting God's apparent indifference to people's lives, a world gone to hell in a hand basket. Ashley leaned against the door, felt the thump of the bass on her forehead. She lowered her hand to pull the handle, but found none. This was a backstage door, a one-way exit for those already inside.

Why had she gone back to Jeff, when college offered such a clean break? Why could she not follow through with all those plans to pack her clothes and be gone? Why didn't she forget about Lucas, and Jen and Connor, and even her mother and Irene? Why didn't she just start over?

Because the past was there in permanent marker, gathered in the damning ledger book God kept, or would have if he existed.

Play me another, she thought. The cast aside waltz. The how fucked am I blues.

She leaned in closer. The bass slammed against the door, hard enough to throw her backward. She staggered. No, not the bass. The door itself, flung open by another person. She felt her nose and checked her fingers. Bright red blood covered the tips.

"I am so sorry!" a young woman called above the music. She clasped her hands over her face, let the door swing shut behind her. "I didn't know you were—hey. Ashley? Is that you?"

Ashley blinked to clear her eyes and looked into her unwitting assailant's face. Familiar though it was, she had to dig to place it in proper context. Lyssa something, whom she'd played board games with a couple of times on Jen's girls nights. "Yeah. 's me."

Lyssa pulled her scarf from around her neck and wadded it up. "Here."

"I don't want to ruin it."

"It got it from the discount rack at Wal-Mart," Lyssa said. "Please. It'll make me feel better."

Ashley wiped her fingers and leaned back her head and pressed the scratchy material against her nose. "It's not that bad," she said.

"Let me see. No, it's not. One side is bleeding a little though. I'm sure the cold air doesn't help. Have you been outside long?"

"No," Ashley said. My, but how easily the lies were coming these days. "You should get back to the concert."

"Nah. My boyfriend is the rhythm guitar player. I've heard this set a dozen times."

"They're pretty good."

"They all seem to think so. Come on." She touched Ashley's wrist gently, but it was enough to remind her of the bruises. She gritted her teeth and let herself be guided around to a side entrance and into a padded chair. "Take a minute to let it stop completely," Lyssa said.

"Are you a nurse?"

"I will be if I can pass organic. But enough about me. How are you these days? I don't mean to pry—really I don't. Am I prying?"

Ashley closed her eyes. Tried to map out paths of conversational escape. But her nose was starting to throb, and the tired was setting in. It was all she could do not to curl up in a ball.

"Maybe a little," she said at last.

"I'm sorry," Lyssa said. "I don't mean to. It's just—we don't know each other very well. But I know Lucas some. If that breakup was half has hard on you as it was on him—."

"I'm fine."

"I know Connor too. You're still with Connor, right? I mean, not like *know* know him. We've had a couple of classes together."

"Oh. Wow."

"I know," Lyssa said. "I ramble. If you ever need to talk, though. Like, I'm sure you're okay. But life gets tough sometimes, you know?"

"I'm fine."

"Right. Okay. So Jen mentioned some things to our small group the other night. Don't worry—it's all confidential in there. Prayer requests, you know. She said you were having a tough time with a relationship you're in. With some married guy. I know it's not my business."

"It's not," Ashley said. She sniffled. Tasted blood in the back of her throat. What she would give to instantly stop bleeding and walk away.

"I know. Sorry. It's just—you don't have to do this. A girl like you who is so smart and pretty. Honestly, I'm a little jealous of all you've got going for you, which is my own spiritual issue. I'll own that much. Can I tell you a secret?"

"It's getting late."

Lyssa slid forward on her chair, plowed ahead. "I did the same thing my freshman year. Had an affair with a married GA. I thought I was all grown up about it, but it was stupid. And it ended miserably. I really don't want to talk about it."

Ashley dabbed at her nose. "Then I wish you wouldn't."

"Okay, right. I'm sorry. I just want to help."

"I'm sure you do," Ashley said.

She lowered her head and examined the scarf, splattered now with blood, and tested her nose. Still crusty, but no longer flowing. She looked at the girl across from her with what she hoped would pass for earnestness. Dropped the scarf into the girl's hand and pressed it there. Lyssa stared back, ignoring with some effort the sticky mess Ashley continued to force into her palm.

"Can I pray for you?" Lyssa asked.

Ashley stood, dusted off her hands. Checked her nose and stepped toward the exit.

"Sure," she called over her shoulder. "Anytime."

And with that she was back outside, the cold air shocking her awake. She stepped into the shadows of the union, out of the streetlamps so that she could see the stars, burning on through the epochs, unfazed by human drama. She half hoped that Lyssa was following through with the threat to pray for her. At this point, it couldn't hurt.

Ashley opened the LinearLife app, tapped at the keys, and stared down at what she had written.

What the hell is wrong with me?

The tears she expected did not come. What the hell *was* wrong with her? The question implied a need for diagnosis, an understanding of just where she was messed up. But what did that matter, really, when what she really wanted was to stop wallowing in that question altogether. A strange clarity washed over her. Before she could talk herself out of it, she closed down the app and opened a new text and, for the first time in months, reached back to Lucas.

CHAPTER 25:
I SUSPECT EVERYBODY
OF SOMETHING

D ent cracked his knuckles as he examined the jumble of cardboard boxes in the bed of his pickup, stacked to three feet over the cab and leaning in every direction. In his haste to get the vermin-harboring boxes out of the parsonage, he had stuffed the pickup bed too full and piled its contents too high. No matter the angle from which he viewed the life-sized Jenga puzzle, the boxes defied any plan he might make for removing the nylon straps that had held them in place, much less for unloading them once they were unbound.

He left that problem for a moment and opened the door to his newly rented U-Stor-It unit. It was an early Christmas gift from Doc, who'd informed him of the rental via an old-fashioned prescription pad, its square page pinned against his windshield by the wiper. On it, Doc quite legibly instructed Dent to store the damned boxes and their scorpion tenants somewhere besides his primary residence, doctor's orders, and to send Lucas by the office for a follow-up visit. Doc had paid the deposit and first three months' rent on the unit. Now, two pickup loads into the endeavor, it was already near to overflowing with boxes, all labeled in Janet's impeccable script, indicating each box's contents and preferred location in the house. *Cookbooks/Kitchen. Towels/Guest Bath. Sermon Files/Church.* Janet's his-and-hers packing system before their final move as a couple was,

Dent could see in hindsight, meant to streamline the post-divorce reckoning. *Knitting Supplies/J's Office. Winter Shoes/J's Closet.*

Art supplies/Leah's Room.

He bypassed the stack for now and reached into the back seat of the pickup, emerging with a box marked *FRAGILE* on every side. The scent of potpourri tickled his nose. It brought to mind their bedroom in Odessa. Janet had complained about the oil-town smell from the moment they arrived. After only a month Dent came home from an administrative council meeting to find the parsonage engulfed in a spiced fog, snifters or candles or dried rose petals on every flat surface. When he complained of allergies, Janet calmly told him to either spend more time in the office or earn a better appointment.

That was three moves and eight years ago, and none of the other towns had anything remotely like the sickly-sweet odor they'd endured in Odessa. Janet probably hadn't opened this box since she'd packed it. But it had moved with them each time, a reminder to Dent of how much she endured for his sake. And now here it was again, in his hands, while she went happily about her business in New Mexico with Mr. Costume Guy and Leah and—very soon, it seemed—a grandchild. If Janet gave him the chance, he just might strangle her.

Instead, he pulled out his phone. Examined his face in the cracked screen. Pressed the home button and brought up Leah's contact info. Since he'd glimpsed her in Tucumcari, he had called her four times—not once leaving a voicemail—and composed at least fifty texts, of which he sent exactly zero. How did you start off a conversation like this without sounding condemning or pathetic? *So tell me how you ended up pregnant at nineteen and how your mother turned you against me. Tell me what I'm supposed to do, since what used to be my family has abandoned me here. Tell me how* to make things right again. Tell me your screwed up story, and I'll tell you mine, and maybe we can forgive each other.

He pressed the call button and waited. Four rings later, Leah's chipper voice informed him that she was unavailable. He ended the call before the message tone.

He carried the potpourri-scented box toward the open door. Looked back and forth from pickup to storage unit. Unwrapped his fingers from the bottom of the box and let it drop onto the pavement. The muffled chink of breaking glass leaked through the cardboard, a pleasing sound to Dent's hearing. He picked it up again, dropped it from shoulder height. Picked it up, threw it down with some force. And again, and again, and one last time with his weight behind it, so that the impact produced a noise more crunch than shatter. He picked up the ruined box and hurled it at the open door of the storage unit.

As it left his hand, he caught sight of a human arm, sheathed in the brown jacket of county law enforcement, emerging from behind the pickup. The Sheriff looked up with mild surprise as the box descended upon him. He leaned back just in time for the projectile to miss his face. Instead, it connected with the brim of his hat, knocking it harmlessly off his head so that it landed on top of the crushed cardboard.

"Careful," the Sheriff said as he appeared from behind the tower of boxes. "I can't dodge quick as I used to."

Dent nodded sheepishly. He felt a sticky liquid fill his palm, followed by a stinging sensation. He opened it to find the skin sliced in at least half a dozed places, some of the cuts flecked with bits of glass from whatever globes he had crushed. He pulled a fast food napkin from the door pocket of the truck and squeezed it and hid his injured hand behind his back.

"Sorry," he mumbled.

"All right then," the Sheriff said.

The wet fog that had greeted him this morning turned to drizzle. Dent frowned and poked at one of the lower boxes. The damp cardboard gave way beneath his finger. Here was his past life, piled high and fixed to ruin. If he put them in the storage unit, these boxes might well freeze and thaw several times over the winter and disintegrate in the spring into pulpy masses covered with slick black mold. He might not be able to salvage anything after all.

Before he could entertain alternatives, however, he heard the scuff of boot heels against bedliner. He looked up just in time to see the Sheriff squeeze the quick-release on the tie-down straps. The tower of boxes swayed one way, then another, until the Sheriff reached his hand into the top row and stabilized it. He swiped his arm forward, sliding the top box off the stack. Dent shuffled under it just in time to catch it knee high. The impact sent pain sliding across his palm. He gritted his teeth, placed the box on a stack in the unit, and went back for another.

Once the pickup was empty, Dent backed it in so that the bumper was just under the U-Stor-It awning. The two men sat on the tailgate, their feet propped up on the low wall of boxes at the edge of the unit. The Sheriff pulled a package of cigarettes from his breast pocket. He shook one out, cupped his hands and lit the tip.

"I didn't know you smoked," Dent said.

"I quit for years," the Sheriff answered. "And then Aubrey died, and riding the wagon didn't seem quite so sensible as it once had." He offered one to Dent, who declined. "I can remember going to a brush arbor revival with my grandpa when I was a kid. The service went on and on, had to be more than two hours. After a time my Grandpa lit up a smoke. The preacher—a Methodist, as I recall—tore into him about the evils of tobacco and sin in the presence of the Lord."

He stopped, smoked for a few seconds.

"What did your grandpa do?" Dent finally asked.

"Finished his cigarette, I reckon. You talked to Lucas this morning?"

"Just for a second. Doc wanted him to come by for a follow up visit."

"Is he walking?"

"Rachel set him up with a scooter. He can put one knee on it and wheel just about anywhere. Why do you ask?"

"I'm wondering if he's mobile enough to be a felon." He pulled a smart phone from his jacket pocket and tapped the screen. Held it out for Dent to see the pictures of Jeff Burke's navy blue pickup. Spider webs ran up from a circular hole on the windshield, and the windows had been smashed in completely on the driver's side.

"When did this happen?" Dent asked.

"Sometime Wednesday morning. Burke had ridden his bike to school and left the truck in the driveway. Crystal found it when she came home over her lunch hour."

"And she thinks Lucas did it."

"No. I think that. Crystal won't say. They have a security system, so it should all be on video. But she says she hasn't had time to go through it yet."

Dent turned that over in his head. Tried not to settle on what seemed most probable.

"You don't look convinced," the Sheriff said.

"Lucas may have done it, and may have not," Dent said. "I can't vouch for him after about 8:30 yesterday morning. But I did see Crystal screaming at Maya Jordan last night before the Hallelujah Halloween."

"Half the town saw it. What's your point? Maya's just a waif of a thing. I don't think she could swing hard enough to do this kind of damage to a pickup."

"Probably not. But what if she was on the security video for some other reason?"

"Like because she was with Lucas?"

Dent shook his head. "Not Lucas. Jeff."

The Sheriff worked his jaw back and forth. Spit onto the damp pavement. "Damn," he said.

"It's only a guess."

"Probably a good one, given that Maya ran away last night. You know anything about that?"

"First I've heard of it." Dent waited a moment for the weight of the news to settle. He brushed his hand over his face. "I wish I knew more to tell you. Poor kid."

"Poor kid," the Sheriff repeated. "Careful what you wish for, Brother Denton. The more you know, the greater your responsibility. I can tell you from experience, you best be cautious uncovering secrets."

"I'm not doing anything illegal."

"The law is my concern," the Sheriff said. "But whether or not you sin in the eyes of the townsfolk is something else. When an outsider starts poking around too deep, the ones with secrets get nervous."

"Like Jeff Burke?"

"Can't say."

"Meaning you don't know?"

"Meaning I can't say." The Sheriff crushed his cigarette on the sole of his boot. "You found out about his parents, I guess."

"I found out Old Mother Earth's ex was his daddy," Dent said. "And that the old man shot himself right in front of Burke and his momma."

"That so?"

"You were there, Sheriff. You signed off on the police report."

"I did. Damned shame."

"Wait," Dent said. "The incident was a damned shame, or signing off on the report was?"

"Both, I reckon."

"Tell me about it."

The Sheriff dropped his hands to his knees. "I don't believe I will," he said. "Not much to tell anyway. A well-placed bullet can do damage that I pray you never encounter."

He pulled the cigarettes from his pocket again, tapped one out. Pressed it with his index finger until it disappeared back into the carton.

"At least Brantley died instantly," the Sheriff continued. "Burke's momma took another some-odd years to poison herself."

"Judy said it was alcohol," Dent said.

"Heart attack, officially. But alcohol was a factor. Drugs too. Jeff was used to supporting himself by then, working odd jobs after football practice to buy food and pay the bills. He could have gone to live with Sarah's parents in Oklahoma City, but he didn't want to leave Earth. Folks figured that sixteen was old enough to make his way if he could, and so a lot of people helped him out those last couple of years of high school. But he did all right on his own too."

Dent turned the story over in his mind, checking its angles for some glint of revelation. Two tragic parents produced the town's golden boy, all the more so because of the widespread investment in him. "So Burke is the model citizen."

"I didn't say that."

"No," Dent said. He fought back a smile. "You suspect him then?"

"Of what?"

"Of something. I don't know."

"I suspect everybody of something, Brother Denton. I'm starting to suspect you of nosiness and bad manners."

"You're not the first," Dent said. He reached his hand back to let the runoff wash over the cut on his palm. The cold water stung his wounds before running out pink between his fingers.

"That revival I was telling you about," the Sheriff said. "I don't recall the end of it directly. I'm sure they had some altar call and a lot of crying and shouting. That's the way those things used to be. But I do remember getting back in the truck with Granddad and having one of the neighborhood boys run up with a message that Irene Ostendorf had just returned from California with a black suitcase and a rifle."

"California?"

"Where she was and why she was there is her business, but she came back loaded for bear. Granddad threw the truck in gear and flew through town to tell my father about it. I asked him why he was driving so fast, and he said he had to, if he wanted to keep Harlan Brantley alive and that woman out of jail."

He paused, returned his hat to his head, made like he would leave. Dent reached out for the meaning of the story, touched only air. "What then?" he asked.

"Can't say. That's what happened. Make of it what you will."

CHAPTER 26:
YOU CAN BLAME
ANYTHING YOU
WANT ON GOD

He bought a lock from Trefz Hardware and clamped it to the handle of the storage unit, debating even as it clicked into place whether the ten-dollar investment to secure his belongings was worth it. Could he name the contents of those boxes? Would he miss anything now stuffed inside? No. In fact, the thought of reopening the unit months from now filled him with dread. What had once been his treasure had been reduced to mere stuff, a worthless hoard for the paper dragons of his past. He made sure the lock was fastened then dropped both keys through a crack in the drainage grate. They splashed into the water six feet below. Instantly, he felt better.

Until he remembered Lucas.

Dent had stopped back by the parsonage on the way home from Trefz', but the house had been empty. He called Irene, who thought he had the wrong number and told him to go jump in a lake, and texted Rachel, who replied that Lucas had left Doc's hours ago. He considered driving by the Burke residence, just in case, but had no idea what he might do if he caught the young man there. Instead he parked in the alley behind Heinmann Theater, where the Last Man Club Tall Tale Round Up was set to kick off in just over twenty-four hours. He found Rob beside the stage, fastening a handrail to the wheelchair ramp leading up to it.

"Hold this," his former coach ordered, patting the rail.

Dent placed both palms on top and steadied it while Rob drove home screws through the brackets. When he'd finished, Rob pulled himself up by the rail, then leaned against it, and then sat on top of it. He hopped back down with a satisfied grunt.

"For Old Mother Earth," he said. "She may be too proud to use it, but if she breaks a hip it won't be on my account." He stepped back. Peered down his nose at Dent. "You get into a fight this morning?"

Dent shook his head.

"You look like hell," Rob said. "No offense."

"None taken."

Rob sat down on the edge of the stage and slapped his hand down on it. "What's on your mind, Dent?"

Dent shifted, trying to hold back the verbal flood he could feel welling up inside. "Long week is all."

"Bullshit," Rob said. "Let's have it."

And all at once Dent was back in Little League, back in the dugout with his old coach. He was Denton or Johnny or J.D., without the degree or the title or the twin shackles of ordination and history. He took in a deep breath. "Well," he said, and the stories started spilling out of him. The boxes and the scorpions, Bud Cockburn and the church, Leah, Old Mother Earth, Lucas and Rachel—all piled together in the biggest pool of word vomit Dent ever recalled producing. He was talking too fast and saying too much and watching it all with an anticipatory sense of guilt. Yet he couldn't stop. He plowed through THE DIRT and his worries over Maya and his conversation with the Sheriff. It was in this last tale that he finally crashed into a narrative wall and went silent.

"That's all?" Rob said.

"Sorry," Dent said. "I shouldn't have—."

"Hang on." Rob jumped to his feet. Lifted an index finger. "Watch this."

Rob trotted back to the tech booth along the back wall and set to work with switches Dent could not see. The house lights dimmed, and a row of overheads came to life. One last adjustment, and a spotlight landed on a wooden stool in the center of the stage.

"Just finished wiring in the light board this morning," Rob said.

"It's incredible," Dent said, and he meant it. The theater's transformation from apocalypse backdrop to gala host site was astounding. It had taken Rob less than a week. "What's your secret?"

"My secret?"

"To the quick turnaround. To all this."

Rob shrugged. "No secret. Just imagination. You have to begin with the end in mind. I think Aristotle said that. Or maybe Steven Covey." He came out from behind the soundboard and walked forward and hopped back up onto the stage. Stood with his hands on his hips and admired his handiwork. "Did I ever tell you about the three-fingered man who taught me how to farm?"

Dent shook his head.

"His name was Elton Grindal, though I never heard anyone call him anything but Sonny. He was a former Marine who'd lost seven fingers in Lebanon, or so he said. But if you ever watched him run a chainsaw, you'd have reason to think he lost them another way. He'd have to wedge the saw between his ankles and grab the pull cord with both hands and yank. He had a thumb on his right hand, and his index and middle finger on his left. It was just enough for him to do most of what he wanted, and not enough for any of it to be safe. Sonny complained all the time that the military discharged him, and he a perfectly good soldier. He talked about the battles he fought and the medals he won all the time. I can't say how much of it was true. But I do know that he loved the Marines. He may have been stuck here in this nowhere Panhandle town, teaching some guy named Rob to farm. But if he'd had his choice, he'd have been on the front lines, lobbing grenades at the enemy."

Dent nodded. "I can relate," he said soberly.

"But see, you've got different eyes," Rob said. He tapped Dent on the chest. "You're looking for good, so you're likely to see it. Sonny, he taught me all kinds of things. And he went out during ice storms and spread salt on church steps so that the little old ladies hell bent on keeping their streak of consecutive Sundays alive wouldn't break a hip. He volunteered at the orphanage—built the strongest dog pen I ever saw, just so those kids could have a pet without it running off."

"Because he was looking for the good?"

"That's the funny thing. He may have looked, but he never saw it. Never appreciated any of it. Drank himself to death, thinking he was some big failure."

"Well."

"Here's what I'm getting at," Rob said. "The life he wanted blew off his fingers and wrecked his plans, dropped him into a life he didn't choose. You could call that a tragedy, and maybe it was. He certainly saw it that way. But if it hadn't been for those lost fingers, those kids would have never had a dog. God knows how many old ladies would have cracked bones on the ice. I never would have learned to farm, which means I would've left Earth before I ever met Em."

"So you're saying that his losing his fingers was some sort of providence," Dent said. "Like God's will, you mean?"

"You can blame anything you want on God, good or ill," Rob answered. "Sonny didn't get medals for taking care of his neighbors. But he wouldn't have taken care of his neighbors if he'd gotten his way in the first place. Did God cause that, or did Sonny just make lemonade out of lemons?"

"I don't know," Dent said. "I guess maybe it doesn't matter which."

Rob smiled. "I guess maybe not." He walked across the room again. Brought down the stage lights and turned up the house. Took his seat next to Dent. His face sobered. "You say Lucas beat in Burke's windshield."

"That's what the Sheriff said."

"But Crystal hasn't turned in the security footage yet."

"No."

Rob picked up his tape measure and turned it over in his hands. Bowed his head thoughtfully. "Try this out," he said. "Crystal comes home for lunch and finds the truck all beat to hell. So she logs on to the camera footage to see who did it. Only she goes back a little too far. And instead of seeing Lucas, she sees an unauthorized woman coming over while she's not there. Am I making sense?"

"That's more or less what I assume," Dent said. "But if it's the girl I think it was, then I'm not sure why Crystal would have thought anything of it."

"You mean Maya," Rob said in a lower voice.

"Yes. She babysits their girls. Why would Crystal think twice about seeing her?"

"Because the girls were with Crystal Tuesday night at a birthday party. Emilia catered it out at the Haurwas place north of town. Jeff was the only one home last night. So if Crystal saw any guests, well." He stopped. Shook his head. "I reckon since you spilled all your worries to me I should return the favor."

"Come again?" Dent said.

Rob pulled the tape measure out to eight inches. Let it snap back. "I did the wiring for Burke's security system," he said. "There are cameras in the bedroom too. I told Jeff that wasn't necessary, but he said he wanted to make sure his family was safe."

Dent hooked one hand over his neck. "So you think—."

"I don't think about it at all. I can't bring myself to, and would hate myself if I did. It's enough to say that, whatever it was Crystal saw, she's going to have a hard time unseeing it. You know what I'm saying?"

"I do."

"Okay." Rob clapped his hands on his knees. Pushed himself up and stretched. "Let's get this mess cleaned up and head on over to the Super Chief. Maybe we can talk Emilia into feeding us."

CHAPTER 27:
THE STORIES WE TELL
BECOME THE TRUTH

The sign on the Super Chief door read *CLOSED*, and so the two men went around to the employee entrance in back. They found Emilia and Rachel seated at the table nearest the kitchen, sharing a plate of fried mushrooms. The two women flashed a speak-of-the-devil glance at each other, but Dent could not say whether he or Rob was the devil in question. Emilia wiped her hands on her apron and motioned for Dent to take her seat.

"Let me go see what we have to make a decent dinner," Emilia said. "If you're done with the stage you've earned it, and if you're not finished yet you'll need it. Rob, could you come help me please?"

Rob groaned. Pulled out a chair. "If it's all the same to you—."

"It's not," Emilia said. She tapped him on the arm. Pointed toward the kitchen. "Let's go."

They disappeared through the swinging doors into the back. Rachel looked down at her plate. Pushed around a stray piece of mushroom batter. Dent waited.

"Haven't heard much from you today," Rachel said, more casually than Dent might have wished.

"It's been busy," Dent answered. He thought about listing off his day's accomplishments and conversations. Stopped himself. "I'm sorry," he said instead. "I'm just sorting things out."

"Well you aren't the only one." She stabbed her fork toward the kitchen. "I can't tell if Emilia is trying to set me up with you or warn me away."

"I don't know either. She's a complicated person."

"Fair amount of that going around these days, it seems. What were you trying to sort out?"

Dent held up a hand. "I didn't mean it like that. You and I—whatever we are is good."

"Whoa!" she said, extending a full stiff-arm in his direction. "I like you, all right? That ought to be clear enough. But I'm not ready for any kind of define-the-relationship talk yet."

"Oh. No, of course not."

"Don't be like that. It doesn't mean that we won't live happily ever after. It just means that there's a lot about you I don't know yet. Now let's try this again. What's been on your mind?"

"Well," Dent said and pondered the complexities of the female heart in the brief silence that followed. At last he pushed onward. "Lucas might be in trouble, and Maya is missing, and my daughter is pregnant."

"You have a daughter?"

Dent nodded. "Leah. She's nineteen."

"Seems like that's something you should have told me already."

"I'm sorting a few things out with her too. She's still a teenager. She lives with her mother in New Mexico. I haven't talked to her much since Janet and I split."

Rachel squared up her shoulders. Stared hard into his face. "I know you're a preacher and that you have to maintain a certain reputation," she said. "I get that. But you can't be ashamed of your daughter just because she's going to have a baby so young."

"No!" Dent said quickly. "That's not it at all. She was born when her mother and I were in college. We didn't even get married until she was four, which to church people was just sin upon sin. So I can't condemn anybody, especially Leah. I think it's more that Leah's ashamed of me."

"Why in the world would she be? You're her dad?"

"But I'm a failure."

"A failure."

Dent nodded. Looked down at his hands. Wondered if he should just confess everything—stalled career, absentee parenting, inability to move on. Hell, he should go ahead confess to her that he'd watched a handful of quite indecent films since the divorce. Then he could ride of into the sunset of pastoral ministry, on through to a new life in retail. Give up trying to be good. What a relief that would be.

"Rachel," he began.

But the jingle of a bell derailed him. Rachel's eyes widened. Dent turned around to see Jeff Burke wiping the soles of his running shoes on the welcome mat. He turned the sign around so that *OPEN* faced out. Unzipped his jacket and stepped toward Dent, but pointed to the east dining car.

"Brother Denton," he said. "Might I have a word?"

He disappeared through the doorway. Rachel stood. "I guess duty calls," she said.

Dent swallowed hard. Wiped his hand over his face. Nodded.

"I'll let Emilia and Rob know what's going on," she said. "You need me to come with you?"

"No. I'll be all right."

"Okay." She cleared the plates. Looked into Dent's face as he stood. "Pay attention in there. And be careful."

Burke had seated himself at the same back table where they'd eaten on the day of the shooting, which seemed both yesterday and forever ago. He sat still, hands folded, staring out the window, wounded and dangerous. Dent took a seat across from him.

"It appears that some pieces of my life are slipping beyond my control," Burke said without moving his gaze. "I'm traveling by bicycle until my pickup is repaired, which is of course not a hardship in a town this size. But now Crystal has decided we need some time apart, which means I am living in a hotel for the foreseeable future." He turned to face Dent. Stared hard into the other man's face. "Then again, I'm just another sad story, Brother Denton. I'm sure you've heard those before."

"Many times."

"And people come to you for spiritual advice."

"They do."

"And you give it to them. Even though you're just another man, like everyone else. You don't know any more or any less of life than I do, and you certainly don't know what it's like to be me."

"I never claimed that," Dent said.

"But you do!" Burke protested. "Every week, a preacher—you or Holloway or Cockburn or whoever—gets up to speak and tells me what I should believe or think or do. But the world you talk about exists only in your head. You don't know what the real world is even made of."

"I have some idea."

"I doubt you do."

Dent rubbed his face. Yawned. "It's late, Jeff. What can I do for you?"

"I guess nothing." He reached into his jacket. Pulled out a yellow envelope. Turned it over to reveal the words Dent feared were there. THE DIRT.

A cold feeling swirled around Dent's neck. "How did you get that?" he asked.

"Parsonage inspection," Burke said. "As chair of the church board, I feel it's important that the church provide our pastor with suitable accommodations. Since you were out today—and, as it turns out, so was your guest—I thought I'd look in on things. Check the water pressure. Test the smoke alarms."

"Stealing is different."

"I didn't steal anything, Brother Denton. This file is church property. It was produced by a former employee of the church. I found it on a table the church owns, inside a house the church holds the deed to. Seeing that it is not fit for public consumption, I decided I'd secure it. Of course, you could file a complaint with Brother Cockburn, but I'm sure you wouldn't want him to know that you've spent your first weeks on the job wallowing around in rumors and scandal."

"I'm in no mood for drama," Dent said. "If I can't help you, I'll be on my way."

"Please sit, Brother Denton. This is a serious matter. Why don't we reason it out together."

"Maybe tomorrow."

"One last thing," Burke said. "A bit of personal history. You know how my father died?"

"I've heard he died in a war. I've heard he dug his own grave and shot himself in it."

"Yes."

"But that's not the truth," Dent said. "I've seen the police report. He died of suicide on Irene Ostendorf's front lawn."

"That report has nothing to do with the truth," Burke insisted. "A war did kill my father—Korea, to be exact. He was an old man already when my mother had me, you see, but the war had damaged him. And in a way, he had dug his own grave already. Don't you see how much more sense that story makes?"

"I can see how you came by it, if that's what you're asking."

"I'm not asking, Brother Denton. I'm opening your eyes to the way the world works. Truth has a practiced element to it, you see. The stories we tell become fact over time. What Crystal knew about my father's death was more true than the facts. I wish you could have appreciated that."

"I never told her—."

"No, but Lucas Lim did. Dropped an envelope off at her work with a copy of that police report he'd obtained from the library. I believe you might have led him in that direction."

"I don't recall discussing it."

Burke folded his hands. Leaned forward. "My point is this. You and your guest have introduced nothing but chaos and confusion since you came into town. I'm disappointed, Brother Denton. Buddy Cockburn had told us you were a reasonable man. Yet you want to rewrite my history before you even know it. You should read your Bible more, perhaps. Search out the way of things, like Jesus did. Wasn't he the one who asked, 'What is truth?'"

"That was Pontius Pilate," Dent said. "Jesus said the truth will set you free."

"Don't you wish it were so," Burke said. He reached for THE DIRT. Thumbed through it to a dog-eared page. "Here is what Reverend Holloway saw as truth. 'Jeff Burke grew up with an alcoholic mother and no father, and has had multiple marriages and numerous affairs. He shows up at church occasionally and likes to be on committees because it gives him a way to control things.' That is certainly not a flattering picture of my character as a Christian."

"No," Dent said.

"Do you think it's the truth?"

"I didn't write it."

"But you read it, and it's in your head. You can't just pretend you didn't hear it, and you can't tell yourself it doesn't matter. You will think of me differently because of what's written here."

"I'll think of you differently because you broke into my house."

Burke smiled. He picked up THE DIRT. Tucked it back into his pocket and stood.

"I certainly hope so," he said.

CHAPTER 28:
YOU NEED TO FIND
THAT GIRL

A nother sleepless night, or near to it.

An hour before dawn, Dent gave up. He pulled on his shoes and jacket and set out for places he knew he should not go. He crossed Main Street and walked through the neighborhoods behind the Super Chief—smaller homes with concrete porches. Rentals, mostly, although a few were occupied by widows who had lived their entire lives in the same house, who now wheeled bottles of oxygen behind them and hoped to die rather than be forced into a nursing home. He passed the high school and the golf course and finally came to the entrance to Carriage Hills. Somewhere behind the wrought iron gates and manicured shrubbery, Crystal Burke would be pacing the floor, wondering if her marriage was over before their third child was even born. Dent wondered too. Wished better for her, if not for Jeff.

He turned away.

Just before 7:00am, he passed the Schugart house, making sure not to linger, lest someone see him and get the wrong idea. A block later, he could see the light through the window of the Sheriff's office. He hustled inside. Rubbed cold from his hands.

"I didn't figure you for a morning person," the Sheriff said.

"Jeff Burke came to see me last night," Dent said. "I was at the Super Chief with Rob—."

"Already heard," the Sheriff interrupted. "Your girlfriend stood on the other side of the wall with her ear to that model train tunnel. Heard the whole conversation between you and Burke. She called me last night."

"I wouldn't call her my girlfriend." He lingered a moment on the word, though, and had to admit he liked the sound. "Wait. She called you?"

"Now don't get your knickers all twisted," the Sheriff said. "She complained about you for ten minutes before she finally got around to her point. If that's not love, I don't know what is."

"Well," Dent said, and had to search for a moment to regain his track. "Burke, though."

"Right. Anyway, Rachel said he stole something out of the parsonage. Wants me to file a complaint against Burke and not tell you she put me up to it."

Dent frowned. "You just told me."

"Damn," the Sheriff said, slapping his desk. "I've never been good with secrets. Do you want to register a complaint?"

"No. It'll just make things worse."

"Good, because you've really got nothing to go on." He picked up a sheet of paper from his desk. "Now Burke, on the other hand, has got a pretty good case against your roommate."

He handed Dent the page, a grainy still from a security camera. It showed a man in an oversized black hoodie swinging an aluminum bat into the windshield of Burke's pickup. His face was not visible, but his right leg was encased in a large plastic and Velcro boot.

"Proof enough," Dent said. "What are you going to do?"

"I have to charge him with destruction of property. No way around that. Burke wants him locked up, but I doubt that'll be necessary. You think Lim will run? Metaphorically speaking."

"Not without Ashley."

"Well then. Judge Gleason is ending his docket at noon today so he can get ready for the Last Man Club Roundup tonight. You better get Mr. Lim here before lunch to book those charges, if he doesn't want to spend the weekend in jail."

"I can try," Dent said, once again bristling at the order. "Why don't you just come arrest him? He's probably at the parsonage now."

"I could, I reckon," the Sheriff said. "But don't you think you've been the subject of enough gossip since you pulled into town? It would serve everybody better and make my job a hell of a lot easier if Mamie Martz didn't get to see blue lights in your driveway."

Dent spent the entire walk home cursing his profession. Pastoral ministry was an exercise in futility. If you weren't a dumping ground for one person, you were an errand boy for someone else. He might as well wait tables at the Super Chief.

He sent Lucas a text asking him to wake up and get ready, but the young man was still sound asleep when he arrived back at the parsonage. Dent tapped his walking cast until he finally awoke, bleary-eyed and disheveled.

"Get dressed," Dent ordered. "The Sheriff wants you to turn yourself in this morning."

"Okay," Lucas said, as calmly as if Dent had asked him to pass the dinner rolls. He was up and ready in fifteen minutes, emerging from the bedroom wearing the black hoodie he'd taken from the church's donation room. He reached for his scooter. "Are we walking or driving?"

"You don't seem too put out by getting arrested," Dent said.

"I figured it was coming."

"But you're not upset by it. I wonder if you appropriately grasp the situation."

"I think so," he said, and shrugged. "I'll get charged with vandalism and destruction of property, but I have a clean record and will be fully cooperative. I think I'll be able to plea bargain down to paying restitution and a fine. Maybe community service. I can survive that."

"And if it's worse than that?" Dent asked. "Suppose you end up in jail. Or suppose your parents find out."

"It could happen," Lucas said. Another shrug. "Dad will just distance himself. Mom will understand, once I tell her the story. Anyway, the goal is what matters."

"The goal?"

"Buy time." He hopped up onto the counter, careful not to bang the cabinets with his boot. "Did you know Maya Jordan ran away?"

"The Sheriff mentioned that. Who told you?"

"Ever hear of Twitter?" he said, and then held up a hand in apology. "Seriously, you may not want to know."

"Try me."

Lucas considered this for a moment. At last he pointed at the kitchen table to an early-model smartphone dredged from the phones-for-troops donation box. Dent picked it up and turned it over. Examined the cartoon kitty that stared out from the bright pink case.

"Ashley's?" Dent asked.

Lucas shook his head. "Maya's She left some passwords stored on it. I was able to restore her profile, including her photos. Some of the things she sent to Burke—I don't even want to know how young she was then. I bet it could put Burke in jail for a long time, though."

"If she was underage—did you send them to the Sheriff?"

"Not yet. Just to Crystal. Only two, though—and not the worst ones, of course. I mean, I just needed to make the point. If the rest of those photos got out...well."

"Jesus." Dent pinched the bridge of his nose. His head pounded. "You know they'll be evidence if there's a trial. You can't pretend you never saw them."

Lucas shifted on the counter. Picked at a seam in the laminate. "I know. But—look, I should have thought it through better. From Maya's perspective, I mean. If I'd known Crystal would confront her, or that she was going to run—she's just a kid."

He started to say more but pulled up short. He watched his dangling feet swing in little circles. When he glanced up again, his eyes went back to the box of old phones on the kitchen table. Dent followed his gaze. Noticed another old smartphone laying off to one side.

"You also found Ashley's," Dent said at last. "And more photos?"

Lucas drew in a sharp breath. Stared hard at the tile floor. "Please don't tell her I know. We only just started texting again a couple of days ago. And I couldn't tell her anything today if I wanted to. All these old phones around, and I can't remember where I left my own. You think it might be in one of those boxes in the storage unit?"

"Surely not," Dent said. He decided not to mention throwing away the keys. "Don't you have some sort of tracker app on it?"

"I turn those things off. I hate the thought of people spying on me." He planted his hands on his thighs. "Promise you won't say anything about Maya or Ashley? At least not yet?"

"If Maya is missing—"

"She might not be," Lucas said. He was sitting on his fingers now, trying to look steady. "Ashley said she might know a place Maya would go."

"What place is that?"

"She didn't say. Or if she did, I haven't gotten the message." He patted his pockets, then held up his palms. "Please, just give me an hour, okay? Let's find my phone and see what Ash has to say."

Dent blew out a long breath, feeling all at once the weight of caring for other people's children. He wondered what he would do if Leah were the one missing, or worse, if her phone and old photos were in that box. "All right," he said after a moment. "Where was the last place you remember having it?"

Half an hour of searching the parsonage turned up nothing but loose change and wayward popcorn kernels. Lucas bore the loss of his phone bravely, saying that he'd rather go ahead and get to the courthouse without it than risk spending the weekend in jail because Judge Gleason took the afternoon off. Besides, the weather forecast warned of a looming winter storm that could render travel impossible for several days. Trapped by ice was one thing. Trapped by ice in jail would be quite another.

Dent parked on the diagonal yellow lines of the loading entrance and left his pickup running. He walked Lucas to the door. The young man said he'd take it from there. He even stuck out his hand and shook Dent's with deep feeling, as though bidding him farewell to face the gallows. Once he was through the door, Dent turned back to the pickup and rolled his eyes. Zipped his jacket against the wind, cutting down from the north. Wondered what he should do.

On cue, he heard his name—not Reverend or Pastor or Brother Denton, nor even the less formal Dent. This was his full name. *John. Wesley. Denton.* He closed his eyes and braced for trouble.

"I see you!" Crystal Burke called. She was lifting the second of her two daughters out of their SUV and onto the courthouse parking lot. She closed the door. Snatched a mittened hand in each of hers and marched toward Dent. She took a few steps past him and turned the girls loose on the dry grass. "Go play," she ordered, and whirled on Dent. The wind pressed her Red Raiders jersey against her swelling breasts and baby bump. She lifted a finger to his chin and seethed. "You son of a bitch."

"Crystal?"

"Don't you 'Crystal' me! You knew, didn't you? You knew what Jeff was up to, and you hid it because of some man code. Or some pastoral thing. Whatever." She whirled to check on her twins, who had climbed atop the war memorial obelisks. "*PaigeandKaylee!*" she shrieked. "Get down from there before I wear you out!"

"Honestly, Crystal," Dent said. "I haven't the foggiest idea—"

"You don't? You two seemed to hit it off just fine the day Old Mother Earth shot that biker, eating together at the Super Chief and all. And then Jeff tells me no, he doesn't trust the new preacher. The new preacher is too nosy. But who does he go to the minute I ask him to leave? *You.* Don't think I didn't hear about you two talking last night. Was that your special table at the Super Chief? Yours and Jeff's?"

"Oh, that," Dent said. His mind wobbled with adrenaline. "That was just, well. He had some things to say."

She lowered her head. Cupped her hands against her face. Dent expected them to be filled with tears once she raised up again, but her eyes were as dry and fiery as before. Only now her expression was calmer, more resolved and dangerous.

"I've never suspected Jeff of being completely faithful," she said coolly. "A town like this, you hear things. But with that girl? And in my own house? Even my own bed."

Now her eyes did begin to water, but in rage rather than pity. Dent began to fear for Jeff Burke's safety.

"Help me understand what you're telling me," Dent said. "Because it's likely that I don't."

"You do too! You know about that Lim man breaking out the windshield. You know that Jeff has lied to me about his parents. You know." She stopped. Drew in a deep breath. "You know about those videos."

"Surveillance videos?"

"No!" Crystal hissed. "The ones Lucas found. The ones that girl sent to Jeff."

"You're talking about Maya Jordan?"

Crystal's head snapped up. "Did he tell you?"

"No. Lucas mentioned pictures. I didn't know about any videos."

She squeezed her fists together in front of her, digging her long nails into her palms. "How could he!"

"I can't say," Dent said. He lowered his head. "You talk to him yet?"

"No. I'm not even sure where he is."

"He told me he was at a hotel."

"He was," Crystal snorted. "I tried to find him this morning, just so the girls could see their daddy for a few minutes. But he'd already checked out. I have no idea where. Dale's Auto Glass called the house and said his truck wouldn't be ready until Monday, so he must still be in town."

"Could he have rented a vehicle?"

"No place around here to rent one, unless he got a ride to Portales. And he doesn't have as many friends as he'd like you to think."

"I'm sure he'll turn up."

"That's what they say about Maya." She pulled her arms in close. "I'm worried for her, Brother Denton. Between you and me, I mean. Jeff has a temper. I'm sure it'll all be fine. After all, he's never hurt me—not really. A bruise or two."

"I believe that counts as hurting you."

"I don't know." She reached into her purse. Pulled out a flash drive. "These are the surveillance videos. The Sheriff asked me to bring them in for evidence."

"I suppose I should get out of your way then."

She shook her head, the wind tossing her long hair into her face. She brushed it back. Handed the drive to him. "You take it."

"I shouldn't."

"Maybe not," she said. "Maybe I shouldn't try to put you in this position, either. But I can't help but hold you responsible, Brother Denton, at least in part. So you can take these videos and give them to the Sheriff, or maybe just shove them up your holy ass. I don't care which, really. I just don't want to have to think about it any more." She looked around, as though noticing how exposed their setting was for the first time. She checked on Paige and Kaylee, who squatted together over the sidewalk, watching a stream of ants working the half-eaten remains of a candy bar. "Do you think anyone heard us talking?" Crystal asked.

"Probably not over this wind."

"But they saw us."

"I would bet someone did."

She wiped her eyes. Looked down at her pregnant belly. "I won't ask you to lie, Brother Denton. But could you not tell the whole truth if anyone asks you what we were talking about?"

"Of course."

Crystal nodded once, as near to a thank-you as she could muster. She collected her children and held their hands and strode back toward the burgundy SUV. He looked down at the tiny rectangle in his hand. Depending on what she'd included from her surveillance video, both her husband and Lucas Lim could be incriminated, albeit for different crimes. But at the cost of how many ruined lives? The word *justice* floated through Dent's head, but found nowhere to land. He put the drive in his pocket as Crystal pulled even with him. She rolled down her window.

"You need to find that girl."

CHAPTER 29:
NOTES IN SEARCH
OF CONTEXT

Sid was jamming out on his electric guitar—this time without his headphones—when Ashley arrived for her Friday morning shift at the music store. Late again—eighteen minutes, by the clock that hung on the far wall between posters of Bob Dylan and Rich Robinson, and this time no excuse. Her mind was simply elsewhere, or maybe several places, scattered through the peaks and plains between Lubbock and Ft. Collins, too far away to get her body to work on time. She pushed the door gently so not to jingle the bells that hung from the handle. Took her place behind the counter. Prepared to be fired.

The lead line stopped mid-phrase. Sid muted the amp. Turned around. "Why do you do that?" he asked as the door closed behind her.

"Do what?"

"Sneak in."

"I don't."

"You do it all the time."

She wanted to argue but couldn't find the will. Instead she shrugged. He stepped back once again and sat down on top of his amp.

"Is it that guy?" he asked.

"What guy?"

"The one you said you were dating. Luke, was it? Or maybe Connor? Whatever his name is, you just say the word and I'll kick his ass." He sat up straight and flexed his scrawny arms. "I'm what you call wiry," he said. "Deceptively strong for a man my age."

"It's no big deal. Just—I don't know, stuff."

"Ah, stuff," he said knowingly. "I feel you. Want to hear something cool?"

"I don't know. I was really late for work. I wouldn't blame you if—."

"Yeah," Sid interrupted. "But listen to this." He turned on a loop from his pedal board and set to work riffing over a blues progression. After only a couple of phrases, he landed on a note that grated against her ears. A few beats later, however, he hit it again, and then again. By the third time, it somehow seemed to work against the backdrop of the loop. Sid muted everything and smiled. "Something I figured out about improvisation. If you hit a note outside the scale you're working with, sometimes you need to go back and hit it again. Makes it seem intentional. What you're doing is creating context. Doesn't mean it belongs in the scale, and you can't lean on it too hard. But you turn a mistake into a part of the musical canvas. So to speak."

Ashley smiled despite herself. "That's pretty philosophical."

"It's what we artistic types do. You scientists wouldn't understand."

"You'd be surprised."

"Always am. Which reminds me. I have a surprise for you." He stepped behind the counter and emerged with a rectangular package, wrapped in a brown paper sack. "Happy birthday," he said.

"It's not my birthday."

"Well then happy whenever-your-birthday-was. Open it."

She picked at the tape with what fingernails she had, finally managing to get one corner started. But she knew what was inside even before she tore into it. It was a green journal, the one from her list of things she wanted. For weeks, she had glanced at it on the bottom shelf of the magazine rack. Beneath the glossy covers of tattooed musicians and painted gear, Sid kept a more literary shelf—novels and classics and a few blank journals for the more introspective customers. They were entirely out of place amid the drumheads and guitar strings, but they somehow fit with Sid's persona.

"Lately you've looked like you could use it," he said. "You don't have to tell me what's going on. It just sometimes helps me to write things down, you know?"

"No," she said. "Actually yes." She laid the journal down on the counter. "I don't think I should."

"Shouldn't write things down?"

"Maybe not." She looked up at his face, focused on the cleft below his nose. Took in a deep breath. "I'm sorry I've been such a lousy employee. You can fire me if you want. That would be okay."

"Not a chance," Sid said. "I've never had someone stick with me at the shop for as long as you have. What's it been, two years? You're just going through a rough stretch, that's all. I get it."

"You don't even know what 'it' is."

"I know enough to tell that you're not yourself. Listen." He moved a step closer, and for a moment she feared he would hug her. But he reached past her. Pulled a tissue from the box next to the cash register. "Shit," he mumbled.

Ashley released her stare and looked over his face. He was crying. Sweat began to flow from her armpits.

"Sorry," he said. "I get this way when it's people I care about, all right? I'm just usually better at hiding it." He blew his nose. Stuffed the tissue in his hip pocket. "Okay, truth is that Shayla is getting pissed that I'm closing every night lately. So I do need the help. But she'd kill me if I fired you because you were in some kind of trouble."

"It's not trouble," Ashley said.

"Then whatever it is. Get through it and we'll pick back up, all right? I can manage a little while longer."

"Thank you," she said. He reached for another tissue, and she paused, her head full of memories. Every mistake she'd ever made. "Hey, Sid?"

"Yo?"

"That thing about wrong notes."

"Ah!" he held up a finger. "But there are no wrong notes. Just notes in search of context." He picked up the journal. Placed it back in her hand. "Take the weekend off," he said. "Go do your thing."

She still had not opened the journal when she arrived back at her apartment in mid afternoon, tired from hours of walking around campus. Her stomach growled as she turned the key, and she thought at first that might account for the strange sound she heard as the latch gave way. But the swing of the door sounded hollow, the creak of the hinges more sustained than usual.

"Hello?"

She let her eyes adjust, walked over and pulled the blinds. Her tent was still erected in the middle of the worn gray carpet, but the rest of the furniture was gone.

She stepped into the bedroom, also barren except for a bedframe leaned up against one corner. She pulled out her phone and typed.

Things that are sadder than an empty room.

She could think of plenty of things to put on the list, mostly dealing with pestilence and war and animal cruelty. But those greater sorrows were nonetheless further away than the emptiness she now inhabited, and wallowing in tragedy would not make her feel a bit better about her best friend and boyfriend running off together. She deleted the title and closed the app and looked around at the bare walls, painted a dark gray and scarred by furniture lines and nail holes. She had lived a brief but irretrievable portion of her life in this space—a season of coping, she supposed. She had found warmth and comfort, but from an indiscriminate source, one that could not sustain her. Another mistake to live down. She cleared her throat. The sound echoed into the corners and came back to her sharpened.

She spent more than an hour cleaning the apartment, empty though it was. Since Connor's furniture was better on every score than the dilapidated bedroom set Ashley had put in storage, they had used his couch and bed and dresser and nightstands. Now all that remained were tiny circles indented in the carpet, pressure points that marked each room's former layout. She wiped down the walls and vacuumed and scrubbed the baseboard until she was satisfied that Connor's presence had been physically erased. Like witness protection. No one was ever here.

The light was growing dim when she remembered she was hungry. She pulled a box of noodles from the pantry and set water on the stove to boil in her lone remaining pot. She ran numbers in her head. If she wanted to make it without a roommate—and the thought of sharing living space with another human being currently made her want to vomit—she would need more income. Irene would give it if she asked, but after all that had happened, did she have a right to ask? No, she decided. Her best option was to ask Sid for more hours, maybe pick up some time as a tutor if he couldn't afford it. It was like everything else in life. It could be done. She just had to do it.

She crossed to the tent and ran her finger along the seam. This time she noticed something she hadn't before—a cream-colored note pinned to the flap with her name written across the front in Jen's swirly handwriting, complete with three perfect stars drawn beneath her name. Her explanation, perhaps, or defense. Maybe her mea culpa. Ashley slid her finger beneath the unsealed flap and raised it up, revealing a triangle-shaped portion of the same loopy script. "...no way...understand...never intended..."

Water boiled over the side of the saucepan, splashed and sizzled on the burner. Ashley strode into the kitchen and lifted the pot. Turned down the heat and counted to ten. When she replaced it, the water instantly began to simmer. She pulled the card from the envelope without reading it. Dropped it into the water. Watched the ink dissolve.

CHAPTER 30:
NO SAY IN SETTING UP
THE RULES

"Turn left," Rachel said.

Dent heard her voice, but the command didn't register, divided as his mind was. Finding Maya Jordan was the mission—of course it was! But Rachel's presence crowded his thoughts and thrilled him, even as they bounced along the back roads of Lamb County in search of the runaway. Dent tried not to feel happy, or at least to feel less happy than he was worried.

"Left!" she called. She thrust her arm across the cab to point.

This time he lifted his foot off from the accelerator, tried to apply gentle pressure to the brake. But the intersection was already upon them, and his foot came down harder than he intended. Their seatbelts locked across their collarbones. Rachel flung her hands forward against the dash, but the centrifugal force threw them off to the right, pinning her against the passenger side door. The pickup fishtailed, enough that Dent feared he might lose control. But it righted itself after a few feet and Rachel cleared her throat.

"Sorry," he said.

"Well."

He glanced down again at the flash drive, which rattled in the cup holder between the seats. Dent did not ask what Rachel had seen when she had scanned through Crystal's video files back at her apartment, and she did not offer.

"About two more miles and you'll turn back east. Be watching for it."

"Yes ma'am."

Dent slowed too soon this time and had to press the gas again to keep from rolling to a stop before the intersection. But he made the turn without flinging his passenger all over the cab of the pickup, which he counted as a win. His tires hit gravel, and he backed off the accelerator. Rachel pointed to an orange-tinted trailer home with a dilapidated jeep parked at an angle in the yard. He pulled to a stop along the road. The wind caught the dust from their tires, sending a cloud billowing toward the trailer. Maya Jordan's mother, Jess Turrell, sat on the concrete steps outside, smoking a cigarette. Her yellowed skin seemed to drape directly over the bones, without any intermediate layers of fat or muscle to give her shape. She neither winced nor blinked as the dust cloud passed across her and dissipated over the curved roof of the trailer.

"He ain't here," Jess called over the wind.

Dent and Rachel exchanged glances. "Who's that?" Rachel asked.

"Whoever you're looking for."

Dent followed Rachel to the base of the steps. Jess looked up at them, shielding her eyes from the wind and dust.

"We need to speak to Maya," Rachel said. "Are you sure she isn't home?"

Dent followed Rachel's gaze to the window to the left of the front door. The blinds were drawn, their bottom edges bunched unevenly and still shivering from hasty deployment.

"No business of yours if she is," Jess said. She shifted, looked to her left down the road. "She in trouble?"

"Not with us," Dent said.

"With who then?"

"I can't say."

"Then I can't neither." She looked back at them, her eyes deep-set and weary.

"Maya?" Rachel called. She stepped over on the packed earth until she was beneath the window. "Honey, we can help, okay? Maya!"

"I told you she ain't here," Jess said.

"I saw someone in the window," Rachel snapped.

"That ain't your business."

"Has she been home at all? Since Wednesday night. Have you seen her?"

"Not that I know of."

"That you know of?"

Jess blew air through her nose. Looked down the road again.

"Okay," Rachel said. She rubbed her hands together. "Think for me. If she was in trouble, where would she go?"

"Wherever she's gone to."

Rachel threw up her arms. Dent stepped forward.

"Was anyone with her?" he asked. "Anyone who might have been forcing her against her will?"

Jess grunted. "She ain't been kidnapped. Don't no one want her."

"I think someone does," Rachel said sharply. "Jess, your daughter may be in danger. We're trying to help."

"Can't be helped," Jess said. "She's old enough to make her way. I can't be responsible for her."

"So you just let her go?" Rachel pleaded. She turned up her palms. "Just abandon her?"

"Don't preach at me," Jess snapped. "I didn't choose how the world works. I didn't get no say in setting up the rules."

Rachel drew a sharp breath, preparing to let loose a torrent of rebuke. Jess bowed up her shoulders. For a split second Dent thought they might physically fight. He stepped between the two women, pulled out a card and slipped it under the cat bowl Jess was using as an ashtray. "Call me if you hear from her."

They pushed their way through the dust cloud and back to Dent's truck, climbed inside and closed the door. The pickup swayed with the wind.

"She ran away," Dent said. "That's all."

"Oh good!" Rachel said. "And here I was worrying."

"I didn't mean it like that."

She picked up the flash drive. Twirled it in her fingers. Glared at Jess, who was still smoking on the steps, staring down the road as if Dent's truck were not parked right in front of her home.

"Jess dropped her off at Burke's house," she said at last. "You could see it in the surveillance video from the outside camera. She pulled into the driveway and waited. Maya got out of the car and went inside, but Burke walked right past her and up to the car window to talk with Jess."

"Well," Dent said, and tried without success to come to a different conclusion than the one lodged in his brain. "You think they have some sort of arrangement? Like Jeff is paying Jess for—."

He did not finish the sentence, and in the silence that followed he felt foolish for even making the suggestion. But at last Rachel nodded. Closed her eyes. Leaned her head back against the window. "You must think I'm naïve."

"No," Dent said. "Not at all. It's a terrible situation."

"I'm not," she said. "Not naïve. I know things happen, all right? I've seen plenty working with Dad. But this?" She leaned forward again. Set her gaze back on Jess.

"It's the drugs, I'm sure. She's trapped by them."

"Then so is Maya."

Dent nodded, acknowledging her without altogether agreeing. He studied her face. Feared she might get back out and confront Jess again. He started the pickup. Eased forward. Rachel let out a long, heavy sigh.

"What?" Dent asked.

She brought both hands up to her face. Split her index and middle fingers so she could see out. Gave a quick shake of her head, as if shedding some thought. "Nothing."

"No. That sigh meant something, and you should know that I'm way off balance because of—well, all of it together. The least you could do—."

She raised a hand to silence him. "I shouldn't have brought it up." She dropped the flash drive back in the cup holder. "You're not the only one sorting things out, okay?"

He drove on, listening to the roar of his tires over gravel. She did not speak. "I guess I don't know what to say to that," he finally said.

"Well," was all she said. When he glanced across, though, he could see her smiling. "Well."

CHAPTER 31:
THE ROUNDUP

Lucas stood on the other side of the room, arms crossed, tapping his front teeth with a fingernail as he looked Dent up and down. Dent turned to the mirror. Saw the same body in the same suit he'd been examining for going on half an hour.

"Just tell me the truth," Dent said, annoyed.

"Really, darling," Lucas said in some indefinable accent. "I can only do so much with the raw materials you give me." Dent threw up his hands. Lucas slide-stepped to block the door. He spoke again, his voice once again Texan. "The truth is that you look fine. Better than you have at any time since I've known you. I don't know why you're so paranoid all of a sudden."

"Long story," Dent grumbled. "And it's a big night. You sure you don't want to go?"

Lucas swung his head side to side. "Judge Gleason said to stay in town but out of sight. The Roundup is not exactly low profile."

"No."

Weariness pressed in on Dent. Rachel was helping Emilia with the catering tonight, and although part of him was relieved not to have that pressure of a companion at Last Man Club's signature event, the bigger part of him dreaded going through the evening alone—smiling and shaking hands and pretending all was right with the world, all the while wondering what had become of Maya Jordan and Crystal Burke and Ashley Hyatt.

"Relax," Lucas said. "Parties are supposed to be fun."

A new storm system rushed into town that evening, driven across the Prairie by the north wind that had sandblasted Jess Turrell's trailer. But these were not the dreary, lazy clouds that had piddled on Dent and the Sheriff outside the U-Stor-It. These were low and dark and threatening, portents of a storm Lubbock stations were calling the Ice-pocalypse. Dent pulled his good overcoat up around his throat. Hoped Maya was someplace warm.

Bad weather did nothing to deter the grizzled citizens of Lamb County from their Tall Tale Roundup, however. The doors had been open for fifteen minutes when Dent arrived at Heinmann Theater, and yet the line still stretched fifty feet out the front door. He slipped toward the end of the line, praying for anonymity. A voice to his right shattered that hope.

"There he is. Hey, Brother Denton!"

Dent composed a good-ol'-boy smile and turned to see the usual suspects huddled on the sidewalk beneath a poster for an upcoming dystopian blockbuster. Jack Schoendienst had been the one to call to him, although the rest—Joe Dick Schieble, Lonnie Chambers, et al—were no doubt party to the hijacking. Dent joined them, casting a wary eye from one old man to another. He was surprised to find no sign of farmer bullshit or practical joking on their faces. They were genuinely worried, which genuinely worried Dent.

Jack put his arm around Dent. "You hear about Jeff Burke?" he asked.

"Not a thing," Dent said, but his voice was unconvincing even to his own ears. "What's going on?"

"He and Crystal had a knock-down, drag-out fight," Joe Dick said. "Lonnie here is their substitute mail carrier. He saw it happen."

Lonnie nodded. Offered nothing more.

Dent breathed in through his nose, out through his mouth. Tried to look grave rather than petrified. "Any idea what it was about?"

"Most likely another woman," Jack said. "He's the school superintendent, you know. All those cute young teachers about. I don't know if you've had a gander at Mrs. Pender down in first grade, but I'd learn my ABCs quick, if it meant—."

"The bigger problem," Joe Dick interrupted, "is that Burke was our emcee for the Roundup. So folks are getting ready to sit down for their dinner as we speak, and we're up a creek. If only we had someone used to public speaking."

"No," Dent said, already backing away. Jack caught him by the arm.

"Just hear us out," he said. "This is a crisis, Preacher."

"It's worse than you think," Joe Dick said. "Tell him, Lonnie."

Lonnie laced his fingers together. Let his hands dangle in front of him. "Old Mother Earth has transformed from wildcard to certain vexation," he said. "She has been talking all over town about what tale she intends to tell, but her story is awash in inconsistency."

"I heard she was going to confess to killing a man back in the '40s," Jack said. "She told Mauri Beth that she was going to tell about growing up with so many sisters in the Dust Bowl. Joe Dick here said he heard something about her being a local spy for the Nixon camp in that '72 election."

"I admit that's far fetched," Joe Dick said.

"Of course our worst fear," Lonnie said, "is that she'll serve up a heretofore unspoken morsel regarding her ex-husband."

The four men stood silently, considering the possibility. Secrets, once spoken aloud, lingered for generations. Dent was just about to excuse himself—what could they reasonably expect from him, after all—when Jack put his arm around his shoulders and ushered him to the side.

"Do we Methodists believe in fate?" Jack asked.

"That's more Presbyterian."

"Okay, then maybe something more sanctified. Providence?"

"What's your point, Jack?"

"You came here at just the right time," Jack said. "When Irene shot at that boy, you were right there to handle the story. And then when Lucas needed a place to stay, you were the one to step up. You and Rachel did the Hallelujah Halloween by yourselves once Annette went down, and yet Rob tells me that no one has put in more volunteer hours renovating the theater this week than you have. It's like all these crises sprang up at once, just as you rolled into town. Now I think there might be a reason for that."

Dent looked at the old man. Searched his face for any hint of duplicity. His aged eyes were as sincere as a newborn's.

"That's kind of you," Dent said. "As for tonight, though—."

"Good!" Jack clapped him on the shoulder. "I knew you'd come through for us. Let's head backstage and get a mike on you. Rob has one of these doohickeys that hangs over your ear. Makes you look like Miley Cyrus."

He kept talking as he moved away. Dent almost didn't follow, almost asserted his right not to get suckered into every blessed job that no one else wanted. He didn't believe in fate. Didn't want to think that every whistle and mouse fart was predetermined by a God who was at best inflexible and at worst cruel. But if the Almighty wanted Dent to make good and free choices, the least He could do is expand the options on the menu.

He lowered his head. Soldiered on behind Jack.

Rob wired him up and tucked the mike down inside his collar for safekeeping during the meal. Dent's nerves were such that he wouldn't have eaten at all, had the hostess not insisted he sit alone at the table nearest the podium. Every time the door to the improvised catering kitchen opened, he was in full view of both Rachel and Emilia, neither of whose vigilance he trusted to wane. He skewered a new potato with his fork, waited until he was sure they were looking before thrusting it into his mouth. Then he stabbed another and held it in midair as he looked over the program for the night. He had settled on Matthew's parables as an opener, how no one ever learned anything from Jesus that didn't come in story form. Trite, perhaps, but appropriate. Low-hanging fruit was all he had time to harvest.

A ripple of applause began at the back of the room and washed forward. By the time Dent laid his napkin on the table, people were standing and blocking his view. It took several seconds for him to understand that Old Mother Earth had finally arrived. The crowd parted, and she shuffled through them without a walker or even a cane. Mauri Beth escorted her at the elbow, hands ready to grab the old woman should she stumble. Just in front of them, Dent could see a tail wagging back and forth. Henry Fifty-one greeted Dent with a single nuzzle of his snout before crawling beneath the table and settling in for the evening.

Irene came round to the chair next to Dent, turned to the crowd and waved once. She spoke to Dent loudly enough for half the room to hear. "What do they want me to do, strip naked and boogie dance?"

"Irene!" Mauri Beth scolded. But the applause faded, and the crowd returned to their dinners. The two women took their seats. The wait staff brought them plates.

"No thanks," Irene said. "As many spices as you got on that chicken, it would run through me like a mess of jackrabbits."

Mauri Beth groaned. Reached her hand in front of her. Moved it in a straight horizontal line, left to right. A second later, Dent remembered what she was doing. The curtain of calm. These days, the idea didn't seem so crazy.

He scanned the program once more as dessert made its way through the audience. Rob signaled to him from the sound booth. Five minutes until showtime, which would begin with a prayer for the meal. He tapped his pocket to reassure himself that the folded Prayer of St. Francis was still there, ready to be his salvation. Then he began running through the acts, making sure he knew how to pronounce each name. He was arguing with himself over *Arampatzis* when he heard a gasp from across the table. Mauri Beth stared open-mouthed at the stage, her curtain obviously in tatters. Dent turned to follow her gaze.

Irene Ostendorf stepped from the top of Rob's ramp onto the flat part of the stage, her hand resting lightly on the guardrail. She patted it once, as if admiring his workmanship, and shuffled toward the podium. Dent scooted his chair back, but the old woman moved faster than he'd anticipated. Before he could even stand, she grabbed the podium and adjusted the microphone and, while the audience leaned forward in wonder, began her tale.

CHAPTER 32:
THE PAIN OF ALMOST

Spring of 1937 doesn't come in like a lion or out like a lamb. It arrives like a street fighter, barreling through with a flurry of punches. The dusters beat against the Plains in all seasons, through cold and heat, like violent men in desperate households. Just before Easter, the air feels like August, with scorching sunlight descending from the sky and bouncing up from the barren soil, swallowing all.

Irene has quarreled with her mother and stormed out into the doomed landscape, where the wind is blowing in earnest. After only a few steps, she can no longer hear her name being called, and she wants to look back to see if her mother still watches her or if her mother's husband, Mr. Randall, is chasing after her. But she locks her gaze forward, remembering Lot's wife, a nameless cautionary tale, petrified and disintegrating. She, on the other hand, has a name—Irene—and she will not look back.

Except when she does.

As soon as she reaches the sunlight, sweat pours out of her body. But it is an open-air misery, still better than the close-in spaces of both her mother's house and her husband's, and without the hopeless conversations that drone through those dual confinements—marriage and money and a little rain, that's all. A little rain in this land of blowing earth.

She steps across the brown grass and into the bare pasture. Two years now since her father died, and nineteen months since her mother took up with Mr. Randall. His unnatural desires have driven

Irene from the house via the only escape she could imagine. She has married too young, and the wrong man besides.

She thinks of her sisters, what she has abandoned them to. Squeezes her eyes shut, but can't shake what she knows. Randall is following her, even now.

She walks on. Her feet sink into the barren soil, plowed and planted twice now without so much as a bushel of grain to harvest. The dirt closes up around her ankles and slides down into her shoes. She tips one way, then the other. By the time she reaches the road, sweat pools beneath her hair and under her arms and in the small of her back. She looks like misery incarnate, and she prays that she will be alone on the road, without kindly strangers to offer help or hurried drivers to coat her wet body with dust. She drapes her apron over her forearm and quickens her pace. Birds screech overhead, fleeing the storm in droves. Already her shadow is blurred, a halo fanning out from edges of black cast by her head and shoulders. But she harbors no illusions of beatification. She is a sinner living in a godforsaken land, bludgeoned by the air itself, swept to desolation by apocalyptic skies. If the light that spreads out from her shadow signifies any message from on high, it is one of ruin.

The wind kicks up behind her, drying her skin and pushing her along toward the tiny wooden house she shares with Harlan Brantley. She shivers, despite the heat, knowing what awaits her there. Still she pretends that all is well and she is safe and all shall be well.

That she will not turn to salt.

A gust of wind slams against her back, carrying a puff of black dust over her shoulders. She stumbles forward, catches herself as the black blizzard swallows her shadow.

The roar of the wind is such that she does not notice the car until it pulls around her and rumbles to a stop in her path—an old Model A, barely holding together with the help of whatever parts Henry could scrounge or improvise. It is an eyesore and a menace to Irene, and she's never talked to anyone who did not share that opinion. But Henry has built it, and he loves it with the devotion of a new father. He throws the passenger door open and climbs over the gearshift and out onto the road.

"Get in," he calls over the wind.

"I can walk fine," Irene answers. "Ain't but a mile to go yet."

Henry looks from her to the sky behind her and back again.

"You don't have time. Come on."

She says no thanks and tries to pass by him. He stands in her way, grabs her shoulders and spins her around. She bristles at the rough handling, especially from one so tender as Henry. She clamps her eyelids down so she won't have to look, draws breath to give him a piece of her mind. But the air is full of dust already. It cakes on her lips and tongue. She opens her eyes just a slit and at last faces the danger. A cloud like the end of worlds billows toward them.

She scrambles into the seat of the car, holds on as he wheels back toward Irene's mother's house, which is nearer than Brantley's and sturdier besides. As they near the house, she thinks she sees the shape of a man, fighting the wind along the road.

"Did you pass Elzie Randall?" she yells.

Henry does not answer.

She tries again. "I thought he followed me out, maybe. I don't think he could survive out in this."

Henry does not slow. He merely grips the wheel tighter, and she understands. He knows more than she realizes about what goes on in that house. Her face burns crimson.

He drives on through the yard. They slide to a stop by the back door and dive out of the car and into the kitchen, already dark as the cloud envelops the house. Her mother looks up as they come in, staring daggers. She whisks the baby up from the floor and stomps into the back room.

"Here," Irene says, shoving an oil lamp and some matches across the table toward Henry. She hurries off to double check the quilts her mother has hung over the windows, to seal them up best she can. In a few minutes, all five rooms will be full of gritty haze.

Henry stifles a cough. Lights the wick. Watches the light begin to glow. His skin is pale, his breath ragged. She reaches with her left hand for a thin towel beside the basin of clean water. A stabbing pain shoots through her ring finger just above the knuckle. She yanks her hand to her mouth and the towel falls. A large brown scorpion skitters across the counter and through a crack in the wall. She turns to see if Henry has noticed, but he is occupied in the struggle for breath. She retrieves the rag, dips it in water, wrings it out. Hands it to Henry as her finger throbs.

"Thank you," he says.

He wipes his forehead, unfurls the rag. Holds it over his mouth and nose. She wants to tell him to go lie down. But even imagining Henry in what once was her bed stabs Irene with the pain of almost having, and it is too much to think about.

"We can't stay here," he says.

"Well we can't leave," Irene answers. "Not in that storm."

"That's not what I mean." He grows paler. His fingers tremble.

She does not answer. Her mind twists.

"There's work out west," he tells her. "In California, they are building their own island for the World's Fair—dredging it up right out of the Bay. Todd wrote to me about it. Can you imagine?"

Dust cakes in her throat. She has seen little of Henry since the wedding, but the thought of him leaving still slices her inside. And the idea of his beginning a new and better life without her grinds salt into that wound. If he asks, could she go with him? Could she leave Harlan Brantley and her mother and sisters and live in sin and never come back? Never look back?

"When?" she croaks out.

He drops the wet rag, looks at her earnestly. "Whenever you're ready."

Her heart crumbles to dust at his invitation, swirls in the currents of wind that leak through the seams of the house. She is disconnecting, her mind letting loose from her body. She floats up from the kitchen, through the low ceiling and tin roof, through the stinging wind and black clouds until she is above it all, looking down on the storm as it savages the Plains. She pities those trapped below, hunkered down in whatever poor shelters they have while cruelty incarnate rakes across the land. The rain may fall on the just and unjust alike, but it falls in unjust proportions, dropping ash instead of water on those already suffering. She cannot quite make peace with this.

"I can't tell you what to do," Henry says through the rag. "Lord knows."

A faint moan hovers for a moment in the kitchen. She blinks. Meets Henry's eyes.

"Hold on," she says.

She pulls a quilt back from the windowsill just enough to look outside without letting Henry see. A shape twists across her vision. She has seen dust phantoms before, but as the shape ekes closer, she can tell that it does indeed belong to a man—a very large man with rounded shoulders and a fat neck. Randall, the fool, stomping back to give her and Henry the beating they deserve. By the time she recognizes his form, he is no more than three steps from the door. He staggers forward, one hand clasping the guide rope connecting the house to the barn.

"Someone out there?" Henry asks. "It can't be Mr. Randall, can it."

She does not see the hat blow away, but Randall's thick arms shoot upward toward his head, then fly eastward, following the wind. He loses his balance and thrashes. One heavy arm falls across the guide line and yanks down hard. Irene hears the *pop!* as the rope pulls free from its anchor. Randall staggers, disappears from view. She waits.

"Irene?" Henry asks. "Who's out there?"

Another minute passes, and another, and after a time she knows Randall is gone. They will find him suffocated on the ground once the storm passes. His death will make some things easier, some things not.

"I don't see anyone," she finally answers. "It's just the storm." She moves back to the table. Sits down across from Henry, looks into his gentle face. "Will your car make it to Albuquerque?"

He rubs his eyes. "Yes. I believe it will."

"Then go on tomorrow. Catch the train to San Francisco. Don't wait on me."

"I'll wait. You're a part of this."

She lifts her stung finger to her mouth and feels the heat in its flesh, which has swollen up and over the edge of her wedding band. She drops her hands into her lap and tugs, but the ring will not budge. In the next room, she can hear her sister Wilma, whimpering between coughs. The girl has not forgiven Irene for getting married and moving out. She never will forgive.

"You go on," Irene says. "The kids are going to need me. Mama's in no shape to handle all that needs handling."

"Well how long then?"

"I don't know. A while." She reaches across to touch his face, but her hand veers away at the last moment. She takes the wet rag instead. Rinses it and returns it to him. "I got to make sure this time before I go. I shouldn't have left them all when I did. I should have—."

He waits for her to say it. *I should have married you.* They both know the future they want. Only she cannot yet figure how to untangle herself enough to cross that bridge.

She does not say it. Henry spreads the cloth over his face so she won't be able to see his disappointment.

"It's okay," he says.

She nods, even manages a smile. But she doesn't tell him what she is feeling. Hope has blown away with the wind, but even now all may not be lost. She will find a way out west. They will have another chance. Surely this will not be the end of possibility for them. Surely they will not have a lifetime to regret this one choice, when all might have been different.

No, they won't.

They will have another moment, one more decision on which their futures hinge.

That is the one Irene will take to her grave.

CHAPTER 33:
FACT IS YOU'RE STUCK

Ashley peered through the darkening gray at the hazy yellow light on the horizon, still five miles or more away and showing no haste. The last bit of warmth from the heater had seeped out the leaky car doors and into the damp November evening, carried away by the early winter storm as it bore down on the High Plains. She worked her knees around the steering wheel and pulled them up into the seat so that her whole body, save her head, was tucked under her old winter coat.

Survival items I should keep on hand:

1) An extra blanket
2) Energy bars
3) Bottled water
4) Toilet paper
5) Battery-powered phone charger

Already, the temperatures had fallen. The rain shifted to sleet and snow. The dead wiper blades dripped ice. If the tow truck did not hurry, the storm would cut off her line of retreat, making it impossible not to go to Earth to see her dying aunt and endure her mother's scolding. And—she could almost admit it—face up to Lucas.

The distant light floated on toward her, ghostly silent.

The belt on her car had snapped almost an hour ago, stranding her a hundred yards into Texas but still thirty miles away from Dalhart and three hours from Irene's ranch. With nothing but endless prairie and the rattle of sleet to distract her, Ashley had plenty of time to regret every horror movie she'd ever watched. Plenty of space to watch her doom approaching. Plenty of silence in which to hear the voice of a God she did not acknowledge, speaking her just condemnation.

Merciful God, we confess that we have sinned against you in thought, word and deed, by what we have done, and by what have left undone.

She stopped there, even though she remembered more. Her church's communion service, recited time and again when she was a child, when her mother would drag her to church. Had Ashley ever really believed? She didn't think so. At least, she'd never had the heart-strangely-warmed, washed-in-the-blood moment that everybody else in Texas seemed to have. But she did enjoy communion, the spiritual made tactile, the mess of life given shape by liturgy. The congregation silent, their natural hierarchies flattened in penitence before God. It was, she had to admit, a pretty dream.

Stop it, she told herself.

Maybe the reunion wouldn't be as awkward as she feared. She and Lucas had been texting back and forth for nearly two days now, ever since her conversation with Lyssa in the Union. Nothing serious, of course. Lucas told her about his impression of Earth, the people and places of her childhood. She caught him up on classes and work. But even those banalities were filtered through the satellites, digitized and sanitized and softened by emoticons. He knew more than she told him, and quite possibly knew everything—the affair with Burke, the breakup with Connor, the lies Jen told. In fact, she assumed Lucas knew these things. In that was freedom, but also terror. She had been naked with him before, sure, and that had felt safe and honest. But now? Having his eyes on her would be like turning a floodlight onto her bare skin, lighting every dark and ugly crevice and leaving nowhere to hide. The thought both thrilled and mortified her.

Her text icon appeared. Lucas. *Tell me you aren't still coming to Earth.*

I have to, she answered. *Irene.*

Her mother had related the sad tale via a video call, between sobs and sips of wine and pulls on her imaginary curtain. Something had happened after Irene told her story at the Roundup—some lesion or rupture or blood clot in her brain, some breakdown in physiology that caused her to crumple on stage in front of God and everybody. Doc and Rachel had stabilized her enough to get her back to their clinic, but it was only a matter of time. Mauri Beth was too distraught to process the collapse, but Ashley figured it to be the result of elevated blood pressure, hammering one too many times against the old woman's aged vessel walls. Leave it to Irene to die from public speaking.

The headlights drew close enough that she could hear the slushy whir of tires on pavement, the faint whine of an engine. A late model SUV materialized, all chrome and shine despite the gritty road. It slowed as the driver noticed Ashley's helpless vehicle. She slid down beneath the coat and, she hoped, out of sight. The SUV traveled on.

Another message from Lucas. *You sure it's a good idea to travel in this storm? I know you love your aunt, but it's not worth dying.*

She rolled her eyes. He should know better than to talk like her mother. She dropped the phone into her lap. Decided to wait him out. Three minutes later, it buzzed against her thigh.

Sorry. Didn't mean to preach. Just want to make sure you're okay.

She tapped the side of the phone with her index finger.

I'm actually stuck, she finally typed. *Belt snapped. Getting towed to Dalhart now.*

Another light, just visible on the horizon. It took forever and a day to finally reach her, but at last the outline of a pickup emerged, made a U-turn to face south. It swung around and backed up to within six feet of her bumper. A wiry man hopped out and reached into the bed. He pulled out a set of battery-powered flashers, trudged into the wind toward the back of the car. As he passed, Ashley could see a tattoo, the fiery head of a bird shooting out from beneath the sleeve of his hoodie. She tensed. He dropped the blinkers onto her car with a magnetic *thunk*. She took in a deep breath. Slipped her feet back into her boots and stepped out onto the blacktop. His face lit up with recognition.

"Raptor girl! That is you, right? The dinosaur tattoo? Oh shit. Tell me I didn't screw that up."

"No," she said. "That's me."

"If you'd let me fix those belts that day in Dalhart—sorry. Never mind. Me being smug isn't going to get you off the road. I'm Carl."

"I remember," she said. "I thought I had a tow truck coming."

"You should, but you don't."

"Listen, I don't want to sound ungrateful—."

"No worries," Carl said. He dropped to his knees in front of the car and looped the chain over the frame. "Wayne just sent the tow rig—I mean like a second before you called—out to handle a wreck down in Channing. I told him I'd come get you and pull you in. It'll be slow going, but we'll still get there ahead of that wrecker. I guess you're stopping in Dalhart tonight?"

"No," she answered quickly.

"Never mind! Creepy question, I get it. I just don't realize these things until they come out of my mouth, you know? The storm's really getting bad, though. And Shallowater was in town tonight for the football game. It's going to be hard to find a place to stay."

"I won't need it."

"You sure? I do some maintenance work for a couple of the motels. I could probably get you a—no, never mind. You're right. Creepy. You ever drive with a tow chain before?"

She shook her head.

"The thing to remember is that you got nothing pulling you forward but me, and you got nothing stopping you but you. You don't have hydraulics without the motor running, so you're going to have to use some muscle on the wheel and pedal. Don't hit your brakes until you see my brake lights. Punch it as soon as you do or else you're going to run up under my bumper. You ain't going to hurt my truck, but it'll beat the hell out of your hood if you let it get away. You understand?"

Ashley nodded. She'd already worked through the physics of the tow while he was securing the chain, but she saw no need to let Carl know he'd insulted her intelligence. If he was not what he seemed, it would be to her advantage if he underestimated her.

"All right," Carl said. "Let's go."

She slipped into her car and, once Carl was back in his pickup, locked the doors. He eased back onto the road. The chain jingled and stretched. Just in time, she remembered to put the transmission in neutral. The two vehicles rolled forward, slowly gaining speed until they leveled off at 35 mph.

She stared out the window, watched the miles tick away, slowly enough to count fenceposts and spot hawks on top of speed limit signs. The storm battered the empty land, left a shine on the blacktop. Her phone buzzed.

You have a room reserved at the Dalhart LampLight under your name. Just in case.

I won't use it.

It's reserved anyway. Do what you want.

I will.

I know. ☺ *Maybe I'll join you. The pastor said I could borrow his jeep. It's four-wheel drive.*

She felt her face go hot, beads of sweat popping out despite the cold. Was she ready to see him? And in a hotel room, of all places? Maybe not, but then again maybe. He would be warm and stable, and he would understand that she was already mourning Irene. Besides, he would be too much of a gentleman to try to take her to bed on this first encounter.

Still.

In the rearview mirror, the round yellow lights flashed back and forth, a set of winking mouse ears. She watched the taillights of the pickup, tried not to let her mind wander. It did anyway, of course, along every kind of regrettable trail. Carl could be taking her anywhere. At this speed, she could not jump out. Even if she could, where would she go? Down an empty road until he caught up with her? Across the plains to take her chances with the cold and wind and snow? She opened her list app. Deleted *toilet paper* and inserted *handgun.*

That was when the loneliness of her situation finally seized her. Who could she call, though? Who could she trust to break through her isolation? Not Connor or Jen, not anymore. Certainly not Jeff Burke, who with a little luck she would never see again. Her mother would flip out if she knew about Carl, and besides was occupied with Irene's last hours. Sid would call the cops. She had only one real option, and was surprised to find herself okay with the risk. She opened up her texting app to reply to Lucas.

You can come. Just be careful. The weath—

The app closed without permission. Ashley frowned at the screen. A half second later, it went dark, leaving only a tiny swirling circle in the middle to indicate that no more could be drained from the poor depleted battery. It blinked once, mimicking the ancient television set Irene used before everything went digital, and with a final flash, faded to black.

Ashley tossed it onto the passenger side floorboard, more in resignation than disgust. Control was leaking through her hands, spilling out into an irretrievable puddle. With no engine running and nothing to distract her, she felt the silence pumping in through every seam. How many miles still to go? At least twenty-five. At their current speed, she had about forty-five minutes left in the car, and that only if Carl's intentions were noble. But how to know anyone's intentions, least of all her own?

She fixed her eyes on the taillights in front of her. Reached behind the seat for her backpack and pulled out the journal Sid had given her. Held the wheel with her knees and thumbed the empty pages.

They pulled off the main road a mile north of town. Two right turns later she could see the sign for Dalhart Auto. She let out a long breath she hadn't realized she'd been holding. Carl pulled onto the concrete slab in front of the auto bay. He motioned for her to follow him inside, through a door covered in credit card logos and warnings about managers not having access to the safe. She carried in the journal and a pen she'd snagged from her backpack, thanked him and nestled into a spongy vinyl chair in the corner of the waiting room to write.

Two hours later, she'd filled the first 29 pages of the journal. The floor was crusty with wet sand and marked by the boot prints of farmers, and the three light bulbs in the ceiling were covered with wire cages. The whole room smelled like orange degreaser. Ashley logged these things on her pages, reported the sights and sounds and smells with the diligence of a social scientist, from the Dr. Pepper clock on the wall to the rusting legs of the furniture to the granules of pumice that rimmed the slow-draining sink.

She wasn't sure how long she'd been scribbling before she noticed that she had transitioned from setting to narrative. She sat upright. Cocked her head and flipped back a few pages. Without so much as an asterisk, she had moved from describing the 2007 Dalhart Wolves football calendar that still hung beneath the television to a summary of her breakup with Connor, complete with a verbatim of the conversation she'd overheard between him and Jen. After that she had written about her parents' divorce and her estrangement from her father. Then about Irene's collapse, as relayed to her by her mother, and a collage of camping memories from last summer, when she and Lucas were still on track for happily ever after.

Her pen had stopped there. Hovered over the page for five minutes or more. She knew what came next, what story she had to write. But how to tell it? She had tried before, if only once. Before the apartment fire, when she worked at the Super Chief, she had unloaded most of her cares one day on Emilia de los Santos—not the whole, bald-faced story of course. But enough for her boss to connect the dots. Emilia had narrowed her eyes and ground her teeth, but little more. Ashley had expected something different, some guidance in interpreting her affair with Burke. Was she a victim? Maybe. But she had made choices too. If she was part victim, she was also part sinner, only without a God to either cleanse her or take responsibility for his shitty, everything-happens-for-a-reason way of doing things. Even with Emilia's patient listening, Ashley could not make sense of it. All she had was this history. This fucked up story to carry. A note outside the scale, grating and dissonant, which still lacked context.

"Ma'am?" Carl said. His volume indicated he'd been trying to get her attention for some time.

"Yeah," Ashley said. She slapped the journal closed. Rolled her shoulders and tried to focus. "Sorry. All set?"

"I wish I could say I had better news. But you ain't going nowhere tonight." He pulled a chair from the only other table in the room. Straddled it and leaned his tattooed forearms on top of the backrest. "We got the old belt off, but it turns out we don't have the right one to replace it. I tried—well, doesn't matter what I tried. Fact is that you're stuck, and I'm truly sorry about that."

"No worries," Ashley said. "My—someone I know already reserved a room for me. I should be all set."

"Well, then," Carl said. "Which hotel is it? I can give you a ride, is what I mean. Got the studded tires on my pickup this afternoon."

"It's a couple of blocks over. I can walk."

"You can, but it's slicker than greased goose shit out there. You'll slip all over the place."

"I'll be fine. I just need to get a few things out of the car."

"You'll be miserable."

"I'll deal with it."

Carl smiled. Bobbed his head up and down. "I was right about you."

"Excuse me?"

He leaned forward. "Can I tell you a secret? I don't get paid to work here at Wayne's. It's all volunteer, which Wayne doesn't always like, but that's the way it's got to be. I'm working off a debt, see. I won't get into the nature of it, unless you want to come to one of our AA meetings—I know. Forget I said that. I just saw it in your face."

"I'm not an alcoholic," she said. "I don't even drink."

"Well I know that! What I mean is, is that you've got your own debts to work off. You don't have to tell me what they are."

"I'm not doing penance."

"Call it whatever you like." He reached into his shirt pocket and pulled out a plastic baggie, its contents clinking together as he reached out with them. He pressed them into her hand. "My sister gave me some extra St. Jude coins," he said. "I think you need them more than I do."

Her first fall came as she was trying to close the car door while hoisting her backpack on over her coat. She had packed only the overnight essentials—toiletries and underwear, an extra shirt, the journal—but that small weight was enough to throw her. Without the normal friction of shoes on pavement, the swing of her arm sent her skidding in an equal and opposite direction as the car door. She managed to grab the handle on her way down, which softened the impact. Still, her left hip and elbow crashed against the asphalt, sending bolts of pain through the rest of her body. She stayed down only long enough to make sure Carl had not seen her fall, then pulled herself up and shuffled around the back of the station toward the Lamplight.

To her relief, straight-line travel in these conditions was doable, if uncomfortable. Sleet rattled against her coat and stung her thighs through her jeans. Pellets flew horizontally into her eyes, forcing her to keep her gaze locked on the path immediately below her. But she could scoot along well enough, an object in motion staying in motion. When she had to turn from parking lot to sidewalk, however, her feet flew out from under her again. Same hip, same elbow. She flung curses into the storm, patted her body to make sure nothing was broken. Climbed to her feet and skidded into the grass, which crunched with blessed reassurance that here her feet could gain purchase.

A glance upward told her she was closer than she'd realized to the motel entrance. Soft yellow light glowed from its lobby windows, and the thought of a warm shower would have made her giddy if not for the new wave of loneliness that engulfed her. Even if he tried to drive up to meet her, Lucas almost certainly wouldn't make it out of Lamb County in these conditions. She closed her eyes. Tried to shake it off. Another night alone was probably for the best.

She gave her name at the counter. The receptionist looked at her computer monitor. When she found the listing, she stiffened. "Oh yes! Your—ah—friend just got here. He's paid for everything and left a card on file."

"He's here?" Ashley said.

"That's not my business, honey."

She flipped to the front tab in a plastic box on the counter and pulled out a paper sleeve with the key card inside. A second later, a loud pop sounded outside, and the building was plunged into darkness. Low green emergency lights flickered on in the lobby and above the service counter.

"Blew a transformer," the receptionist said. "Happens at least once a winter. The lock readers all run on battery power, so your key should work."

Ashley nodded and thanked her, but the old clerk had already marched away into the room behind the desk. So much for Texas hospitality.

She followed the clerk's directions to the stairwell and climbed to the third floor. In the hallway, she stopped to collect herself. Leave it to Lucas to anticipate her wishes. He must have gotten on the road about the time her phone went dead. She lifted a hand to her mouth, chewed on a cuticle. Tried to parse her feelings. Thought of how warm Lucas' body would be on this cold night. How gentle his hands, how bruised her heart.

She counted down rooms by the emergency lights until she got to hers, directly across the hall from the vending area. The cold drink machine popped and whirred, the happy recipient of some of the hotel's precious back-up power. But the snack machine lay dark and emptied. Someone had laid out its gears and springs on a newspaper and slid the greasy mess beneath the machine along with a hammer, pliers, and a half dozen assorted screwdrivers. The rows of empty coils reminded Ashley that she hadn't eaten. Oh well. The free breakfast started at 6:00am. Hopefully the power would be on enough for something warm.

She inserted her card into the reader and opened the door and stopped short. A pocket flashlight lay on the bedspread, illuminating a few feet around it. A pillow was propped against the wall-mounted headboard. No one was in the room itself, but the bathroom door was closed. Ashley waited, one hand draped over the door handle. Was there a couch? Yes. She could sleep there, maybe. A compromise. She would not be so vulnerable, but neither would she be alone. Fatigue descended over her. She let the door close behind her and walked across the room.

Before her backpack hit the patterned cushions, she heard the bathroom door swing open. Her heart thumped against her chest, though not entirely in fear. A smile tugged at the corners of her mouth. She forced it away, waited until she felt as though she could control what Lucas might see in her face. When at last she turned around, the blood in her veins froze, and hope drained away in an icy rush.

Jeff Burke leaned against the doorframe of the bathroom, mean and victorious, his long fingers curled around Lucas' phone.

CHAPTER 34:
NO TELLING WHAT YOU'RE
HEADING INTO

"How is she?" Dent asked.

Rachel shook her head. "Doc thinks it won't be long now."

She turned her hands over. Pressed them against her thighs. Leaned forward, nearer to the propane lantern that cast its white light from the table between them.

Hushed voices wafted in from Doc's waiting room, where the masses had gathered for Irene Ostendorf's death watch. Dent had waited among them for a time, thinking he could help shield Mauri Beth from the crush of hangers-on and well-wishers that pretended to be there for her support. They reacted to every update in the old woman's condition, gasping or smiling as reports on Old Mother Earth went from bleak to promising to bleak again. After a time, Dent realized how superfluous his presence was. These people had seen preachers come and preachers go, and they functioned just fine without clergy. Besides, Mauri Beth seemed to like the attention, even from those who only came for the spectacle.

And what a spectacle it had been. When Old Mother Earth collapsed on her way back to the ramp, half the audience thought it was just another part of the show. Some even applauded, until they realized the gravity of the situation. Mauri Beth had been the first to reach her, with Dent on her heels. By the time Rachel arrived from the kitchen, her skin was already a faint blue.

Dent blinked away the memory. Stared at the lamp. "I would have thought the power going out might thin the crowd some," he grumbled.

"Maybe they'll leave when the lights come back on," Rachel said through a yawn. "Rob ought to be here with that generator any minute.

She raised her hands to her face, fingers split around her eyes. In spite of the inner voice telling him to see the bigger picture, Dent couldn't help but size her up for what she might be feeling toward him. But her posture revealed only the weight of her task and a little sadness. He wanted to put his arms around her. Thought better of it.

"Where's your dad?" he asked instead.

"Up in my apartment. He's having a hard time. Doesn't like to cry in front of people."

The crunch of tire chains sounded outside. Rachel sat up straight and dusted herself off. Prepared to abandon Dent to these new arrivals. But when the door flew open to reveal Rob and Emilia, she settled back onto her perch. Lucas hobbled in behind them, Dent's laptop in hand.

"Grab your coat, Reverend," Rob said, and tossed a pair of insulated work gloves toward Dent.

Dent traded his dress shoes for the pair of rubber boots beside Doc's back door and shuffled out onto the ice. The freezing rain had already fused the generator's feet to the bed of his pickup, and they had to chisel them loose before they could unload it. Dent filled it with gasoline while Rob connected it through the portal below the breaker box. The entire process could not have taken more than fifteen minutes, but Dent's every extremity was already approaching numb. He could almost feel the relative warmth of the great indoors. But when Rob pulled the start cord of the generator, the plastic handle at the end of the rope snapped off in his hand. Rob lifted his arms to heaven. Looked up into the sleet. "You have got to be shitting me!" he called.

He snagged a screwdriver from inside his pickup, fished out the frayed cord and tied it around the shank. This time he handed it to Dent, who planted his foot against the generator's steel tubing and tried again. This time the engine sputtered for a few seconds and finally came to life. A dim light showed from the window in the patient room. Rob gave Dent the thumbs up sign.

They entered Doc's offices in high spirits, laughing even. But the face that greeted them seemed unconcerned with their heroics. Even by greenish-white light of the propane lantern, Lucas Lim was pale.

"What?" Rob said. "If the generator isn't working, you best tell me before I get these coveralls off."

"No," Lucas said. "I think that's okay. Emilia went to get the fireplace going in the waiting room. Rachel is checking on Irene."

"Then what's the matter?" Dent asked.

"Rachel still has service on her phone, so she let me get on her hot spot."

"Uh-oh," Rob said teasingly. "You know nothing good ever comes from the internet."

"I'm serious," Lucas said. He turned around the laptop. A series of white and blue text bubbles alternated down the screen. "I told you I lost my phone, right? Well, I think it must have fallen out of my pocket at Burke's house when I—when I was there. Because when I signed in to my texting on your laptop and tried to send Ashley a message, I found this whole conversation she thinks she's been having with me."

Dent pressed his fingers against his forehead. "Only it's not you."

"Clearly, no," Lucas snapped. "I think Burke must have my phone. He's setting her up."

"Can you warn her with that contraption?" Rob said with a flip of his hand toward the laptop.

"I've tried," Lucas said. "She isn't responding."

"Police?" Dent said.

Rob shook his head. "This storm will occupy every law enforcement officer in the Panhandle tonight. They won't have manpower to chase down a tip from a paranoid ex-boyfriend. No offense."

"None taken," Lucas said. He turned to Dent. "Do you think your truck would make it to Dalhart in this?"

"I don't see how," Dent said.

"We can throw some sandbags in the back. I've spent a lot of time in Colorado, so I know how to drive in winter. Please, Dent! I'll pay for damages if there are any."

"I know you would. But it's a fool's errand for you to try. You'd be in the ditch before you got three miles out of town, and you not able to walk."

"He's right," Rob said. "You'd have to have chains to get anywhere on this ice, and besides, you're in no shape to travel." He looked up at Dent. "You, on the other hand, can borrow my truck. Leave yours with me, just in case. And you better take Rachel with you. I don't imagine there's much she can do here. And there's no telling what you're headed into."

Darkness enveloped the road northward out of Earth. The storm had knocked out power throughout the Panhandle, leaving the headlamps on the pickup as the only man-made light for miles in any direction. The world was silent save for the rumble of the chains and the roar of the engine. Dent thought more than once that Rachel had fallen asleep. Each time he looked across, however, he could see her sitting straight, lost in whatever thoughts the black night dredged up in her. They stared ahead through the windshield, watching by the headlights as pellets of ice fell to earth at a slant, shimmering like bullets.

Rachel laughed softly.

"What?" Dent asked.

"Did you ever expect to be here?" she said. "I mean, was this what you had in mind when you started your pastoral career?"

Dent almost laughed himself, so relieved was he to hear her speak. He considered the question. "Not quite," he said at last. "I figured I'd be preaching at a big church by now, maybe doing some good deeds. You know, fighting economic injustice and ending poverty and stopping all forms of discrimination and abuse."

"Is that all?"

Dent shook his head. "I also expected to be happily married."

"Most do."

They rolled on for a long moment, listening to the rattle of sleet against the roof of the truck. When she spoke again, her words nearly caused Dent to swerve off the road.

"I had an affair with Paul Wayne Pearson," she said.

He lifted his foot from the accelerator and let the truck right itself. Reminded his hands to grip the wheel lightly. "Well," he said.

"Do you want to know about it?"

"I don't know," Dent said. "I guess it depends on whether or not you want to tell it."

Rachel waited several seconds. Pulled off her gloves and reached down to let the heat from the floorboard vents warm her fingers. Her face, mostly hidden in the dim dashboard lights, now disappeared entirely into darkness. He thought he heard her sniffle, but when she sat up straight her cheeks were dry.

"He wasn't serving as Sheriff at the time," she said. "He'd taken a leave of absence to care for his wife. Poor woman had developed Parkinson's at 55, and it took her fast. In less than a year she was confined to bed and out of her mind."

She pulled her gloves back on. Patted her hands together in some sort of internal pep talk. Soldiered on.

"I had just come back to town to work at the clinic after splitting up with this guy I'd been living with in Lubbock since college. So I was still—what was your phrase? Off balance. I'd go by to check on Aubrey, and Paul Wayne would be sitting on his front porch, as sad as any man I'd ever seen. One night, we ran into each other at a high school football game. He walked me home, and I asked if he wanted to come upstairs. It went on for maybe two months. We never talked about ending it. We just both sort of knew when it was over, I think. Aubrey died a few weeks later, and Paul Wayne went back to being Sheriff Pearson."

Dent waited for more. When none came, he squinted ahead into the darkness. Drove on into the sleet.

"Aren't you going to say something?" Rachel asked.

"Well. Like what?"

"Whatever it is preachers are supposed to say when someone confesses their sins. Absolve me or condemn me. Throw me out of the damn pickup if you want. I did it, and I can't change it. Not any of it."

"I don't think I'm in any position to judge."

She shook her head. "I was hoping for better than that."

Dent cursed himself internally. After all these years of pastoral experience, could he not find a more suitable response than *I shouldn't judge*? He searched his memory for something more appropriate, but only a single phrase rang in Dent's mind, clear as the starry Panhandle sky he knew was somewhere above this storm. He held the wheel with both hands to keep himself from fidgeting. A rectangular green sign told him he had eleven miles to Dalhart. Not enough time to say all that he was thinking. Too much time to bottle it all up. He opened his mouth and spoke, the words so strange to his ears that he wasn't quite sure he had said them. A glance at Rachel's gaping expression told him he had indeed spoken them aloud, and that he could not take them back.

"I love you."

He'd said *I love you.*

"Not what I was expecting," Rachel said at last. "Wow."

"Sorry," Dent said. "Too soon."

But it was nevertheless true. He wanted to say more, to justify the feeling or at least give it some nuance. Words failed him, though. He kept opening and closing his mouth, breathless and silent as a beached carp.

"Anyway," she said slowly. "I thought you'd want to know something that the Sheriff told me, while we were together. About Irene and Harlan Brantley."

Dent opened his mouth again to say yes, but produced nothing but a helpless gurgle. He nodded.

"All right then." She straightened. Collected herself. "Promise you won't tell anyone?"

This time he kept his lips pressed together. Shook his head.

"The official story is that Brantley committed suicide on Irene's lawn, right? Sarah Burke is there, and Jeff is in the car, and Brantley just goes crazy and shoots himself. But Paul Wayne told me that, given the angle and nature of the shot, there's no way Brantley could have pulled the trigger himself. The entry wound was on the side, here." She reached across and touched Dent's head, just above his ear. "And it wasn't the .410 shotgun that they found next to Burke. What killed him was a bullet from a rifle. He guessed it to be a thirty-aught-six."

Dent grunted. Felt his words returning. "That's Irene's gun."

"Bingo. He thinks that Brantley might have been threatening to shoot Sarah or even Jeff. Irene saw it and put a stop to it."

"I don't know about that," Dent said. "I have a hard time imagining Paul Wayne looking the other way on a murder case, even for someone so worthless as Harlan Brantley."

"Paul Wayne wasn't the Sheriff then, though, remember? His daddy was. He was a deputy. He could have told the truth, but he'd have had to call his daddy—who is also his boss, mind you—a liar in public. And he'd have to do the same with my daddy."

"Meaning?"

"My father did the autopsy. I saw it in the Book of Knowledge."

They drove on, beneath lightless street lamps and past the city limit sign. The entire town was dark, save for the few places with back-up generators. Combined with the low visibility and treacherous roads, it was enough to throw Dent completely off his bearings. He kept his eyes peeled ahead and left Rachel to look for Ashley's old car. When he glanced her way, he saw her staring back at him.

"So did that really happen?" she asked.

"I suppose," Dent answered. "I don't think Paul Wayne would lie to you, although I'm surprised he ever said anything in the first place."

"No," she said, waving away the story. "I mean the other thing. What you said. Did that really happen?"

He released the wheel with one hand, wiped it over his face. This was one of those moments on which their future hinged. They might talk about this night with their friends or even their children—my god, the thought of that! Or each of them might revise the story in a convenient way, grinding it down into nothing but a weird interaction during a stressful situation. Excitement and fear tingled in his every extremity, even as they turned his mouth to cotton. He took a long drink of cold coffee. At last he found his words.

"Yes. It happened. And I meant what I said."

They watched each other a long time from across the hotel room, maybe half an hour or an hour or a week for all Ashley could tell. Her sense of time abandoned her the instant she saw Jeff blocking her exit, his face triumphant as though he was just the cleverest of boys. She spent the first several minutes staring at his Adam's apple as she positioned the muscles in her own face. When she scanned him downward, she could see that his jeans were ripped at the knee and covered with mud. The hole in the fabric revealed a nasty scrape, dark with unevenly clotted blood.

"This?" Burke said, lifting his knee. "Just a party that got out of hand. I'm fine. Don't you worry."

She fixed her eyes on the collar of his shirt. Noticed scratches on his neck.

"I'm not here to hurt you," he said.

She let that hang in the air between them.

"Think about it and you'll realize it's true. Did I ever force you into anything? Did I ever try to overpower you?" He waited for her answer. Gave up after only a few seconds this time. "No, I did not. I made invitations, which you accepted. Every time. All these years."

She took a deep breath through her nose. Welded her face into a defiant glare. Looked up into his eyes for the first time and saw he was terrified.

"No," she said, her voice even.

"No what?"

"No to whatever it is you're going to ask me to do. I'm finished."

"Finished. With me, you mean? All right. I will honor that, of course I will. But the question is how finished you can be."

Her hip and elbow throbbed, the bruises from her fall tightening the longer she remained motionless. "Completely finished," she said. "As in forever."

"Well now," Burke answered. "That's fine. But you see the problem isn't your resolve. It's your presence." He took out a pocketknife, unscrewed the tiny bolts holding Lucas' phone together and slipped the blade into its seam. It cracked open, and he pried out the battery. Dropped the pieces onto the carpet and ground his heel into the tiny circuit board. "You can't go back to Earth."

"I have to."

"You don't." He rubbed the knuckles on his right hand, bruised and cracked. "I wish it didn't have to be this way, Ashley. Truly. I wish we could have kept our love separate from everything else."

"Love."

"I would call it that," he said. "I would. You call it what you like. But you can't go back. Things are all tangled up now—Crystal and the kids, even."

Ashley's face burned. "Your wife knows about us?"

"I think she might."

"That isn't my fault."

"It doesn't matter. I'm not concerned with the path that brought us here. I'm just showing you the way leading out."

She bit the insides of her cheeks. Coaxed just enough moisture into her mouth to allow her to speak. "I won't say anything to anybody," she said. "And I won't cause your family any trouble. But I am going to see Irene as soon as my car is fixed."

"No you're not."

He stood straight and took a hard step in her direction. She flinched, in spite of herself.

"You understand, I think," he said.

"I understand what?"

"That peace the plan. But it is not the priority. I can't let you go back to Earth, not now nor ever. Take off your clothes."

Her insides turned to ice. The world took on a strange red hue, and she had to fight to stay steady on her feet. But stay she did, and she kept her voice even. "Fuck off."

"That's an awful word for a pretty girl," he said. He was smiling now, more comfortable by the minute. "Relax. I'm not even going to touch you, if you'll help me out. But I need to get a shower, to clean up these scrapes. I can't risk you running away."

"I'll give you my shoes then."

"All right."

She slipped out of them. Kicked them hard in his direction. He let them bounce off the wall and picked them up. He unscrewed a bottle of water from the nightstand. Poured half in each shoe. He thought for a second. Shook his head.

"That's enough to keep you from going outside the building. But not enough to keep you from going outside the room. I'm afraid I'm going to need the rest."

"No."

He stepped toward her again, but this time with more than a feint. He grabbed her by the shoulders and picked her up as though she weighed nothing. Threw her into a seated position on the couch. He reached down and grabbed the hem of her jeans and pulled hard. She slid forward, reached out and dug her fingernails into his injured knee. He buckled, let go with one hand. She pulled her toes back and brought her foot up hard into his crotch. He lurched forward, an agonized groan rising in his throat. But he did not let go. Instead he grabbed her pinky toe on the foot he still held and twisted until it snapped. The pain overtook her—only for a second, but enough for him to yank the jeans the rest of the way off. He trudged into the bathroom. Stuffed them into the sink and filled it full of water. He emerged again, still angry, but wary now. He studied her, weighing whether or not stripping her of underwear and hoodie was worth the injuries he might receive.

"That'll do," he said at last. "I'm going to clean out these scratches. When I come back out, we'll try to work through this peaceably."

He picked up her coat from the bed. Returned to the bathroom and stuffed it into the filled sink along with the jeans. Then he shut and locked the door.

Ashley pulled off her sock as quickly as she dared. Her pinky toe jutted out at a right ankle to its neighbors. Intense as the pain was, she would not let herself cry. Instead she pulled the hood of her sweatshirt around and stuffed it into her mouth and, before she could think too much, grabbed the toe firmly and yanked it forward. It snapped back into place with a loud pop. A half second later, her muffled scream tore out through the hoodie's fabric. She looked down again at the swollen knuckle, the skin around it burning hot and bright red.

But above it, back toward the center of her foot, the velociraptor flared and snarled. She would fight harder next time. She would make him hurt. She would earn the claws tattooed on her body. She could not win, not against a man of his size and strength. But she could resist hard enough that he might have to kill her, hard enough to make the coroner remove his hat, so amazed would he be at the fight she put up, here at the end.

No, not that. Martyrdom was for the pious. She needed another way.

She shoved her hands into the pocket of her hoodie to still their shaking. Her fingers brushed against something she had not expected but instantly remembered. The St. Jude coins Carl had given her. She pulled open the baggie and grabbed one, turned it over in her hand. Bit into it with her eyeteeth. The metal was hard enough. It was the wrong size—not quite the same diameter as a quarter. But the thickness would work, she was almost sure. She would figure the rest later, make up a lie about a drunk boyfriend who threw up on her clothes.

But first.

She put the key card between her teeth and opened the door as quietly as she could. She stepped outside, thrust the card into the slot and pulled it out. The light blinked green, engaging the hidden ratchet, and she was able to close the door without a click from the bolt. She fought to steady her hands and got to work. Seconds later, she'd slipped two coins into the space between the frame and the door just above the lever. Then she took a long stride toward the torn-up vending machine and grabbed the hammer. She inserted another coin, lightly tapped it until it was nearly flush with the others. Repeated the action near the top, then the bottom, and then at the midpoints between the other stacks. On the other side of the door, she could hear Burke turn off the water to the shower. He called her name. She swung the hammer faster, speed now more important than stealth. She brought the last stroke down a split second before Burke rattled the handle on the other side. She stepped back, breathing hard from the effort, and raised her middle finger to the closed door.

"My god," a low voice said from a few feet away. "Awesome."

Ashley took another step away from the door, but did not need to turn her head to know who her admirer was. "Hi, Carl."

"Hey—I don't know your name. You aren't wearing pants."

"No."

"Sorry. Creepy, I know." He threw up his hands. "The hell with creepy. You okay?"

"I think so, yeah."

"This guy you're with—it's not going well, huh."

"No."

Burke pounded on the door again. Called her name, not loud but seething.

"Sir?" Carl yelled through the door, his voice contorted into some fake Midwestern accent. "Sir, this is Joe Dale, the maintenance man. Can you hear me?"

Silence for a long moment, and then, "I hear you."

"Good," Carl said. He winked at Ashley. "I seen what that girl did to the door, but I couldn't get to her in time. She's got you locked in tight. I'm going to have to go get my tools, so you just hang on, brother. I'll have you out in a minute." He stepped toward the door and examined Ashley's work. Whispered to her. "So the coins create a pressure lock, right? Puts so much force on the bolt mechanism that it won't turn. That's flippin' genius! Where did you learn to do that?"

"Colorado State. Freshman dorm."

"Wow." He backed away to the vending machines. Glanced down at Ashley's legs. "Is he hurting you? 'Cause I'll kick his ass if you need me to."

A smile tugged at the corners of Ashley's mouth. She shook her head. Looked down at her swollen toe, which the talons of the velociraptor seemed now to be carrying.

CHAPTER 36:
YOU DON'T KNOW ANYTHING

Rachel spotted Ashley's old car parked to the side of Dalhart Auto, but too late for Dent to safely make the turn into the station. Instead he coasted past it and into the parking lot of a farming supply company. No sooner had he killed the engine, however, than a lanky grease monkey appeared from inside the station with a set of keys. He unlocked the car and climbed into the backseat and began rifling through a suitcase.

"Let's go," Rachel hissed. "While he's distracted."

Before Dent could answer, she was out of the car, tire iron in hand. He crawled out the driver's side and hustled around the truck, trying to catch up to her without falling on the icy blacktop. As she approached, the man began to climb back out of the car. Rachel held the tire iron aloft. The man saw her just in time to duck behind the open door. He threw up his arms, clutching a pair of women's blue jeans in his left hand.

"The hell, lady!" he screamed.

Rachel kept her weapon cocked and ready. "Where's Ashley?"

"Who?"

"Ashley Hyatt. The woman who owns this car—and those pants."

"Right, okay. Ashley." He stood slowly, beating the air between them as if he were doing push-ups. "Raptor girl."

"I have no idea what you're talking about."

"Right. Okay. Shit, lady!" He took a deep breath. Blew it out sharply. "You can hit me with that thing if you have to, all right? But I'm not telling you a damn thing unless you tell me why you want to find Ashton."

"Ashley."

"Right."

Dent finally caught up and slid to a stop beside Rachel. "We think she might be in trouble," he said. "And God help you if you're contributing to that."

"What?! No, man. Listen—no."

"Are you working for Jeff Burke?" Rachel seethed.

"Who? No. Lady—lady, can we please put the weapon down?"

"It's a tire iron."

"I know what it is. Just—." He extended his arms, palms down, and made slow cool-it gestures. "This Ashley you're looking for. I maybe know her. Yea tall? Velociraptor tattoo?"

Dent looked at Rachel. She shrugged back at him. "We don't know about the tattoo," he said. "But there's a man who might be after her."

"Let me guess. Jerry Burke?"

"Jeff."

"Whatever." The man lowered his arms. Stood up straight and relaxed his shoulders. "A big smile spread across his face. "I feel you, yo? But she took care of him already. And the raptor—wait til you see it, man."

They shuffled along back to the motel. Carl stopped in the lobby to retrieve a battery-powered lantern. He led them to Room 329. Rapped on the door with his oversized knuckles.

"Raptor girl?" he called. "Ashley?"

The door opened a crack, and a small hand reached out from behind it. Carl placed the jeans in her grasp.

"Mr. Asshole is across the hall," he said once the door had closed. He turned and lifted his lantern. Dent counted five perfectly spaced sets of coins wedged between the door and the jamb to room 328. He reached across and pressed his fingers against it, but the door had no give whatsoever. Carl nodded in appreciation. "Badass."

Ashley emerged from the room, fully dressed except for one bare foot. She stared past the trio at the opposite door. Clicked on her own flashlight and pointed it toward Dent's feet, still clad in Doc's rubber work boots. She raised the light slowly, looking him over toe to head—his rumpled gray suit, his untucked oxford, his damp wool overcoat. Finally she reached his face. He squinted but did not look away.

"I'm sorry," she said. "You are?"

"Call me Dent."

"Oh, right," she said. Her face brightened. "Lucas has told me about you—well, I think I was talking to Lucas at the time. When did Jeff steal his phone?"

"He didn't exactly steal it," Dent said. "We're still sorting that out ourselves."

"We?" she moved the light to her left, skimming past Carl and landing on Rachel, whose face she recognized. "You're the nurse," she said. Her lower lip quivered ever so slightly. "Irene?"

"Oh honey," Rachel answered. "I'm sorry."

She stepped forward, arms outstretched, but Ashley slipped away from her embrace. She dropped her arms. Let the light fall straight on her feet, onto the fierce tattoo and her swollen toe.

"You're hurt," Rachel said.

"I think it's just dislocated."

"That's a lot of swelling," Rachel said doubtfully. "Can I take a look?"

Ashley shrugged. Walked back into the room and settled onto the couch. Rachel sat on the bed across from her, tenderly lifted the injured foot onto her lap while Dent held Carl's lantern over it. Rachel asked mothering questions, the way she had with Lucas. Where was the pain on a scale of one to ten? Was she warm enough? Able to wiggle her toes? Hurt anywhere else? What was she doing, out in a storm like this? What had happened with Jeff?

The technique that had worked so well on Lucas did nothing to pry open Ashley's interior world, however. She offered polite vagaries when she answered at all, sometimes deflecting the questions and sometimes staying silent as though she had not heard. Dent watched her face, clearer now that his eyes were adjusting to what light was in the room. She didn't even wince as the nurse worked her foot over. After a few minutes, Rachel gave up on conversation. She laid Ashley's foot on the bed and went with Carl to get some ice, if not from the machine downstairs then from the icicles that hung from the awning.

Ashley stood. Opened the curtains to reveal the dark world below. She raised her arms above her head and stretched. In the pale light of the lantern, Dent could see the pale skin where her sweatshirt rose above her waistline. Noticed something small he couldn't make out. Another tattoo, just above her hip. She lowered her hands and smoothed out her clothes and turned again toward him. He met her eyes. Waited.

"She never answered," Ashley said.

"Who? Rachel?"

"Yes. I asked her about Irene, and all she said was 'Oh honey, I'm sorry.' Does that mean Irene's dead?"

"Not when we left," Dent said, but knew even as he said it that his voice was too cheerful, too full of hope. This woman had endured enough lies. "Doc doesn't expect her to make it through the night though."

Ashley nodded. "So she'll be dead by the time we get back."

"I don't know. Probably so."

"Okay." She cried softly, but only for a few seconds before she wiped her eyes and started again. "How's Lucas?"

"Well enough to get into some trouble on your account."

Her eyes shimmered, but not from sadness this time. For a fleeting moment, Dent though she might smile. "What kind of trouble?" she asked.

"He beat the hell out of Jeff's truck. Smashed his windshield and windows. Got himself arrested."

This time she did smile. "So how bad was it?"

"I'll let Lucas tell you about it," Dent said. He stopped. Tried to read her face. "You are going to see him, I assume."

"I think so." She trained her eyes on the carpet between them. "The more immediate problem is across the hall."

"I guess it is."

Her expression hardened, dark lines cast in relief by the greenish glow of the lantern. "I found something, the last time I saw him," she said. She slipped the blue Beta Club bracelet from her wrist and handed it to Dent. He gave a somber nod. "Do you know where she is?" Ashley asked.

"Lucas said you might."

"She's just a kid."

"High school senior," Dent said.

"Still a kid."

"I know it. I'm just trying to tell the story the way it is. Burke's wife found out about her, and she disappeared."

She pressed her lips together. Breathed in through her nose. "As in ran away, or as in was taken?"

"I don't know."

"You think Jeff killed her?"

"No," Dent said, but too quickly. It was a reflex answer. Did he really know that Jeff Burke was incapable of mortal violence? Just because a thing was too horrible to imagine did not mean it wasn't still plausible. "Do you think he might have? Killed her?"

"Before tonight I would have said no. But at this point..." She trailed off. After a few seconds she turned back to Dent. "Do you have kids?"

"A daughter. Maybe a year or two younger than you are."

"Better keep her away from guys like Burke."

He swallowed hard. Tried to sound like a competent father. "I do what I can."

She stared into his face, and he could imagine how old and beaten he must look to her. But there was no pity in her expression. Her eyes were dry now, and cold.

"If I do tell my story, there's no going back," she said. "Once I make the first accusation, I'll be the center of every rumor in Earth."

"So will Burke."

"He's a man. And he has power. It's different."

"Well," Dent said. "We can't just leave him in that room to rot. Tempting though that is."

"No. We can't."

He shook his head. Looked down at his hands. "I know it's hard," he said. "All the things you've had to hide."

"You don't know anything."

"Maybe I don't."

"There's no 'maybe' to it."

Dent leaned back. Studied her face. She stared at the thin bulb that gave what light the room contained, her eyes dancing with exhaustion. She stifled a yawn, and so did Dent. He felt his eyelids getting heavy. Dropped his elbows on his knees and leaned forward as if to pray.

"Lucas is right," Ashley said. "I think I know where she is."

Dent straightened. Tried to clear his head. "Who?"

"The other girl. From the high school."

"Oh, right—sorry," he said. "Maya."

Ashley glared at him. "Don't do that. Don't say her name like that."

"Like what?" Dent said. "That's just her name."

"And if you only say it in the same context as Jeff Burke, she will always be connected with him, understand? She'll never not be the girl he went to prison for."

He nodded. "I get it."

"Do you?"

Before he could answer, the door to the room opened and Rachel and Carl strode inside. Dent tried to shake off the fatigue that had gathered behind his eyes. He wiped his hand across his face. "I suppose we better deal with Mr. Burke," he said.

"We won't have to," Rachel answered. "He's gone."

CHAPTER 37:
HERE AT THE MYSTERY
OF DEATH

Carl broke the blades off two flathead screwdrivers trying to knock out the St. Jude coins and release the pressure on the door. Each time, he held the jagged shank up in something near to triumph and uttered a respectful, "Badass!" Finally, he was able to dislodge one set, and then a second. The rest of the coins fell to the floor after the third. Carl stepped back. Let his hammer swing in his fingers. Cracked his neck.

"Okay," he said. "All right." He bounced up and down on his toes like a boxer before a fight. Then in a sudden motion, he stepped forward and swiped his master key in the card reader. Yanked on the handle. Flung the door open and, in one giant step landed in the hallway behind Rachel and Ashley, fists up.

Dent caught the door before it closed again and pushed his way inside. Freezing rain was blowing in through the open window, coating the metal heater box and desk chair with a thin layer of ice. The curtain rod had been pulled from its sheetrock anchors on one side and now dangled, bent and worthless, from the other. Dent scooted across the icy carpet to the window and looked out. One of the heavy curtains that had hung from the rod lay crumpled, fifteen feet below the window and stiff with ice.

The others crowded around to look. Rachel took his elbow.

"We were chipping ice from the awning when Carl spotted it," she said. "The best we can figure, he tried to lower himself by the curtain."

"Didn't work," Carl said. "Dude busted his ass."

Dent stared harder at the ice below them. Sure enough, spider-web cracks fanned out from three pressure points, presumably foot, butt, and elbow. Dent winced at the thought of the impact.

"Where do you think he went?" he asked.

"I'd guess back toward Earth," Rachel said. "But not far after that." She pointed south along Main Street, to where the headlights of a police cruiser shone on the rusted tailgate of an old jeep, the front of which was planted inside the sign of the First United Methodist Church.

"I'm afraid I don't follow," Dent said. "Except that it's a Methodist church."

"I can't be sure from this distance," Rachel said. "But I think that's Jess Turrell's jeep. You remember, the one we saw in her yard when we were looking for Maya."

"You think she drove him up here?"

"I think it's her jeep," Rachel said. "Beyond that is as much a mystery to me as to you."

Dent clapped his hands together. "All right then. I'll go check it out."

"I'm coming with you," Rachel said. They looked to Carl.

"Sorry, y'all." He raised his palms. "AA hasn't cure me of hating cops. You going with them, raptor girl?"

Ashley thought for a moment. Nodded.

"All right then," Carl said. "Pick up some St. Jude coins on the way out. Save me at least that much clean up."

Dent shuffled toward the cruiser while Ashley went with Rachel to retrieve her gloves from Dent's pickup. As he approached, he could make out the insignia of Dallam County Sheriff's Office on the driver's side door. Inside, the deputy tapped out a report on his iPad. Dent rapped on the window, and the young officer virtually threw the tablet onto the floorboard as his right hand went to his sidearm. He studied Dent for several long seconds before his face and arms relaxed. At last he opened the door and stepped out.

"What can I do for you, sir?" he asked.

Dent searched his tired brain for the right explanation, but everything that came to mind sounded weak or insubstantial. At last, he thrust his gloved hand forward and introduced himself as John Denton, the Methodist pastor.

"Deputy Chastain," the young man said. He eyed Dent doubtfully. "I thought the pastor here was a woman."

"She is. Sorry."

"Are you a friend of hers?" Deputy Chastain said. "I'm trying to put this together, sir. Hell of a night to be out."

"Right. I know her, but I'm here helping another friend." He waited, knowing the silence was getting awkward and unsure how to pull it back. Finally, he said, "Earth. I'm the pastor in Earth."

The deputy held up a finger and dove back inside the car to fish for his iPad. He punched the screen a few times before turning it around to show Dent a headshot of Jeff Burke, his profile pic on the school district website. "We think this was the driver of this vehicle. Is he one of your flock?"

"I'm afraid so."

"Then you know he's in trouble."

Dent listened to the sleet on the hood of his jacket. Carefully searched for words. "I have my suspicions."

"The owner of this jeep called Sheriff Pearson earlier this evening to file a complaint. According to her, the suspect beat her up and stole her vehicle. Said she'd lost a couple of teeth and had a broken arm. You heard anything about that?"

"No."

"According to your Sheriff, she may also have been pimping out her daughter to Mr. Burke. Maybe others. I don't suppose you know anything about that either."

Dent tried to keep his face neutral. Paul Wayne already knew, then. "Not that I can say right now," he answered.

The deputy nodded as though he'd expected as much. He pulled a card from inside the iPad case and handed it to Dent.

"I've done about all I can do here, at least until the storm lets up," the deputy said. "If you run into your friend, be careful. We're considering him hostile. But if he'll listen to you—."

The radio crackled from inside the vehicle. The deputy again crawled inside his car and this time closed the door. A moment later he rolled down the window. "I've got another call. House fire a few blocks over." He flipped on the blue lights. "Call me if you find Mr. Burke. It's best for everybody if we can get him in peaceably."

He put the cruiser in gear and disappeared down one of the side streets. Once it turned the corner, Dent's eyes began to adjust anew to the low light. He walked around the wreckage, trying not to step on the shards of glass that had frozen, jagged side up, into the sheet of ice. He shuffled closer. Squinted beneath the buckled hood at the busted radiator. Reflected on the collateral damage a life gone off the rails could cause. He half hoped Burke was alive and well enough to receive the justice due him. Half hoped he was not.

As he backed away, the heel of the rubber boots caught on one of the shards thrust up through the ice. He tipped backward, knowing with awful clarity that falling here would be akin to diving into a pool of upturned box knives. Yet how fitting was it, to wish another human being dead a moment before being sliced and diced himself. Instant karma. What a life.

He slipped and hopped backward through the field of shards, hoping against hope to make it far enough that he would fall on less deadly debris. He skated on his heels and windmilled his arms, oddly comforted by the fact that no lights illuminated his predicament. He watched the jeep move further away, the ruined church sign pass through the corner of his vision. And an idea struck him, a sudden burst of understanding about where he fit in the laws of physics that was as near to divine inspiration as anything he'd ever experienced. The back panel of the church sign was still intact, meaning the spray of glass could have fanned out on either side, but could not have landed directly behind it. He shifted his weight with all his might and fell, finally, into the narrow flower bed behind the sign—right next to the bloodied form of Jeff Burke.

"Brother Denton?" Burke said, his voice watery and weak. He rolled his eyes. "Of course."

Dent felt for his cell phone to use as a flashlight, but knew before he even reached into his pocket that the screen, damaged in his showdown with the scorpion, was now shattered beyond use. He slid back a few feet. Tried to focus through the darkness. Burke's left ankle bent at an unnatural angle. His arm was wrapped in a makeshift sling, made from what appeared to be an old Cowboys' sweatshirt. Dark blood trickled from his nose and forehead, and more blood—the source of which Dent could not locate—puddled around his knee.

"How bad are you hurt?" Dent asked.

"Bad enough," Burke said. There was a gurgling sound in his throat. "You see how far I managed to run."

"You could have called for help. The deputy was just on the other side."

"With more accusations about things nobody understands. I don't expect you to either."

"To understand?"

"No." He leaned his head back onto the bricks. Winced. Dent very nearly pitied him. "I didn't do anything wrong," he said at last.

"That's not for me to decide."

"Who decides then? God?"

"I suppose so. Maybe the state."

"The state can kiss my ass," Burke said. He tried to push himself up with his good leg. He rose up maybe an inch before the heel slipped on the ice. He landed in more pain than he was before. Settled in again. "I only played what cards were dealt me. Tell me why that's not good enough for God."

"We should get you some help."

"Why is that, Brother Denton? Why does God want so much and give us so little?"

"It's a good question."

"So you don't know either," Burke said, with a hint of triumph. "All right then, answer me this. Is God responsible for this world?"

Dent got to his knees. Looked out over the dark down. Three or four blocks over, he could see the orange of a house fire mixing with the blue and red flashes of emergency lights, all reflected off the low clouds. "I suppose that depends on what you mean by responsible. I don't think he causes everything to happen. But I do think he has an obligation to the world He created."

"That doesn't make it better." Burke shifted to one side. As he changed position, Dent could just make out a shard of white collarbone lifting through the skin near his neck. "You say God doesn't cause everything that happens to happen. All right then. He's off the hook for some things. But if he is responsible to the world—protecting us, righting the wrongs, and so forth—why does he seem to do such a poor job of it?"

"I'll get the deputy."

"Answer me first."

"I don't have an answer."

"Well then," Burke said, with what looked to Dent like a smile. "I guess I plan to find out soon enough."

He closed his eyes. Made a swallowing noise. Dent stood and tried to take in Burke's injuries. The ankle was likely broken. The collarbone definitely was. And so much blood around his leg. Had he sliced an artery? There was no way he could walk, and no way Dent could carry him across this ice. Ashley and Rachel had still not made it back, and the deputy was long gone.

A horrible and thrilling thought occurred to Dent. The deputy had been only a few feet away and had not seen Burke. Why should Dent be expected to find what law enforcement could not? If he walked away now, Dent would leave no tracks in the ice. No traces of guilt. Ashley would not have to reveal her secrets. Maya would not have to worry. Even Crystal would be free, if devastated by it all.

Burke's shoulders slumped, and Dent squatted down and listened. His breathing was strong, if labored. Dent had seen enough of hospital trauma to know that the man was not yet in his death throes. But neither would he survive much longer, not out here.

Dent turned. Walked down the street to the south. Wondered, as he always did here at the mystery of death, what it would be like to die.

CHAPTER 38:
HENRY ON THE OTHER SIDE

Irene is dying.

Her mind's eye sees this clearly, even though her body no longer responds to her commands. She is not afraid. She is along for the ride, drifting through her memories, knowing where she will land before the end comes.

And so she arrives at the moment again, the one to which all roads lead and from which all roads progress. She has relived it all her life, and she is not the least bit surprised to be here now, at the very end—and not as an observer. She returns to it fully, gives herself over, relives it.

She approaches the church from the east, drawn forward by the inevitability of what has happened and is happening. She slides the tiny black overnight bag beneath the stone bench and takes a seat and settles in. To her left, the whitewashed walls of St. Jude's Catholic Church blaze forth in apparent glory. But it is all bluster. If the clouds hovering over the Bay manage to roll across the sun, she will be able to pick out the church's flaws. She will trace the cracks in the walls and see the bird droppings on the grate below the bell tower and inspect the slightly uneven windows on either side of the entryway. Direct sunlight declares the glory of the house of the Lord. A softer illumination reveals the truth.

She shields her eyes from the glare and checks the front door. It rests unevenly against its frame, as it has since before she and Henry began using St. Jude's as their rendezvous point. The priest has tried covering the poor construction with shrubbery and filing down the edge of the door itself to make it fit within the frame, all to no avail. The door stands perpetually ajar and impossible to lock. Irene could go in any time she likes—in fact has gone in on occasion to pray with these Catholic strangers. Now, however, there is no time for detours. What she will do, she must do quickly.

She looks northward along the path. No sign of Henry. She smooths her skirt with sweaty palms, looks around the garden. Eyes the church door as she fishes in her handbag for a cigarette. She taps her suitcase with her heel, just to reassure herself. She wishes she could have packed more, shoved the sea and the shore and the whole of the city into her little bag. As it is, she has brought with her less than the overnight would hold—two changes of clothes, an extra pair of shoes, what money she could get her hands on. What she packed for this trip to California was mostly hope. When Henry does not come with her, she will return with mostly space.

A movement catches her eye. The door easing open just a crack, then falling back against its frame. Someone is watching. Judging, perhaps.

Where is Henry? He usually arrives before vespers begins, rolling toward her on his bicycle. She expects to see him any minute, although she hopes he will be on foot. If he has his suitcase with him, she will have her answer and no need for explanation.

But this is love talking in its child thoughts and child speech. She has seen too much to think life can ever be simple again. She has watched the very earth blow away from the Texas Panhandle, and she has seen the devastation war can wreak on the home front. So many young men are dead, her brother included. Who can say what tomorrow holds? Optimism is an unnatural business in these dark times.

A cloud passes over the sun, and Irene looks back at the doorway to remind herself of the defects she knows are there. She notices something else, hidden behind the shrubs. Henry's bicycle. Her heart leaps into her throat, and a fool's hope overtakes her. They will go off together, despite all that's happened in these years since he left Earth. They will board the train this very night and pass through the Sierra Nevada on their way east. They will get off in a place where no one knows them or their current spouses or their pasts—Albuquerque, perhaps—and get married and begin a new life as a legitimate couple, without sorrows and poor choices to haunt them.

It will not happen, Irene knows. However much she might wish for different, this scene played out a certain way and so became fixed in time, just like the moment in the kitchen when she put off going to California. She wrote her part in this drama all those years ago, and Henry had written his. She cannot escape this outcome. Not even now, as her body fails.

Not yet.

She glances again at the door, and now Henry appears, pale and anguished. He steps into the garden.

"I'm sorry to make you wait," he says. "I needed to think on our situation a little more."

"Well."

"It's not as simple as you wish it was, Irene. I've got Trudy to think about, like it or not. I can't just leave her to fend for herself. You know how it is, being responsible for someone."

"Surely I do."

"I just don't know," he says. "I just don't see any way. I want things to be different—God, but I do. It doesn't matter though."

"No."

"It doesn't matter what we want."

"I know it."

"You do?"

"I do."

She looks out across the Bay, toward what had been Treasure Island before the War, now covered with planes and hangars and other machinery of the Navy. What once was the world of tomorrow has been sacrificed to preserve today. Treasure Island is nothing more than a swath of useful earth, stripped bare like the soil in Texas and just as likely to die.

Henry shuffles his feet and tries to speak, but a cough doubles him over. He spits a dark red glob onto the grass. "You're not worried about what might happen?" he asks. "If we tried to do this?"

"No."

"Well, that's you then. I just can't."

"Why not?"

He wipes his hand across his face. Coughs again. His face pulses with guilt and fear that she has never in all her years been able to parse. She sees another future take shape in her mind, one of destitution and shame. She sees their return to Earth to face the ghost of Mr. Randall, the wrath of their rejected spouses, the gossip from their neighbors. She sees Henry's lungs wither in the dusty air, his body waste away, and everything she wants to save erased by time and wind.

She blinks away the glare reflected on the church wall. She is in love with a coward. And so is Henry.

He lowers his eyes. Kicks at the ground.

"So will I see you again?" he asks.

"Well."

A thin laugh bubbles up from inside him, and he has to fight off another cough. He pulls his bicycle out and stands beside it. Looks in her direction, but not at her. It pains him to know that she will not cry—she can see that much. He wipes his face, fumbles with his shirt sleeves. Straddles the bicycle and takes a deep breath.

She watches him. Thinks of things to say, pleas and reasons and farewells. None of them fit quite right. He is slipping away. She has become part of the garden, a wilting flower, rooted here and withering in the sunshine.

And now Henry steps on his pedals and pushes forward, his frail body laboring to set the machine in motion. Now Irene watches him catch his balance, and anger fills her senses. She hates him for choosing others over her. Wishes he would fall. Wishes he would show the hurt that she knows he carries. Wishes he would stay just a little longer, since so little time remains.

He doesn't though. He leaves her there, alone. Pedals away for what she knows will be the last time.

This is hell, she thinks. *This place of regret from which I cannot move.*

She stiffens. Tries to accept her fate, which surely is just. It is a story she cannot change.

Yet change the story does.

A few yards ahead, Henry stops. He has never done that before in any version of memory or dream. She stands to watch, chides herself for what little hope she clings to. But Henry gets off his bicycle and lays it in the grass—another change in the script. He stands firm on the sidewalk. His lungs are not heaving, nor his legs shaking. And now she understands that this is not the Henry of her regret. He is something more, Henry on the other side. Henry made whole and strong. He is beyond his mistakes or responsibilities, a witness now to things accomplished. Maybe to things redeemed.

Oh God, Irene thinks. Oh God, let this be real.

He extends his hand.

She steps toward him. Reaches back.

CHAPTER 39:
LET US BE FREE
OF THESE BONDS,
OF WISDOM MOST OF ALL

Once they were back in Earth, Dent dropped Rachel off so she could get cleaned up. He made Ashley drive from Doc's to the parsonage, just to make sure she knew how to handle the manual transmission of Rob's pickup as well as she claimed. She did—and even better. When they pulled into the driveway, Lucas hobbled out calmly, as though seeing his ex drive up in a borrowed 4x4 made all the sense in the world. Dent loaded them with food and blankets for the trip. Sent them on their way. Put on his own, better fitting boots and inched his way back to Doc's.

The old man was in the now empty waiting room, seated on the coffee table maybe three feet from the fireplace. Rachel had changed clothes and curled up on the couch. In the yellow glow of the flames, he could see her orange hoodie peek out from beneath the blanket.

"Evening, Reverend," Doc said without looking up. He peeled two more sheets off the stack of papers at his feet and fed them into the fire. "Beer is on the front deck. Reach out there and get you one."

Dent did, and carried another in for Doc, who twisted off the cap and took a long drink. He held the bottle at arm's length. Examined the label.

"My Daddy drank whiskey when I was little," Doc said. "One of my first memories is smelling it on him when I was sitting on his lap. I might have been four years old. By the time I was in junior high school, he'd added gin, vodka, and tequila to his favorites. Then when I graduated medical school, he showed up at the reception looking like he'd swallowed a cheap liquor store and chewed up the bottles. It got worse as time wore on, is what I'm saying. Drank himself to death, the way I've seen a thousand other people do. I'm sure you have as well, Dent."

"A few."

"Well." He took another drink of his beer, wiped his lips. Dropped more sheets into the fire. "I never have let myself turn to drink, and I don't aim to in my old age. But tonight may be enough to do it."

"Might be," Dent said.

They sat in silence for several minutes, watching the fire. Doc finally rose and stepped onto the porch. He came back with a large cottonwood log with marks from a hydraulic splitter still visible in its end. He dropped it onto the coals and stood over it, opening and closing his hands toward the flames.

"Rachel tells me Burke is in pretty rough shape," Doc said.

"He is. Broken bones and frostbite. Lost quite a bit of blood. But the EMTs seemed to think he'd pull through."

"That's what Rachel said. I'm not sure how I feel about that." He tilted his bottle toward his daughter. "She said you probably saved his life by getting that deputy. How'd you know where to find help?"

"House fire. I could see it from where Burke had crashed."

"Like a moth to the flame," Doc said. He sat again. Continued his burning. "He busted up Jess Turrell pretty good. The Sheriff said he'll go to prison for it."

"He should. I hate it though."

"You feel sorry for him?"

"No," Dent said quickly. And then, "Yes."

"Clarity is not your strong suit, Preacher."

"I'm not saying he doesn't deserve the pain he's got or the punishment he'll get," Dent said. "But I do pity him."

"As much as you pity Jess Turrell? Or Maya Jordan? Or Ashley Hyatt?"

"No." Dent felt his face and ears go hot. "What kind of question is that?"

"A realistic one. From somebody who's used to seeing the best and worst of what people do to each other." He sat back. Watched Rachel sleep. "You think Maya or Ashley will have to tell their stories, now that Burke's going to be locked up for something different?"

"I don't think they have to. But I think they will. Ashley will, anyway."

"You think?"

"I do. Rachel told her about the pictures Lucas found on that old phone in the parsonage. They had a long talk about it while I was with Burke. I'm not sure exactly what was said, but when we were on the way home Ashley told us she'd press charges, but only if we left Maya out of it."

"I doubt anyone gets left out, now that Jess is in the mix."

"Maybe not," Dent said. He stretched his arms over his head and yawned. "Doesn't diminish Ashley's courage."

"I suppose not," Doc said. He rolled up about ten sheets of paper. Stuffed them in between the logs. They fell back as the ends began to burn, and when they unfurled Dent could see the purple ink of an old mimeograph machine.

"You're burning the Book of Knowledge?" he asked.

"I figure it's time," Doc answered. "The evil men do lives on after them. Isn't that in the bible?"

"No. Shakespeare, I think."

"It's the truth, whoever said it. And I'd be happy to know I didn't contribute to the problem. What time is it?"

Dent reached for his phone, but remembered before his hands hit the bottom of his pocket that it had been ruined in his fall. He stood and leaned toward the fire. Peered at the clock on the mantle. "Five o'clock almost."

Doc nodded once. "Then it's been twenty-two years now, to the hour, since Ana died."

"Rachel's mother?"

"And Emilia's," Doc reminded him. "And my wife. Got up to let the dogs out one morning and died on the porch. Her heart just had so many beats in it, and she hit that number. Irene is dead now too."

"I know it."

Doc picked up the last of his fifty years of notes. Tossed them to the flames. "Then let us be free of these bonds that so bind us," he said. "The bond of wisdom most of all." He took up a steel poker and jabbed at the logs, eyes fixed but unseeing. "Are we fools, John?"

"Probably," Dent said. "The evidence would suggest as much."

"It would indeed." He turned toward Dent, a crooked smile taking shape over his mouth. "I'd hoped that burning that book would help. That being a fool would somehow feel better."

"How did you think it would feel?"

"I don't know. I think I thought it would be happier. Are you happy?"

Dent looked down at his unopened bottle, now sweating in the heat from the flames. A fleeting prayer shot through his mind so quickly that he did not have time to turn it into words, and anyway words had so often failed him. Rather, what rose up within him—rose up to God, he truly believed—was a great hope for this old man in front of him, for Lucas and Ashley, for Crystal Burke and so many in town that he still barely knew. For his daughter and her child, soon to be born. For Rachel, asleep on the couch and lovely. All was not right with the world, to be sure. But perhaps all would be, if not here then somewhere. If not now then someday. He felt

his answer before he said it, but was still surprised to hear the words
come from his own mouth.

"I believe I'm on my way."

CHAPTER 40:
I JUST WANT HER TO KNOW
IT'S NOT HER FAULT

Lucas slept on, contorted in the passenger seat in a manner that would have looked uncomfortable even without his various casts and braces. His left foot extended straight out across the floorboard and behind the stick shift of Rob de los Santos' pickup. His right was propped up on the dash. The rest of his long body lay across the seat, his head flopped over against a rolled-up sweatshirt. He had moved maybe half an inch since they'd made the turn onto 84 at Amherst. What must it feel like to sleep so soundly?

"Lucas?" she said, but her voice was lost in the grind of tire chains over the icy pavement. She leaned forward. Draped her arms over the steering wheel and took in the early morning sky. The pastor had loaded them down with coffee and snacks, made sure they had candles and blankets. He'd also thrown a jack and a flathead screwdriver into the bed of the truck, just in case the roads cleared before the return trip and they needed to take off the chains. And while his kindness warmed Ashley's heart, she nonetheless doubted his sunny prophecy. As they rolled along, the growing daylight revealed more low gray clouds, heavy with ice and snow. They were two hours into a sixty-mile drive, and Lubbock just coming into view.

Sweat beaded on her cold palms. What she was doing was the height of irrationality—slipping out of town in the wee hours of the morning, bargaining with that preacher and leaving her mother to mourn Irene alone. Taking to the road in such awful weather to look for a girl she barely knew who might not even be where she expected to find her.

And then there was Lucas, which still made no sense. She had not invited him, nor had the preacher. He just assumed that he would go with her even before he knew the errand—"to help a girl," was all Ashley had said—and so he'd inched across the frozen driveway and into the passenger seat of the truck.

Was there meaning in the ease at which he leaned back into her life? Was he being smug? Or timid, or maybe stoic? She had not even told him where they were going. Was he a sucker, or some kind of codependent, or was he really motivated by bravery and love? Too many possibilities. Too many questions, and no clear path to answers. He would not understand what she felt. He would be no help if they wrecked, not in his condition. And he might do more harm than good with the girl, might scare her just by being there. Bringing him had been a mistake. This whole trip probably was.

Ashley rolled her shoulders. No point second-guessing now. The road before her was treacherous enough.

The power was out at the apartment building, its entryways dark and security lights dimmed by the backup generator. Most of the residents had opened their curtains to invite in the paltry morning light. Ashley counted the windows, four up and three across. In that room, the curtains were closed tight. The sliver of a girl's face appeared through the gap at the near end. Ashley breathed out slowly.

"Lucas." She reached out this time, shook his good arm. His eyes popped open, and he tried to straighten himself. Winced and groaned. Looked around at his surroundings—the pickup, the parking lot, the apartment building. The semi-bionic paraphernalia on his limbs.

"Where are we?"

Ashley lifted her bare foot. Lowered it again onto the rubber floor mat, which was cooling by the second now that she'd turned off the engine. Flexed her toes, and was surprised anew by the pain in the smallest of them.

"Lubbock," she said at last.

"Lubbock?" Lucas repeated. "All right. Should I ask why?"

"Trying to help a girl," she said again, and this time tried to offer more. She had the first word on her tongue a dozen times, but she could never quite get it out. Where could she start? How much did he already know? What did she *want* him to know? She might tell about Maya and Jeff and Jen and Connor and maybe even her own litany of poor decisions. But if she was going to climb that mountain, first her feet had to gain purchase on the slope, and the base might as well be covered with grease.

She looked away, toward the building.

Maya.

He followed her gaze to the fourth-floor window. A young woman pulled back the curtain another inch and held it there. She lifted the other hand to her mouth. Chewed on her nails.

"Who's that?" Lucas asked.

"Her name is Maya."

He sat up straighter. "Maya Jordan? The kid that ran away?"

"Don't say it like that."

"Sorry."

"It makes it sound like it was her fault."

"No. Sorry. I know."

"She's just a kid in trouble. I don't think she had any idea what she was getting into."

"With Burke, you mean?"

"Yes."

The silence swelled between them, and she could sense the emotion rising within Lucas. She was afraid of what he might do next, that he would try to hold her hand or touch her leg. She braced herself.

"So are you going to go talk to her?" he asked.

"I'm going to try."

"And convince her to come back with us."

"Maybe. I don't know if she will. I just want her to know it's not her fault. I want her to know she can move on."

"And you're going to tell her all that?"

"Yes."

"And you think she'll believe it?"

"I hope so." An unwelcome sting burned around her eyes. She pressed the injured toe into the underside of the brake pedal.

"Do you believe it?" Lucas asked. "For yourself, I mean."

Ashley blinked away the tears. Looked up past the window to the brightening sky above the roof of the apartment building. Nodded, once.

CHAPTER 41:
SWEPT CLEAN

Thirty minutes before the normal Sunday worship hour, the front had passed to the south and east, giving way to a newborn yellow sun that illuminated the icy prairie with terrible brightness. Dent had slept maybe two hours when his eyes popped open, his brain flashing a warning that he had not officially cancelled church. He went through his mental list of mass communication options, but none of them were available at this point. The cell towers were still down, as were the TV and radio stations. Common sense said that no one—not even the most die-hard of Methodists—would brave such impossible conditions. But Dent had been a pastor long enough to know how little common sense bore on the decisions of church people. He dressed in jeans and a sweatshirt. Made his way across the sheen to the church and unlocked the doors and went into the sanctuary.

On this first Sunday of November, Earth United Methodist Church had planned to celebrate their saints. Every church had its quirky traditions—Veterans Day fish fries, Fourth of July gospel singings, Valentine's Day wild game dinners. As such productions went, Earth's investment in All Saints Day was among the most theologically sound that Dent had encountered—certainly more so than the Odessa Mother's Day chili cookoff and mule drop, which, in hindsight, had a considerable lot to do with Janet's negative evaluation of her prospects as a preacher's wife.

The concept of the All Saints service was clear enough: honor those who had died while allowing the congregation both to express their grief and to proclaim their hope in resurrection.

All week prior, the United Methodist Women had been gathering mementos of family and friends for whom the bell had tolled—Purple Hearts, grainy sepia photographs of men in bowties and women with horn-rimmed glasses. Even collars and chew toys to memorialize family pets. No way to hold the service today, though. They would have to pack everything away as soon as the ice melted so that they would have room for the flowers at Irene's funeral. And then they'd have to drag it back out and do the All Saints' service next Sunday, when they would gather to mourn their dead and, though it could not yet be spoken aloud, begin to make peace with all that had happened these past few days.

The glass doors to the narthex swung open. Dent squinted against the light, but knew by the figure's movements who had entered before he could see her face.

"Fine display you got there," Rachel said. She pulled down the orange hood of her sweatshirt and shook out her hair.

"Can't say I expected to see you again this morning," Dent said, fighting off what was sure to be a goofy smile. "Decided to give church a try?"

"Don't get carried away. I just couldn't sleep. And I thought you might be here by yourself this morning."

"Well," he said. The goofy smile came out anyway. He decided to own up to it. "I'm glad you came."

"I wanted to tell you that Doc got a call from Lucas on the landline. Maya is safe. Ashley was in talking to her. He didn't know when they'd be heading back. I thought that might be a relief to you."

"It is. Thanks. Can I get you—." He tried to think of something reasonable to offer, since the power outage left him no way to make coffee or tea. The only thing that came to mind was what he had in his office. "Candy corn?" he said.

Now it was Rachel's turn to hide her smile. Dent pretended not to see.

She tromped ice from her boots. Walked to the front of the sanctuary. She scanned the tables, finally picking up a tarnished gold pocket watch, carved with the initials HB. She wound it, listened for its ticking. Placed it back on the table and moved to the window to gaze out over the old cemetery. "Will they bury Irene here?" she asked.

"I haven't heard," Dent said. "There's still space in the family plot, but she told me once she'd just as soon be cremated and her ashes sunk in Doc Schugart's pond."

Rachel laughed. "I'm sure there's more than one version of her wishes out there."

"Likely so."

She thrust her hands into the pocket of her hoodie. Glanced behind her. "I came by for another reason too," she said. "I brought something to show you."

Her hands emerged from the pocket with a small journal, its brown leather cover worn smooth from years of handling. She peeled back the front cover and ran her finger down the binding. Turned the book around. Gave it to Dent with both hands, as if it were an offering. Inside, on what appeared to be the title page, were the words "Dream Book," written in perfect script and surrounded by a hand-drawn border of honeysuckle vine. Dent turned the page to reveal a sketch of a smiling, dark-haired woman in a wedding dress, holding an infant. Opposite that was another drawing, this one of a young man clad in a tuxedo and a cowboy hat, with a stethoscope dangling from his neck.

"Wow," Dent said. "Where did you get these?"

"Will you believe it if I tell you?"

"Try and see."

"Dad made it."

"Doc?" Dent said. He remembered the train sketch at the Super Chief. "I forgot he was an artist."

"The best in town, although no one knows it. Keep going."

Dent turned a few pages in, revealing a two-page spread of the couple in a convertible, driving along a highway that connected the Space Needle on the left with the Statue of Liberty on the right. The caption read, "Drive Coast to Coast." He thumbed through a few more pages, some with sketches and some without. Most of the blank pages had a caption in one corner—"Float the Colorado" or "See China's Great Wall."

"Whenever they thought of something they wanted to do together, they wrote it down and left the page blank," Rachel explained. "Once they did that thing, Dad made a sketch. I think this started as a way of setting goals for themselves, but it ended up being more of a journal. Look."

She reached across and flipped through a few more well-worn pages—Emilia's return home, her marriage to Rob, Rachel's college graduation, the first day of business for the Super Chief. The last few had only captions. Buy an RV. Travel the country. Spoil our grandchildren.

"You can't tell Emilia I showed you," Rachel said. "And you sure as hell can't tell Dad I even have this."

"He doesn't know?"

She shook her head. "He placed it in Mom's casket at the visitation. In his mind, Mom was dead, and so were their dreams, and he just needed to buck up and start over. I stole it before they closed her in."

"Lucky you didn't get caught."

"Part of me wishes I had." She swept her fingers over the calloused cover. Stuffed it back into her pocket. "So what now?"

Dent checked the clock on the back wall of the sanctuary, which read five minutes after worship was set to begin. That seemed like a safe enough time to close up shop. He scanned the tables behind him. Relics of the saints. Artifacts from past lives. You never knew how people would grieve. Some denied their losses. Some buried themselves with the dead. How many ever really moved on?

"My turn to show you something," Dent said. "Let's go."

He barely touched the accelerator, inching along with one tire on the slowly thawing blacktop and the other on the edge of the grass, where his truck could sink in for better traction. The trickiest part was the entrance to the U-Stor-It facility, which required him to ease to a stop in front of a card reader to raise the gate. He managed to get through without damaging anything expensive, but decided not to press his luck by backing up to the unit. Instead he pulled parallel to it and put the transmission in neutral. Let the pickup roll to a stop.

"So we're here," Rachel said. She held up the hacksaw and bolt cutters Dent had given her before they left the parsonage. "You want to tell me what the plan is now?"

"It's not really a plan," he answered. "More of a direction. Come on."

They took turns cutting into the shackle of the lock, trying to notch out a wedge big enough to get the nose of the bolt cutters into. Forty minutes and three blades later, the metal finally gave. Dent lifted the rolling door to his unit. One of the bolts on the joints between panels caught on a box, gashing it open. Broken glass and shredded potpourri leaked onto the ice and concrete. Dent pulled on his new leather gloves—an early Christmas present from the Sheriff—and swept up the fragments. Then he gingerly loaded the box into the bed of the pickup.

Rachel crossed her arms. "You still haven't told me what we're doing here."

"Just start pulling out boxes."

"What are we looking for?"

"Whatever I don't need."

Rachel dragged the boxes out one by one, eventually creating a half-moon shape around the pickup so that Dent could inspect their contents. Most of what he found—old VHS movies, back issues of *National Geographic*, shards from Janet's scrapbooking hobby that never materialized—could be loaded into the pickup bed for immediate deposit in U-Stor-It's oversized dumpsters. He took three loads behind the building before they finally reached the back wall of the unit. He kept next to nothing. Felt better by the truckload.

After the fourth trip, he came back to find Rachel sweeping out the unit with a broom she'd freed from the ice next to the empty office shed. She'd lined the three remaining boxes up at the edge of the blacktop for Dent to examine. One turned out to be a collection of mission trip t-shirts, which he immediately ticketed for donation. The second was full of school-age memorabilia for his daughter—Leah's yearbooks and academic awards, a copy of her valedictorian speech. The pay stub from her first part-time job, off-centered in a dollar-store frame. Wristbands from her induction into the Beta club.

"You can't throw that away," Rachel said.

Dent shook his head in agreement. "I need to make a trip to Albuquerque once it thaws."

"You think she'll see you this time?"

"I have to keep trying."

Rachel slapped him on the shoulder. "Good for you! Check that last box and let's get out of here."

She slid her box along the ice, skating behind until she reached the passenger side door. Dent pulled out his knife and cut the tape on the one left beside the unit. He lifted the flaps to find a stack of unused photo albums, still wrapped in their cellophane, stuffed into one end as placeholders. Lined up in the other end was a series of hardback notebooks, some with worn covers and others almost new. Janet had kept a journal for most of the time they were married, even though she neglected the habit more and more as they marched toward divorce. He had never before read even a single page in them. Yet here they were, his ex-wife's innermost thoughts laid out before him.

Dent stared at them for a long moment, wondering what they could tell him that he didn't already know. She had obviously not thought them worth the trouble of moving. And supposing he did find out where things went wrong in their marriage? An autopsy helped the living assign blame. It didn't bring back the dead. Enough to know that he had loved an imperfect and at times deeply troubled person. At least he and Janet had that in common.

He steadied himself against the lowered tailgate and heaved the box into the pickup's bed and slammed the tailgate shut.

"Ready?" Rachel called.

He looked back at the storage unit, empty now and swept clean of the artifacts of his past life. All that available room caused his stomach to do a little flip. He pulled down the sliding door.

"Okay," he called back to Rachel. "All right. Let's go."

THE END

AFTERWORD

All the writers I know have a deep passion for language and story, coupled with a ridiculous desire to share such things with the world. In short, we write to be read.

Which is where you come in.

If you enjoyed this book, please leave a review with the website or store at which you purchased it. Those reviews help other readers find it, and so on down the line. And ultimately, sharing with other book lovers is what keeps me at my keyboard, day in and day out.

You can also find my weekly blog about things overlooked and undervalued at www.mondayspenny.com[1].

Thanks for reading!

---

1.   http://www.mondayspenny.com

Don't miss out!

Visit the website below and you can sign up to receive emails whenever Eric Van Meter publishes a new book. There's no charge and no obligation.

https://books2read.com/r/B-A-TIRU-EZHAC

BOOKS 2 READ

Connecting independent readers to independent writers.

About the Author

Eric Van Meter writes stories that reflect the quirky, rhythmic, hilarious ways that people try to cope with being human. He began *Earth* while bicycling across Route 66, listening as folks shared their rich experience in one of the most rural places in America. In between doomed efforts to master various musical instruments, Eric blogs at www.mondayspenny.com, where you can find "St. Anthony and Buddha Bike Through the Desert," his award-winning non-fiction essay on the aforementioned bicycle trip.

Read more at https://www.ericvanmeterauthor.com.

About the Author

Lightning Source UK Ltd.
Milton Keynes UK
UKHW012242081122
411848UK00001B/122

9 798201 897840